Other Women

Jean Levy has worked in genetics research, the pharmaceutical industry and in academic publishing. She is currently completing a doctorate in Linguistics. She studied Creative Writing at the University of Sussex and lives with her husband in the South Downs.

Also by Jean Levy

What Was Lost

JEAN LEVY

OTHER WOMEN

CANELO

First published in the United Kingdom in 2020 by The Dome Press

This edition published in the United Kingdom in 2021 by

Canelo
Unit 9, 5th Floor
Cargo Works, 1–2 Hatfields
London, SE1 9PG
United Kingdom

A CIP catalogue record for this book is available from the British Library.

Print ISBN 978 1 80032 513 5
Ebook ISBN 978 1 80032 231 8

Look for more great books at www.canelo.co

Printed and bound in Great Britain by Clays Ltd, Elcograf S.p.A.

1

*All men lie. To their mothers, to their wives, to their lovers.
And they quickly learn that no lie stands alone. Its very
existence requires the support of other lies, which, together
with that first dishonest moment, shift the world towards a
false reality. There can be no return from this disagreeable
state other than through guilt, confession and disgrace.*

Women also lie. Mostly to themselves.

From *A Natural History of Lies* by J. Clarke

Storm

Across the steep wooded slopes, at a point where the Western Weald meets the Hampshire Downs, the forest waits for daybreak. The air is thick. Dry. Suffocating. The dense cloud overhead seems determined to hold on to the night. But, at last, a patch of grey dawn breaks through, casting its shadows deep into the dry cracks that streak across the forest floor. Bracken and bramble are in crisis, their lowly roots denied sustenance by the giant thirsts rising all around them. But they will prevail, for the deluge, long-promised, is here. A burst of dry lightning heralds its arrival. Deep in the forest something cracks and falls. Then the rain. At first, tight and hardened by drought, the alkaline soil proves impervious to the few drops that find their way down through the ancient canopy of beech and yew, hornbeam, hazel, sweet chestnut and alder. But more is to follow. Much more. And soon the parched ground is awash, tiny rivulets running in all directions, gouging their way towards the dried bed of a river-in-waiting. Withered leaves and tree litter are carried along with the flow. The riverbank swells, begins to crumble, flooding dusty burrows, dislodging tiny underground stores of hazelnuts and acorns, uncovering a single antler, a badger skull, a rusted can. And, close beside it, the slim fingers still delicate, a pale hand emerges from its shallow woodland grave.

Hedgehog

There are few untrodden places in the ancient woods of the southern counties. Over the centuries, footsteps have penetrated into the deepest gullies, the most perilous slopes, the most inaccessible clearings, in search of food, shelter, solitude. However, today, Watkins is only seeking food. And a recently drenched woodland is sure to provide it. Not everybody knows how to feed off the land. The supermarket chains have stolen that knowledge and wrapped it in cling film and recycled plastic. But Watkins is a seasoned forager and he knows where to look. After such heavy rain, dry roots and dormant mycelia spring forth with new life, so there is every possibility that his favourite mushrooms will be taking the opportunity to pool their resources and spread their spores wide. He can hear the stream close by, its girth swollen by the storm. The clearing should be straight ahead. Then half a dozen paces towards the water's edge. That's where they've been every year for as long as he can remember. He can already taste the damp, nutty smell of fresh hedgehog fungi. And, yes, there they are. Right where he's been expecting to find them. What he hasn't been expecting to find is the girl's body, lying on the bank, face down, mud streaked across her naked back, her legs awkward as if she's been trying to slither down to the water to cleanse herself. Watkins pauses, considers running away. Then he pulls out his mobile phone. The signal is weak but he manages to get through. Tells the people that need to be told. Then he kneels down beside the mass of mushrooms and uses his razor-sharp knife to cut their stipes, carefully, so as not to deplete the underlying matrix.

Ants

'DI Sam Barnes. NCA. You're the Attending Officer? Sergeant Boakes?'

'Yes, sir. DI James was here earlier.'

'Is that the guy who found her?'

'Yes. Leonard Watkins. He was foraging.'

'Foraging?'

'For mushrooms. He's given a statement.'

'Right. I gather the dogs are on the way. I suggest you get a wider area cordoned off, before the ramblers start hiking through with their lunch boxes. Who's the pathologist?'

'Dr Moran, James Moran.'

'Ah, yes. James. How long does he think she's been here?'

'About two days. Possibly three. Just before the storm. Probably buried and uncovered by the rain.'

'Right. How the hell did they get her here? It's bloody impenetrable.'

'They might have brought her along the riverbed. According to Watkins, it often runs dry in the summer. So, probably not much to be found now. There's been some ant activity.'

'Nice. Anything else?'

'Yes, sir… the ant activity. It's clustered around a large wound.'

'A knife?'

'Of sorts. Dr Moran believes it's the result of… He believes the young woman was recently operated on to remove a child. A baby.'

'Jesus, fuck! Don't you just love this job? I'd better get over there and take a look.'

'Better watch out, sir. One of the young officers is projectile vomiting.'

Body

'James. Hi. How's it going?'

'Ah, Sam. I thought I might be seeing your lot here sooner or later. Get fed up with cyberporn, did you?'

'Couldn't bear to spend any more of my life trolling around the rancid web. There's a limit to how many freaks you can deal with in one lifetime. Although this might be turning into a joint exercise. So, what's the story?'

'Victim is a young woman who has recently undergone a C-section. Full-term or thereabouts. The wound was left open. Placenta and cord still partially adhering to the wall of the uterus. It's a bit of a mess. You might like to wait until after the clean-up. Don't want any more heaving around here. Contaminating the crime scene.'

'I'm good. What do you think's going on here?'

'Well, the external incision is clean. Apart from the wildlife. Whoever did this probably considered completing the job and sewing her back up, but something went wrong. Can't be sure, but it looks like the uterus ruptured during what might have been a natural birth. The incision is longitudinal so was probably done as an emergency to remove the child. I'll be able to get a better picture back at the lab. The mess on her arm is probably the result of an attempt at transfusion, pulled out post-mortem. Death probably a result of hypovolemic shock. Judging from her colour, she bled out during the delivery.'

'So, somebody fucked up a DIY Caesarean and buried the evidence? Any sign of the infant?'

'Not as yet.'

Director

'Ah, yes, the Downs body. Nasty business. Any further developments?'

'Not much more than you already know, sir. SOCOs are still at the scene. And the dogs are on site sniffing around, but there's not much hope of uncovering anything after all that rain. Forensics believe the body was transferred to the site prior to the storm and interred into a shallow grave. Quite near to where it was found. The bank of the river has fallen away along that stretch, so it will be difficult to pinpoint the exact location. Bloodied dressings have been found downstream. They're checking the DNA with that of the woman... the girl: she can't be much more than a child herself. As yet, there's no identification. And nothing much to go on. Painted nails – nothing special. There's a small heart-shaped tattoo on the left shoulder, so that can be checked for point of origin. And there are several piercings – all the usual places. The jewellery's been removed. There's still no sign of an infant. It might be worth investigating local antenatal records, although that would be a mammoth task. Sir, can I assume we're linking this to the existing Hampshire investigation? The body, the pregnancy, would confirm practices way beyond mere sex trafficking, but...'

'But you believe there's a link?'

'Yes, sir. We're checking out a series of IP locations. In the Winchester and Guildford areas. Trying to establish links.'

'Guildford? That's conveniently close to your home territory, isn't it, Barnes?'

'Yes, sir, very conveniently close.'

'And you are continuing to maintain your cover? The teaching post?'

'For the time being, sir, yes. It's as good a place as any to investigate cybercrime and sociopaths. And although, unsurprisingly, the movement of foreign staff and students into the UK has not proven to be the significant trafficking route anticipated by some amongst us, there is a healthy air of sedition to keep me occupied.'

'Quite so. Well, Barnes, liaise with forensics and keep me informed. And keep as much of this out of the press as possible. Preferably all of it. Has the individual who discovered the body been briefed?'

'Briefed and debriefed, sir.'

For everything there is a single truth but many non-truths. The phoney, the fabulist, to be successful, must recall with absolute certainty which of these non-truths has been substituted as truth. A liar with a poor memory is doomed to failure.

From *A Natural History of Lies* by J. Clarke

Sophie was happy with things the way they were. Mostly. But there was one exception. She wished there was a garden at the front of her house, an any-shaped outcrop of nature that distanced her from the world outside. But there was no such thing. Instead, Sophie's front door opened directly onto the street, which, apart from denying her a garden, guaranteed a constant stream of daytime passers-by staring into her lounge as if her life was a display in a department store. And there were steps, two steps that led from her front door down onto the pavement. It was almost impossible to single-handedly manoeuvre the pram in and out of the house. And when Laura got a little older it would be a worry: the steps and the main road being that close. Sophie fretted about it, but Jonah was not that bothered, probably because men don't concern themselves with such issues. They have other things to worry about; as far as Jonah was concerned, child safety fell within the mother's domain.

In the early days, Sophie had made a few attempts at threshold horticulture: potted bay trees either side of the steps; snowdrops, crocus corms and thyme eased into the mean promises of soil between the bricks and paving stones. But, invariably, they had been vandalised. Even stolen. And, anyway, Jonah had disapproved of the scent of thyme and bay wafting in from the street and ravaging his home. Jonah had also disapproved of the scent of cinnamon, curry plant, garlic, cloves and cardamom, lavender, baby wipes, dishwasher tablets, peppermint and cabbage. But Sophie understood: people smell things differently. So that was that.

Sophie did have a small concrete garden at the back of her house. Its measly dimensions owed to the fact that, at some point in the distant past, priority had been given to the construction of a line of flat-roofed garages, which had reversed, windowless, into the existing row of Victorian properties, leaving their terraced residents with a diminishing display of disappointing rears. As always, Sophie had rallied. Despite this horticultural privation, she had accumulated a vast array of terracotta pots, which she had squashed into every opportunity in the vestige of backyard that nestled beyond her kitchen window. Throughout the year, she religiously cultivated a rich, potted, non-aromatic, shade-loving flora, supplemented in the summer months with a dozen or so tomato plants and a few etiolated sunflowers that cast even more shadow upon her dank little garden. Even at the height of summer, the damp cement, the terracotta pots, the sunflowers and the tomatoes encouraged the growth of moss and algae. Sophie loved the green and blue tenacity of these lowly plants, although Jonah always referred to their lush colonisation as mildew.

All things considered, Sophie hated the front of her house and, if the truth be known, she would have rather lived somewhere else. But all requests for relocation were denied. As far as Jonah was concerned, they could not move from their small, cramped, terraced house to a bigger house with a proper garden, where Laura would eventually be able to run and play, because they did not have enough money to better themselves after Sophie's unplanned pregnancy. Sophie couldn't really argue with that; she could have been more cautious. But some innate awareness of the proximity of her thirties, and of her declining reproductive opportunity, had encouraged laxity. The pregnancy was definitely her fault. So, that was that.

-

It was twelve thirty, early-August. With the washing loaded and Laura enjoying her morning nap, Sophie had just started tending her pots. She was engrossed in snipping axillary shoots from her tomato plants, when she heard the front door open and close. She stepped into the kitchen to investigate. Jonah was in the dark passageway, puffing and cursing and removing the large suitcase from the cupboard under the stairs. She kicked off her gardening shoes and approached him, the kitchen scissors in one hand and a posy of tomato shoots in the other. 'Why are you home,' she asked. 'I thought you were in Bournemouth today. Are you going somewhere?'

He did not look up. 'I'm leaving,' he mumbled.

'What do you mean, you're *leaving*?'

'I'll come for the rest of my things tomorrow.'

'What things? What are you talking about?'

He balanced the case upright and met her eyes. 'There's no way this is good for either of us.'

Sophie clenched and unclenched her hands, an activity which caused the tomato posy to disintegrate and the scissors to spin onto the floor and come to rest beneath a radiator. She grappled for words. 'But, what about Laura?'

Jonah recoiled from the pungent smell of crushed tomato leaves, the cocktail of alkaloids loved by some, unloved by others and loathed by Jonah. 'The longer this goes on the worse it will be for her. I'll send money.'

Sophie fell back against the wall, wiped her hands down her jeans. '*Money?* I don't know what you're talking about. What's happened?'

Jonah turned away and started to haul the suitcase up the stairs, crashing it against the slim spindles with all the disregard of a person who no longer owned them. Sophie hurried after him.

'*Jonah*, you'll wake Laura. Tell me what's happened. We can talk about it.'

They did not talk about it. Sophie asked him where he was going, if she would be able to contact him. What if something happened to Laura? Jonah said nothing. Sophie repeated her questions. Several times. But still Jonah said nothing. So, Sophie became silent, stunned, forced to stand and watch Jonah coldly and methodically arrange his clothes into the case: jeans, socks, shirts, boxers still in their presentation pack. The Arran jumper her mother had given him the Christmas before she died. Finally, he crushed three pairs of shoes, his library book and his phone charger into the top section, then tried to force the latches closed. That was never going to happen. So, he opened the case, pulled out the Arran jumper and, with this removed, secured the latches. Eyes down, he edged past Sophie into the en-suite and emerged moments later carrying his washbag, grabbed the handle of his case and made to leave.

Sophie threw herself in front of the door to prevent him doing so and, her voice trembling with suppressed tears, asked him again where he was going.

He paused before giving her an answer she'd never expected: 'There's somebody else.'

Sophie got out of the way.

She propped herself against the doorframe and watched Jonah bumping the case back downstairs, this time holding on to the banister and gouging channels into the wall opposite. She needed to do something, took a moment to rush in and check that Laura was still asleep, then hurried down behind him. By the time she reached the bottom of the stairs Jonah was already dragging the case down the two doorsteps. In her haste, she wrenched her ankle as she stepped off the bottom stair and saved herself from falling only by catching hold of the scratchy newel post. She sagged against it, trying to make sense of what was happening. But there was no sense to be had. No sense at all. Through the doorframe she could see Jonah balancing his case as he rearranged the boot of his BMW, which was parked immediately outside on the double yellow lines. The driver's door was hanging open, obstructing much of the pavement. She limped forward.

Clearly, Sophie was painfully ill-prepared for this situation. It was not that she was a particularly naïve person, it was just that she had always trusted Jonah; trusted him in a way that caused her never to have suspected adultery. As she pursued her abandoning partner, she became so overwhelmed by the mix of revelation and emotion that she was barely capable of functioning and as she hurried, shoeless, down the two doorsteps and across the pavement towards him, she felt her twisted ankle fail her. Pointlessly, she grasped the air ahead of her, tripped and stumbled forward. Unable to cancel her increasing momentum, she tumbled down the kerb towards Jonah, the whole weight of her small frame impacting his shoulder. Jonah spun round to push her away but was thrown off balance by the weight of his suitcase as it pivoted back against his elbow. As Sophie's arms folded around his chest and his hands flailed around her, lifting her and hugging her in an attempt to pull himself back, he too began to tumble. Trapped in their inappropriate embrace, they both fell heavily backwards towards the traffic and dangerously close to the path of an oncoming petrol tanker. The dismayed driver overreacted, swerved, narrowly missed an oncoming cab and came to a standstill just by the traffic lights. His frantic reaction caused a sequence of insurance-worthy bumper collisions, a bruised cyclist and a buckled bicycle wheel, but it had guaranteed a safe distance between the wheels of his tanker and the plummeting couple.

Unfortunately, though they were saved from a crushing end, all was not well. With Sophie's weight added to his own, Jonah's trajectory towards the ground had been harsh and unstoppable and all that had prevented his head striking the unforgiving road surface was the sharp corner of his toolbox, which he had removed from the boot and placed behind him to make room for his case. Sophie both heard and felt Jonah's skull break as she landed on top of him. Automatically, she pushed away from him and felt herself roll off and down towards the gutter just as Jonah's suitcase landed beside the toolbox, burst open and emptied its contents over Jonah's unconscious body. A young woman on the pavement screamed and fell back onto Sophie's steps. Horns sounded. Someone yelled.

Sophie lay still. She could smell the warm, dirty tar of the road beneath her cheek. She could hear shouting and car alarms. She tried to remember what was happening. Pulled herself up. She didn't think she was hurt. Just her ankle. Jonah was lying a short distance away. His head was covered in shirts and socks but she knew it was him. He wasn't moving. Somebody touched her hand and told her not to move. She glanced up to see the driver of the tanker leap down from his cab and hurry over. He threw himself onto his knees, started to pull away the contents of the case to investigate Jonah, uncovered his head and instantly vomited over Jonah's outstretched arm. With the shroud removed, Sophie could see a thick pool of blood collecting beneath Jonah's neck and running with the camber of the road towards her. His face was turned away from her but she could make out one of his ears with an attached patch of scalp lying on the road just beyond his head. She felt a numbing wave rise through her, felt someone's arm around her encouraging her to turn away. She tried to resist but she was made of nothing. 'Is he all right?' she asked the arm that was holding her.

'There's an ambulance on its way,' said someone.

'He's still breathing,' said someone else.

Moments passed. Sophie watched Jonah from her sitting position. He continued to not move. The pool of blood stopped getting bigger and started to seep into the dry road surface. Blood that ought to have been inside Jonah. A police car arrived and parked in front of the BMW. One of the police officers pulled out a blanket and arranged it over Jonah's legs. Another officer led the distressed lorry driver to the patrol car, radioed for assistance, then hurried over to deal with the traffic that was building up on both sides of the road.

Sirens drew closer then stopped abruptly as an ambulance manoeuvred its way into the space behind the truck. Yellow-clad people leapt out and ran to investigate. One yellow man assessed Sophie then joined the others who were tending to Jonah. She couldn't see what they were doing to him. A policeman squatted beside her, took down details: 'Jonah Royston... 39... 76 Tanner Street... Sophie... will he be all right?'

Passers-by had congregated. Some of them were now managing to divert their attention away from the carnage and were taking the opportunity to glance in through Sophie's open door, others were peering in through her lounge window. Some responsible parents overcame their desire to look and pulled their children away.

Assisted by the gentle breeze, some of the lighter items of Jonah's clothing were now dispersing themselves across the carriageway. Sophie could see Jonah's green corduroy jeans emerging from under an ambulance wheel. His library book had flapped open and the slip of paper that was marking his place was spiralling away towards the traffic lights. A second police car arrived. Two more officers, one man, one woman. Sophie felt herself being helped to her feet, encouraged towards her front door. She resisted. The female officer squeezed her hand. 'They'll take care of him. We need to get you inside.'

Sophie turned. Jonah was on a stretcher. He was being lifted into the ambulance. She checked the ground around the toolbox to make sure they hadn't overlooked his ear and his tuft of hair. Jonah had always been very vain about his thick, black hair.

'Why can't I go with him?'

'They'll be working… helping him en route to A&E. We'll follow on after,' said the policeman. 'Let's get you some shoes first, shall we? Have you injured your foot?'

'I twisted my ankle.'

'Are you alone in the house?' said the policewoman.

'Yes. I want to go with him.'

—

They walked towards Sophie's front door, Sophie between the two officers, slowly to accommodate her ankle. The crowd fell back, silent. The young woman who'd screamed was still sitting on Sophie's top step, rubbing her eyes repeatedly, as if she was trying to suck the images back out of her mind along the same route that they had entered. She jumped up as they approached, pushed her dark hair away from her face. 'The suitcase fell on them and pushed them over,' she said.

'Did you see that happen?' said the policeman.

'Yes.' She handed him a scribbled-on business card. 'That's my mobile number.' Her hand was shaking. She looked at Sophie. 'Can I do anything? Make tea or something?'

–

Sophie allowed herself to be led up into her hallway and on into the kitchen, watched the woman from the step filling the kettle, the female officer fetching her shoes. The other officer stepped back into the street to see if anyone else had witnessed the incident, but apart from the tanker driver who was already making a statement, nobody had seen what happened other than the woman from the step, because these things happen so fast. So, he organised the recovery of Jonah's belongings and the removal of his car from the double yellow lines then stepped back inside to make a few calls. Sophie tried to hear what he was saying, but her head was still full of car alarms and the sound of Jonah's skull imploding.

'I'm Sally Browning,' said the policewoman. 'Sophie, is there anyone that could accompany you to the hospital? A friend? A family member? Is there a neighbour I could fetch?'

Sophie tried to think. She wanted her mother, but she was gone. 'My sister, Josie, lives in Cork. I could phone my friend, Katie, but she'll be at work. And Mrs Davies next door is on holiday. All month. The other side is students, but they've gone home for the summer.'

'What about your husband's family?'

'He doesn't have any family. And... we're not married.'

'I could come with you,' interrupted the woman from the step. She offered Sophie a mug of tea. 'I'm Suzie... Kay.'

Sophie opened her mouth to reply just as a high-pitched scream came reverberating through the hallway. Officer Browning glanced towards the stairs. 'Is there a...?'

2

'Laura!' Sophie leapt up, pushed the mug away, causing dollops of tea to explode upwards, and ran into the hallway but, just through the door, her ankle failed her yet again. The already-startled police officer turned from looking up the stairs, dropped his phone and caught Sophie as she stumbled towards him. He lowered her onto the floor as his colleague hurried to help.

'I'll go up, Pete,' said Officer Browning. 'Sophie, let Officer Clark take you back to your chair. Shall I bring Laura downstairs?'

'Yes. Please.'

Suzie Kay hurried into the hallway clutching a tea towel. 'There's a baby?'

'I forgot about her.' Her eyes wide with desperation, Sophie watched Officer Browning disappearing up the stairs, Officer Clark checking his phone and retrieving her gardening scissors from beneath the radiator. 'Suzie, I forgot about her.'

'No, you… You've had a bad shock.' Suzie helped lead Sophie back to her chair.

'I'd get them to look at that ankle,' said Officer Clark, returning to the hall to communicate this latest development.

Sophie clutched at her stomach. 'What if I'd gone in the ambulance and she'd been left on her own?'

Suzie Kay crouched down and took Sophie's hands in hers. 'You mustn't think such things. She's called Laura, right? What a lovely name. How old is she?'

'Eleven months.' Sophie took a deep breath. 'Jonah wanted her to be called Laura. It was his mother's name.' She could feel Suzie Kay's fingers touching hers. Clean and soft. Her own fingers were still covered in a film of pulped tomato leaves. 'She needs her lunch. My hands are filthy.'

'I'll get a cloth. Are you still feeding her?'

'Only before bedtime.'

Suzie Kay fetched a damp cloth, waited as Sophie wiped her hands and exchanged it for some kitchen towel.

Sophie looked up into Suzie's dark brown eyes. 'Jonah was leaving me,' she said. 'When will I know what's happening?'

'They'll let you know.'

'What about his ear? It was lying in the road. And some of his hair.'

'Yes, I… They can stick ears back on. It's just skin and cartilage.'

'Are you a nurse?' said Sophie, grasping at the possibility of things returning to the way they were.

'No. But my mum had a dog with a stitched-on ear.' An abrupt, nervous laugh. 'I work in a travel company. In Guildford. This is my day off.' She glanced up. 'Here comes Officer Browning with your baby.'

-

With Suzie Kay's help, Laura was lunched and settled in her playpen in the lounge. The two officers stepped in to join them. 'Mr Royston has been transferred to Southampton General,' explained Constable Clark. 'He's being taken straight to theatre. Transport is being arranged, Ms…?'

'Denham. Sophie Denham.'

He nodded. 'I've explained that there's a young infant involved. Do you have a child's car seat that can be transferred? Social Services are unable to supply one at such short notice.' He handed her Jonah's car keys. 'Mr Royston's car has been parked in the back road. In the correct permit zone. There doesn't appear to be a child seat inside.'

'Perhaps you have another car?' suggested Officer Browning.

'I don't drive. Jonah always removes her seat in case he has to pick up equipment. It's in the kitchen.'

Constable Clark turned his attention to Suzie Kay. 'Ms Kay, if you would be so good as to provide a statement, you can be on your way.'

Suzie Kay disappeared into the kitchen with the two officers, and for the first time since Jonah's disastrous exit, Sophie was alone with her daughter. She watched the little girl chewing her sock, oblivious to the unfolding crisis. Only this morning she had been living her normal life, with her ordinary parents living together, like ordinary parents do. And now this. She had no way of understanding the changes this day had forced upon her innocent world. Even if they mended Jonah's skull, sewed his ear back on and he made a complete recovery, he'd decided to leave them. He'd found someone else. They must have been meeting up for weeks – maybe months – Jonah and this other woman. Spending carnal lunchtimes at her place. Sweaty hotels. Then coming home as if everything was normal. Admittedly, he'd complained about her reduced libido since Laura's birth, about her getting up in the middle of the night to check Laura was still breathing, but things had been better lately. At least she'd thought they had. She glanced up as Suzie Kay stepped into the room.

'Sophie, would you like me to come to the hospital with you?'

Sophie longed to say yes, but this poor woman had already been exposed to enough of her catastrophe. 'I'll be fine. I'll phone my friend. She lives in Portsmouth. She'll probably drive over. But, thanks for everything.'

'Glad I could help. Look, this is my mobile number.' She handed Sophie a business card: *Horizon Luxury Travel Services. Suzannah Kay – Consultant*. An additional telephone number was scribbled along the bottom. 'Call me if you need to talk, OK?'

–

The two officers confirmed that Sophie's transport would arrive within the hour, then left to confront another of those aberrant things that the police spend their days dealing with. Sophie thanked Suzie once again then hobbled to the front door to watch her cross the road and disappear into the everyday crowd. Things outside seemed to have returned to normal. The petrol tanker was gone and the traffic lights were executing their usual routine, directing cars whose drivers knew nothing of the events barely two hours before. There was nothing that might indicate Jonah's exit and subsequent misfortune other than some pieces of broken headlight and a few sweepings of sand, cleared into the gutter along with any remaining traces of Jonah's blood and lorry driver's vomit, waiting for time to wash it all away. Sophie experienced a stultifying wave of nausea, steadied herself against the doorframe, turned to retreat into her hallway and caught sight of a man loitering by the students' front window. He was tall, lanky in fact, stooping the way some tall people do, apologetic about their height. He had a buckled wheel in one hand; his other hand was resting on the saddle of a one-wheeled bicycle. He was wearing a crumpled linen suit, light grey, a navy T-shirt, trainers, a bike helmet and bicycle clips. He nodded apologetically as she caught his eye.

'I'm waiting for my brother. The police said the people here were away so… I hope your husband is all right.'

'They've transferred him to Southampton. I'm waiting for transport to take me there. An hour, they said.' She noticed the man's left eyebrow was red and swollen, forcing his eye to be half-closed. Another wave of nausea rippled through her. 'Were you hurt?'

'Went over the handlebars.' A half-smile. 'Bit of a crash landing. Punched myself in the eye.'

'Oh, did the paramedics see to you?'

'I told them I was OK.'

Sophie wrung her hands a little, uncertain how to end the conversation, uncertain as to whether she ought to end the conversation. Whether she wanted to end it. If it ended, she would have to go back inside and be alone. Close the door against the sand in the gutter. And wait. 'Will your brother be long?' she said.

'He has to pick his sons up from Summer Club. He said he'd be here by five.'

'That's ages. Do you want to come inside while I wait? I don't suppose anyone will steal your bike if you leave it there.'

He looked uncertain.

'I could make a quick cup of tea.'

'That would be great. If it's not too much bother.'

'It's no bother. And I could do with the company.'

–

Sophie tried not to limp as she led the man through her hallway. She wasn't sure it was the right thing to do, asking a stranger into her house. Particularly a tall, broken stranger carrying a bent bicycle wheel, and wearing bicycle clips. But anything was better than being alone. And besides, she'd left the front door wide open. So, she could see her transport arrive… and possibly so that she could grab Laura and make a dash – a limp – for it.

'The name's Sam,' he said. 'Sam Barnes. Did you hurt your foot?'

'I twisted it. Before the accident. I don't think it's anything serious. I'm Sophie.'

He followed her into the kitchen, dithered for a moment then propped his wheel against the back door and removed his helmet. 'Why don't you sit down and I'll make the tea.'

He stepped past her and picked up the kettle and, as he did so, Sophie caught a hint of his aftershave. Fresh and a little spicy. Jonah never used aftershave. Just an electric razor, bland soap and unscented deodorant. And toothpaste that smelled of nothing. She sat down and watched Sam Barnes filling her kettle. 'I'd better fetch the baby. Laura. I need to get her ready to go to the hospital. I don't know how long I'll be there.'

'Ages, probably.' He glanced back along the hallway. 'Where is she?'

'She's in the lounge. In her playpen.'

'Are you OK carrying her? With your ankle like that? Do you want me to fetch her? I'm not too mucky. And I've had loads of practice.'

'Do you have children?'

'Just my brother's two. I'll go get her, shall I? Then I'll have a look in your freezer. See if I can find a quick fix for your ankle. Before your lift arrives.' He loped off and returned moments later, carrying Laura and a large, floppy blue bear. 'She was just dozing off. The bear wanted to come too.'

'She doesn't usually like strangers.'

'Sensible girl.'

Laura seemed quite happy to be fixed into her highchair by this tall man. She clutched her bear and watched Sam Barnes make tea, hand her mother a mug, then root around in the freezer. Sophie also watched him. She noticed he was in the habit of running his fingers backwards through his blond hair in order to push it away from his eyes. He clearly needed a haircut and possibly a stylist. Jonah had always disapproved of poor grooming.

'OK!' he announced. 'Would you prefer petit pois or Brussels sprouts? For your ankle. It'll reduce the swelling. Have you got a clean tea towel?'

'In the bottom drawer. Petit pois, please.'

'In that case, do you mind if I take advantage of your Brussels sprouts?'

Sophie laughed, in a way she'd thought she never would again. She watched him wrap the packet of peas and hand it over. She leant forward and touched it against her ankle and shuddered at the sudden cold. She watched him fold the sprouts into another tea towel and hold it against his temple, lowering himself into a chair and sighing with relief. And there they sat, opposite one another across the kitchen table, sipping tea and indulging Laura, with their various swellings being reduced by a vegetable medley.

And time passed. And during that passing time Sophie experienced whole periods of not hearing the sound of fracturing bone repeating itself. She asked him about his brother's children.

'Jesse's wife died five years ago. The kids were really small. I'd just come back from Hong Kong and I didn't have a job so I put off finding one and looked after my nephews.'

'Have you got a job now? I mean, are you still…?'

'The boys are both at school now. So, I've gone back to teaching. North Surrey Uni. English. That's what I was doing in Hong Kong. I'm part-time so I can fit in with the boys' school times. And clubs. Obviously, today has had to be the exception.'

'Oh, I'm sorry.' Consequences. 'I did Biological Sciences at uni. But I never thought of teaching. Before Laura was born, I was working in Communications at Portway Biotech. I'm supposed to be going back in September. Jonah's a computer engineer. He has his own company.'

'Blimey. That sounds impressive. Did you say "Jonah"?'

'Yes, like the man who lived in a whale.'

He picked Blue Bear off the floor and handed it to Laura. 'I always wanted to teach. And you know what they say: *Those who can, do; those who can't, teach*. Fortunately, I couldn't do anything else. So, my choice of career was literally a no-brainer.' He checked his watch. 'When did they say your lift would be here?'

'An hour. I'd better be getting ready. My ankle feels much better now.' She lifted her ice-pack and got to her feet. 'How's your eye?'

'OK, but I'll probably have a hell of a shiner by the morning.'

'*Hell of a shiner?* My granddad used to say that.'

He smiled. 'I'm a bit of a crime fiction buff. Especially the post-war stuff. People were always waking up with a hell of a shinerin those days. Although please don't tell the Head of English that I'm a secret wannabe detective. Especially a nineteen-fifties detective. I'm not supposed to stoop lower than the Bard.'

'Don't worry, Sam. Your secret's safe with me. Would you keep an eye on Laura while I collect her things? She seems to have taken a liking to you.'

Sam Barnes watched Laura while Sophie fussed around getting ready. Then he plucked up his bicycle wheel and hovered awkwardly beside the sink. 'I hope it all goes OK. I think there's a car pulling up outside. I'd better get back to my bike. Jesse won't be long now.'

Sophie's stomach churned as she collapsed back into the day's trauma. She wanted to say to Sam Barnes why didn't he wait inside and just pull the door closed behind him when he left. But that would have been ridiculous. Trusting her house to a stranger. Perhaps he would accidentally leave the door open and when she got back she'd worry there was someone inside the house, hiding upstairs.

'Thank you so much for waiting with me,' she said instead. She wanted to tell him to call round sometime. For a cup of tea. But that would also have been ridiculous. And inappropriate.

Suddenly a police officer was standing on the top doorstep. 'Apologies for the delay, Ms Denham. I'm Sergeant John Wilkes and this is PC Tyler.' Sophie could see an unfamiliar female officer standing beside a police car that was parked immediately outside. Right where Jonah's car had been earlier. 'Mr Royston was transferred to Southampton General and is currently undergoing surgery.'

'I thought Social Services were taking me.'

'Social Services have been unable to locate a driver at short notice so we've undertaken to drive you there. Perhaps clear up a few details on the way. If I might have the car seat? That is assuming you have not made alternative arrangements for your daughter.'

Sophie frowned. 'What details?'

Officer Wilkes presumed to step inside. 'Mr Royston had no documentation on him at the time of the accident.' His tone was almost accusatory. 'We were hoping you might have access to his driving licence or passport. Some record of his national insurance number?'

'I think Jonah keeps his licence and insurance papers in the car. But I've no idea where he keeps his passport. He was in Latvia for four weeks recently. Perhaps he keeps it in his business premises. I don't remember ever seeing it.'

Sergeant Wilkes did not respond. He just gave Sophie one of those policeman looks that made her feel she might have committed some felonious act that had temporarily slipped her memory. Sam Barnes took a step forward to stand beside her. 'I'm a close friend. Samuel Barnes. Is there some kind of problem, officer?'

Sergeant Wilkes glanced at Sophie. 'Nothing for Ms Denham to worry about, Mr Barnes. Probably an administration glitch. But, in the absence of documentation, the hospital has been unable to locate any of Mr Royston's details: his blood group, any existing medical conditions.' He cleared his throat. 'And, there appears to be nobody by the name of Jonah Royston registered as living at this address.'

3

'I don't know what that means,' said Sophie.

'It means, at the very least, that Mr Royston is absent from the electoral roll,' said Sergeant Wilkes. 'Only an Emily Denham is registered as living here. And according to Council Tax records, this residence is listed as single occupancy.'

'Emily Denham was my mother. This was her house. She died the year before last.'

'As I said, Ms Denham, probably an administration glitch. It will undoubtedly all be resolved. Our most immediate concern is to take you and your daughter to Southampton. If I might have the child seat?'

Sophie pointed into the kitchen. 'It's behind the door.' She watched Officer Wilkes haul Laura's car seat outside and looked at Sam Barnes. 'Jonah thinks voting is a waste of time. And I don't remember ever receiving any election papers.'

'I wouldn't worry about that now. Why don't you fetch Laura and I'll help get your things into the car?'

'But how can my mum still be listed as living here? I registered her death.'

'That kind of information probably doesn't filter through to the electoral roll. It's a different bunch of pen-pushers. I think you're legally obliged to complete those election papers each year, but they're hardly going to throw you in jail for not doing it. Although they might get a bit shirty over you not paying enough council tax. Don't worry about it right now. Does Jonah have any medical conditions they ought to know about?'

'No. He's rhesus positive. I had to have injections when I was pregnant. But I don't think—'

'Sophie, just tell them what you know.'

Sam Barnes helped load things into the car then returned to guard his bicycle and watch as Sergeant Wilkes pulled away. Sophie tried unsuccessfully to placate Laura, who was currently red-faced and screaming. 'She'll quieten down in a moment,' she yelled.

Officer Tyler glanced round and forced a smile then resumed staring at the windscreen. Eventually, Laura calmed and the car became unpleasantly silent. Sophie had never been relaxed about extended periods of silence, a shortcoming that, in the past, had provided many instances of her blurting out the exact wrong thing. And, right now, the silence was becoming oppressive. She leaned forward. 'Jonah is rhesus positive,' she said.

'I imagine they would have discovered that by now,' said Sergeant Wilkes.

Sophie slumped back into her seat and tried to focus on the scenery: the rows of shops, houses, recycling bins, graffiti, then trees and hedges. Then the motorway. Increasingly unfamiliar. She had absolutely no idea where she was from one minute to the next. Such ignorance comes of not being a driver, of being conditioned to simply sitting and being taken places, usually by Jonah, occasionally by Katie. Katie was always pressuring her to learn to drive but Jonah had always discouraged it: they couldn't afford to run two cars, and the insurance premium on a BMW with a new driver would have been extortionate.

God, she needed to break the silence or she'd go mad. Again, she leaned forward. 'How will I know where to go when we get there?'

Officer Tyler inclined her head. 'We'll escort you to Reception and you'll be directed from there. Mr Royston will undoubtedly be taken to Intensive Care during the post-operative period.'

'Do you know how he is?'

'I believe his condition remains critical,' said Officer Wilkes. 'The surgery is likely to continue for several hours.'

Sophie glanced at Laura's sleepy eyes. Perhaps she should have waited at home. She wanted to ask how much longer before they arrived at the hospital, but good sense told her that was verging on infantile. Yet again, she addressed the back of their heads. 'We moved into the house the year before last, after my mother died.' No reply. Sophie resumed looking through the window.

Officer Tyler broke the silence. 'Where did you live previously?'

Did that sound like an attempt at friendly conversation? Not really.

'We rented a flat. The other side of town.'

'And Mr Royston's place of work is nearby?'

'Jonah rents some space at the Business Centre. He mostly has clients in London and the South, but he often takes contracts abroad. He was in Africa for six weeks in the spring. He missed Laura's first Easter.'

Silence resumed. Then Officer Tyler turned in her seat. 'Does Mr Royston have any clients that need to be notified? You're likely to have quite a long wait. Making a few phone calls would occupy some of the time.' Another attempt at a smile.

'I wouldn't know how to contact his clients. Their details are probably on his phone.'

'Mr Royston did not have a phone with him when he arrived at Accident and Emergency,' said Officer Wilkes. It sounded snappish.

'He probably left it in his car.' She was beginning to feel uneasy.

'And you have no house phone,' said Constable Tyler.

OK, now she was scared. 'How do you know that, Constable Tyler?'

Officer Wilkes was quick to reply. 'We've been trying to trace Mr Royston's records. On behalf of the hospital. But, also, regarding his involvement in today's unfortunate traffic incident. Perhaps you would forward details once you've retrieved them from his car.'

Officers Wilkes and Tyler escorted Sophie and Laura to the brightly illuminated reception area and left them in the care of a youngish woman, who introduced herself as May Barnet, Family Support. Her face was rigid with sympathy and compassion. She fussed over Laura then bustled Sophie along the main concourse, past shops brimming with consumer opportunities, and on into the hospital Costa. Sophie took a quick look around her: tables, chairs, food cabinets filled with the usual quick-satisfaction carb snacks. Tired, worried people. Waiting. An air of resignation. A place to be because you had no choice: just like Sophie had no choice.

'This would be the best place to wait,' said Mrs Barnet. 'It's open twenty-four hours and it's less-stressful than the Intensive Care Unit. I'll take you there shortly. There's a nice restaurant on Level B. And the Chaplaincy is on Level D, if you feel you need to chat to someone about the situation.'

Sophie's stomach took a dive. The last time she'd been encouraged to visit the hospital Chaplain was when her mother was unconscious and about to die. It had been a mistake. The Chaplain had offered to pray with her and it had made her angry. What was she supposed to be praying for? For her mother not to be dying? For her mother not to have developed cancer in the first place? For her mother to rally and open her eyes one last time and, amidst the pain, have one more cherished conversation with her daughters? Or perhaps for God to realise that allowing Emily Denham to suffer in this way was not her, Sophie Denham's, idea of Divine Love. God's punishment for mankind's sin, the Chaplain had said. And all because a pair of unlikely miscreants had pissed him off way back at the beginning of time. No, seeing the person you loved most in the world being dealt that fate was incompatible with praying to a benign creator.

'Can I get you a coffee?'

Sophie looked up. 'Yes, please. Is it all right if I use my phone?'

'Sure. Although not in Intensive Care. Can I get anything for Laura?'

'No, it's OK. I've brought supplies. Will the people in Intensive Care be able to tell me how the surgery is going?'

'I'm sure they'll let us know as soon as there's any news. I'll just get our coffees.' She wandered over to the counter and Sophie took the opportunity to phone Katie.

—

Katie Hurst had been Sophie's closest friend for much of the last decade. They had met on an induction course in the days well before Jonah had entered the scene, and had spent several years sharing dates and holidays. Katie had met her husband around the same time that Jonah had been contracted to install a new computer system in the biotech company Sophie worked for. Katie had been married within the year and was filing for divorce before her third anniversary. Sophie and Jonah had chosen not to marry. Actually, Jonah had chosen not to marry. He had experienced a messy break-up not long before and was feeling bruised and cautious. And what did it matter? They had enjoyed a modestly happy relationship. At least, Sophie had believed it to be a modestly happy relationship until Jonah's announcement earlier that day.

Lately, though, she had suspected that Katie was reluctant to spend time with her when Jonah was around. Perhaps she'd had an inkling about Jonah's intention to leave. Perhaps she had known about this other woman. Although, surely, she would have told her? But then people don't, do they? People know about infidelity and feed it life by staying silent.

May Barnet chatted to Sophie over their coffees. Sophie got the impression that her conversational skills were the result of some course in how to fill time in a potentially tragic situation. She also seemed to have majored in pulling faces and waving at babies. It was beginning to drive Sophie to distraction when, fortunately, Katie came bursting into the cafeteria. They hugged.

May Barnet looked on, apprehensive. Substituted. She attempted to introduce herself, but Katie dismissed her with a brief handshake then hurried round to appreciate Laura. 'Have they told you anything, Soph? Have you got to wait here?'

'He's in surgery. Then they'll take him to Intensive Care. We'll be able to wait there.'

'I'm afraid they don't allow occasional visitors in the ICU,' said May Barnet.

Sophie sensed a contest for her soul. 'Perhaps, May, if you could show me the Intensive Care Unit. Katie could stay here and look after Laura while we're away. Then I'd know where to go when Jonah comes out of surgery. And I wouldn't have to take up any more of your time. There must be so many other people that need you.'

May Barnet's mouth twitched a half-smile. 'Of course. If Mrs Hurst is happy to wait with your daughter.'

—

The lift down to Level B was almost as big as Sophie's spare room, although instead of a bed there was a porter and an elderly man on a trolley. The lift came to a halt, the doors opened and the elderly man was wheeled out and away. Sophie stepped out into the lift area behind May Barnet and was briefly reminded of her twisted ankle. She followed her over to a set of swing doors and, as they opened, the smell of disinfectant hit her like a baseball bat.

'Is it all Intensive Care on this level?'

'Good gracious, no. There's all sorts here.'

It had been a stupid question. Sophie was an expert at stupid questions. So, she decided to say nothing, always the safest option, and followed May Barnet along identical corridors, reading signs, fearing that, without a guide, she would never find her way back to the lift and would be lost for ever in a super-sanitised hospital maze. The smell seemed to be intensifying. When Jonah came round after the surgery, it would be sure to drive him insane. She ought to mention his olfactory intolerance to the nursing staff.

May Barnet came to a sudden halt in front of some wide swing doors, stroked a card across a security panel then led the way through into a world of humming and beeping and distant voices. She directed Sophie towards a reception desk where they waited in silence. Presently, a woman in scrubs came over and explained that Jonah would not be out of surgery for some hours and that a room would not become available until nearer the time. Then she hurried away to respond to a buzzing noise.

On the way back to the lift Sophie recognised nothing. She recalled a fable in a long-ago storybook, about some hero finding his way out of a labyrinth by unwinding a trail of thread as he went in to kill a monster, then following the line of thread back out to safety. He might have been carrying the monster's head with him on the way out. Although the monster's head might have belonged in another story. Perhaps the head had belonged to Samson. She couldn't remember.

Back on the ground floor, May Barnet presented Sophie with a business card, told her to call if any problems arose, then wandered away towards Reception. Sophie inserted the card into her purse, behind the card Suzie Kay had given her earlier. She wondered if she would ever see her again, if she would recognise her if she passed her in the street. Her memories of the day were such a jumble. Hadn't she said it was her day off? Yes. She worked for a travel service in Guildford. Poor woman, becoming embroiled in Jonah's calamity like that. You can never know what the fates are going to throw at you.

–

By the time Sophie returned to her pitch in Costa, Katie had managed to locate a highchair and was coaxing Laura into eating baby-grade macaroni cheese.

'Hi. Any news?'

'Not really. It's likely to be hours yet. You ought to go home.'

'Sophie, don't talk rubbish. Anyway, I'm getting really good at this feeding thing. Quite a lot of it's gone in her mouth. I hope the highchair isn't covered in antibiotic-resistant germs. There're messages everywhere about disinfecting your hands with that squirty stuff.'

'And have you? Used the squirty stuff?'

'No.'

'No, neither have I. Do you want me to take over?'

'No, just sit. And tell me what happened.'

Sophie sat down, looked at Katie and sighed. 'He was leaving us. No explanation. Just that he'd found someone else and that was that: case, clothes, washbag, library book. He didn't even take a look at Laura before he dragged his case outside.' She described the sequence of events from the moment she ran out after him. Katie continued to manoeuvre stodge into Laura's reluctant cheeks. Sophie frowned. 'You don't look that surprised.'

'I'm not. Well, I'm surprised about the accident and his ear but, well, he's a shit.'

Sophie gaped at her. 'I didn't realise you thought that.'

'I didn't think you'd want to hear it. It's just stuff Paul told me. Last time we – air quotes – spoke. He said Jonah told him he should never have let himself be coerced into marriage. Because marriage and kids are a liability when you want to move on. And that's why he refused to, you know, marry you.'

'But men always say things like that.'

'I saw him.'

'What?'

'Right after Easter. When he was supposed to be in Africa. I didn't tell you because Laura was so little. And...'

'Where did you see him?'

Katie held the macaroni spoon still. 'You remember I attended that seminar? In Exeter? Hoping to find my new man. Well, I went to this restaurant for a supper-cum-shag with this jerk I'd just met and Jonah was in there. With this flaunty woman.'

'Exeter? No, he was in Mauritania. It probably just looked like Jonah. They say everybody has a doppelgänger.'

'That's what I thought. Anyway, I suggested to the jerk that we have a quick cocktail and then go straight to the hotel for the shag. Jonah's BMW was parked outside.'

'Are you sure?'

Katie handed her the spoon and reached for her mobile, scrolled down her photos then held the screen towards Sophie. And there, unmistakably, was an image of the back of Jonah's car: the *Royston Computer Solutions* bumper sticker; the offending boot that earlier that day had played its part in Jonah's miserable fate. Katie swiped back to the previous photo and held it steady. 'I took this through the window.'

Sophie frowned. It was definitely Jonah. She wasn't sure she recognised what he was wearing but it was definitely his thick, black hair. His dark eyebrows. The woman opposite him was laughing. They were holding up their glasses, ready to clink. And then she noticed, pulled Katie's hand closer to be sure, narrowed her eyes in disbelief.

'Katie, he's wearing a wedding ring.'

4

The hours passed slowly, punctuated by an expedition to the ladies' to put Laura into her sleeping bag, a trip to the restaurant on Level B and several returns to those two incriminating Exeter images. As the evening plodded by, Laura slept in her pram and Katie and Sophie lounged uncomfortably on a couple of hard chairs. Sophie ventured over to the Neurological Unit twice and was given very little information. On both occasions, she managed to find her way back to the lift without the need for a ball of thread and, along the way, she did a lot of thinking about Jonah clinking glasses in Exeter when he should have been in Mauritania. Perhaps they were jumping to conclusions. Perhaps he'd come home via Exeter to visit some company or other. A company that woman worked for. And she'd taken him to dinner. Perhaps wearing a wedding ring was Jonah's way of not getting involved. He wouldn't have bothered to mention it. He never discussed his business affairs with her. It was almost midnight when Sophie nudged Katie and insisted she go home because she had to go to work within hours and this was really her dilemma and hers alone.

'I'll phone in sick.'

'No, Katie! People who phone in sick never get promoted. And I can't see me getting away from here for hours. I'll ring you as soon as there's any news.'

'Will you be all right on your own?'

'Yeh.'

Katie rubbed her eyes. 'Sophie, what are you actually doing here? I mean, surely you're not going to let him move back in with you?'

'Well he didn't actually manage to move out, did he? And he is Laura's father.'

Katie shrugged. 'OK, Soph. Phone me the minute you need me.'

'I will. And drive carefully. I don't want you finishing up in a ditch because you're exhausted. That would be something else to hold against Jonah.'

'Perhaps it would help tip the balance.'

'Yes, well, don't do it.'

Sophie watched Katie disappear towards Reception then settled back into her uncomfortable chair, determined to stay awake, just in case someone attempted to steal Laura. Babies had been stolen from hospitals in the past, albeit usually newborns. She was surprised, therefore, to be jolted awake by a woman in scrubs and informed that Mr Royston was now in Intensive Care and a surgeon was available to discuss the situation if she came straight away. She jumped up and checked Laura was still in her pram, checked her watch: one twenty. Laura hadn't stirred since falling asleep at around eight. At least Jonah had presented her with this situation when Laura was still young enough to be contained in a pram.

Back on Level B, Sophie left Laura with the woman in scrubs and was escorted into a side room, empty apart from a bed, a person whose head was swathed in bandages – presumably Jonah – and a mass of equipment to which he was attached. Even his eyes were bandaged over and the place where his mouth ought to be was blocked by a fat tube, which fed into the machine that was breathing on his behalf. No chair. She waited. After a few minutes, a doctor walked in, shook her hand and introduced himself as Ben Donovan: grey haired, weary, green scrubs, a red splodge just below his knee. Nice manner. He explained that Jonah's skull fracture had caused some damage to the surface of his left dorsal cerebral hemisphere. The protective layers had been ruptured causing leakage of cerebrospinal fluid and, obviously, some moderate bleeding into the intracranial space. They were not able to anticipate the extent to which neurological function might be compromised by this. It had been necessary to remove fragments of bone and a small amount of superficial brain tissue and he was being held in an induced coma for the moment. Did she have any questions?

Questions? Yes, she did have questions. For a start, what did removing bone and brain tissue mean? If you remove fragments of skull bone, does the person's skull grow back or does it always have a hole in it? Was the small bit of brain they removed the bit that contained all Jonah's intelligence? Would Jonah still be able to do his puzzles with a piece of his brain missing? He loved his puzzle books. What was she thinking? She'd been a biologist once. Those higher things, like intelligence and memory, they all functioned deep inside the brain, not just immediately under a skull fracture. Didn't they? She needed to ask. But all she heard herself say was: 'What about his ear?'

'The ear has been reattached. The attachment will most likely prove successful. Quite a clean detachment, involving only the exterior part of the ear. The tympanic membrane, the eardrum, has been compromised, although there appears to be no middle or inner ear damage. There may be some unilateral hearing loss.'

Sophie felt a wave of nausea. She looked at the person lying there, looking like an early Hollywood version of the Invisible Man. 'How long will he be in the coma?'

'Several days. Once you've stayed with him for a while, you might consider returning home. There can be little virtue in subjecting yourself and… is it a son or daughter?'

'A daughter. Laura.'

He smiled. 'There's little to be gained in subjecting yourself and Laura to any more discomfort. So, I would suggest that you return home to wait. We'll notify you of any changes in your husband's condition. And, of course, you may phone in for updates. We're hopeful that, although Mr Royston's condition is critical, he will make a fair recovery.'

'Fair?'

'It's unlikely that such an injury will not carry consequences, although many head injury patients do return to a normal life. He will probably need a period of rehabilitation. But let's cross that bridge when the time comes, shall we?'

Sophie sighed. It was pointless asking anything else. Futile. Too many permutations of good news and bad news and nobody knowing. So, she thanked the surgeon and he left. She lingered for a while trying to deal with the tirade of thoughts that were crashing through her mind but she was too tired to organise them into any kind of logical order. It would be better if Laura woke in her own room. She wished she hadn't insisted Katie left. She couldn't phone her now: she was probably asleep, dreaming away the trauma she had been dragged into. She'd call a cab. There were approved numbers by reception. So, that's what she did. The cab driver was apologetic about the fare. It was double rate after midnight. And it wasn't officially morning until seven o'clock. Sophie shrugged: money was the least of her concerns. Of course, that situation was about to change.

–

Sophie suffered a restless couple of hours, drifting in and out of dreamy sleep, with each transition being filled with the kind of madness that revels in fear and doubt: Jonah's detached ear lying in the gutter; Laura stolen from her pram; peeling Jonah's bandages away and discovering that his head had degenerated into a mass of macaroni cheese; Sam Barnes unloading the dishwasher wearing nothing but her Cath Kidston apron. Right, enough was enough! She sat up and checked the alarm clock: seven twenty. Laura was stirring.

Sophie turned towards Jonah's side of the bed, touched his cold pillow. She was used to sleeping alone when he was on his trips, but today his half of the bed looked more than unslept in. It looked left. Just like her. Last night she had been desperate to rationalise; today she wasn't feeling that generous. Perhaps, even if his Exeter stopover had been legitimate, perhaps his clinking-glass supper had proved to be so enjoyable that he'd decided to embrace West Country life permanently. Perhaps that woman *was* his *somebody else*. Sophie pictured her sitting at home wondering why he hadn't contacted her. Why he wasn't there with her to start their new life together. Perhaps she'd been trying to call him. She needed to check Jonah's mobile for incriminating evidence, but she didn't want to do that right then. Instead, she concentrated on getting herself and Laura ready for the day, and that way she managed to put off thinking until almost nine thirty, when she phoned the hospital and was told that Jonah's condition was unchanged.

The doorbell rang.

Sophie's heart skipped several beats. She bundled Laura into her playpen then hurried through to the front door. This time her heart almost stopped completely: Officer Wilkes was standing on her top step, Officer Tyler on the pavement below, holding Laura's car seat. Sophie wrung her hands. 'Is it about Jonah? They said there was no change.'

Officer Wilkes held up his hand. 'No, no. We gather Mr Royston is as well as can be expected. We're returning your car seat.' His attitude seemed to have mellowed. 'And we were hoping you might be able to provide us with Mr Royston's car details. There are a few problems related to yesterday's traffic incident. If we could come inside?'

Sophie stepped back and directed the two officers into her lounge, invited them to take a seat, glanced at Officer Tyler, who gave her a convincing smile. OK, that was unexpected.

'What's this all about, Officer Wilkes?'

'Ms Denham, might we ask how long Mr Royston has owned his vehicle? The black BMW?'

'About three years, I think.' How could they expect her to know such things at a time like this? 'Isn't the road tax up to date?'

'No, no, the vehicle's documents are in perfect order. The problem arises from the fact that the vehicle does not appear to belong to Mr Royston.'

Autopsy

'James! I'm not interrupting anything am I?'

'No, Sam. Come and join us. I… Good God, what happened to you? Have you been wrestling with international crime lords?'

'I came off the bike. Is that the failed Caesar?'

'Yes, minus the fauna.'

'So, what can you tell me?'

'Not that much, I'm afraid. Dental records, fingerprints, DNA… not previously on record. Actually, her teeth were perfect. Facial recognition provided nothing. There are indications of previous pregnancies. A nicely reworked low transverse C-section scar just above the pubic hairline. I missed that at the scene. The uterine wall seems to have ruptured along the site of a previous incision.'

'Does that often happen?'

'Under normal circumstances it rarely happens. Usually, it's only when there's an insufficient gap between pregnancies and the uterine scar fails to heal prior to subsequent implantation. Perhaps due to an infection. There's no knowing the circumstances under which the previous procedures were carried out. How aseptic they were. We're checking microbiology. There's a lot to choose from given her circumstances of late. But in this case the rupture was undoubtedly due to a twin pregnancy with the attachment of a second placenta over a previous Caesarean scar. So, we're looking at a case of *placenta accreta* in a multiple pregnancy, most likely a twin pregnancy. The detachment and subsequent rupture would have caused the haemorrhaging that necessitated the emergency section.'

'So, you think at least three pregnancies including this twin pregnancy? How old would you say she is?'

'Difficult to be sure. Skull sutures, epiphyseal fusion, tooth eruption... I wouldn't place her much older than eighteen. Maybe younger.'

'God Almighty! Do you think someone's been using this child as a baby factory?'

'She was well-nourished. No signs of long-term maltreatment. Although there's bruising and recent, unhealed vaginal tears, possibly due to abusive sexual activity immediately prior to the start of labour or possibly during it.'

'Good God, now there's something to colour my dreams for a while.'

'We're checking for foreign DNA. The strange thing is there are no signs of older wounds. No signs of previous abuse. The recent injuries seem inconsistent. If this girl was part of the prostitution-baby-farming network you lot suspect, it would be unlikely that they would risk the sexual health of one of their breeding stock. In addition, the fact that the outfit behind this was organised enough to be able to call upon some reasonably competent surgical back-up, would not only suggest the involvement of individuals with more than a basic knowledge of obstetrics, but it would imply that there are others like her.'

'A review of disgraced medics hasn't turned up anything.'

'Perhaps you should check out a few from the ranks of the undisgraced.'

'Yeh. So, have you been able to determine ethnicity?'

'Blood markers suggest a Central European origin. And the tattoo ink would seem to confirm that. Quite likely manufactured in the Czech Republic.'

'Recent? The tattoo?'

'No, loss of symmetry and fading would suggest it was done several years ago.'

'Right. Thanks, James. Keep me posted on that. I'll put someone on to checking Europol's Missing Persons data. Possible child abductions. So, what would we be talking about here? Six years ago? Probably longer if she'd been put to work before the pregnancies.'

'At least six. As I said, there doesn't seem to be any history of tissue damage so it would have to have been softly, softly. It's likely this lass was well cared for. Her unfortunate fate has probably been a financial inconvenience as much as anything else.'

'Right. Well, I'd better get back to HQ and give Short the good news…'

'Sam, there is one other thing, before you dash off: the nail varnish. I checked it against our database. It appears to be identical to varnish found on the body of a young woman, early twenties, washed up in Plymouth last year. Thought to have fallen off a boat, possibly dumped at sea. She'd been in the water for some time. There was no identification. Central European markers. Might just be a coincidence. It's not uncommon… the varnish, that is.'

'Were there any signs of previous pregnancies?'

'There was a lower section scar – I've requested more images – but there were also previous compound fractures of the long bones. And she was HIV-positive.'

5

Sophie fought for vocabulary. 'What?'

John Wilkes flashed a look at his fellow officer. 'Preliminary enquiries have revealed that the car is registered as belonging to a Robert Perrin. Mr Perrin is also the sole name on the insurance policy.'

'I've never heard Jonah mention anyone called Perrin.' She watched Officer Tyler wander over to engage with Laura. What on earth was going on?

Officer Wilkes continued. 'DVLA records have Mr Perrin listed as residing along the Topsham Road south of Exeter. We were hoping you might be able to explain the confusion.'

'Exeter?' She ought to tell them about the clinking-glass woman, but she already felt unbearably foolish in front of these uniformed people. 'I'm sorry, I can't explain it.'

'Perhaps, if we might take a look at Mr Royston's driving licence. You believe it might be in his car along with his insurance documents? Officer Tyler will watch your daughter. If I might accompany you.'

Sophie put her hand across her mouth. That had always proved to be an efficient way of preventing herself from saying the wrong thing. And, at the moment, everything she said was likely to be the wrong thing. She fetched Jonah's keys and followed Officer Wilkes out into the street, averting her eyes from the sand still in the gutter. They walked in silence through the narrow shortcut to Jonah's car where a brief search revealed his wallet on the floor behind the driver's seat, his sunglasses and mobile phone beside it. Officer Wilkes scooped them up then asked Sophie if she would check the glove box, so she climbed into the driver's seat, leant across and retrieved a wad of papers and an unfamiliar silver iPhone.

She eased herself back onto the pavement. 'I've no idea why Jonah has two phones. I've never seen this one before.'

'I would imagine it's one he uses for business purposes.' Officer Wilkes took another cursory glance inside the car then pushed the door closed. 'Shall we go back to the house? You look as if you need to sit down.' That sounded positively empathic. In fact, it was nothing less than alarming.

Back inside, both officers watched Sophie investigate Jonah's wallet. She discovered his driving licence in a zip pocket, pulled it out and looked at the photograph: a younger version of Jonah, slim around the neck, very short hair. Both ears intact. Her eyes strayed to the details alongside:

1. PERRIN
2. MR ROBERT BRIAN
3. 16-03-76 UNITED KINGDOM
4a. 29-03-15 4c. DVLA
4b. 28-02-25

Then a long number and a signature and the Exeter address Officer Wilkes had mentioned. Sophie thought she might be losing her mind. She pulled out Jonah's Mastercard, Visa card, his AA Breakdown card. They all carried that same signature. Even his library card belonged to Robert Perrin. Why had she never noticed? She tried to think back. Jonah always paid in cash whenever they went out to dinner or shopping. He said he liked to feel the money in his hands. She looked again at the photo, re-read the details, then handed the licence to Officer Wilkes. 'It's not even Jonah's proper birthday,' she said. But it occurred to her that it was probably Robert Perrin's proper birthday.

Officer Wilkes noted down the details. 'We'll forward this information to the hospital. It would be in everyone's interest if the medical staff were made aware of your partner's true identity. His medical notes may be important.'

'And then what?'

'We'll ensure that there's no criminal explanation for Mr Perrin adopting an alternative identity, which, if it has not been used fraudulently or to procure loans or benefits, is not likely to be regarded as a criminal act. Mr Perrin's car insurance, road tax and licence are all valid. Preliminary checks have revealed no outstanding fines.' He paused to gauge Sophie's response 'We'll check with the Inland Revenue to ensure that the dual identity is not associated with any attempt at tax evasion. Would you have access to his tax returns?'

'They're probably in his office.' Sophie shook her head. She couldn't believe that she'd spent the last five years of her life living with somebody who didn't exist. Then she had a thought. 'But Jonah's company is called Royston Computer Solutions.'

'We'll check with Companies House, but as long as he has used his correct name in the documentation, there is nothing to prevent him calling his company whatever he chooses.'

'Do you think Robert Perrin is Jonah's correct name?'

'The evidence is tending to that conclusion. This *is* a photograph of your partner, is it not? The person you have known as Jonah Royston?' He handed back the licence.

'Yes, it's him.'

Officer Tyler got to her feet. 'I wonder, Sophie, do you have Laura's birth certificate? Is her father listed as Jonah Royston?'

'Yes. But I registered her birth. In the hospital. And I gave her father's name as Jonah Royston because that's what I thought it was. I think he signed a form. I can't remember.' She glanced over at her daughter and recalled those first euphoric, panic-filled days of motherhood, wanting to do everything right for this minute person she and Jonah had created. Jonah had agreed that Laura should share his name but, looking back on it, had he simply not disapproved? So, now her daughter was named after nobody. 'Does that mean that Laura's birth certificate isn't legal?'

Officer Wilkes seemed uncertain. 'I would imagine that might be the case but only because the father's name is erroneous. Essentially, Mr Perrin encouraged falsification of the certificate. I'm not sure of the legal repercussions. However, I believe that any surname may be chosen when registering a new child, including a surname that belongs to neither parent. I suggest you obtain some legal advice: a solicitor or the Citizens Advice Bureau.'

Sophie felt numb. How could he have done this to her? It was bad enough that her mother had died never knowing her granddaughter, but worse than that she had died believing her daughter was living with someone who didn't exist. And that address in Exeter? He'd never mentioned anything about... 'Will you check that address? In Exeter?'

'As I said, Ms Denham, our involvement will depend upon any perceived possibility of fraud. Mr Perrin will not be the first person to have used a dual identity for non-fraudulent reasons. We'll check with the Passport Office. You said your partner spends long periods abroad. That might be significant. In the meantime, you can contact me on this direct line.' He handed her a business card.

The two officers left. Sophie stood back from the window and watched them drive away before wandering over to Laura's playpen, lowering herself down onto the floor and allowing herself the tears that were way overdue. Her sobbing waxed and waned as she fought to hold on to a past that was collapsing around her...

Five Years Earlier

Sophie had been surreptitiously watching him for the best part of an hour. All he'd said when he carried in his heap of boxes, and apologised for his intrusion, was that he'd try not to disturb her; that he just needed to make a few adjustments to the system; that he might have to interrupt internet access briefly but he'd give her good warning. He didn't look like a computer geek. More like an executive on his day off: smart casual, expensive watch, perfectly-styled dark hair. No wedding ring. Sophie felt needy. She looked back at the screen in front of her. Just one sentence and she'd changed that more times than it had words. She checked her phone – five past eleven – got to her feet, smoothed her skirt and prepared to interrupt. He glanced up as she approached.

'Sorry,' he said, 'am I disturbing you?'

Absolutely. 'No, not at all. I was just wondering if you'd like a coffee. I'm just off to the machine. I could bring you one. If you like.'

'I, er… actually, I'm a bit of a coffee wimp. I…'

Such amazing, brown eyes. 'It doesn't really taste much like coffee. And there's hot water so you can dilute the horror of it. I could bring you some.'

Eyebrows to die for. 'Or you could nip down with me. Then you'll know. I'm Sophie, by the way.'

'Great! I'm Jonah. I'll just pause this…' He smiled. 'Then I'm all yours.'

Sophie had never seen anyone add sugar to a cup of hot water and then drink it but, ten minutes into their acquaintance, this Jonah could do nothing wrong.

'So, how long is this going to take you... with the computers?'

'I should be finished by the end of the day. Maybe a trip back in a week or so, to make sure it's all running smoothly.'

'Oh!' *Panic. Action required.*

'Do you have to come far?' *Did that sound too obvious?*

He put his head to one side. 'Interesting question. I've just sold my flat so I'm a bit itinerant at the moment. Moving between motels.' He sighed. 'Possessions in storage. I'm staying at the Premier Inn tonight, sorting out a few local contracts for the rest of the week.' He grinned. 'Take my word for it, hotel life is a lot cheaper than paying a mortgage... and having to replace gutters and the like.' He took her empty cup and tossed it with his own into the recycling bin. 'We'd better be getting back. Before somebody notices we're enjoying ourselves.'

Sophie gave a little laugh, stepped through the door he was holding open for her and heard herself say, 'If you like, I could show you around town this evening. Show you the best places to eat. If you haven't got anything better to do.'

–

Sophie (mostly) wasn't in the habit of sleeping with a guy on a first date. But this, well, it was different. She'd never felt so at ease with a new person. She watched him, still sleeping. It wasn't yet dawn but he seemed to be already glowing with a new day. She pushed back the duvet and climbed out of bed slowly so as not to disturb him, pulled on her dressing gown and crept through to the kitchen. She put the kettle on, checked the sugar canister, selected the two matching cups and put them ready, felt his arms close around her waist.

'I tried not to wake you.'

'Why? Are you bored with me already?'

'No, I'm not. Where have you got to be today?'

'Wisley. Late morning.'

'Oh. How late… morning?'

'Late enough. Why don't you call in and say you woke up with a migraine?'

'OK.'

6

Sophie was jolted from her melancholy by a plastic duck that hit her squarely on the back of her head. Laura was standing a few inches away, staring through the bars at her, wearing that same look of infant apprehension she had worn when she first heard the coffee grinder. Parental responsibility triumphed.

'Laura, shall we go feed the ducks?'

Laura's apprehension became uncomplicated frowning.

'We like feeding the ducks, don't we?' And, besides, anything would be better than sitting in a house full of lies.

Sophie spent the next ten minutes preparing to leave and avoiding Jonah's two mobile phones, but the temptation proved too great. So, with Laura secured in her pram, she fetched them from the lounge and set them alongside one another on the hall table: Jonah's familiar Samsung and the sleek, unfamiliar iPhone. She turned on the Samsung – 91% charge – and recalled Jonah squashing the charger into his case. She didn't remember seeing it lying in the road so most likely it had been loaded back into the suitcase with his other belongings. She scrolled down the list of calls but most of them were to or from her. She picked up the iPhone, tried to turn it on and found it was password protected. She poked in various combinations of numbers but after several failures she gave up. She couldn't remember how many tries you have before you become locked out. Frustrated she placed it beside the Samsung, pulled open the front door and positioned herself for the nightmare of manoeuvring the pram backwards down the steps.

'Can I help you with that?'

Sophie half-turned. Sam Barnes was standing on the pavement, clutching a large bunch of pink roses. She was shocked at how delighted she was to see him.

'I thought these might cheer you up,' he said. 'It's also my attempt to thank you for your kindness yesterday. How's the ankle?' He paused. 'I hope your… I hope Jonah is OK.'

Sophie couldn't quite manage to speak. She was not at all sure she could remember how to breathe either. She thought to put the brake on the pram. Silence hung in the air. Awkwardly. Sam Barnes took a step forward. He looked different. As if he hadn't just been thrown over the handlebars of his bicycle. He was wearing that same grey suit, still crumpled, but he'd combed his hair. His brow was no longer swollen but his eye was black and yellow and numerous shades between.

'My goodness,' said Sophie. 'You've got a hell of a shiner.'

There followed several moments of mutual dithering. Then Sophie came to her senses.

'Jonah's in intensive care but they're hopeful he'll recover. My ankle's much better. We were just about to go and feed the ducks. You're welcome to join us… if you're not too busy.' She inclined her head towards the roses. 'But we'd better put those in some water first. They're beautiful.' She stepped to one side so that he could squeeze in past the pram, wafting that same fresh, spicy, intoxicating aftershave that she imagined must drive his young female students to distraction. It was the perfume of a more sophisticated and urbane man than the scruffy English teacher who had, only yesterday, been thrown into her troubled life. She closed the front door, instantly shutting out the bright August sunshine and casting the hallway, the pram and her disgruntled daughter into semi-darkness. Laura's protest was instant. Sophie hurried to unstrap her, carried her into the kitchen, inserted her into her chair, glanced up and realised that, yet again, Sam Barnes was standing by her kitchen sink.

'Do you have a vase or something? Maybe a bucket?'

'Sam, you have no idea.' Sophie strode over, pulled open the larder door and stepped inside. She flicked on the light and cast her eyes around the shelves. Sophie's mother had been a collector and, apart from her house, she had bequeathed to her two daughters many things, most of which Jonah had regarded as useless 'tat'. Josie had removed her mother's jewellery and her fine antiquarian library over to Cork but Sophie had stubbornly hung on to her mother's extensive collection of vases, jugs and teapots, most of which were now crammed into cardboard boxes and packed away in the depths of her spidery larder. She reached up and selected a white pottery vase – plain, hand-thrown, big enough to accommodate her pink roses – returned to the sink and watched Sam Barnes unpeeling the bunched-up cellophane; watched him trying to release the long stems from their thick girdle of florist's tape. Noticing her gardening scissors beside the kettle, she plucked them up and held them towards him. 'Here!'

He turned, saw the scissors and threw up his hands in a mock gesture of surrender.

'Oh, sorry!' She turned the scissors. Handed them over, watched him cut the tape, half-fill the vase with water, remove an inch or so from the bottom of each of the stems and arrange them in the vase until they were perfect. Then she noticed the sachet of plant food lying beside the discarded cellophane. She held it up. 'You've forgotten something.'

He rolled his eyes. 'Bugger! I reveal myself as a person who rarely receives flowers.'

'We could pretend it never happened. But it does make things last longer.'

'Well, then, perhaps I should keep it and add it to my tea.'

She heard herself laugh. 'I've got a mini watering can,' she said. 'We can add it with that, without disturbing your beautiful arrangement.'

He smirked. She smirked back. She fetched her watering can, handed it over, studied his expression as he filled it and added the plant food. She recalled her early days with Jonah, the way he had once made her laugh. She couldn't remember when the laughter turned to smiles, when the smiles faded. Perhaps that's when you know that your relationship has gone stale. When the laughter dies.

He dispensed the contents of the can into the vase then stroked the foliage back into place. 'There! Windowsill? Coffee table? Playpen?'

Sophie indicated the kitchen table. 'Thank you so much. They're really lovely. Do you fancy that walk in the park? The ducks will be hungry by now.' That might have been overfamiliar, in fact the whole last twenty minutes might have been overfamiliar but, given the revelations of the last twenty-four hours, she didn't care. So, it was agreed: the park, the ducks and possibly a coffee at the café beside the boating lake.

–

Sophie sipped cappuccino and watched Sam Barnes playing peek-a-boo with Laura and her stuffed clown. He was a really nice guy: he looked after his nephews, made tea, arranged flowers. He fed ducks; fed Laura raspberry yoghurt. It seemed his gallantry knew no bounds. It wasn't until midway through her second cappuccino that Sophie started to wonder why such a nice guy, probably well into his thirties, was still single. Then the thought struck her: perhaps he wasn't. She had been so fixated on her own unravelling relationship that she had allowed herself to flirt. Because flirting was what it was. She had allowed herself to flirt with this man, who might just belong to somebody else. He wasn't wearing a ring, but that's something men can get away with. It allows them to keep their options open. She was instantly overwhelmed by self-loathing, a state of mind clearly visible from the outside. Sam Barnes stopped peek-a-booing.

'What's wrong?'

'Nothing,' she lied.

'Are you sure? You've gone a bit pale.'

'No, really. I just suffered a bit of a reality check. I suddenly remembered yesterday.' She hurried the rest of her coffee. 'I ought to be getting back. Give Laura her lunch.'

'OK. Mind if I walk back with you? Make sure you don't go wandering off in a fugue.'

She smiled. 'I'm not going to do that. But, yes, please walk back with us. If you have the time.' She frowned. 'How did you get here today? Without your bike.'

'Caught a train. It's still possible – if you have a strong constitution and you don't need to be anywhere in a hurry.'

'Oh, where do you live?'

'In my brother's attic. This side of Dorking.'

–

They strolled back at a leisurely enough pace, Sam with his hands in his pockets, Sophie pushing the pram. She was desperate to interrogate him about his possible wife-stroke-partner but asking him outright would be completely unacceptable.

'Are you married?'

He laughed. '*What?*'

'Oh, I'm sorry. Sometimes I think I'm thinking something and then I hear it coming straight out of my mouth. I'm really sorry. It was rude. And…'

'No, I'm not. I nearly was. But it all went horribly wrong. I'm still smarting about it.'

'Oh. When did that happen?'

'About eleven years ago.'

Sophie pulled the pram to a halt. 'Eleven years!'

'Once bitten, *et cetera*.'

'But you've got a girlfriend?'

'Nope. No significant other half. As I said, once bitten…'

Sophie's head teemed with conflicting sentiments: eleven years was a ridiculous amount of time to nurture a lost romance; he should move on; it was terrible that such a lovely human being had no one; she was delighted he had no one… what? Why was her mind thinking that? 'I'm so sorry. I shouldn't have asked you anything as personal as that.'

'That's OK. By now I can almost talk about it without weeping. We're nearly there. I'll help you inside. The Princess seems to have fallen asleep.'

'Have you got to get back? For your nephews?'

'No. Jesse's collecting them. He's working from home today.'

'Oh. What does he do?'

'He's an architect.' An abrupt laugh. 'He's the successful brother.'

'Is he older than you?'

'No, I'm the oldest. By twelve minutes.'

Sophie paused to consider. 'You're twins? Are you identical?'

'No. Jesse's got a beard.'

-

Sophie held the door and Sam lifted the pram plus sleeping baby up into the dark hallway, secured the brake then took a couple of backward steps. 'I'd better be getting out of your hair.' He fumbled in his trouser pocket and pulled out a folded slip of paper. 'That's my mobile number. If you ever need anyone to arrange flowers or help with an essay on postmodernism...'

'You could help when she wakes up. We've got brioche, and Marmite and mozzarella.'

'Oh. Do you think that's... what with Jonah...?'

'I'd rather not be on my own. My friend's coming over later. But that's not until...'

'I'll put the kettle on, shall I?'

-

Once again, they sat opposite one another, chatting about nothing and sipping tea. But periods of awkward silence began to assert themselves. Sophie wanted to ask him things, tell him things that would be inappropriate to tell a person she hardly knew. To start with she wanted to tell him that Jonah wasn't Jonah. And she wanted to tell him… she peered at him over her cup and the words just happened. 'He was leaving me.'

'What? You mean Jonah? Jonah was leaving you?'

'Yes. But he isn't Jonah. He's Robert.'

'Robert?'

'Yes. The whole five years we've been together, I've known him as Jonah Royston. But Jonah Royston doesn't exist. He's really Robert Perrin. And yesterday, just before the accident, he came home, packed his case and said he was leaving.'

Sam's jaw seemed to suffer a momentary spasm. Then he recovered. 'Sophie, why?'

'Apparently, someone else came along. If you're interested, I'll tell you the whole weird story. Then when you've heard it, you can run straight out of the house, catch your train and never darken this kitchen table again. I won't try and stop you. In fact, you can make a run for it now if you prefer.'

7

Sam stayed and Sophie told her tale of infidelity and brain damage. And Sam listened without interrupting. A couple of times he shook his head in disbelief but said nothing. She got as far as showing him Jonah's driving licence and inaccessible iPhone, when a piercing scream from the hallway declared Laura's disgust at being excluded.

Sam leapt to his feet. 'Point me towards the Marmite. You fetch the girl.'

Four ounces of mozzarella, several brioches and a lot of Marmite later, Laura was back in her playpen and Sophie and Sam were beside one another, on the sofa, sharing a bottle of Pinot Grigio blush. With ice.

'So,' said Sophie. 'You haven't made a break for it?'

'I was wondering if there was any more.' He sat back and folded his arms. 'Or if it was just a simple case of you being totally screwed over by a complete wanker. It's bloody Pinteresque.' He glanced over at Laura, who was trying to pick an embroidered eye out of Blue Bear. 'Does he own any part of this house?'

'No, it's jointly mine and my sister's. Josie lives in Cork. She grows cows. Well, she buys calves and sells them when they're ready to eat. So, Jonah hasn't any claim on the house. Although he did pay for the new bathroom.'

'Well, he'd have a job taking that with him. Tell me, if he'd left you not knowing his real identity, you'd never have been able to chase him up for any support for Laura, right?'

'I know the name of his company. And he said he'd send money.'

'Nice guy. Sophie, what are you going to do about this long-term?'

Sophie had no idea what she was going to do about it any-term. Yesterday morning she'd been living with a man she thought she loved, but the last twenty-four hours had changed all that. It was as if Jonah had died. No, worse than that, it was as if he'd been erased from existence: past, present and future. All that remained of Jonah Royston was sitting there in her playpen: Laura Emily Royston. 'I don't know what I'm going to do. He's still Laura's father. And when he comes out of hospital, this other woman might not want him any more.'

Sam stared at her. 'Surely, you'd not let him move back in with you!'

'I don't know. He'll have to go somewhere. There's the address in Exeter. But perhaps it's rented out.' It occurred to her that his other woman might have been his tenant. Perhaps Jonah was her landlord. And that clinking-glass supper was just Jonah checking out… She could feel her bottom jaw wobbling, her glass being eased from her hand, Sam's arm across her shoulder pulling her towards him. She didn't resist. She just let herself lie against his fresh, spicy, warm shirt, sobbing out a few semi-coherent words. 'You'd better go. I don't want to drag you any deeper into my disaster.'

'Too late. Think about it: how can you expect a Knight in Shining Armour, such as me, how can you expect me to leave you to sort your way through a mess like this? Besides, my students are on summer vac so I've got the next six weeks free. I was going to try reading *War and Peace*, but your story's far more interesting. You can call me whenever you need moral support or someone to boil you an egg. And I'll nip straight over.'

—

Sam stayed through the afternoon. At one point, Sophie left him watching Laura and adjourned to the garden to phone for an update on Jonah and to water her tomatoes. Intensive Care had obviously been informed of Jonah's actual identity, therefore there was initial confusion as to exactly whom Sophie was asking about. Eventually, she was told that Jonah's condition was unchanged. Presumably that meant his situation had not deteriorated; only her situation had done that. She filled her watering can and, as she did so, wondered at what point she would start to think of Jonah as Robert Perrin. Sam stepped outside to join her.

'She's still abusing Blue Bear. Any news?'

'No change.'

He rubbed a tomato leaf lightly between his fingers then lifted them to his nose. 'I really love the smell of tomato leaves, especially that twirly bit right next to the tomato.'

'Obviously not a botanist, then?'

He smiled. 'Jesse has allotted me a modest herb garden full of dandelions.'

She plucked a tiny tomato, handed it over and watched him pop it into his mouth. 'Gardener's Delight. The smell is due to the chemicals released when you break the tiny hairs on the leaves. Some of them act as insect repellents. What do you think?'

'Delicious! You obviously have green fingers.'

'I'd love to have a herb garden. Mint and marjoram and masses of chives with their pinky–purple flowers. But Jonah hates smells so I have to grow unscented plants. And I have to pick the tomatoes and remove their twirly calyx and store them outside until the smell goes away.'

'What do you mean, Jonah hates smells? What smells?'

'All smells.'

'You know, the more I hear about this guy, the more I'd like to murder him. Look, I've been thinking, let's take another look at that phone of his. The one that's password protected. I've had an idea.'

Sophie followed him back inside and handed him the phone.

'Can you remember what numbers you've already tried?'

'Different birthdays. Why?'

'Well, did you try his actual birthday? The one on his licence?'

'No.'

'Do you mind if I try?'

Sophie shook her head then watched him key in four numbers. The home screen opened with an image of a beach somewhere she knew she had never been.

'How did you do that?'

'I entered the day and month of his date of birth. From his driving licence: 1-6-0-3.'

'But how did you know it?'

'I remember noticing it. You know, 1603: when James the Sixth of Scotland became James the First of England and Ireland. That's a date every school kid has to learn. Shall I go talk to Laura while you check his call history? There's only 14% battery.'

'No, stay.'

So, together, they checked Jonah's calls and messages. There were a lot of missed calls, several to and from a handful of Exeter numbers. And there was a single text message to the mobile of a person Jonah addressed as *Darling Heidi*. It had been sent early yesterday morning and simply read: *Together soon*. A pink heart had been sent in reply.

Sophie noticed Sam frowning. 'That's probably her,' she whispered. 'The woman he was with in Exeter. Perhaps he was moving down there to be with her. She's probably wondering where the hell he is.' Worried that something terrible had happened to him; unaware that something terrible actually had happened to him. And unexpectedly, through the hate and resentment, Sophie started to feel sorry for this other woman called Heidi.

—

Katie arrived just after five thirty, hurried straight through to the kitchen and dumped a bottle of prosecco, a potted lavender and a bunch of cut coriander onto the work surface. 'Sophie, now the freak's out of the way, you need to start making up for lost time. Is there any news on the Jonah front? I thought we could get takeaway curry and sprinkle some of this coriander on top.

You can leave the tubs in the kitchen overnight so it stinks by the morning.' She turned as Sam walked into the kitchen. Gave Sophie a bemused smile and waited.

'Katie, this is Sam Barnes. He fell off his bicycle yesterday.'

'Really? How careless.'

Sam walked over and shook hands. 'Actually, it was more a case of being *knocked* off my bike yesterday. But Sophie invited me in for a cup of tea and calmed me down.'

'Really?' Another bemused smile. 'Are you staying for prosecco and curry?'

He flashed a panic-stricken glance towards Sophie. She rolled her eyes. 'Don't let her scare you. Katie, coffee first then prosecco, right? I ought to get Laura sorted before I become incapable. Sam, coffee?'

'I'll do it. You tell Katie your news. You might get her to sit down first. Go to the lounge so you can keep an eye on Laura.'

So, Sophie pulled Katie into the lounge and, when they were safely out of Sam's earshot, Katie whispered, 'Do you want him or can I have him?'

'Katie, shut up! He'll hear.'

'No, he won't. Do you fancy him. He's clearly attracted to you.'

'Don't be ridiculous. I can't just pretend Jonah doesn't exist.'

'Yes, you can. He'd already decided to go off with his new trollop. So, if he survives, she can have him. When did Jonah ever make you a hot drink? He's gorgeous. I love the black eye. He could do with bulking up a bit. And, perhaps a good stylist...'

'He's very strong!'

'Really? And how would you know that?'

'He lifted Laura's pram up the steps. And... I don't fancy him. How can I fancy anyone at a time like this? He's just been very kind.'

'Haa! Sophie Denham, mistress of self-delusion. Anyway, what's the news he mentioned?'

Sophie sighed and, after a brief interlude of frowning, she relayed the day's revelations.

Katie became silent and listened. Sam brought in coffees and also listened. When, finally, Sophie had exhausted her story, silence descended and hung in the air until Katie turned to Sam and said, 'There's no way she should let him move back in. Daughter or no daughter.'

'I couldn't agree more. He chose his path yesterday. I saw the contents of his suitcase all over the road. He had no intention of coming back. You should try speaking sense to her.'

'Excuse me,' interrupted Sophie. 'But…' She sighed. 'Look, I'm very grateful to you both but this is something I'm going to have to work out on my own. And when I make my decision it will be in Laura's best interests.' Silence resumed.

Sam started to collect up the cups. 'Well, in the meantime, phone me if there are any developments. I'd better be getting back. It's my turn to put the kids to bed.'

'Do you want a lift?' asked Katie. 'Where do you live?'

Sophie tried to deny the upwelling of possessiveness that was overwhelming her and was relieved to hear Sam say, 'No, I'm fine. I'm catching a train in forty minutes.' She jumped up and followed him into the kitchen, thanked him again for the roses, for listening to her ramblings, and apologised about Katie's brashness.

'I like her,' he said. 'Despite the fact that she frightens me.' He touched Sophie's arm. 'You have my number, right? You'd better give me yours so I can know it's not someone asking me if I want to claim PPI. I'll just go and say goodbye to Laura and the scary person.'

—

Sophie saw Sam to the front door then returned to the lounge braced for interrogation, which was immediate.

'Is he married?'

'No, they're his brother's kids. His brother's wife died.'

'God, this is unbelievable! Do you know whether he's involved with someone?'

'It did come up in conversation. And, no, he's not. Well, at least he said he's not.'

'Well, have you arranged anything? Not just call me if you need me stuff. Have you actually arranged to see him again? If I were you, I'd ask him to move in straight away. He'd make a great replacement father. Laura gets on really well with him…'

'*Katie!*'

'What? Don't tell me you've not been thinking exactly the same thing.'

'Look, I met Sam yesterday. Under traumatic circumstances. A traffic catastrophe is no basis upon which to build a new relationship. Particularly when your old relationship is still happening.'

Katie flopped back into her chair like a belligerent adolescent. She folded her arms. 'If you let a guy like that slip through your fingers, you're an idiot. In fact, I'll go so far as to say, that if you don't pull your act together, then I'm going to make a play for him. Where does he live?'

OK, that was annoying. 'With his brother.'

'Where?'

'I'm not telling you.'

'Why? Isn't that what friends are for, Ms Delusional Denham.'

Sophie glared at her. 'No. Friends are for not keeping quiet about witnessing their best friend's partner wining and dining another woman when he's supposed to be in Africa!'

There was a pause during which Katie formulated her defence. She sighed. 'I couldn't tell you, Soph. You'd still not got over losing your mum. And Laura was so little. And you seemed to be happy for the first time for ages. And I thought it might have just been a business supper. Although, I admit it didn't look like it. I'm really sorry.'

Sophie exhaled stress, walked over and lifted Laura out of her playpen. 'Come and help. And don't say anything else about Sam Barnes this evening. Or I'll punch you.'

Services Rendered

'Dr Matthews, please be assured that, as I explained over the telephone, there is not the slightest possibility of the unfortunate young woman's fate being linked to yourself or your practice. Her remains have been disposed of according to our exacting protocols.'

'Well, Thaddeus, I hope you are confident of that. Because, as I am sure you realise, I know rather more about your organisation than would be convenient for yourself – and the hierarchy that you service – if I should find myself under threat of exposure.'

'Quite. We are, indeed, fully aware of that, Dr Matthews. This whole episode has been regrettable. However, the Organisation has significant resources at its disposal to guarantee that no traces will be found and no blame apportioned.'

'I repeat: let us hope that is the case. And may I also remind you that I cautioned you that it would be inadvisable to let the father…'

'The *sponsor*,' insisted Thaddeus Jones.

'The father, the sponsor, whatever grandiloquence you prefer. I warned that it was inadvisable to allow the *sponsor* access to the girl at such a late stage in the… *confinement*. This in itself would have been manageable, but the man took advantage of the situation to satisfy some perverse proclivities. However… *experienced* these young women are, there are limits to what a late pregnancy can tolerate. Her death was not unrelated to what she was exposed to during parturition. I should have been notified immediately it became clear that the membranes had ruptured.'

'Unfortunately, the doula was not alerted until the situation was quite advanced, by which time the sponsor had left. You were informed immediately.'

'And this sponsor, who I presume will be billed for extra services rendered, is now the parent of two healthy young females? Well, God help us all, Thaddeus.'

8

Sophie woke just after nine with a hangover. She glanced at the clock, leapt out of bed and ran into Laura's room to see why she wasn't awake. She was awake, but she'd clearly decided that trying to attract her drunken mother's attention was a lost cause so was, instead, dedicating her time to pulling the fitted sheet off her cot mattress. Sophie hated days like this, days that started late, because lateness builds upon lateness exponentially, and today was going to be no exception.

So, after a late breakfast, Sophie made a late call to the hospital to see if there had been any change in Jonah's condition – she referred to him as Mr Perrin; no point in complicating matters – and was informed that his condition, although still critical, appeared to be stable. The nurse also mentioned that Sophie's sister had phoned earlier that morning to enquire about Mr Royston but had been advised that the hospital was not at liberty to provide information to anyone other than direct relatives. Sophie thanked her for the update, cancelled the call then sat in a daze trying to recall phoning Josie to tell her about Jonah's accident. She couldn't remember doing any such thing. The last conversation she'd had with Josie concerned her holiday plans: she'd been about to go to the Greek Islands with her husband, Francis. That was about four weeks ago. Josie and Francis had probably finished island-hopping and were now back in Cork. Sophie phoned straight away.

Indeed, Josie had returned last weekend. She told Sophie she and Jonah should consider an Aegean holiday. The food was fantastic. Maybe when Laura was a little older. Although the

Greeks really love babies. Sophie interrupted to mention Jonah's accident and to apologise for not calling sooner. Things had been chaotic. And had she phoned the hospital for an update? Josie was shocked to hear about Jonah and, no, she hadn't phoned. How would she have known to phone? And, anyway, they probably wouldn't have told her anything if she had. Did she need her to come and help?

Sophie chose not to tell Josie about Jonah's double life or about his leaving, promised to phone in a couple of days, ended the call and took a moment to consider the possible identity of the non-sister who had phoned Intensive Care. Could it have been his other woman? But how could she have known about the accident? And how could she have known about Josie? Had Jonah spent sweaty, clandestine afternoons, titillating her fancy with family details of the woman he was about to abandon? She was disturbed from her festering by a text reminding her about her appointment with the hygienist. She phoned and cancelled it. Dental hygiene was the least of her worries.

–

The day got even later. Late lunch followed by a late trip to the supermarket. Late latte at Starbucks. Late, late, late. But, then, what difference did it make? There was no Jonah to feed, no job she had to go to, nobody checking her obedience to a timetable. And Laura was hardly going to take her to task over trailing an hour behind schedule. Two hours behind schedule. No, when you're on your own, time takes on new significance or, rather, it loses all significance. But, more than anything, that lack of temporal obligation made Sophie realise how isolated she would be without Jonah: just empty days and suppers for one with no one to bicker with. She couldn't expect Katie to give up her time. There'd been other friends when she was working but she hadn't seen much of them since Laura was born. They all had their own child-free lives to lead. Wrapped in self-pity, she had almost reached home when she caught sight of Officers Wilkes and Tyler standing outside her door. She wondered whether this was going to be the hostile or the amicable police officer duo.

'Officers, I'm sorry, have you been here long?'

'We were on our way here when we spotted you walking home. We have some more information. It would probably be best if we came inside.' Officer Wilkes helped lift the pram up the step. 'Not the most convenient arrangement,' he observed.

Once inside, Sophie transferred Laura to her highchair, offered tea of numerous origins, which was declined, then, adopting her most determined expression, braced herself for this latest update on her faithless partner. But, whatever her determination, assumed or otherwise, Sophie was totally unprepared for what she was about to learn.

Officer Wilkes cleared his throat. 'Ms Denham, a quick check with Devon County Council… and Exeter City Council… revealed that the Topsham Road address on your partner's driving licence is the home of a Mr and Mrs Robert Perrin. Further enquiries have revealed that Mr Perrin and his family have resided at this same address for almost fifteen years.'

'Mrs Perrin? Family?'

Constable Tyler straightened her skirt. Sophie could feel her lips tingling. Sergeant Wilkes continued.

'Officers from the Exeter constabulary called round to notify Mrs Perrin of her husband's current circumstances. They discovered that Mr Perrin does, indeed, own his own company, Royston Computer Solutions, and that he spends several weeks, occasionally months, at a time away from home, working on overseas contracts. As I said, he and his wife have lived in their Exeter house for almost fifteen years. Along with their two daughters.'

Sophie turned to locate the nearest chair, collapsed into it and tried to comprehend what she had just been told. 'Two daughters? Are you sure?'

'The officer obtained a recent photograph.' Sergeant Wilkes removed a folded sheet from his breast pocket and handed it to Sophie. 'This is a photocopy.'

Sophie looked down at the clear image of Jonah, smiling at the camera, in his arms a small dog, some kind of minute, off-white pom-pom of a Pekinese.

'This must be very difficult for you, Ms Denham,' suggested Officer Tyler.

Difficult? It was bloody impossible. Sophie handed the sheet back. 'Jonah doesn't like dogs. He says they smell. But I suppose that's a very small dog.' Almost too small to smell. And definitely too small to be a dog. 'Did they tell her where he was when it happened, Sergeant Wilkes?'

'Sorry?'

'Did they tell this Mrs Perrin, that I've never heard of up until just now, did they tell her he was in Surrey when the accident happened? Did they tell her about me?'

'I'm sorry, Ms Denham, we have not been informed as to whether Mrs Perrin was made aware of her husband's alternative address and of…'

'…his alternative life?' Sophie threw her head into her hands. 'This is ridiculous. Why would he do this to me? Why would he do this to this other woman?' Then realisation: Mrs Perrin was not the other woman. She, Sophie Denham, was the other woman.

Officer Wilkes seemed to be at a loss. Time became vacant. Then Officer Tyler took it upon herself to pour a cup of water and hand it to Sophie, as if what Sophie needed right then and there was a little supportive rehydration. That was not at all what Sophie needed. What she actually needed was for someone to tell her exactly what to think next.

'Ms Denham,' said Officer Wilkes, 'as yet there appears to be nothing incriminating in Mr Perrin's decision to adopt a dual identity.' He cleared his throat. 'False identities are often used for the purposes of pursuing a discrete romantic liaison: on-line dating and such-like. If this is the explanation, then this would be a purely domestic issue and as such the police would not be interested in pursuing further enquiries. But, just to be certain, perhaps you would let us have the details of Mr Perrin's business premises.'

'The address is on his business card.' Sophie fetched Jonah's wallet and, with some trepidation, checked the pile of cards forced into one of the sections. 'I'm sure he must have one of his own amongst all these. Ah, here it is.'

'Thank you,' said Officer Wilkes. 'I'm sure our enquiries will need go no further. On the other hand, there are numerous counselling agencies that might offer assistance.'

'You mean people that might act like referees when me and Mrs Perrin fight over ownership of Jonah?'

'It's a very difficult situation,' repeated Officer Tyler.

Sophie shook her head. 'No, it's not difficult at all. Jonah was leaving me. That's why he was packing his case into his car. I didn't realise it at the time but, clearly, he was going back to his wife. She probably has no idea about me and Laura. She probably believed he's been working abroad on his various overseas commissions and instead of that he's been falling into the road in Surrey!'

At that point, the situation seemed to have run out of conversation. The two officers hovered. Sophie wanted them to go away.

'Is there anything else, officers? I ought to put the shopping away.' Then an unwelcome thought popped into her head. In her new role as the other woman, Sophie was now a marriage breaker, the person Jonah-stroke-Robert was shacked-up with behind his wife's back. 'Do you think that, if this Mrs Perrin finds out about me, do you think she'll come here and do something terrible? Because I know I would. I'd want to murder me.'

Sergeant Wilkes held up his hands. 'No… no, I don't think there's any reason for you to be concerned. Adultery is not that uncommon, as I'm sure you know. Mostly people just accept it and move on. If everybody took extreme action when they discovered their partner was unfaithful, there'd be bodies all over the place!' He attempted to laugh and clear his throat at the same time. 'I'm sure you have nothing to worry about. On the other hand, you might be advised to seek legal counsel to protect your and your daughter's interests.'

At that the officers left. Sophie unpacked her shopping onto the kitchen table then sat down beside it, bereft and incapable. She poked a tub of melting ice cream, rubbed her finger along the condensing droplets of water, glanced over at the freezer. It was too far away for her bloodless legs to carry her. Laura started to cry. Sophie sat and looked at her. Babies were inconvenient at a time like this. The crying became screaming. Sophie felt she might go mad if she didn't do something to make it stop. Of course, that is the evolutionary purpose of baby screaming: to get you to do something before your head explodes. Sometimes the strategy goes badly wrong, but, on this occasion, it worked. Sophie pulled herself up, put the ice cream in the freezer then carried Laura outside to look at her garden, now lusher than ever due to last week's downpour. And, as she stood in her small yard amidst its brief daily sun-trap moment, she could smell the calming scent of her tiny new lavender plant. She was definitely going to acquire more of those, Jonah or no Jonah. Because, hell, what kind of freak abhors the scent of lavender?

9

Katie phoned late afternoon and suggested Sophie get herself and Laura into their glad-rags and meet for tea-cum-supper in Pizza Express. Sophie paused: she wanted to say yes, but she didn't want to use up all Katie's good will too soon. This would be the third day Katie's evening had been commandeered by her. She would thank her but decline.

'Sophie?'

'Katie, I can't expect you to...'

'Don't talk crap, Soph. There's no way I'm going to let you sit there on your own feeling sorry for yourself.' There was a moment's hesitation. 'Unless, you're not on your own? Is the skinny hero coming over? Is he there now?'

'No, don't be daft.'

'Well, has he phoned? You did give him your number, didn't you?'

'Yes, I did. And, no, he hasn't.'

'Oh, well. He probably will. Bring your phone with you. We can eat outside. Take advantage of a rare summer evening. It'll probably be snowing by the end of the week. So, meet you there, six o'clock. Right?'

–

The advantage of a late day is that six o'clock arrives earlier than usual. So, with time to spare, Sophie woke Laura from her afternoon nap and dressed her for pizza. She opted for the pushchair, which would be easier to get back up the steps after a glass – hopefully two – of prosecco, then pushed her way slowly towards the town centre, enjoying the late-afternoon sun and the promise of conversation. She chose a table to one side, parked the pushchair close by a large topiarised bay tree and took advantage of Jonah's absence by ordering fresh mint tea.

She took a look around. Only one other outside table was occupied, by two women. Sophie sipped her tea and listened to their conversation: apparently, holidays in hot and exotic places were imminent. It occurred to her that she had never been anywhere hot or exotic with Jonah. In fact, over the last five years, the only holiday they had taken was a week in Edinburgh, the second autumn they were together. It had been freezing. They'd spent most of the week in their hotel room, eating and making love. The following year, and perhaps the year after that, she had suggested they go somewhere warm, but Jonah had argued that he was not a fan of catching the sun which is why he never returned from his trips overseas with a tan. Sophie realised now that the actual reason for his absence of tan was that the climate in Devon is no more tropical than that in Surrey.

'Hi, Soph. Are you aware that Laura's eating that bay leaf?'

'What? Oh God!' Sophie pulled the leaf away, stuck her finger in Laura's mouth to retrieve the piece that was missing. Laura screamed. Katie gave her her car keys. The screaming stopped. Sophie sagged back onto her chair. 'God, Katie. I'm just not with it.'

'Well, at least it proves she hasn't inherited her father's no taste-no smell affliction. That's something to be grateful for.' They acquired a highchair, ordered salads, baby pizza and two glasses of prosecco. 'So,' said Katie, 'what's new?'

'There's a Mrs Perrin.'

'What?'

'That Exeter address is the home of Mr and Mrs Perrin and their two daughters. Unsurprisingly, Mr Perrin is a computer engineer who goes off on long trips to foreign places. So, presumably, when Robert Perrin is away setting up computers, he's actually here being Jonah Royston.'

'And when Jonah Royston's telling you he's in bloody Africa, he's really in Exeter being Mr Family Man? What a total bastard! Did you say two daughters? How old are they?'

'I don't know. But the police said he's been living in that same house for fifteen years.'

'Sophie, that's awful.'

'Yeh. It means that for the last five years, I've just been Jonah's *piece on the side*. There I was, feeling venomous towards that *other woman* you saw him with, and all the while, the other woman was me.'

The prosecco arrived.

'Well, at least you're not left wondering who this other person is.'

'I'd prefer not to know. I could have just spent the rest of my life hating this unknown woman, but instead of that I know that I've facilitated Jonah's adultery. What will his wife think of me when she learns he's been having a baby with me when he should have been driving his daughters to school and helping them open their Christmas parcels? He was with me last Christmas. How could he even think of doing that to his daughters?'

'But he wasn't with you all the other Christmases, right?'

'No, he was always held up in some out-of-the-way place trying to uncrash computer systems. Every December, just in time for Christmas. I was stupid not to realise.'

'OK, let's change the subject. Haven't you heard anything from Sam?'

'No.'

'God, I hate men!'

–

They were just rounding off their salads when Sophie's bag vibrated. She stared at it. 'What if it's the hospital? What if something's happened?'

'Well, you need to know, whatever it is.'

Sophie pulled out her phone just as it stopped vibrating. 'Oh! That's the third time that number's called.'

Her phone pinged a new message: *Sam here. Are you OK?*

She looked at Katie. 'It's Sam.'

'So, call him back, you dope! Can Laura have this last bit of pizza? It's been on the floor.'

'Yes. Wipe it first.' She called the last number and waited. 'Hello, is that you, Sam? It's Sophie… Oh, it's been on silent… Oh, how long have you been there?' She glanced up at Katie, who rolled her eyes. 'I'm with Katie. We're in Pizza Express… Yes, I mean, no… OK, bye.' She ended the call and swigged down a mouthful of bubbles. 'He's been waiting outside my door.' Katie raised her eyebrows and smirked. Sophie gave a frustrated sigh. 'He's coming here. Do you think he's stalking me?'

'What? Good Lord, you spend five years living with a guy who, quite apart from being an adulterous bastard, has discouraged you from driving and forced you to live a fragrance-deprived life. And now this decent individual, who shows signs of really caring about you, you call him a stalker? What the hell's wrong with you?'

–

Sophie took Laura for a clean-up. When she returned, Sam was already there, chatting to Katie. Sophie noticed she was being overly vivacious, doing her pick-up laugh. Sam jumped up and moved the pushchair out of the way. Laura shrieked with excitement. Sophie felt herself do the same, although not audibly. 'I'm sorry I missed your calls,' she said. 'You shouldn't have come all the way over just to check I was OK.'

Sam helped feed Laura into her pushchair. 'Katie's just told me your latest news.'

'I didn't think you'd mind,' said Katie. Sophie said nothing.

A waiter brought three glasses of prosecco. 'My treat,' said Sam. 'I'm student-free until the end of September. So, this is by way of a celebration.'

'I've always envied you teaching people,' said Katie, 'with your disgustingly long holidays. While us normal people just get two pathetic weeks. Are you planning to get away to some tropical island or a secret retreat in the Andes? Climb Mount Kilimanjaro?'

Sam glanced at Sophie's silence. 'No, I've just got planning permission on a piece of land I bought last year. My brother's drawn up some plans for a five-up and big spaces down. So, I'm going to start digging next week. I've acquired a small spade.'

Sophie smiled. 'That shouldn't take you long.'

'Actually, Jesse's organising a team of brawny builders. They're starting on the foundations next week. He said I can work on the vegetable patch.'

Katie gave her pick-up laugh. 'You should ask Sophie about that. She knows about plants.'

They chatted and watched Laura falling asleep in her pushchair. 'I ought to get her home,' said Sophie. 'She's really been messed around this last few days.'

'I wouldn't worry too much,' said Sam. 'Kids are more flexible than you imagine. I'll get the bill.' Katie reached for her purse but he held up his hand. 'My treat, I insist.'

'But you haven't eaten anything,' said Katie.

'I had a Mars Bar earlier. I couldn't eat another thing. Are you both walking back to Sophie's place?'

'No, I'm parked round the corner.' Katie gave Sophie a sly look. 'Will you be all right walking back, Soph?'

'I'll make sure they get home,' said Sam.

'OK. Soph, call me tomorrow. Not too early. Unless it's urgent. Thank you so much, Sam. My turn next time.' With that she stroked Laura's sleepy cheek and left.

Sam watched her go. 'She's not that bad when you get used to her, is she?'

–

They strolled back in the balmy evening air, carefully avoiding any mention of Jonah and his Exeter family. The streets were deserted.

Anybody who wasn't at home watching the TV had been sucked into the bars and restaurants in the town centre, so they were alone with their easy conversation and the occasional passing car. It all seemed so clear and fresh. One of those nights when your senses just seem to be working overtime: the colour of the sky turning to dusk, the crisp sound of their footsteps, the perfume of night-scented stock drifting over the rooftops... mingling with that intoxicating aftershave.

Sam carried the pushchair into the hall then made tea while Sophie put Laura to bed and phoned to check on Jonah. When she walked into the kitchen, Sam was sitting at the table guarding the teapot. She sat down opposite him.

'Would you like something to eat?'

'I'm fine.'

'Chicken pâté, toast, bistro salad?'

'Well, if it's not too much bother.'

'It's not. The pâté's in the fridge. Top shelf. Salad's in the bottom drawer. I'll make the toast.'

'OK. But, while I eat, I want you to tell me what the cops told you.'

'I thought Katie brought you up to date.'

'I want *you* to tell me.'

So, Sam ate and listened. And finally Sophie said. 'When I phoned the hospital, they said he's critical but stable. There seems to be a logical conflict in that statement. But at least he's not any worse.'

'Sophie, why are you still worrying about him? He's Mrs Perrin's problem now.'

'He's Laura's father.'

'He also has two daughters in Exeter.'

'I feel sorry for them. His wife's been sharing her husband with me, all through the last five years of her daughter's lives. Perhaps if I hadn't been working at Portway when he came to set up the computer system, perhaps he would never have strayed. I encouraged him.'

'If you'd known he was married, would you still have encouraged him?'

'I don't think so.'

-

Time passed and the evening grew old. Sophie glanced at the cooker clock and suppressed a yawn. 'It's almost eleven. What time's the last train?'

'Eleven fifty. There's plenty of time yet. Shall I make coffee?'

'No, I don't want anything keeping me awake, with all those horrible thoughts running through my brain.'

'Don't you have a book to read? I've got crates of them you could borrow: Agatha Christie, Harry Potter, *The Complete works of William Shakespeare*. Everything that's been Booker short-listed since it started… 1969, I think. Does Laura usually sleep through?'

'Usually. That's a lot of books. Where do you keep them all?'

'Mostly on the floor. Jesse's building me the new place in the hope that I'll take them with me. Do you have a TV in your bedroom? You could watch some episodes of *Friends*. They're good however many times you've seen them. They've certainly helped me through some difficult nights.'

'Eleven years ago?'

'And the rest.'

'Sam?'

'Yeh?'

'Don't go.'

Disembowelment

'Sir Hugh, I came immediately I heard the news to assure you that…'

'That you intend to do the honourable thing and disembowel yourself in my presence?'

'…to assure you, Sir Hugh, that I have launched a thorough investigation into the unfortunate mishap. And that all those that bear any responsibility will be dealt with appropriately. And severely.'

'Jones, there has clearly been a major cock-up! And your reassurances are utterly inadequate. A disaster such as this threatens our entire operation. Not only have we lost one of our valued assets, but I gather that there has also been a breach in the absolute host anonymity that our process requires. Am I to understand there was contact between the sponsors and the girl?'

'Only a brief contact. An administrative… an error of understanding. I can confirm that this had nothing to do with the regrettable outcome and that the situation is now contained. I am informed by the obstetric team that the unfortunate young woman suffered a very rare complication which caused her not to survive the delivery, after which a cluster of unique circumstances seem to have led to her inappropriate disposal. I have scheduled a meeting with the operatives involved to discuss this further. I am also informed by the Source that the woman has not been identified. And we are confident that she will remain unidentified.'

'Well, Jones, let us hope you are justified in your optimism. Otherwise, I fear we must revert to the disembowelment option.'

Mimicry is a form of dishonesty and within the Plant Kingdom, the orchids are the most-accomplished liars of all. Within the Animal Kingdom, there are no liars greater than man.

From *A Natural History of Lies* by J. Clarke

10

Sam stayed. Their transition from sitting opposite one another across the kitchen table, to climbing the stairs, to making love was surprisingly untraumatic. The choreography was near perfect for a first performance, although effected with mutual speed. And afterwards, as they lay quietly together, it was as if that was the way things were always meant to be. Sophie loved the feel of his slim body against hers, wanted that feeling to last for ever, wanted the lies of the last five years to, please, go away, although Laura was part of those lies and she didn't want her to go away; she wanted her to belong to Sam and herself. She ran her fingers across his chest towards the silver chain around his neck, lifted a small oval medallion.

'Do you always wear this?'

'Why, did it distract you?'

'Did I seem distracted?'

'No.' He laughed. 'My mother gave it to me to keep me safe. It's a St Christopher. He used to be the patron saint of travellers but then the Pope decided carrying Jesus wasn't a miracle so he got demoted. Now he just brings good luck. I'm too superstitious to take it off.'

'In that case, I'll just have to get used to it.' She let it drop back onto his chest, pulled herself up and kissed him.

He stroked a strand of hair from her eyes. 'Are you tired?'

'No.' She kissed him again. 'I'm wide awake.'

Numerous theories have been postulated regarding the activity of the human mind during sleep. Obviously, dreams are an inconstant feature of the sleeping brain, and would appear to be a scramble of recent experiences, thoughts and fears, together with the kind of surreal creativity that borders on the illogical and the absurd. But there are also suggestions that, on some completely different mental level, logical thought and problem-solving may also proceed during sleep. Occasionally a question with no answer, a dilemma which has proven insurmountable can be fathomed during a good night's slumbering. For instance, in the past, Sophie had often found such to be the case with the *Guardian* cryptic crossword. Her mind was clearly more rational when she was asleep than when she was awake. So, it was no surprise to her that, when she awoke alongside Sam after their first night together, she was convinced that her life had suddenly fallen into place and all its chaos had been brought to order. Of course, life never lets you get away with such optimism.

–

They ate breakfast at the rickety table in the backyard and the sun beamed down and confirmed their happiness.

'I'll nip back and have a word with Jesse. Collect some clothes.'

'Bring enough for ever.'

Sam smiled. 'Sophie, you don't really know anything about me.'

'Yes, I do. I want you here. With me and Laura.'

So, with a promise to return by late afternoon, bearing groceries and an iPhone charger, Sam left and Sophie began transferring Jonah's remaining things to the spare room. She remembered the suitcase in the boot of the BMW but decided to leave it there for the time being. She didn't want its bloodied contents to disturb her breathless euphoria, although she did suffer a brief interlude of tearfulness as she collected up the odd photos she had of Jonah with Laura, of Jonah and her before Laura and one of him standing beside her mother. She wasn't ready to part with them so she slipped them beneath the T-shirts in her bottom drawer. Then, with Laura down for her morning nap, she commenced the tedious job of checking the CDs. Mostly hers.

The doorbell sounded. Her stomach took a dive: it was way too early for Sam, so probably the police with another revelation. What else could there be? She hurried through and discovered Suzie Kay standing on the bottom step, a tight spray of bright purple orchids in her hand – *Dendrobium* – tied with a white ribbon. They were Sophie's permitted favourites: Jonah had always been relaxed about orchids because for all their elaborate morphology they offered no fragrance, no affront to his olfactory sensitivities.

'Hello, Sophie. I thought I'd call in and see how you are.'

'Suzie, I've been meaning to call you but things have been really chaotic.' She stepped back to invite her in and suffered a sudden dread that traces of her too-soon sexual encounter might be obvious, signs that just three days into Jonah's mishap she had moved his replacement in. 'Are they for me? I love orchids. And they last ages.' Obviously, a lot longer than her grief over her abandoning partner. Suzie followed Sophie into the kitchen. Fortunately, breakfast had been cleared away and a quick check of the work surface confirmed that this was a house most likely occupied by a woman on her own.

'Do you fancy tea, coffee, something cold?'

'I'd love some iced water, if that's OK?'

'I'll have some too. We can go and sit in the garden. Laura shouldn't wake for another hour or so. I hope you've got over being dragged into my disaster.'

'I was pleased I could help. How is… how's Jonah?'

'He's stable. More than you can say for me.' She filled glasses, added ice.

'Have you been to see him?'

'Not since Wednesday night. And he was swathed in bandages then, so it could have been anyone. They're keeping him in a controlled coma. They had to remove a piece of his brain.' She noticed Suzie's increasing pallor. 'Are you OK? You've gone a bit pale.'

Suzie's eyelashes effected a nervous flutter. 'I'm not too good with conversations about blood and brains. I'll be OK. Just don't mention, you know...'

'OK. Shall I put my orchids in water first?' She hurried to the larder, selected a slim cylindrical vase – opaque glass – arranged the orchids. 'I'll cut their stems later. Give them a chance to get used to their new surroundings first.' She feared she might be demonstrating too much happiness, noticed Suzie looking at Sam's pink roses. 'They're from a friend. It's sad they don't allow flowers in hospitals any more, isn't it?' She threw her hand across her mouth. 'Oh, I'm sorry, I mentioned hospitals.'

Suzie smiled. 'No worries. Show me your garden.'

–

Sophie watched the colour slowly return to Suzie's cheeks as she sat chatting and taking in her surroundings, appreciating the sunflowers and pansies, the tiny outpourings of white alyssum. She tried to take a guess at her age. Even Sophie was not crass enough to ask that question. She estimated early-twenties, still pretty with the hopefulness of youth. Her clothes were smart – professional – although she seemed a little nervous for a person who spent her days advising people about their dream holidays, their once-in-a-lifetime exotic honeymoons.

'I feel terrible that my disaster ruined your day off. Still, we'd never have met if it wasn't for poor Jonah.'

'Do I remember you saying he was leaving you?'

'Yes. I suppose he still is.' She ought not give details. But she did. 'He was going back to his wife. We've been together five years and he was married all that time and I didn't know. And probably his wife had no idea about me either. He'd been juggling lies about overseas trips to set up computer systems and all the time he was going between us. He owns a house in Exeter where he spends half his time with his wife, Heidi, and his two daughters.

And, to top it all, Jonah Royston isn't his real name. He's really Robert Perrin.'

Suzie's mouth dropped open. 'That's terrible. And you never suspected anything?'

'No. My mum always said if you look for the bad in people, you'll always find it, so I suppose I've always made a point of not looking. But then the police ran a check because the hospital couldn't find Jonah's medical records. And they discovered his car was in someone else's name.' She sighed. 'So, I've spent the last five years living with a man who doesn't exist, who's the father of my child.'

'Does his wife know about his accident?'

'The police told her. So, probably by now she knows about me. I feel awful for her. I know he's treated me as badly as he's treated her, but it's worse in her case because they've been together for at least fifteen years. And at least Laura's young enough not to remember him. His other daughters have probably looked forward to him coming home each time. I wish there was some way I could tell them I knew nothing about Jonah having a family.' Sophie paused for breath. 'Anyway, there's not much anybody can do about anything until Jonah recovers. Do you fancy some lunch? The freezer's bursting with opportunity.' She knew she was sounding too jolly but she couldn't help herself.

'I'm OK. I've not got much of an appetite at the moment. I've had a bit of a tummy bug over the last couple of days. I'm over it now. I don't think I'm contagious.'

'Poor you! Actually, you probably caught something off Laura. Babies are storehouses of bugs. Every time we go to toddlers' group we come home with something new. It really used to piss Jonah off. But I've got some nice bland quiche in the freezer. Good comfort food when you're recovering from baby bug.'

Suzie laughed. 'OK, bland quiche sounds great.'

Laura joined them for lunch and, true to predictions, Suzie recovered her appetite. They chatted about holiday packages and Sophie fantasised about traipsing along a golden shoreline with Sam quoting lines from Keats and Coleridge.

'Did they give you any idea how long Jonah would be in hospital?'

Sophie snapped back to reality. 'Not really. The doctor mentioned rehabilitation.'

'And then you think he'll go and live with his wife?'

'I suppose. Although there's always the possibility that she'll tell him to go to hell when she finds out about me.'

'But you wouldn't want him back, would you? Sorry, I'm being too nosey.'

'No, you're not. And no, I don't want him back.' She could feel her cheeks flushing. 'I've decided to move on. Actually, I *have* moved on.'

'There's somebody else?'

'Yes. Someone I've only just met. Please don't judge me badly, Suzie. I know it's a bit quick, but I've never been more certain.'

Suzie nodded. 'What a crazy mess!' She got to her feet. 'Sophie, thanks for lunch. I'd better be getting back. I'm babysitting later.'

'Well, try not to catch any more baby bugs. Perhaps you'd like to come over in the next week or so. If the weather's still good, we can go feed the ducks.'

'I'd really like that. I'm free Wednesdays. And alternate Saturdays and Sundays.'

'OK. How about next Sunday?'

11

With Laura confined to her playpen, Sophie carried a small stack of Jonah's CDs up to the spare bedroom then returned to do a quick scan for any Jonah-related paraphernalia. She spotted one of the monogrammed handkerchiefs she had given him for his last non-birthday lying on top of the DVD player. She picked it up and ran her fingers across the embroidered JR. Well, he wasn't likely to be needing that any more. She carried it upstairs along with his Folio copy of *Lord of the Rings*, his puzzle books and the pewter tankard that he always took over to the Fox and Gander for his monthly skittles matches. It occurred to her that the people in his skittles team would probably start wondering where he was. She ought to find a way of contacting them. She paused to consider Jonah's piled-up possessions. There wasn't much there really, at least not much that might declare five years of a man's life. But, then, he probably kept most of his things in his Exeter house. Along with his real life. A tiny pang of regret caused her to wander over and pick up a framed photograph of herself and Jonah taken at Katie's doomed wedding. They were both smiling at the camera, her head full of hopes for the future, his head full of the knowledge that he had a wife and two little girls waiting for him to come home. Two little girls deceived. And she'd played a part in that deceit. She had to make up for it somehow because, if she didn't, then who was she to ever expect happiness? She heard Laura politely protesting her imprisonment and hurried downstairs to pre-empt any possible descent into rage.

–

Sam returned just after three, with two bags of groceries and a bulging hold-all. He handed Sophie one of the grocery bags and kissed her cheek. Her heart experienced a flurry of extraordinary beats.

'Did you see your brother?' she managed to say.

'No, Jesse's taken the boys over to Grandma Buckley.' He dumped his hold-all at the bottom of the stairs. 'Sandi's mother.'

'Was Sandi Jesse's wife?'

'Yes.'

'How did she die?'

'Ovarian cancer. I came back to the UK when Jesse told me she'd been diagnosed. I'd spent years feeling sorry for myself about my blighted love and it kind of brought me to my senses. Made me feel like a self-indulgent arse.' He took her free hand and pulled her towards the kitchen and suddenly Sophie's lungs didn't feel capable of supplying her with the air she needed.

'Is Laura in her cage?'

'Yes.' She tried to control her breathing. 'Does Jesse know you're staying here?'

'I left him a note.'

'What about your nephews, if you're staying here?'

'He's already made arrangements, so we can be free to start on the house on Monday. I've brought the plans over to show you.'

Suddenly Sophie felt a little panicky. No, she felt *very* panicky. That same stranger who, just three days ago, had been waiting outside her house, holding a bent bicycle wheel, was now standing in her kitchen. His clothes were in a bag at the bottom of her stairs. She'd made love to him wrapped in the same sheets that Jonah had slept in the night before he dragged his case downstairs and outside into brain damage and a controlled coma. It was all happening too fast. And she had encouraged it. With indecent speed. She started to empty vegetables onto the table. Pea shoots, radishes, carrot sticks. She really ought to change the sheets. Wash away any last remnants of Jonah.

'I thought you might have a couple of suggestions about my library. It's very open-plan at the moment. That's how Jesse does things. No walls where they're not needed: *Open Space No Waste*, that's his battle cry. But I'm not sure I want to see my books when I'm eating pasta. I think a library ought to have walls. Don't you?'

Cashew nuts, new potatoes, purple grapes. His arms closing around her waist.

'Has anything happened, Sophie?'

'No.' Cantaloupe melon, baby leeks. Caesar dressing, yellow peppers, spring onions. 'The woman who witnessed the accident came to visit.'

'The woman you were saying goodbye to just before you spoke to me?'

Sophie pointed to the orchids, still with their stems unsnipped. 'She gave me orchids.' She was aware of a slight tremor in her own voice. Felt him easing her round to face him.

'Are you all right? Soph, if you're having second thoughts, tell me. There's no pressure. This is all a bit fast for me too.'

Her heart was racing. 'I'm not… I…' Her blood was pulsing through her neck so hard she could hear it. Uninvited images were invading her thoughts: blood and sand and bandages. And Jonah's ear sliced away by the sharp corner of a metal box. She could feel tiny tremors, rising deep inside and rippling outwards, across her shoulders, down into her fingers, every small sound an echo, every breath inadequate.

'OK, Sophie, don't be frightened. It's a panic attack. Just breathe slowly.'

'Laura!' She grasped his shirt. 'I forgot her!'

'Laura's fine. Let's go and see her, shall we? Just concentrate on walking. That's right.'

–

They sat in silence watching Laura pursue her ongoing attempts to remove Blue Bear's eye. And gradually Sophie calmed sufficiently to construct coherent sentences. 'I'm so sorry. Everything… I didn't know what anything meant.'

'I know the feeling.' He kissed her hand. 'It was probably a delayed reaction to three days ago. I'll make some tea. Or would you prefer a drink drink?'

'Tea's good. I'm so sorry. I couldn't breathe.'

'But, you were breathing. Just too much. It makes you feel faint. Then you panic about feeling faint. I'll just be a sec, OK?'

-

Sophie calmed sufficiently over tea to be able to tell Sam to take his things up to her... to their bedroom and take advantage of the drawer space recently vacated by Jonah. She watched him hauling his hold-all up the stairs, put away the shopping, checked Laura was unlikely to choke in the next five minutes and hurried upstairs. She discovered Sam in the spare bedroom, holding his toothbrush and a tube of toothpaste. He turned as she stepped in.

'I'm sure there was a bath in here last night. I must have been disorientated after all the excitement.'

She pointed across the landing. 'The guest toilet's there, the bath is in the ensuite. And you're an idiot.'

'But I'm a sexy idiot, right?'

'Right. Do you need coat hangers, sexy idiot?'

'No, I think my scrunched-up T-shirts are OK in the drawer.'

-

By the evening, Sophie was restored to romantic bliss. So, with Laura asleep and the debris of supper cleared away, Sam spread the plans for his new house across the kitchen table.

Sophie was impressed. 'Did Jesse do this?'

'Yeh.' He pointed to one side of the large empty area on the ground floor. 'The library's going there. I'm thinking of asking him to add a wall here. More books. And I thought it might also help prevent the first floor from falling in. So far, Jesse's not had any of his masterpieces collapse, but I'm not sure I'm ready to risk it. That bit there's going to be the gym. He sees my guests using it more than me.'

'It's all very big.'

'Jesse prefers big and open. He likes to cook and argue with his guests while they lounge around drinking champagne.'

'Does he cook?'

'Like a professional. Sometimes he lets me come down from the attic to peel potatoes.'

'Is it really an attic?'

'It's a big attic. Three rooms. Panoramic vistas. As soon as I'm gone, he's going to convert it into a granny suite. That's why he's so keen to design my dream house for me.'

Sophie felt a brief echo of doubt: why on earth would Sam be so ready to leave his vast attic and move in amongst another man's leftovers? 'This place must seem like a hovel compared to what you're used to.'

'I'm not used to anything, Sophie. Watching Jesse struggle with his private griefs, I've learned to appreciate what I have in the here and now.'

She studied the plans without seeing them. 'Does Jesse have girlfriends?'

'Occasionally, but he's not interested. He's still horribly shell-shocked. One minute he had a wife he loved and two little boys, and the next he was a widower and a single parent. I came back home and did what I could to help.'

She chewed her lip. 'What made you move to Hong Kong in the first place?'

He studied her expression, clearly deciding whether to give her the unabridged or abridged version. She would later learn that what he provided was the significantly abridged version. 'Nothing that spectacular. I fell for this older woman. And after she'd encouraged me to sign away half my life, she returned to her partner.'

'Eleven years ago? You must have been very young.'

'Twenty-seven. A wide-eyed young idiot. My mother was still alive then. She saw right through her from the start. But I wouldn't listen. I'd spent years filling my head with romantic poetry, most of which was more relevant to the eighteenth century than third millennium Surrey. So, I was easy meat. Much of the reason I quit the UK and went to the colonies was to escape my own embarrassment.' He exhaled. 'So, two fucked-up brothers, Jesse due to hateful fate and me due to my own stupidity.'

'I'm sorry that happened to you, Sam. But don't tell me you've avoided relationships ever since.'

'I've not avoided them, but I have run a mile every time it looked like things might get serious. Until about twenty-four hours ago.'

'Not quite love at first sight, then?'

'Maybe not. So, what do you think of my library proposal?'

'I think I have no idea. Shall we open another bottle?'

'I'd prefer you conscious.'

'I have quite a tolerance.' She laughed. 'You'd be surprised.'

Sam collected a Provence rosé from the fridge, rummaged in the cutlery drawer for a corkscrew and set about opening the bottle. Sophie turned her attention back to the plan. She noticed an insert in the top right corner:

J&S Barnes Architectural Services
Living Space

She'd seen it before. 'Is that your brother's company? Jesse and Sam Barnes?'

He looked up from pouring. 'No. Jesse and Sandi. Sandi was a draughtsman. I'm not involved in his business, although, if he ever needs any help beating up difficult clients, I get his back.' He laughed at Sophie's expression. 'I'm joking. Do you want ice?'

–

Later that evening Sam demonstrated a unique ability to recite Shakespearean sonnets whilst making love. He explained that he had always found that the Bard's unfaltering iambic pentameter imposed structure upon what could have otherwise been a more random performance: unstressed stressed unstressed stressed… five times per line. All fourteen lines. With the occasional essential pauses. Sophie failed to disagree.

12

It was as the dawn broke and Laura mumbled dreamtime protests from the next room, that Sophie woke with a very clear idea of where she had first seen those words: Living Space. She checked Sam was still asleep then eased herself out of bed. Treading as lightly as possible, and avoiding the creaky third stair from the top, she hurried down to the hall table, plucked up Jonah's wallet, carried it into the kitchen and closed the door before turning on the light. She flipped open the wallet, pulled out the tight pile of business cards and splayed them out across the work surface: restaurants, an office cleaning service. And there it was.

> J&S Barnes Architectural Services
> Living Space

She turned it over. A date and time was written on the reverse. Why on earth did Jonah have Sam's brother's business card? Did he need an architect? But why Sam's brother? She heard the creaky stair, forced the cards back into the wallet and pulled out Jonah's driving licence.

Sam walked into the kitchen, his hair unruly. 'Couldn't you sleep?'

'I woke up thinking about Jonah's driving licence. At any point over the last five years, he risked me seeing his photo alongside his real name. What was he thinking?'

'Some people get off on the risk. Sophie, love, come back to bed.'

'As far as I knew, his birthday was last month, not March. He probably made sure he was with his real family on his proper birthday.'

'Sophie, the lies are over. Put it away. Let's have a lie-in. Until Laura wakes up.'

They returned to bed and Sophie spent the next two hours mulling over the various reasons why Jonah would have been needing architectural services. Would it have been for his business premises? Would he carry on renting them if he was going back to his wife full-time? She remembered him moving into them just after they started living together. Perhaps he had wanted an architect to work on his Exeter home, perhaps new premises down there, but then he would more than likely have contacted an architect based in Devon. She wondered whether to ask Sam why his brother's business card was in her ex-partner's wallet. She could feel him warm beside her. Asleep. There was probably some simple explanation. She was relieved when Laura woke and forced her to stop thinking about it.

–

After breakfast, Sophie helped Sam to finish unpacking and told him to put his hold-all in the spare room. She hurried downstairs to check Laura and returned moments later to discover Sam standing in the spare room, holding the framed photo from Katie's wedding. 'Is this Jonah?' he said.

'Yes. I don't suppose you'd recognise him from the accident.'

'I just remember seeing someone on a stretcher.'

'Well, that's Jonah. It was taken at Katie's wedding.'

'Good Lord, is she married?'

'She was. They spent most of their time arguing.'

'What about?'

'Everything.'

–

The day trundled by, with a walk to the park, pub lunch and a leisurely stroll home for Laura's afternoon nap and some serious time together. Sophie's mobile vibrated on the bedside table. It was Katie. Was everything all right? Had there been any developments regarding Sam? Sophie found it very difficult answering questions about Sam owing to the fact that he was lying there beside her, so she reassured Katie that all was well, excellent even, and that she would phone tomorrow. Katie asked if that was code for he's standing next to me. Sophie said yes, sort of, and speak later. Sam watched her slip the phone under her pillow...

'*My mistress' eyes are nothing like the sun...*'

Sam's brother phoned late afternoon and, from what Sophie gathered, they were having a similarly coded conversation which might have been Jesse wondering where the hell Sam had been for the last few days. The call ended. Sophie waited.

'Jesse was making sure I'd be on site tomorrow morning to meet the Project Manager.'

'Is he expecting you home?'

'He was, but now he's not.'

'Is he cross?'

'Sophie, I'm thirty-eight. And Jesse is not his brother's keeper. But, for God's sake, make sure I set my alarm.'

–

Sophie stood at her bedroom window watching Sam hurrying away towards the station, his hair still crazy with the night. She grabbed her phone and texted Katie: *On my own now.*

Katie texted back: *NOW? It's 7:20. Did he stay over?*

As Sophie's finger hovered over the 'Y', her phone rang. She brought Katie up to date with developments, although she didn't mention Jesse's card in Jonah's wallet. She still wasn't sure what she thought about that. Katie said to let her know when she was free for coffee then rang off.

As Sophie carried Laura downstairs for their sunny-day pyjama breakfast her eyes fell on Jonah's two phones lying on the hall table. Perhaps Jesse's number would be in the call history of Jonah's iPhone. So, straight after porridge, she hurried to dump Laura in her playpen, fetched Jonah's wallet, checked Jesse's card and memorised the last three digits of the contact number. Then she turned on the iPhone, punched in the year of ascension of James I and noticed 2% battery just before the screen went black. She turned on the Samsung: 16% battery. There had been a lot more than that a couple of days ago. She needed to collect Jonah's charger from the BMW. In fact, she needed to retrieve the entire case and all its bloodied, vomited-on contents, which by now were probably incubating all manner of toxic organisms. She startled as the letterbox spewed onto the doormat. Another consignment of junk mail, no doubt. Oh, and a letter. She put down the phone, wandered over and eased the envelope from the heap. It was addressed to Mr J. C. Royston. She frowned: what was the 'C' all about? Had he added a pretend middle name to his pretend name? No, it was probably only an initial with no name belonging to it. She slid her finger along the top of the envelope and pulled out an invoice from Ace Van Hire, thanking Mr Royston for his custom. Immediately beneath this gratitude, was a note informing him that he was to 'forfeit the deposit of £100 paid to secure hire of a Thames van for pick-up on…' Last Thursday's date had been added in red biro, followed by 'paid in cash' written in the same red biro.

She carried the letter into the lounge, where Laura was now working on Stuffed Clown's trousers, collapsed into the sofa and considered the meagre piles of Jonah's possessions now in her spare room. He could have fitted all that in the BMW. Why would he need a van? Then realisation dawned: he'd intended to take other things. The TV, the Bose equipment. The new freezer. Everything he'd paid for. Take them to his real life in Exeter, although, how he would ever have explained his sudden acquisition of all that stuff, she couldn't imagine. Perhaps he was going to store everything. He'd probably admit to the TV straight away. Give it to his daughters for their room. She tried to picture them, Jonah's other daughters. Tried to imagine Laura one day meeting up with her half-sisters, constructed a mental image of the three of them together, Laura on the biggest sister's lap. All of them blessed with Jonah's striking brown eyes. She suffered a crippling wave of regret that her daughter would likely never know those sisters, glanced over at the playpen and was dismayed to see Laura asleep on top of a pile of toys. Her mobile rang. It was Josie.

Josie suggested that, if she needed to get away, she should come over. Maybe wait until Jonah was back on his feet and they could both come to recuperate. Watching cows could be very relaxing. Sophie promised to keep that in mind. She knew she ought to mention Jonah's wife. And Sam. But thinking about Sam becoming her lover, when she was on the phone to her sister, induced those same panicky vibrations she'd felt yesterday. And this time Sam wasn't there to make her breathe slowly. She promised yet again to keep Josie posted and ended the call. Her phone rang in her hand. It was Sam. He was going to lunch with Jesse and the Project Manager but would be back soon after. Jesse was going to drive him because he'd forgotten his wallet that morning and his Railcard was inside. It was probably on the bedside table. The call ended but hearing Sam's voice had calmed her tremors.

She slipped the invoice between the pages of her plant catalogue, lifted Laura from her playpen and carried her up to her cot, carefully so as not to wake her. Then she wandered into her room to check that Sam's wallet was there and, before she could stop herself, she was rooting through it, looking for evidence. Of course, she didn't expect to find anything incriminating. Right up to the point when she discovered Jonah's business card.

13

Sophie stood staring at the words written in bold across the top of the card: *Royston Computer Solutions*. A cocktail of emotions rippled through her: surprise, confusion, panic. But mostly she just felt deceived. All over again. She slipped the card into her jeans pocket and returned the wallet to the bedside table. She wanted to phone straight away and ask Sam what the hell. But he was probably at lunch by now. She'd have to wait. Concentrate on normal things. She tidied the already tidy kitchen, snipped an inch or so off each of the rose stems, to perk up the blooms, off the orchids to give them a chance. Sam arrived just after three. Sophie opened the front door and peered out along the street. 'I thought Jesse was driving you?'

'He dropped me off at the end of the road. He's on his way to pick up the boys.' He stepped inside and stooped to kiss her but she made as if she needed to pick the junk mail off the doormat. He watched her scoop up the multi-coloured envelopes and set them down on the hall table, then followed her into the kitchen. 'Is anything wrong, Soph?'

She concentrated on filling the kettle. 'Why do you ask?'

'You seem a bit edgy.'

'Well, that's probably because my cheating partner is in hospital with a broken head.'

He pulled out a chair next to the highchair. Sat down. Laura threw her brioche on the floor. He picked it up, watched Sophie making tea. 'They were marking out the plot this morning,' he said. 'And they've been digging the foundations this afternoon. The ground's as hard as concrete. Even after all that rain.' Sophie said nothing. 'Sophie, are you cross because Jesse didn't come in to meet you?'

'No. Why would he?'

'He would have, but he takes the boys swimming most Mondays. Sometimes I go too.'

'Will they be disappointed you're not there?'

'Not really. You and Laura could come next week. Do you take her swimming?'

Sophie transferred mugs to the table and sat down opposite him. 'No. I can't swim.'

'Oh!' He pulled his mug closer. 'I'll teach you.'

She ignored his offer and just sat and looked at him for a long moment before easing Jonah's business card from her pocket and prodding it towards him. He frowned. She frowned back. 'It's Jonah's business card. It was in your wallet.'

'You looked through my wallet?'

'Yes. I didn't expect to find anything. What's your game, Sam? Do you know Jonah?'

'No, I don't know him. Sophie, why did you go through my wallet?'

'To check you could be trusted.' She could feel her eyes pricking with tears. 'And clearly you can't.'

'Sophie…'

'I think you should leave. Go and collect your things and… and…' Sam jumped up and hurried round to her but she pushed him away, threw her hands over her eyes. 'I can't take any more lies, Sam. Not from anyone. But especially not from you.'

'Sophie, there's a simple explanation. Listen, love…'

Laura started to cry. Sam went to pick her up but Sophie leapt to her feet.

'Don't touch her!'

He stepped back. 'She's upset to see you like this.'

'*I'll* pick her up. You can work on your explanation. Would you like more time?'

Sam sagged back onto his chair and watched Sophie consoling her daughter. 'No, I don't need more time. Look, Sophie, it's a bloody ridiculous coincidence. Jonah came to the college to set up the new staff portal. You said he had clients around London. It was about four... no, three weeks ago. There's a tech station in the library. I had a pile of exam papers to mark so I was holed up in one of the meeting rooms. I approached him and asked if he knew anything about technical drawing software. Jesse's looking to upgrade his system. I gave him one of Jesse's business cards and he gave me one of his to give to Jesse. I stuck it in my wallet and forgot about it. Probably if you search through Jonah's business cards, you'll find one of Jesse's.'

'It was in his wallet.'

'Jesse's card?'

'Yes. Why didn't you tell me you'd already met him?'

'Because I didn't realise I had.' He looked at the card on the table. 'At the time, I didn't register the name of his company. I was more concerned with reading hopeless essays. So, when I heard the name Royston, I never made the connection. It was only when I saw that photo of him yesterday... it was only then I realised who he was. And I was just scared to say. I'm sorry, I should have told you straight away. And I'm sorry you felt the need to go through my things.'

Sophie put Laura back in her chair. She couldn't think of anything to say so she stood by the sink and drank her tea. Sam watched her.

'Did you find anything else to concern you?'

'No.'

'Good.' He sighed. 'Do you fancy feeding the ducks?'

'No.' She chewed her lip. 'I didn't want to not trust you.'

'I know. I think the trouble is this has all been too fast. It probably would be best if I helped with supper then went back to the attic for the night. Give you a chance to properly decide whether you want me crowding you like this.' He attempted a smile. 'We could probably both do with a good night's sleep.'

Sophie felt her legs weaken. 'You haven't been crowding me. Will you come back?'

'If that's what you want, then, yes. There's a meeting with the Planning Officer tomorrow at four o'clock, so I'll be back after that. OK?'

Sophie wanted to say please, don't go. But this thing with Sam really was happening too fast. 'OK. You can leave your things here.'

\-

The afternoon, Laura's bedtime and then supper hurried by. Sam made hot chocolate and chatted about his students but something started to irk Sophie. She just couldn't work out what it was. But then, as Sam started to collect up their cups, it occurred to her exactly what was troubling her. 'Sam, why were you cycling past here the other day? I mean, Jesse's place and the college are miles away. Is it another ridiculous coincidence?'

He paused and looked at her, his face expressionless. The silence seemed to last too long. 'I suppose it is a coincidence. I was cycling over to Eashing to put some flowers by my mother's headstone. I do it every year on her birthday, which just happened to be that day. Her family are all buried there.'

'Oh. I'm sorry.'

'Sorry my mum died seven years ago or sorry you still think I'm up to something?'

'Sam, I don't think that.'

'Right. Well, I'd better get a move on if I'm going to catch that train.'

\-

Sam phoned from the train to check that Sophie had remembered to lock the doors. She told him yes, she'd checked everything and was already in bed. Just falling asleep. They said goodnight then Sophie locked the doors and went upstairs to her empty bed.

Ends

'That you, Sam?'

Sam appeared in the archway. 'Yeh. Why are you still up?'

'Couldn't sleep. Came down for a drink.' Jesse watched Sam walk over and pour himself a brandy, drink it down then pour another. 'I wasn't expecting to see you. Have you and... have you had a row about something?'

Sam emptied his glass and poured another. 'You could say that.'

'Would you like to talk about it before you become unconscious?'

'No.'

'Did you tell her you're...?'

'Of course not!'

Jesse sighed. 'You know it can't work, don't you, lying to her like that?'

'Fuck off, Jesse. It's my problem, so just stay out of it.' He sat on the sofa opposite, pushed his hand through his hair. 'I couldn't tell her even if I wanted to.'

'You guys make that spook shit up! I know what you do and the nation hasn't crumbled into chaos... no more than usual, anyway.'

Sam shook his head. 'The guy she was living with...'

'The one who smashed his head in?'

'Yeh. He's peripherally involved in the trafficking-prostitution racket we're investigating.'

Jesse stared across the divide. 'What? Are you fucking mental? You're letting yourself get emotionally involved with... you've fucked a woman who's been living with a suspect? Is the child his?'

'Yes.'

'Sam, you need to walk away *now*!'

'I can't.' He slugged back the brandy and put the glass on the floor.

'What do you mean, *you can't*?'

'I just can't.' Sam threw himself back in the chair. 'There's too much at stake. And she's no idea what he's involved in. The kind of people who might come looking for him.'

'So, you're setting up house to protect her from the bad guys, are you?'

Sam closed his eyes. 'That's part of it.'

'Well, you need to negotiate your way out of *it*. Before it's too late.'

'It's already too late.'

'For fuck's sake, Sam! What the hell's wrong with you? Can't you just screw a woman and walk away?'

Sam opened his eyes. 'No. Clearly, that's one of the big differences between us.' He immediately sat up. 'Jesse, I'm sorry, I didn't mean that. I'm not thinking straight.'

Jesse dismissed the insult with a mouthful of brandy. 'Sam, mate, you need to think this through. The longer you carry on hiding the fact that you're investigating her partner... her ex-partner... and the longer you carry on lying to her, the more traumatic it will be when she finds out. You know what women are like, she'll convince herself your whole relationship is one big ploy to catch the bad guys. And *you* need to be sure it isn't.'

Sam rubbed his hands down his face. 'If I tell her the truth now, it'll not only be the end to my being able to check out the bastard's contacts, from the inside, it will also be the end of any possible relationship with her.'

'And are you sure which of those two ends would be the worst?'

'No, I'm not sure.'

14

There was a long-ago, ghostly anecdote, once told to Sophie and Josie by their great-grandma. They had listened wide-eyed and fearful, watching the old lady's wrinkly lips, as she told them how her beloved father had contracted smallpox and had been sent to an isolation boat in the Thames. How she had woken as a small girl in the middle of the night and had seen his faint shape move across the end of her bed. She had pointed with her sinewy finger to demonstrate how the ghostly corpse had paused to bow and then had flowed away. She told the girls how she had known in that instant that this apparition was her father's farewell and how her mother had received notification the next evening that he had died the night before. The girls had mostly discounted the story as the fantastical ramblings of a very old lady but stories like that linger on in the depths of your subconscious. And then, when you have no idea that they are still there, when your thoughts are running wild, they ease their way to the surface of your mind and haunt you...

–

It was still dark when some slight movement, perhaps no movement at all, perhaps a prod from a sinewy finger, caused Sophie to wake and see a faint shape drift past her bedroom door. With no time for fear, her immediate concern was Laura. She hurried into the next room and discovered her daughter sleeping peacefully, her small features illuminated by the dim light beside her cot. Sophie sagged down onto the floor and imagined the great-great-granddad she had known only through an old woman's reflections. She watched the dark corridor outside but there was nothing. She thought of Jonah, his head that harboured so many lies, swathed in bandages. Perhaps something had happened. Perhaps he had wanted to apologise to her for the unhappiness he was causing her, before he was gone. These were not the things Sophie would normally think, but it was the middle of the night and she *was* thinking them. She hurried back to her room, turned on the light and phoned the hospital. The phone rang for some time. She hoped it wasn't disturbing desperately ill people. Eventually someone answered. Mr Perrin's condition was unchanged.

Sophie went back onto the landing and turned on the light, returned to her bed and sat going over the day: Sam. She'd upset him. Declared her distrust. What if that had been Sam's spirit calling out to her. She crushed her mind's suggestion that such things were possible. But at ten past three in the morning, alone in her bed, all things were possible. She couldn't phone him. Not in the middle of the night. So, she sat, watching her bedroom curtains, and waited for the daylight to gather and drive away her fears.

–

By late morning Sam hadn't called. When the phone did finally ring, it was Katie. She was about to have lunch with a potential client, in Guildford. She could drop round for coffee at around two thirty. If that was convenient. Sophie said yes, please come, she'd be on her own, then she went to the kitchen to make lunch. The doorbell rang. She hurried to open it and found herself confronted by two large men, one bearded and bald, one ginger with a nasty-looking mole on his cheek. The bald one was standing on her bottom step, the ginger one on the pavement. She felt anxious. Vulnerable.

'Sorry to bother you, love,' said the bald man, 'but we need to contact Mr Robert Perrin and we believe 'e is resident at this address.' He placed a foot on the top step and, as he did so, Sophie was overwhelmed by the stench of stale beer and cigarette smoke. She immediately relaxed. These men were obviously members of the Fox and Gander skittles team, wondering what had happened to Jonah. Odd that they knew him by his Exeter name. He must have assumed she'd never go to watch him play. She briefly explained that Robert would not be competing in the foreseeable future due to being unconscious in hospital with brain damage following a road accident, the Neurological Unit at Southampton General. And would they please apologise to the other team members on Jonah's behalf.

Ginger man looked irritated, but bald man stepped down onto the pavement, his face affecting an ugly attempt at sympathy. 'Sorry to 'ear that, love. Please give Robert our good wishes, would you? And when 'e comes round, tell 'im Joe and Col arsed after 'im.' With that the two men left.

Sophie watched them walk away towards the town centre then carried Laura through to give her lunch. As she was clearing away, the doorbell rang once again. She hurried through, desperate to find Sam standing on the top step. She pulled open the door. It was Sam, but it wasn't. For a start, Sam hadn't had that designer stubble last night and as far as she knew he didn't own any clothes that were half as decent as those that were on the Sam that was in front of her: expensive chinos…

'Hello, Sophie. I'm Sam's brother.'

'Jesse? Is Sam OK? Has something happened?'

'No, nothing like that. Do you mind if I…?'

Sophie invited him in, led him through the hallway and into the kitchen, offered coffee. 'My daughter's just had lunch. It's a bit of a war zone in here.'

He smiled, checked one of the chairs for debris and sat down. 'I just wanted to have a chat with you. About Sam.'

Sophie looked at him, uncertain. 'What about Sam?'

He sighed. 'Look, this is difficult. I just wanted to say, well, to say… I don't want to see Sam get hurt.'

'I wouldn't…'

'He was devastated when he got home last night.'

'Oh, I didn't mean to upset him. It's just… did he tell you how we met?'

'Your partner's accident?'

'Yes, but other things I've found out about Jonah… about my partner, it's made me suspicious of everybody. Then a couple of things made me suspect something was going on that involved Sam.' She told him about the business cards.

Jesse frowned. 'Actually, Sam did give someone my contact details. I think I've booked a meeting.' He pulled out his phone and checked. 'September the fourteenth? Royston Computers. Is that your partner's company?'

'Yes, but I don't suppose he'll be making that meeting. I'm sorry I upset Sam.'

Jesse shook his head. 'My brother's a bit… well, someone let him down.'

'Eleven years ago?'

'Has he told you about it?'

'Not much. He said she was an older woman.' Sophie made coffee and listened.

'Yes, she was older. Amelia. She was South American. She got pregnant. So, Sam signed away his life and then, when she was about six months gone, she went back to Argentina. She phoned to tell him her half of the house would be sufficient to cover any future child care. My mother helped pay her off then hired a private investigator. It turned out she was actually married to an English guy in Buenos Aires. He wasn't able to have children, so they came across to the UK to find a nice blond father for their child. And a significant amount of child support. And that was pretty much that.'

Sophie handed him a mug and sat down opposite him. 'Couldn't she just have opted for AI?'

'I think it was the child support that tipped the balance.'

'What about the baby?'

'Sam's never seen him.' Jesse gave her a cautious look. 'When Sam discovered the extent to which Amelia had used him, he fell apart. Booked himself into a hotel just outside Brighton and swallowed a bottle of fine rioja and a fistful of temazepam. Fortunately, there was a fire and they discovered him when they were checking the rooms. I probably shouldn't be telling you all this, but… I don't want anything like that to happen to him again.'

Sophie shook her head to drive away the image of Sam in his hotel room, swigging down sleeping pills. She watched Jesse's awkward silence. Wondered how people with such perfect stubble managed to stop it turning into an actual beard.

Jesse cleared his throat. 'As far as I know, he's avoided any serious attachment since Amelia. Right up until now. Sophie, if you think this relationship is just your reaction to the situation you've found yourself in then… Christ, I shouldn't be doing this. I… has Sam told you *anything* else about himself? Apart from Amelia?'

'Only that he teaches English. And he has a lot of books.' That didn't sound much to know about a person she'd just encouraged to move in with her. She got to her feet. 'I'm just going to put Laura upstairs. She missed her morning sleep. I won't be a minute. Then we can talk some more. Are you in a hurry?'

'Not really. I've got a meeting at four.'

Sophie hurried Laura into her cot then returned to the kitchen. Jesse looked up. 'Sophie, I'm sorry to do this to you.' He ran his fingers through his hair just like Sam. 'And I'd prefer it if Sam didn't know I told you about him trying to top himself. OK? But I need to tell…'

'Would you like another coffee?'

'What? No, I'm fine. I…'

'Did Sam tell you that I discovered Jonah's been living a double life and that, when the accident happened, he was leaving me to go back to his wife and children?'

Jesse looked startled. 'No, he didn't. That's awful.'

'I can't believe I was so gullible. But, Jesse…'

The letterbox scraped open. 'Soph, it's me!'

Sophie explained that her friend was dropping by for coffee then ran to open the front door. Katie strode in. 'Hi, Soph, I thought I'd better not ring the bell in case Laura was asleep. I could murder a coffee.'

'How was your meeting?'

'Well, there's businesses you can punch life into and then there's miracles. We charge more for miracles. And these stupid sods are willing to pay for one. So...' She stepped into the kitchen and paused. 'Have you had a makeover or something?'

Sophie laughed. 'It's not Sam. It's his brother, Jesse. Jesse, this is my best friend Katie. She's known for saying exactly what she thinks. Without thinking about it first.'

Jesse got to his feet and offered his hand. Katie frowned and accepted it. 'Good Lord. Sophie, why don't you try and make Sam look like this?'

Jesse failed to suppress a smile. Sophie offered Katie a chair. 'Do you actually want coffee or have you just called round to embarrass me?'

'Both will do me. Is Sam here?'

'No. Jesse just nipped over for a chat.'

'What, a chat about Sam behind his back?'

A brief anxiety flashed across Jesse's brow.

'Jesse was just checking that my intentions towards Sam were honourable.'

'What?'

'I wanted to make sure my brother wasn't going to get hurt.'

Katie gaped at him. 'What kind of freak are you? What do you think Sophie's likely to do? Steal his virginity then move on to the next guy she can find with a bad-hair day?'

Jesse stared speechless. Sophie sighed. 'Katie, Jesse's just concerned about Sam.'

'Why?'

'Because... Look, can we just change the subject? Everything's fine. Sam will be back later.' She felt her cheeks flushing. 'He's been staying over. And...'

'And his big brother's just checking out the facilities?'

'He's not his big brother. Jesse's twelve minutes younger than Sam.'

Katie effected one of her legendary attitude reversals and said, 'That was clearly a very creative twelve minutes.'

Jesse looked confused. Sophie glanced at him and rolled her eyes. 'Jesse, would you like to change your mind about the coffee?'

'I don't know. What did I say about the coffee?'

'That you didn't want one.'

'Oh. Yes, I'll change my mind, if that's OK.'

–

Jesse handled Katie's intrusive questioning stoically, hurried to finish his coffee and left to attend his meeting. Katie sat back and folded her arms.

'So, why's Sam's brother so concerned that you don't transmute into the bitch from Hell. With a baby?'

Sophie rubbed her eyes, painfully aware that she had spent most of the night thinking about floating spirits. 'Katie, don't you have to go back to work?'

'I'm currently in the hotel lobby writing up my report. Tell me what's going on.'

So, Sophie supplied a few brief snippets of Sam's history, taking care not to mention the hotel. Katie listened, and when Sophie's summary came to an end, she said nothing. Sophie folded her arms. 'Aren't you going to offer some kind of annoying opinion?'

'Nope. I'll just offer to stand by you when it all falls apart.'

'That's equivalent to an annoying opinion.'

'Soph, the last thing you need at the moment is to get yourself involved with a guy whose life is as stable as a train wreck. What about Laura?'

'It was you who pointed out how good he is with her.' She supressed a yawn. 'And I'm in love with him.'

'Well, that's always a good basis upon which to redirect your life. Look how well being in love with Jonah turned out.'

'I never felt this way about Jonah. I'm just scared I've ruined everything. I found one of Jonah's business cards in Sam's wallet and accused him of knowing Jonah already and being involved in some kind of… I don't know what.'

Katie frowned for a moment then slowly shook her head. 'You went through his wallet? That's a good start, Soph. Really great. Make more coffee.'

Tales of the Riverbank

Thaddeus Jones was seething; he was barely able to maintain his accent. 'Mr Mann, Mr Sokolov, would you kindly explain to me why the body was disposed of in this way? Do you not watch the television? Read crime fiction? Bodies buried in woods are always discovered. Men walking dogs. Children. Gypsies. The Source assures me that the NCA are already involved. So, we are now faced with a most difficult tidy-up operation. Exactly why did you break from procedure? The nautical route has always proved to be efficient in the past, has it not?'

'Mr Jones, we regret to say that neither of the boats was available, on account of them being already at sea for vacation purposes. And Mr Sokolov and myself were advised this 'ad to be an emergency disposal. Already dead. And in a bloody state, they said. So, we 'ad to do some quick thinking and, because of 'is time in 'iding, Mr Sokolov was familiar with the burial site. And 'ad it not rained so 'eavily and the riverbank 'adn't fallen into the river, the local wildlife would of thoroughly seen to the remains before they was discovered. Badgers and foxes and the like. Voles.'

'Yes, yes. Well, there's nothing to be done now, other than to sit this one out. Have you made any progress with this computer man, Perrin? Confirmed that he is the administrator?'

'We 'ave, Mr Jones. Apparently, Mr Robert Perrin's official residence is down in Devon, but we've discovered that 'e spends arf 'is time living in Surrey under the hassumed name of Jonah Royston. And 'is other woman that lives in Surrey 'as this mornin' informed us that Mr Royston is in 'orspital 'aving broken 'is skull.'

Thaddeus Jones tapped his fingers together. 'Well, make sure it doesn't mend until we've worked out what to do about him. Surrey, you say?'

'Yes, Mr Jones.'

15

Straight after Katie left, Sophie staggered upstairs and fell asleep with the baby monitor next to her pillow. Laura would probably wake up any minute but any precious moments of sleep were worth… The doorbell rang. Sophie staggered back downstairs and pulled open the front door. It was Sam. She would have said hi but she had lost the ability to speak.

'Good Lord, what's happened?'

Sophie closed her eyes and sagged towards him. He caught her just as she was about to collide with the open door. She was vaguely aware of being helped upstairs, of her head sinking into her pillow. She woke an indeterminate amount of time later, sat up and knocked the baby monitor onto the floor. Sam walked into the room.

'You're awake at last.' He picked the monitor off the floor.

'Is Laura awake?'

'Almost three hours ago. I've given her rice pudding.' He sat down on the edge of the bed. 'She's in the playpen gurgling at Clown-face. Personally, I think it looks like something out of a Stephen King movie. She's trying to force her rattle up his trousers but I think they're attached at his knees.'

Sophie rubbed her eyes. 'She's such a picky-pokey baby. I had to take her to A&E last month because she'd stuffed a peanut up her nose.'

'Yeh, it's all excitement with kids. Jake stuck a baked bean down his ear when he was about the same age. Why were you so tired?'

'I woke up about three o'clock and couldn't get back to sleep.'

'Me too. Come on, let's think about supper.'

She caught his hand as he got to his feet. 'Sam, I'm sorry I doubted you.'

'No worries.' He took a deep breath. 'You're forgiven.'

–

Sam helped make a Caesar salad with added chicken, spring onions, yellow pepper and cherry tomatoes, in fact with so many things added that it was hardly a Caesar salad at all. But it tasted excellent. As did the white burgundy. They retired to the TV to let their food digest before going to bed. Sophie kicked off her shoes and nestled against Sam's arm.

'Sam?'

He pressed the mute button. 'Mm?'

'Jesse called round to have a chat.'

'He told me. We had a brief, heated exchange about it. I was wondering when you were going to mention it.'

She pulled herself up. 'I wasn't thinking of not telling you.'

He pulled her back down. 'So, did he tell you all about my wayward past?'

'He told me a few things but mostly he was just checking me out to make sure I wasn't going to break your heart.'

Sam said nothing. Sophie sat up and turned to face him.

'He told me about the baby. Sam, I'm so sorry that happened to you.'

He sighed. 'Did he also tell you about my trip to Brighton?'

'Did he tell you he told me?'

'No. Did he?'

'Yes. And I'm glad someone set the hotel on fire.'

Sam took her hand and placed it across his heart. 'So, now you know: I'm an emotionally-destroyed, scruffy wannabe fifties detective with a son I'm never likely to see. Do you think I have the right to foist my fucked-up life upon you, given your current fucked-up circumstances?'

'Sam, I've spent the whole of the last five years being lied to. So, whatever happens between us from now on, it can't possibly be any worse than that.'

—

As well as a familiarity with the first- and second-generation Romantics, Sam also had an impressive repertoire of modern verse, although the metre often proved quite hectic, so he preferred to recite the more contemporary poetry post-coitally. Therefore, as they lay beside one another in the dark, waiting for sleep, he stroked Sophie's arm and asked... *What was that sound that came in on the dark?*...

'Who wrote that?'

'Harold Pinter.'

'Do you ever write poetry?'

'Nothing I'd bother to commit to memory.'

Silence. Then: 'Sam, will you help get Jonah's case in from the car. His charger's in there somewhere. I need to charge his Samsung in case there are important missed calls.'

Sam leaned over and put the light on. 'Sophie, that's not your problem.'

'No, but Jonah used to play in a skittles team at the Fox and Gander. And two of the team members called round today, wondering what had happened to him. And they were scary. I don't really want anyone else like that coming here to ask about him.'

'Do you mean the Fox and Gander pub, by the station?'

'Probably.'

'Didn't you ever go there with him?'

'No.'

'Right. Look, there's an emergency faculty meeting tomorrow at eleven. I'll nip in there when I get back and tell them they're a man down. And you've got to stop thinking of him as Jonah. It's not his name, Sophie.'

Sam carried Jonah's case through to the backyard and set it upright in the shade, checking its catches to ensure that it wasn't likely to repeat last week's emptying-out performance.

'Don't open this until I get back. The car smells of putrid dustbin.' He hurried away and reappeared a few minutes later with a tied refuse sack and a small light-blue overnight bag. Sophie stood at a safe distance and frowned.

'Was that bag in the boot as well? I've never seen it before.'

She went to pick it up but Sam stayed her hand. 'Not now, Soph. Wait until I'm back.'

–

It was well after two thirty when Sam strode into the kitchen, looking harassed. 'Sorry, Soph, the meeting ran on for ages. There's been some kind of compromise with the college portal. The one Jonah-cum-Robert set up. I didn't tell them I was currently romancing his ex-partner.' He took a deep breath. 'And then, when it looked like things couldn't get any worse, I nipped into the Fox and Gander to confirm that he-who-is-difficult-to-name will not be fulfilling his skittle commitments and, firstly, they had never heard of Robert Perrin or Jonah Royston. And, secondly, they have no skittles team and have never had a skittles team. So, God knows who those two guys were that called round. What did they look like?'

Sophie attempted descriptions then sagged into a chair. 'He's been in that team ever since I've known him.'

Sam pulled out the chair opposite and sat down. 'And in all that time, he never once asked you to go and watch him play?'

'Well, I didn't miss much, did I? And, yes, I do remember him asking. When we were first together. And I told him I hated skittles because my dad used to be in a skittles team and he was always coming home drunk and rowing with my mum. Jonah was probably just making sure I'd never want to go with him so he could do whatever it was he really did when he was supposed to be playing. He probably can't even play skittles.'

'It's not difficult. It's like idiot bowling.'

'Have you played?'

'I wouldn't admit it if I had.' He stretched across the table to touch her hand. '*Oh! What a tangled web we weave when first we practise to deceive.*'

'I've always wondered who said that.'

'It was Sir Walter Scott in *Marmion*, his epic poem about knights and lust and dishonest nuns. So, nothing as fucked-up as all this. Did you open the case?'

'No, I waited. Like you said.'

'Good. Check Laura. I'll go and investigate. You can watch from the door.'

–

Sam leapt back as the case fell open and the stench of hot putre-faction filled the air. Apart from a fair amount of blood and filth and vomit, it contained most of the things Sophie had watched Jonah cram into it those few eventful days ago. The rest of its festering contents were obviously in the refuse bag. She stepped over to take a look, cast her mind back to that day: Jonah cherry-picking the things he was going to transfer from his false life to his real life. Most were beyond salvaging. She was glad he hadn't managed to cram the Arran jumper in with the rest of his things. Avoiding any major deposits of organic matter, she picked out the charger and decided to deal with the rest later when Laura was asleep. The blue overnight bag contained money.

'What the— Did you know about this, Soph?'

'No! I told you, I've never seen that bag before. Is it real?'

'Yeh. It's mostly new twenties. There must be over thirty thousand here.'

'Do you think we should tell the police?'

'Well, that would be assuming it isn't legitimately Jonah's money. Money he's been paid in cash. The interest rate is so low at the moment, you might just as well drive around with it in the boot of your car.'

'Do you think that's the explanation?'

'No, I don't.'

'Do you think he was doing something illegal?'

'Possibly. In the great criminal plan of things, thirty thousand's not that much.'

'You know about things like that, do you?'

'I've watched a lot of TV.' He looked at her and smirked. 'All alone in my attic.'

She returned the smirk. 'Actually, I mentioned your attic to your brother and he said it was a very unsatisfactory way to describe your luxury penthouse.'

'Really? And did my luxury brother offer any other opinions?'

'Yes. He said that your scruffy, Bob–Dylan–in–the–sixties look was an affectation. And that beneath your tramp–like exterior you are the most intellectual and cultured twin. By far.'

Sam shook his head. 'Ah, Jesse, the man who reveres the reader of books whilst never attempting to read one himself. Come on, let's put this loot upstairs with the rest of his stuff.'

'We could borrow some of it to buy Laura a birthday present.'

'Sophie! Until we know where this has come from, we leave it alone. Do you need money?'

'Nearly. Jonah usually gave me cash each month and I'm only getting a bit of maternity pay.'

'Well it's just as well you have a scruffy live–in lover on lecturer's pay. We'll almost be able to afford to eat.' He frowned at her. 'Are you going back full–time?'

'No. Mondays, Tuesdays and Thursdays. And Wednesdays after Christmas.'

'What about Laura?'

'She's booked into Rosemead Nursery.'

'What's their record on losing kids?'

'Don't say that! I can't bear to think of leaving her there.'

After supper, Sophie set Jonah's two phones on charge then went to the lounge to remind Sam about the case and bin bag that were currently attracting a variety of nocturnal insects towards her back yard. She found him going through her abridged CD collection. He held up a handful of unmarked discs. 'What are these? They're not labelled.'

'They're probably things Jonah recorded. They can go in the bin.'

'Jesse would freak if he heard you say that. I'll take them over to his waste management centre.' He put the dozen or so CDs to one side. 'There's not much of Jonah here, is there? Not that would suggest he's been living here for the last five years.'

'He keeps his papers and equipment in his office. I've never been there.'

'In five years, you've never been to his office or watched him not play skittles?'

'No. Come and help with his case.'

—

Outside, the light was fading, so Sam dragged the suitcase towards the back door to take advantage of the light flooding out from the kitchen, set it flat on the ground and lobbed it open. Sophie emptied the bin bag on top. A smell that was both sour and appalling filled the chill evening air. 'This is disgusting,' she said. 'I'm going to throw it all away.'

Sam handed her a fresh refuse bag. 'I'll throw, you catch.'

It felt strangely treacherous, consigning Jonah's clothes to the world of waste, and, as she watched Sam checking the pockets of Jonah's battered green cords, Sophie felt her knees weaken. 'They're too messed up to recycle, aren't they?'

Sam eased the bag from her grasp. 'Shall I do the rest?'

'That's almost all of it anyway.' She picked up Jonah's washbag and placed it on the small pile of things she considered salvageable.

'I ought to take this in to him. He hasn't got anything with him.' She lifted a crushed pack of boxers. 'And these are probably worth keeping. I'll take them out of the packet. I bought them for him last Christmas.'

'Very nice. Although, I beg you never to buy me underwear with frogs on it.'

She forced a smile. 'I'll ask Katie to drive me over with some of his things.'

'What? Soph, I'll take you there. I'll borrow a car from Jesse.'

'Do you drive?'

'Ah, it's just one insult after another!'

'I'm sorry, I…'

'Jesse has a Z4, a vintage camper, a Toyota hybrid, a Range Rover, three vans and a truck. I haven't bothered to buy my own car because his drive already looks like a car park.'

'That's a lot of cars for an environmentalist to own.'

'He says he can only drive one of them at a time. Which means there's always one for me to borrow.' He knotted the bin bag and placed it against the wall. 'What about the case?'

'I never want to see it again.'

'Right. Let's go take a shower.'

—

Once again Sophie woke at three o'clock. Fortunately, Sam was there to fend off the ghouls. She felt his arm work its way across her waist.

'Sam, when Heidi Perrin finds out about me… if she doesn't already know about me, do you think she'll divorce Jonah?'

'I've no idea. Can we not worry about it right now?'

'But I'll feel really guilty if I'm the reason her marriage is ruined.'

'Sophie, Jonah is the reason her marriage is ruined!'

'Well, I'm going to go and talk to her. At that address on Jonah's licence.'

Sam sat up and leaned over her and, in the bright moonlight flooding in through the open curtains, she could easily make out his look of disapproval.

'I want to tell her I didn't know Jonah had a family. And I want to see her. And his house. Where he lives his proper life.'

'Sophie, that's crazy! You have no idea what this woman is like. What if she doesn't know about you and suddenly you're standing on her doorstep, telling her she's been sharing her husband with you for the last five years? What if she turns nasty? And what if she's not there? She might be staying in Southampton to be close by.'

'Sam, I'm going to do it. And I'm going to take Laura with me.' Sam threw himself back onto his pillows and said nothing. 'There's a Family Support woman at the hospital. Do you think she'd tell me whether Heidi's visited him? Or if she's called? They've not mentioned anything about anyone else calling. Apart from some woman who phoned last week, pretending to be my sister.'

Sam sat back up. 'You never told me about that!' He pushed his hand through his hair. 'For God's sake, Sophie! This is complete madness. And exactly how are you thinking of getting to Exeter?'

'I'll catch a train.'

'Don't be ridiculous!' He exhaled exasperation. 'I'll drive you there.'

'That's not necessary. I don't want to drag you into it.'

'I'm already dragged into it.' He rubbed the sleep from his eyes. 'Look, when we take Jonah's things over, we'll ask this Family Support person if he's had visitors and go from there. OK?'

'OK. And I'll ask in Intensive Care.'

'Right. It's twenty past three. We should try and get some sleep.'

Silence. Just the humming of the house preparing for another day. Sophie stroked her finger down his arm. 'I don't know about you, Mr Barnes, but I'm wide awake now.'

16

Sam nipped over to the building site that was destined to become his prize-winning eco-home and returned late morning in Jesse's Range Rover, parked behind Jonah's BMW and hurried round to collect Sophie and Laura before a traffic warden discovered his lack of permit. With Laura's car seat in place, they pulled away.

'Someone's going to notice the Beamer's not moving,' said Sam. 'We ought to shift it before it's nicked. Does Jonah have parking at his business premises?'

'Probably.'

Sam sighed and concentrated on avoiding a cyclist, who suddenly chose to turn right across the front of him. 'Bloody cyclists!'

Sophie laughed. 'And how's *your* bike, Sam Cyclist?'

'I'm picking it up on Monday. New wheel and brake cable, two new mudguards and a new top-of-the-range blinking saddle light.'

'Did that get broken as well?'

'No, somebody pinched the last one from the college bike rack. Jesse said I should keep this for the time being.'

-

May Barnet was waiting in Reception. Sophie introduced Sam and Mrs Barnet, showing no sign of disapproval, shook Sam's hand then waved repeatedly at Laura as he wheeled her away to the cafeteria. As the lift doors closed, Sophie was quick to declare herself. 'Since we last met, I've discovered that Jonah, I mean

Robert, I've discovered he's married. I was wondering whether his wife's been to see him?'

May Barnet held the lift doors as Sophie stepped out, waited until they closed then answered. 'We have been informed that there is a…' She paused, searching for the appropriate euphemism. '…*complication* regarding Mr Perrin's circumstances. Obviously, our major confusion was his actual identity.' She showed no sign of leaving the lift area but instead adopted a sympathetic inclination of her head. 'This must have been most distressing for you. As far as I know, Mrs Perrin has phoned most days to ask after her husband. She is being kept informed of any changes in his condition. I have advised the Intensive Care staff to continue to regard you, also, as a major contact.'

Sophie felt that Mrs Barnet might not have offered this advice had she been aware of Jonah's intention to leave, and the extent to which Sam had taken his place. 'Mrs Barnet, would you know if Mrs Perrin knows of the circumstances of her husband's accident?'

May Barnet straightened her skirt. 'I gather that all telephone conversations have been very abrupt. Just enquiries regarding his condition.' She indicated towards the double doors. 'I believe Dr Donovan might be available to update you regarding Mr Perrin's progress.'

–

Sophie handed over Jonah's things then she and Mrs Barnet were shown into the same side room as before: subdued lighting, white linen, the sound of the ventilator. Nothing seemed to have changed and yet in Sophie's world, outside of this place, everything had changed.

'Would you like me to wait with you?' said May Barnet.

Sophie considered saying yes, please, but really, she needed to spend some time with Jonah on her own. Just to watch him. 'I think I'm OK. But it would be great if you could check my friend in the coffee shop. Make sure he's managing with Laura.'

Mrs Barnet clasped her hands together then left. Sophie moved closer to the bed, stared at Jonah's bandages, watched the monitors supplying information she couldn't comprehend, listened to the distant voices filtering in from outside. A wave of panic rippled through her. What if Jonah's wife wouldn't take him back? Would they, whoever *they* were, would they expect her to take him back? She didn't want him back. She was with Sam now. She watched the bedclothes rise and fall as the ventilator breathed, and became overwhelmed by an inconvenient wave of regret...

One Year Earlier

Sophie watched Jonah holding his daughter for the first time. She felt very emotional; missed her mother more than ever.

'She looks just like you. I wish you could have been here.'

He looked up. 'If I'd thought she was going to arrive today, I would have cancelled the trip, but she seemed to be happy where she was for the next few days. And the traffic was awful driving back.' He stroked his daughter's dark curls. 'She's beautiful, Sophie.'

'Her eyes are blue but the midwife says they'll probably be brown with her colouring.'

'That often happens.' He frowned. 'Somebody told me that. What shall we call her?'

'I'd like one of her names to be Emily. After my mum.'

'My mother's name was Laura.'

'Laura Emily Royston.' Sophie smiled. 'It suits her.'

Six Months After That

'Are you sure you've packed your insect spray? And your mosquito tablets?'

'Stop fussing, Soph. I'll phone you as soon as I get to the hotel. But don't start worrying if you don't hear from me straight away. Things are a bit primitive out there. That's why they need me.' He kissed Laura's mop of curls and handed her over. 'There's a good girl. I'm counting on you to look after Mummy while I'm away.'

Sophie smiled. 'It seems so far away this time. And I still think six weeks is ages. She'll probably be crawling by the time you come back. Why does it have to be so long?'

'Sweetheart, we've been through this. I'm pretty much starting from scratch out there. I'll get things sorted as fast as I can.' He kissed Sophie's cheek and then stooped to pick up his case. 'Remember, Africa's only a phone call away.'

'OK. Love you. And don't run off with any dusky maidens.'

'Love you too. Take care of my girl. And don't forget, when the clocks go forward, you'll be an hour ahead of me.'

Three Months Later

'You've only been back six weeks. You're missing everything she does. She hardly recognised you last time you came back.'

'Of course she recognised me. She was just angry with me for being away for so long. But she forgave me as soon as I gave her Clown.'

'But these trips seem to be getting longer.'

'Bigger contracts mean more money. We can't afford for me to turn them down. And when I come back, I've got a couple of big UK jobs lined up. So, I'll be home most nights. And I won't miss anything. I'll buy her a bike and teach her to ride it.'

'Idiot. She has to learn to walk first.'

'Oh, yes. Thank goodness one of us knows all that baby nonsense. I'm just a proud but inexperienced father. I'll phone you both every day.'

16 (continued)

'… Liar!'

'Sorry?'

'Oh! Dr Donovan! I'm sorry… I've brought in some of Jonah… Robert's things.' Another wave of panic, this time accompanied by nausea. 'How is he?'

'He's recovering from the surgery very well. And we're optimistic about his prognosis. The indications are that we'll be able to release him from the coma in the next few days. He'll continue to be sedated, but we will then be in a position to assess any long-term damage arising from the brain trauma.'

Sophie could feel the nausea getting worse, her throat closing over. Clearly there were outward signs of her crisis.

'Ms Denham, shall we step outside. It can be quite airless in here.' Dr Donovan ushered her into the corridor.

She did not turn to take a last look at Jonah but instead garnered her strength to ask, 'Dr Donovan, will Robert be able to care for himself once he leaves here?'

Dr Donovan bowed his head slightly to look at her, a movement that suggested he was in the habit of wearing spectacles. 'Mr Perrin is likely to require some period of rehabilitation, after which he might need a degree of assistance.' He folded his arms. 'I gather there is a certain confusion over his permanent address?'

Sophie saw no virtue in denial. 'He was leaving me and our daughter when the accident occurred. I've since discovered that he's married and has two other daughters. I have to presume that he was returning to his wife.' She paused to breathe. 'I intend to contact Mrs Perrin and offer my help in transferring his things to his family home.' The statement had exhausted her but at least it seemed to have driven away the nausea.

Dr Donovan cast a glance towards the side room. 'Obviously, we are not able to involve ourselves in Mr Perrin's private circumstances. However, we will do what we can to prepare him to return to his previous life, however complex he may have made it. Will you continue to concern yourself with his recovery?'

'Yes, but I'll have a better idea of my involvement when I've spoken to his wife.'

Dr Donovan nodded sagely. 'Ms Denham, I wish you every good luck with that.' He shook Sophie's hand then left. Sophie walked over to take another look through the sheet of glass that now separated her from the man she had lived with through the better part of her twenties. She wondered why he had chosen her as the instrument of his adultery, feared it might be because he saw her as easily persuaded, easily deceived. Someone her grandad used to call a *sucker*.

—

Back on the ground floor, Sophie found May Barnet sitting with Sam and Laura. She had stopped smiling and was instead straight-faced, listening intently to what Sam was saying. Two empty coffee cups were on the table. Sam pulled out the chair next to him and Sophie sat down. She offered Mrs Barnet another coffee.

May Barnet waved her hand to signal no thank you – the hand waving was clearly an important means whereby she communicated. An attempted smile flickered across her face and was gone. 'I'd better be getting along. Sophie, you have my contact details if you need me.' She got to her feet. Sam jumped up, feigning his tall-person, apologetic stoop, which Sophie no longer found convincing. Mrs Barnet gave an abrupt nod and then, with a quick wave to Laura, she was away towards reception.

'What did you say to her, Sam?'

'What?'

'It must have been something because you managed to obliterate the plastic smile.'

'Well, I did get the impression she disapproved of the speed with which you have readily given your all to another man.' He raised an eyebrow. 'Either that or she was full of regret that I was no longer available.'

Sophie shook her head. 'You might be beginning to irritate me.'

'Really?'

'No. Let's go home.'

–

Laura fell asleep as soon as they left the hospital complex so, whilst Sam was negotiating traffic, Sophie took the opportunity to interrogate him.

'Did you sleep with many women when you were in Hong Kong?'

'Only prostitutes. And they were mostly awake.'

'Sam!'

'I had a few girlfriends but I was always careful not to get involved.'

'What about since you've been back?'

'Ah, *I wonder, by my troth, what thou and I did, till we loved?*'

'Don't change the subject!'

Sam laughed. 'I didn't. I suppose this conversation was bound to happen, wasn't it? But I thought I'd have more time to get my story straight. For your information, Ms Denham, I've had a few dating flings. I enjoyed the best part of a year entertaining a GP who I knew was moving to Canada to join her fiancé. And earlier this year I spent four blissful months with a visiting history lecturer who eventually returned to her husband in Durham. She nearly didn't go but I managed to persuade her. Any particular reason why you ask?'

'No.' She concentrated on watching the road ahead. 'I knew you must have had loads of women because you are too good at making love to have spent years being celibate.'

He snorted. 'Would you have preferred it if I'd spent the last decade being celibate.'

Sophie didn't answer. Instead she checked her bag for nothing.

'Soph, we're good, right?'

She looked at him and frowned. 'Will you really drive me to Exeter?'

'Does my sex life depend upon it?'

'Sam!'

'Yes, I will.'

'Tomorrow?'

He flashed her a grimace. 'I'm supposed to be choosing doors tomorrow.'

'I didn't think Jesse favoured doors and walls.'

'He permits doors for bedrooms. And occasionally toilets.' He watched Sophie poke around in her bag. 'OK. We'll go tomorrow. Do you think you'll want to stay over?'

'I won't know until I get there.'

–

That evening Sam helped Sophie re-check Jonah's call histories, although, in truth, she had no idea what she was looking for. There were a lot more missed calls on the iPhone: probably from clients. Sam wrote down a few numbers that might be worth following up and Sophie revisited Jonah's message to Heidi and felt herself collapse into a renewed state of dread. Thank goodness Sam had been passing at that very moment. Thank goodness he'd been waiting outside as she watched Suzie disappearing into the crowd. Thank goodness he was there with her now.

17

I haven't hope. I haven't faith.
I live two lives and sometimes three.
The lives I live make life a death
For those who have to live with me.

Guilt by John Betjeman

'Pram's in the car. I'm parked on the lines so we'd better hurry. I've booked us into the Crown Hotel in Topsham, so we'll have somewhere to hang out. It's an old coaching inn. But we don't have to stay if you decide you want to come home. Have you packed enough for staying over?'

'Yes. Have you?'

'Yes.'

—

Within no time at all, Sophie was en route to the West Country, without the slightest idea what she might find there. With Laura sleeping much of the way, they opted to drive straight through and arrived at the hotel just before one thirty. Sam checked in as Mr and Mrs Barnes and arranged for afternoon tea to be sent to their room, which was everything a room should be. Such a shame about the purpose of their visit. Nevertheless, Sophie experienced a brief burst of holiday excitement and decreed that they should stay over whatever happened in the next few hours.

So, they ate sandwiches, drank tea, fed Laura and braced themselves for the next stage of their West Country adventure, which took them north-west along the Exeter Road then the Topsham Road, neither of which were lined with the Devonshire cottages Sophie had expected. In fact, Jonah's real-life postcode directed them towards some significantly detached houses, set back away from the road and masked from the traffic by many lush and long-established trees. Sam took the liberty of pulling into the Perrins' drive and waited for Sophie to change her mind and want to leave, which she did straight after he cut the engine. 'Sam, why did you let me come here? I must have been out of my mind, thinking it's all right to do this.'

'Yes, you thought it as recently as twenty minutes ago, when we left the hotel.' He undid his seat belt. 'And it would be even crazier to have come all the way here and then leave without ringing the doorbell.'

'But, Sam, what if…' She caught her breath. 'Someone's opening the front door!'

They watched as a slim woman approached. Sophie couldn't recognise her from Katie's photo. She was wearing shorts and a vest and far too much gold jewellery, and as she drew close Sophie noticed her blonde ponytail flicking from side to side as if she was on a treadmill. How could Jonah possibly have a wife that looked quite so athletic?

Sam stepped out of the car to greet her. 'Mrs Perrin?'

'Why yes, I thought you were lost. We often have people pulling in off the road to ask directions.' She bent down to smile at Sophie. 'What can I do for you?' Her accent was unsuccessfully-cultured West Country.

'I'm Sam,' said Sam. 'We were hoping to have a quick chat with you about…'

'My husband?'

Sam frowned. 'Well, yes. A chat about your husband.'

Sophie stepped out of the car and hurried round to stand beside Sam. 'Hello, Mrs Perrin. I'm…'

'Sophie?'

Sophie nodded as non-hysterically as she could.

'You know about Sophie?' said Sam.

'I always know about Robert's little deviations. Why don't you come inside and we can have our chat over a drink or two? But, Sam, would you mind moving your car further in because you're blocking the entrance. Us girls can wait for you inside.'

Sam helped Laura into Sophie's arms then she left him re-parking and followed Mrs Perrin into her spacious hall and on into a vast open-plan kitchen-diner which was both impressive and naff in equal measure. 'What an amazing space,' enthused Sophie as sincerely as she was able to. She heard the front door close and turned to see Sam striding in to join them.

'Well, here we all are,' said Mrs Perrin. 'What would you like to drink? Coffee? Coke? There's a cold cava.'

'I'm driving, so I'd better go for the Coke,' said Sam.

'Me too,' said Sophie. She watched Jonah's wife walk over to the huge fridge and pull open the door to reveal enough food to feed a small village. 'Did Robert tell you about me and Laura?'

'Not really. That would be sick, wouldn't it? No. As brilliant as he is with his computers, he's not very inventive with his passwords.' She poured two Cokes and handed them over before helping herself to the bottle of cava. 'So, what has it been? Close on five years, isn't it? But I didn't know about Laura until just ten minutes ago. He doesn't usually let things get as complicated as that. She looks just like him, poor thing.' She handed the bottle to Sam. 'Would you open that for me, Sam. I've just had my nails done.'

'I'm sorry we had to meet like this,' said Sophie. 'I never knew he was married.'

'Don't you worry yourself about it.' Rosemary tickled Laura's cheek. 'Such a lovely name. My eldest daughter's also called Laura. Robert chose it. Named her after his mother.'

Not only did that last snippet of information reveal to Sophie the extent to which Jonah had belittled her and Laura's lives, but the flippancy with which his wife offered it caused her to fear that at any minute she might pull out an axe and cleave them all asunder. She watched Sam hand Mrs Perrin the opened bottle, watched her pour herself a large goblet of sparkling wine and, once again, felt the need to apologise.

'Heidi, I'm really sorry about all this.'

And, for the first time, Mrs Perrin looked surprised. 'Who's Heidi?'

Sam broke the silence, 'We investigated your husband's text messages. One of them was to someone called Heidi. Apparently, he was leaving Sophie to go to her. And...'

Sophie recovered her voice. 'And when I discovered he was married I assumed he was returning to you and that you were Heidi.'

'Well, I'm afraid I've never heard of this Heidi. I'm Rosemary. Shall we go and sit down?' She directed them towards a cluster of soft chairs, one of which was occupied by a small, white, immobile dog. 'So, Sophie, Robert was leaving you, was he?'

'Yes. He was loading his car when the accident happened. I ran after him and I tripped and nudged him against his case and he fell back onto his toolbox and broke his head open.'

Rosemary Perrin actually laughed. 'What a come-uppance! Fate is such a sick joker. Look, I hate to spoil your noble conclusions, but I wasn't expecting Robert back for another month. Let me see, Bahrain. Yes, it was Bahrain this time. That's what I told the detectives.'

'You mean the police that came to tell you about the accident?' said Sophie.

'No. Actual detectives. Fraud Squad, I think. Two of them called round to speak to Robert. Just over two weeks ago. Something about bank accounts. I told them they'd have to wait until he was back from Bahrain.' She smiled at Sophie. 'I never let slip that was code for his other woman in Surrey. I gave them one of Robert's business cards. And then, a few days later, two more came. It must have been the day before the accident. They looked like a right pair of thugs. Probably Special Branch. Goodness knows what Robert's got himself into.'

'Can you describe them?' said Sam. 'The two from Special Branch?'

'Well, they were both very muscular,' said Rosemary. 'One of them was bald with a beard and disgustingly filthy teeth. And the other one had this really unsightly mole on his face. They asked about Robert's clients. I told them he handled all his business on his laptop which he had with him. They wanted a photo.' She shrugged. 'Anyway, Sophie, it looks like this Heidi is your replacement as well as mine. But I wouldn't be too upset. You're just one of a long series. Although you have been his longest. Most of them don't last out the year.'

Sophie shook her head in disbelief. Sam stood up and took Laura from her. 'Soph, I'll take her for a walk in the garden, shall I? Is that OK, Rosemary?'

'Sure. Don't fall in the pool.'

Sophie watched Sam step outside. She could feel herself trembling, could feel Rosemary Perrin patting her hand like her grandma used to.

'Sophie, you're better off without him. I've often thought of contacting you and spilling the beans, but my life here is OK. My daughters have all they want. So, it was never in my interest to upset the apple cart.'

'But why is he like it, Rosemary?'

'I don't know. We'd been married a good few years when I started to suspect he was leading a double life. I suppose when he decides to move on they're actually triple lives. He always calls himself Royston – his mother's maiden name: Laura Royston – and it's his company name so it never changes, but he likes to vary his Christian name. He's been Jonah with you, hasn't he? But sometimes he's Isaac and I think once he spent a few months as Noah. Always very biblical. I think he sees it as a way of getting back at his mother's religious mania. Very old testament: no lies, no stealing, no adultery, no coveting your neighbour's donkeys or whatever. He told me once that she used to lock him and his brother in their room and starve them until they confessed their sins and repented. There was no Commandment about persecuting children, so as far as she was concerned it was acceptable. I suppose that can turn a kid into a strange adult.'

'I didn't know he had a brother.'

'Lives in Cape Town. We haven't heard from him for a couple of years.'

'Is Robert's mother still alive?'

'She's in a home. Early onset Alzheimer's. Personally, I think she always had it. Robert goes and sits with the desiccated old crone every Sunday when he's at home. Probably confessing what he's up to, just to drive her battier.'

'God, I had no idea.' Sophie leaned back to catch sight of Sam. He was showing Laura the roses, lifting her close so she could smell them. Speaking on his phone at the same time.

'He seems like a nice guy,' said Rosemary.

'Sam kind of fell into my life just as Jonah… Robert fell out of it.' She paused. 'Rosemary, what's going to happen when Robert is discharged from hospital?'

'They said he was in a coma.'

'It's an induced coma. I think they're going to let him regain consciousness in the next few days. And, when he's recovered enough, they'll send him to a rehabilitation unit.'

'And then what?'

'Presumably, he'll come here.'

'What, permanently?'

'I suppose so. He probably still regards this as his proper home.'

'But I don't want him back home. Not all the time. And half his stuff's with you, isn't it? He moved his business premises to be near to you.'

'But he was leaving me. He was hiring a van to bring his stuff here.'

'Not as far as I know, he wasn't. Perhaps he was taking it to Heidi.' She tugged at her ponytail. 'Do you know what kind of state he's going to be in?'

'The doctor wouldn't commit himself.'

'God, I'm not going to nurse the bastard! Sophie, we need to find this other woman of his. Perhaps she'll have him.'

'But he's never actually lived with her, apart from nights when he was working away, which were probably…' The front door crashed open and two girls ran in and demanded food. They turned to consider Sophie.

'Laura, Issy, this is Sophie. Sophie, these are my daughters,' she glanced up. 'And this is Zane, my personal trainer and *handy* man.'

Sophie gaped up at the tanned, blond, muscular younger man that was offering her his hand. He was so bronzed he was approaching orange, a perfect stereotypic hunk. She instantly realised why Rosemary didn't want Jonah home on any kind of permanent basis. She shook hands then watched Zane sweep Rosemary into his arms and kiss her.

'Rosie, darling, Issy did ten lengths today. Straight.'

'She looked like a walrus,' said the older girl. Obviously Laura.

'That's wonderful, Issy,' said Rosemary. 'Girls, why don't you grab supplies and go and watch TV? Zane will bring you some shakes later.'

The two girls considered the proposition, then invaded the fridge and disappeared back into the hallway. Zane walked over and re-opened the fridge door.

'How old are they?' Sophie asked.

'Twelve and fourteen. Zane's really good with them. More than you can say for Robert. They'd be ecstatic if they knew they had a baby sister.'

Again, Sophie leaned back to catch sight of Laura and Sam, still on the phone. 'Doesn't your pool have a fence around it?'

'No, but it's alarmed, so we'll know if anyone falls in. Zane, darling, would you go and introduce yourself to Sam. He's in the garden with Robert's latest daughter. Give us another ten minutes.' Zane finished pouring his Coke, winked at Sophie then hurried outside. Rosemary watched the door close behind him. 'Now,' she said, 'where were we? Oh yes: Robert. I suppose, if he recovers, I'm in the most difficult position because he owns half this house. Do you have your own property?'

'Yes. I've discovered Robert's not even listed as living there.'

'No, he avoids signing anything official in his pretend names.'

'Well, he's Jonah Royston on Laura's birth certificate.'

Rosemary raised her eyebrows. 'Oh dear. Is that legal? He doesn't usually break the law, just most of the Commandments.' She glanced into the garden. 'I take it you'd prefer not to have him back?'

'Yes. I'd prefer not, but I think for both our sakes, we need to find Heidi. I have her mobile number at home. I'll try contacting her tomorrow. We're staying over at the Crown Hotel in Topsham. Rosemary, were you upset when you discovered Robert's affairs?'

'At first I was. I had two little girls not even old enough to go to school. But, what could I do? He was successful enough to have bought this house. And a divorce would have meant selling it.' A smile. 'So, I developed my alternative strategy.'

'Does Robert know about Zane?'

'They're what you might call *acquainted*. Zane has a yacht over in the Dart Marina. And Jonah's always very specific about when he's going to be here. So, Zane knows when to make himself scarce.'

'But, what about Issy and Laura?'

'They adore Zane and they know not to mention him. In case it upsets Daddy.'

–

Rosemary continued to stupefy Sophie with her pragmatism until, eventually, Sam and Zane joined them. And, whilst Jonah's two older daughters looked after their baby sister – without realising she was their baby sister – Sam chatted to Rosemary about her husband's business, mentioning that he had installed the new college portal and they were now not able to call him back to solve the data crisis they were experiencing. Rosemary was dismissive. She was not in the least *au fait* with Robert's business enterprises. His equipment had all been transferred to his Surrey premises, which he had insisted was more convenient for contracts in London and the South-East. As far as she knew, the only clients he still had in the West Country were Kalmus AG, an Anglo-Dutch pharmaceutical company, and a boatyard, the mention of which provided Zane with the opportunity to talk about his 51-foot Jeanneau, *Sweet Dreams.*

'Rosie and I just sail up and down the coast when the sun shines. We're teaching the girls to crew. We'll take you out some-time, if you like. When things settle down.'

-

Driving back to their hotel, Sophie thanked Sam for sharing her encounter with Jonah's other life.

He tugged a lock of her hair. 'My pleasure. Besides, it was very revealing. Your errant ex-lover may be totally unscrupulous, but I approve of his taste in women.'

'Did you think Rosemary was attractive?'

'Yeh, in a slightly vacuous, footballer's wife way. But she's not in your league, Mrs Barnes. You're far more upmarket than that.'

'You can be very annoying.'

'Sweetheart, you have no idea.'

Silence.

'Sam… those two men Rosemary thought were Special Branch, they're the same two I thought were in Jonah's skittles team, aren't they? Why do you think they're looking for him? Do you think it's about that bag of money?

'You told them what happened to him, didn't you?'

'I said he was in Intensive Care. In Southampton.'

Good News

'Nadya, did you ask Mrs Hanson about Galina?'

'Yes, she said, at last minute, she has gone to America to help with her babies. The sponsor parents asked for help for finding a nursemaid and the Organisation suggest that Gally is a perfect choice. Mrs Hanson said I am to tell everyone her goodbyes and that she will write to us of her good news when she is settled. She said also that the sponsors are very rich and Gally will have her own apartment. I wish that could happen to me.'

'Me also. I am always a mother-to-be but I am never to be a mother. I have only five more weeks and then I must say goodbye to my boys. And then I will be back to the hard work. I think I will be in time for the Masked Ball. I have been requested. Is good I will not see their faces.'

'But you will recognise their smells and their noises. I am receiving visitors for only two weeks more. Mrs Hanson has insisted. I am glad this year I am too far gone to be invited to the ball. Although, Petia, you will enjoy usual privileges after. So, that is also good news.'

'Yes. It is true. But I am sad, Nadya. This time I cannot stop remembering the other babies. Where they are. I am sad that they will never know they have these brothers. Mrs Hanson said that such thoughts are normal but I must keep them to myself. She said that, before she was doula, she also had sponsor babies. Many years ago now. She believes that she will one day be a grandmother many times.'

'As will we, Petia. As will we.'

18

The following day, Sam opted to take the coastal route home, the first part of which was plagued by horse-boxes. Sophie expressed a hatred of all things equine and pledged never to buy Laura a pony, not even a plastic one. Eventually, after well over an hour of frustration, Sam decided to stop for lunch at a fine hotel he had previously visited in Lyme Regis. From her seat by the window, Sophie stared out across the English Channel and tried to come to terms with the revelations of the last twenty-four hours, realising above all else that she was now faced with the burden of discovering the identity of Jonah's other woman. The other woman that wasn't her. She glanced round to see Sam watching her, his expression serious.

'Sam, do you think Jonah is properly crazy?'

'Depends what you consider crazy.'

'What do you mean?'

'Well, if we were all living in caves and grunting at each other, with no names and no rules, then he'd probably be quite a catch. But because we do have names and rules, he's a disaster. So, no, he's not crazy, he just lacks obedience to the system we all have to live by. And a lot of people get away with that. Problem I have with those people is that their exploitation of the rules depends entirely upon everyone else obeying them.'

'But what on earth would make him call two of his daughters the same name?'

'OK, I've changed my mind. He's properly crazy.'

That evening, Sophie did another sweep of the house to make sure that anything that might, even remotely, be regarded as Jonah's was packed into her spare room ready to be transported away. She remembered the BMW. 'Sam?'

He looked up from scrutinising the DVDs.

'Why don't you move Jonah's car to his business premises? Then you can use his permit instead of paying for parking. His office address is on his business card.' She put her head to one side. 'You had one in your wallet, remember? I presume you put it back.'

'As a matter of fact, I did. I'll drive it over tomorrow.'

Mid-morning, Sam drove the BMW over to the Business Park. He eventually returned and discovered Sophie walking Laura around the pots in the backyard. She looked up and smiled. 'She's almost walking. You've been ages. I was wondering where you'd got to. Did you move your car to the back road?'

'Yes. Soph, listen, I found this in Jonah's car. It was down beside the passenger seat.' He handed her a credit card.

Sophie looked at it, read the name on the front, knitted her brow. 'Suzannah Kay? This was in Jonah's car? How's that possible?' Sam took Laura and followed Sophie inside, watched her place the card on the table, pull out a chair and sit down to study it. She looked up at him dumbfounded, reached for her phone, opened her latest message and showed it to him. 'She sent this, about twenty minutes ago, asking whether I was still up for feeding the ducks. We arranged it last Saturday.'

Sam eased Laura into her chair, took the phone, read the message then Sophie's reply.

'Soph, where did you put Jonah's mobiles?'

'Why?'

'Just… where are they?'

'In the middle drawer, with the tea towels.' Sam fetched Jonah's iPhone, opened text messages, scrolled down to the exchange with Heidi and laid it on the table alongside Sophie's phone that was still displaying Suzie Kay's text. He pressed 'i' on both phones. The displayed numbers were the same. Sophie shook her head in disbelief. She fetched her purse and pulled out the card Suzie had given her that day, the day of leaving. And there it was again, the same number, written in Suzie's shaky hand. 'I don't understand. Two people can't have the same mobile number, can they?' It was a stupid question. She was just hoping the obvious explanation wasn't true.

'Soph, Suzie's name's on the card.'

'Heidi?' Sophie banged her fist on the table. 'Can't any of these sodding people use their proper names!'

—

The wait for Suzie to arrive was tense. Sophie practised not revealing what she knew in the first five seconds. She would talk about her trip to Exeter. No, that would introduce the subject of Jonah. She would talk about Sam. No, even that would introduce the subject of Jonah. Why was everything about Jonah? She would offer tea. Because tea introduced nothing.

As it was, when Suzie stepped into the hallway the first thing she said was, 'Hello, Sophie, how's Jonah?'

The moment Suzie asked that question, all Sophie's anger fell away. She felt so sorry for this young woman caught up in Jonah's deceit. 'They're going to bring him out of the coma anytime soon,' she said. 'Probably tomorrow or Tuesday. So, they'll know more after that.' She bustled Suzie into the kitchen where Sam was filling the kettle. He threw a questioning glance. Sophie nodded an I've-decided-not-to-kill-her reassurance, so he stepped over to shake hands.

'Hi Suzie, I'm Sam. Shall Laura and I leave you two to chat?'

'No,' said Sophie. 'You can stay and make tea.'

Sam made tea, Suzie amused Laura with two plastic egg cups and Sophie stayed on the subject of Jonah's improvement, praised the Intensive Care Unit then, when they were all seated around the table, she looked straight at Suzie and said, 'Suzie, was it you that phoned the hospital, pretending to be my sister?' Suzie's face froze for a brief flicker of time then tears fluttered onto her cheeks. Sophie pulled the credit card from her pocket and slid it across the table. 'Sam found this in Jonah's car. We were wondering how it got there.' Suzie began to sob into her hands. Laura watched her. Any resentment that Sophie might have been harbouring dissolved into the space between her and this *other* other woman. Laura continued to watch, her mouth turning progressively further down at the edges.

Sam intervened: 'Suzie, it would be best for us all if you told us what's going on.'

Suzie lowered her hands and managed to splutter out a few words. 'I… I think I'm going to be sick.' Her hands flew back across her mouth.

Sophie hurried round to her. 'Another baby bug is it, Suzie?'

'Not really, Sophie. I'm pregnant.'

'Ah!' declared Sam. 'Another Laura!'

Suzie resumed sobbing. Laura started to whimper in sympathy. Sophie flashed Sam a look of desperation, asked if he would take Laura to the lounge for a while. Give her and Suzie a chance to sort things out. Sam said nothing. He just lifted Laura out of her chair and carried her towards the lounge. Sophie heard her daughter's distress lessen the further she was taken away from the tension that now had to be dealt with. 'Suzie, I'm not cross.' She handed her some tissues. 'Tell me about you and Jonah. He was *Jonah*, was he?'

Suzie wiped her face. 'We've been together about three months. And, yes, he was Jonah. Sophie, I didn't know about you and Laura. He told me he'd been with this abusive woman for years and he was desperate to leave. I said he could move into my flat with me.'

And bring my TV and freezer with him, thought Sophie.

'I came with him to pick up his case that day. We were going to go straight to my place. In Guildford. He told me to wait on the corner, but I walked along to see what your house was like and that's when I saw you falling down the step and the case pushing him over. He said terrible things about you. But, as soon as I met you, I knew they weren't true.' She choked out a flurry of sobs. 'Then Laura cried and I realised how much he'd been lying to me.'

Sophie pulled her chair round and sat close. 'Listen, Suzie. Sam and I went to Exeter to visit Jonah's wife...' She gave as accurate an account as she could of the picture that Rosemary Perrin had painted of her faithless husband, of her initial desolation and her subsequent survival strategy.

Suzie listened in clear disbelief. 'Has she visited him since the accident?'

'No. And I'm not sure she intends to. Suzie, you have to stop caring about him. He's a serial adulterer. He moves from one unsuspecting woman to another and then, after a few months, when the fancy takes him, he moves on again.'

'But he was with you for more than a few months, wasn't he?'

'Yeh.' She gave a quick little laugh. 'But that's because I'm so damn interesting. How did you meet him?'

'My company commissioned him to set up a new mailing system. We got chatting about all sorts. He told me his job took him all over the world. He said he'd just been in Africa setting up the internet in village schools.'

'God, he has a real saviour complex, doesn't he? How many weeks are you?'

'Only six, nearly seven. I was going to tell Jonah that evening. I thought he'd be happy he was going to be a father.'

Sophie thought it best not to comment because there was no comment that could fail to be hurtful. Instead she busied herself collecting up the mugs, but as she was loading them into the dishwasher a rather obvious question tumbled into her thoughts. 'Suzie, Sam and I read Jonah's message to you. On his mobile.'

'God, I'm so embarrassed.'

'Don't be. It's just... why did he call you Heidi?'

'It was our joke.' Fresh tears started to squeeze their way onto her cheeks. 'Jonah said we should take a holiday together. Stay in a hotel with a nice view and just get used to being with each other. And I said the Swiss Alps were quiet and very beautiful in the off-season. And inexpensive because there was no skiing. And he said skiing was the last thing he wanted to do with me and he'd rather go somewhere in the UK. But he was going to call me Heidi from then on. We were booked to go to Edinburgh at the beginning of September. I'll go to my mother's instead. Break the news that she's going to be a granny.'

Sophie stared at her. 'What a bloody sicko! I'm sorry, Suzie, but how on earth do women like us fall for that kind of crap?'

Suzie stayed for the rest of the afternoon. Sam and Laura joined them in the kitchen and the conversation actually strayed away from Jonah, thanks to Sam's various Far-East anecdotes. Sophie watched Suzie allowing herself the occasional bright-eyed laugh at Sam's jokes, and felt the stirrings of possessiveness, which she instantly suppressed. She even invited her to stay for supper but Suzie confessed that she needed to be in work early the following morning and getting ready to leave the house took longer at the moment, due to the need to retch into the toilet. She ought to catch the next train. She hadn't driven over because she felt too nauseous. Sam offered to drive her home and, after a brief and courteous refusal, she accepted his offer. Sophie instantly feared that Suzie might, on the journey back to Guildford, decide to revisit her role as replacement mistress. But good sense told her to pull herself together. Her fears were reawakened when Sam failed to return home after an hour. Then two. When she finally heard the front door open, she was ready for confrontation.

Sam stepped into the kitchen. 'Sorry I took so long. I nipped back to the attic for some bedtime reading.' He handed her a beautiful leather-bound book. 'And a chat with Jesse about tiles. He said he'd like to cook supper for us. Next Friday. Is that OK?'

'I think so. What bedtime reading?' She read the gold lettering pressed into the volume in her hands: *The Complete Works of Samuel Taylor Coleridge*.

'I thought we'd start with the Romantics and then work our way through the Laureates.'

Sophie flicked through some of the gilt-edged pages. 'You might have mistaken me for one of your students, Mr Barnes.'

He took the book and placed it on the table. 'Miss Denham, if I was discovered doing with one of my students what you are only too keen for me to do with you, I'd lose my job.'

19

Sam drove out to the garden centre where Sophie acquired a large lavender, a peppermint and several varieties of thyme. As with all flourishing garden centres, this particular horticultural outlet also offered an array of pet supplies, sweets, toys, books and numerous unnecessary scented gifts. Sam alighted upon a tasteless pink unicorn, which Sophie thought looked too dangerously like a horse, but which Laura loved, and a book on garden design to assist Sophie when she was conceptualising his new garden. Driving home, Sophie lay back and inhaled the confusion of intense aromas wafting around the car. Next time she'd buy rosemary and, in the autumn, she'd plant honeysuckle and jasmine along the back wall, to hide the garages. 'I'd love a proper garden,' she said, 'so I could plant apple trees and rows of sweet peas. And giant pumpkins. And I'd have a parterre garden crammed with herbs.'

'You'll have a proper garden when we move into our new house. You can come over with me this week and get an idea about the layout. The plot's just over an acre, so you'll be able to have a whole orchard of apple trees if you want.'

Sophie stared at him. '*Our* house?'

'Yes. Yet again I'd like to risk losing all I have on a beguiling woman. We can rent out your mother's house.'

'*Sam!*' She could feel the stirrings of panic, that even the strong fragrance of lavender couldn't calm. 'Can we please slow down a minute?'

'I'm only doing thirty.'

'No! I want you to not say things like *our* house.'

'Why? Laura needs a place where she can have garden parties with her friends.'

'Sam, it's all too quick.'

'OK.'

'It's just that my life's a complete mess at the moment.'

'Right. No more mentioning our dream house. With its parterre garden.'

Sophie watched him grinning at the road ahead. 'I really want it to happen. I just don't want to talk about it, in case it makes it go away.'

'That sounds like a good case of Sophie logic. We're almost home. I'll park on the pavement and unload the forest.' But, as he was about to turn into Tanner Street, he caught sight of a police car parked outside Sophie's house. 'Soph, don't panic. The cops are outside. I'll park round the back and go ahead. See what they want.'

'Do you think something's happened to Jonah?'

'The hospital would have phoned. Just get Laura into her pushchair and follow me round. I'll come back for your plants later.'

—

Sophie watched Sam disappear into the narrow shortcut. After a few minutes, she took the pushchair from the boot, negotiated Laura into it and walked round to the front of her house. The door was ajar. Sam hurried to help her up the steps. 'Don't worry. They're just following up a few tax anomalies related to Jonah's business. Sergeant Wilkes and Detective Inspector Blake. Just act normal.'

Sophie carried Laura into the kitchen, trying to act normal, although, at that moment, she could no longer remember what normal was like. And she was concerned that they'd sent a detective rather than just two ordinary... what were they called... ordinary *uniforms*.

Sergeant Wilkes bowed his head in recognition. DI Ron Blake introduced himself disagreeably: 'Ms Denham,' he said, 'We have obtained a warrant for an immediate search of Mr Perrin's business premises. If you could let us have appropriate keys, it would prevent our having to resort to forcible entry.'

Sophie's brain began racing with crazy thoughts, supreme amongst them that bag full of money in her spare room. She felt Sam's arm across her shoulders and somehow that focussed her mind. She made deliberate eye contact with the unfamiliar policeman. 'Could you give me some idea what all this is about, Inspector?'

Inspector Blake paused to ask Sergeant Wilkes to move the car and wait for his call, watched him leave then fixed his eyes on Sophie. 'In the first instance, Ms Denham, it would appear that Mr Perrin may be involved in fraudulent activities. Records from the Inland Revenue list Royston Computer Solutions as employing four people. You are included in this list. The other three people, despite holding bank accounts and having National Insurance numbers, are untraceable and may be bogus individuals. Over the last three years, significant amounts of cash have been briefly deposited into their accounts. There is evidence that money has been transferred overseas via a complex of online transactions.'

Sam interrupted. 'Do you intend to interrogate Ms Denham regarding all this?'

'Questions may well arise following the search of Mr Perrin's business premises.'

Sophie held Laura closer. 'What questions? I don't know anything about Robert Perrin's business. I've certainly never been employed by him. He's given me cash each month, but that's been for housekeeping. Are you aware that he has a wife and an additional home elsewhere?'

'A warrant has also been acquired to search his Exeter residence.'

Sophie carried Laura over to a chair and sat down. 'I've no idea what all this is about. Jonah has lots of clients but, as far as

I know, he works alone. I thought everything was above board. Although…' She glanced at Sam. 'Inspector Blake, there is one thing. When we were emptying Jonah's car, we found some money.'

'Money?' said Detective Blake.

Sam touched Sophie's shoulder. 'Soph, I'll take Laura. Go up and fetch the bag. And bring Jonah's keys. They're on the bedside table.'

—

As Sophie was retrieving the blue bag, she noticed once again the framed photo taken at Katie's wedding. She picked it up and studied Jonah's smiling face. Nothing about that face suggested that he was anything other than a clever, hard-working man who had come into her life and had wanted to stay. She lay the photo face down, grabbed the keys and returned to the kitchen. Laura was in her highchair. Sam and Inspector Blake were deep in conversation.

Sam turned to smile. 'Inspector Blake's an Arsenal man, so this is likely to be a short friendship.' Inspector Blake laughed.

Sophie couldn't help but marvel at the levelling power of football. She handed over the bag. 'I'm afraid we both touched some of the notes. But we resisted the temptation to help ourselves, so it's all there.'

'And this was in Mr Perrin's car?' asked Inspector Blake.

'Yes,' said Sophie. She handed him Jonah's keys. 'His car key's also on there.'

—

Inspector Blake left. Sophie threw herself into a chair. 'I should have told him about those two thugs that called last week. Perhaps the money's theirs. And now I've given it to the police. My God, I feel like a gangster's moll. And why does talking to policemen always make you feel guilty? You might want to make a break for it while you can still avoid being sucked down into this criminal underworld that I'm part of.'

'It's too late. I'm already hopelessly incriminated. Shall I go and collect your plants?'

Some time later, Sam wandered into the yard to find Sophie on her knees, squashing a peppermint into the soil around the base of a tomato plant, her face a picture of grim determination.

'Soph, is it OK if Jesse calls round later? He's got some tile samples for me to look at.'

She looked up. 'Yes. Will his boys be with him?'

'I don't think so. They're with Grandma Buckley. He's coming straight from the warehouse.' He pointed to a lone, unplanted thyme. 'Where are you going to plant that?'

'I need more pots.'

Sam stepped over and picked it up. 'It smells fantastic. Why don't you put it inside?'

Sophie paused briefly for doubt, overcame her obedience to Jonah's no-soil-in-the-house directive, pulled Sam back into the kitchen, took the thyme and placed it on the windowsill next to Suzie's orchids.

'Should we invite Jesse to stay for supper?'

'He'll probably refuse. He's a committed hermit. But he might stay for a drink.' He grinned. 'You might want to wash the compost off your face before he gets here.'

Sophie repaired herself then hurried to the lounge, where Sam was coaching Laura in walking between toys strategically placed around the room. She started to tidy up but, as she piled up the magazines, she remembered Jonah's invoice from the van hire company, retrieved it from her plant catalogue and handed it to Sam. 'I think Jonah was planning to take the TV and loads of other stuff to Suzie's place.'

'But he would have needed to show the hire company his driving licence and that's in Robert Perrin's name.' Sam shook his head. 'If the cops come back, we'll mention it.'

Jesse arrived bearing a box full of tiles and a bottle of Meursault. He handed the latter to Sophie, leaned over to kiss her cheek then gave the box to Sam. 'The floor tiles you chose were obviously the most expensive and the ordering period's three months. But that shouldn't interfere with the schedule. The others are also expensive but mostly in stock.'

Sam peered into the box. 'Do I get mate's rates?'

'Possibly. Sophie, the wine's been in a cold box but it could probably do with a bit of a chill before you open it.'

'I wouldn't worry about that,' said Sam. 'Sophie puts ice in everything.'

Jesse gaped. 'In Meursault?'

'Ignore him. He's just being annoying. I have a wine cooler. Will you stay for a glass?'

Jesse looked at his watch. 'I'm picking the boys up at six thirty. I promised them McDonalds. But yes, just a quick one.'

They carried the tiles into the kitchen, where Laura was busy smearing herself in banana. Sophie located the wine cooler, made her daughter presentable then sat and watched Sam and Jesse comparing tiles. It was the first time she had seen the two brothers alongside one another and it was almost disturbing to see such an accurate copy of her lover standing beside the original. She offered the Meursault for Jesse to approve the temperature. 'It's fine,' he said. 'But I won't be offended if you want to drink it with ice.'

They turned as the letterbox flapped open. 'Sophie, it's me.'

Sam rolled his eyes. 'Talking about being offended… You'd better fetch another glass, Soph.' He hurried to invite Katie inside.

'Hi, Sam,' she said. 'I've come round to hear the news because Sophie seems to be unable to write texts of more than three words.' She followed him into the kitchen and came to an abrupt halt. 'Good God, they're both here!'

Jesse got to his feet. 'Hello, would you like a glass of Meursault?'

'Now, there's something you don't often hear! Am I interrupting something?'

Sophie walked over and hugged her. 'If I said yes, would you leave?'

'No.' She caught sight of the box of tiles. 'What's all this?'

'We're choosing tiles for my new house,' said Sam. 'The one Jesse's building.'

Katie gave him a withering look. 'Don't you like colours? They're all white.'

'Ivory,' said Jesse. 'Different textures.'

'Really?'

–

Sam and Jesse opted for cautious silence whilst Katie interrogated Sophie about her trip to Devon, listened to the details of Rosemary Perrin's Zane Alternative and her obvious reluctance to have Jonah living with her on any kind of permanent basis.

'Well, you did tell her there was no way that you're letting that skunk back into your house, didn't you? And, if she didn't collect his things, you'd burn them?'

Sophie noticed Jesse grimacing at his brother. She exhaled frustration. 'No, Katie, I didn't tell her that.'

'Why didn't you? She was expecting him back anyway, wasn't she?'

'Not exactly.' She glanced at Sam. 'I don't know if you've told Jesse about Suzie…'

'I have.'

'Suzie who?' said Katie. 'What do you all know that I haven't been told?'

Sam got ready to be annoyed, but Sophie pre-empted the anger. 'It seems that Jonah wasn't actually going back to his wife. He was just moving on.'

'What?'

'Do you remember me mentioning a woman called Suzie Kay?'

'No.'

'She witnessed the accident. She came in and made tea...'

Sophie explained and the wine disappeared. Eventually, Katie sat back and folded her arms. 'God, Soph, how do you do it? You must have MUG written right across your forehead. Let's hope your latest acquisition proves to be less of a problem.'

Sam stared at her, speechless. Jesse, however, was moved to voicing his disgust. 'That was a very unpleasant thing to say in front of my brother.'

'Would you have preferred me to say it behind his back? And anyway, it's true. People just seem to crap all over Sophie. And to be honest, she's fallen straight into this relationship with Sam without pausing for breath. I don't want to see her hurt again.'

Sam shook his head. 'I'm not going to hurt Sophie...'

'And, if you ask me, there's something too good to be true about you conveniently falling off your bike like that, straight into Sophie's ruined life.'

'*Katie*, my life is *not* ruined.'

'But it's not just about you, is it? It's about you and Laura. I know I said positive things to start with but aren't you worried how eager he's been to move in here?'

'Katie,' said Sam, 'just in case you haven't noticed, I'm sitting *right here*!'

'And I think you could show more grace when expressing opinions about things you know nothing about,' said Jesse.

'Hooray!' sneered Katie. 'It's the Übermenschen Duo!'

Sophie jumped to her feet. '*Katie!* Have you gone mad?'

Laura started to cry. Jesse tried to hand her a rusk but the crying became screaming. Sophie hurried to pick her up. The kitchen became silent. Jesse got to his feet.

'Sam, we'll sort the order out tomorrow. I'll leave the tiles here for you to take another look. If that's OK with you, Sophie. And—'

'If you go now,' interrupted Katie, 'Sophie will blame me.'

'That's really not my problem,' said Jesse. 'My problem would be having to carry on suffering the presence of an interfering woman who experiences a meltdown every time she doesn't approve of something.' He turned to Sophie. 'Thanks, Sophie. I hope to see you soon. Sam, on site tomorrow, OK?' With that he left.

Katie rapped her nails on the table. 'I didn't mean to upset anyone.'

'It sounded pretty deliberate to me,' muttered Sam.

Katie slumped in her chair. 'Sophie, do you want me to leave?'

'No, if Sam can stand it, so can I. You can help put Laura to bed. I'm cooking pasta. You can stay and criticise it.'

—

Salmon and broccoli tagliatelle was about to be served when the doorbell echoed along the hallway. Sam hurried through to prevent a repeat that would be sure to wake Laura. He walked back into the kitchen moments later, carrying another bottle of Meursault and trailing his brother. Sophie looked up from transferring pasta to a serving dish. She glanced at Sam but he just shrugged his shoulders. 'Jesse, is everything OK?' She inclined her head towards the yard. 'Katie's having a cigarette.'

Jesse's brow furrowed. 'Does she smoke?'

'Not usually. Has something happened?'

'I've left the boys in the car park. I've just come back to...'

The door flew open and Katie stepped in followed by a waft of cigarette smoke. 'Who the hell was that at the door? Soph, you should disconnect that doorbell or at least stop it ringing directly under Laura's room. You...' She noticed Jesse and became silent.

Jesse took a step towards her, his confident poise now diminished to a faltering display of his brother's feigned awkwardness. 'I've come to apologise. My behaviour was outrageous. I shouldn't have said... what I said. I realise that you were only trying to protect your friend. Please accept my apologies.' He turned to Sophie. 'I've brought another Meursault in case I ruined the first one.' With that he bowed his head and left.

Katie's eyes remained fixed on the hallway. 'Soph, did that just happen?'

Sam banged the Burgundy down on the table. 'Go after him, you stupid woman!'

Katie glared at him then hurried towards the front door.

'Ask him if he'd like some pasta,' called Sophie. The front door banged shut and Laura's stereophonic scream came resonating along the hallway and out of the baby monitor. 'Damn! Sam, would you cover the pasta and put it in the oven?'

By the time Sophie returned, the kitchen table had been extended, the two functional garden chairs had been brought inside and Jesse's two copper-headed sons were sitting opposite their father, eating Happy Meals. Katie was washing bistro salad and the Burgundy was waiting. 'She's asleep,' said Sophie, smiling at the two boys.

'Sophie, let me introduce my sons.' Jesse got to his feet and extended his palm towards the oldest boy. 'This is Benjamin, who is seven and prefers to be called Benz, because he wants me to remember to buy him a Mercedes for his seventeenth birthday. And this...' he indicated the smaller boy, '...is Jake, who is six and wants me to buy him a Ferrari, preferably before his seventeenth birthday.' Both boys said hi then returned to their burgers.

The rest of the evening went surprisingly well. Sophie was impressed with Jake and Benz, their conversation and behaviour seemed way beyond their years. She watched them engaging with their father and uncle almost as equals, two little boys who probably had no memory of their mother. Perhaps just a memory of missing her. She wondered what memory of her Laura might have if she was suddenly no longer there and it made her feel sick. But at least she'd have no memory of Jonah either. She wished she could say the same for herself.

'Soph, come back, wherever you are! Jesse's about to go.'

She looked up. 'Oh, sorry Sam, I was just…'

'I should get the boys home,' explained Jesse. 'They've had too many late nights lately.' His statement elicited protest.

'Daaaad, I'm nearly eight years old. And Sam usually lets us stay up when you're out.'

'Oh, does he?'

'Just the once. And that, if you remember, was because you were both throwing up.'

'No negotiations with the under tens, I'm afraid,' said Jesse, getting to his feet. 'Both of you, thank your hosts.'

Benz pushed himself away from the table. 'Thanks, Soph. Is Sam living here now?'

Katie snorted into her hand.

'Yes, I am,' said Sam. 'And Sophie and I would be very pleased to have you visit any time you'd like to drop by.' That seemed to satisfy both boys, who allowed their father to herd them towards the front door.

'I'll walk to the car park with you,' said Katie, grabbing her bag.

–

Sophie closed the front door as quietly as possible. 'Well, that was exhausting.'

'I thought the boys were perfectly behaved.'

'No, I mean Katie and Jesse.'

'Oh, that. Yeh, there's a bit of chemistry there. Certainly, in Jesse's case. I've never seen him behaving as weird as that. He's—' The telephone interrupted their conversation. Sophie ran to stop it ringing. She returned a few minutes later looking ashen.

'It was the hospital. Jonah's regained consciousness.'

'Sophie, it's not your problem.'

But, somehow, Sophie knew that it was.

Most lies are intentional. However, some few lies are accidental, told by those who mistakenly believe they are telling the truth. But those failed truth-tellers are, in time, still branded liars. So, take care with the truth. It is not always obvious.

From *A Natural History of Lies* by J. Clarke

The Unnamed God

The afternoon sun was already casting its long shadows across Parliament Square. Sir Hugh Grenville checked his pocket watch and grunted with frustration: time seemed so impatient to be over these days, so keen to become history. He tossed the *Times* crossword aside and poured himself a large whiskey. A larger whiskey. He carried it over to the window to observe the street below, watched the red top of a number 87 choke its way past the plane trees en route to Aldwych. Glared at the newspaper. Always one bastard clue that remained impenetrable. One obscure word whose final purpose, just prior to its timely extinction, was to distinguish those who know from those who don't know. And he really couldn't care less. He was disturbed from his thoughtlessness by a limp knuckle rapping against his door.

'Come in! Yes? What is it, Jones?'

Thaddeus Jones slithered into the room. 'I trust your weekend went well, Sir Hugh?'

'Yes, yes, thank you, Jones. You have something to report?'

'Indeed, sir. In fact, I have a number of things to report. We have now confirmed the identity of our *Deus Innominatus*. The eponymous website located on the dark web appears to be administered by a computing consultant called Robert Perrin who operates mostly in London and the South-East. His company is registered in the UK as Royston Computer Solutions.'

'Perrin is a common enough name. How sure are you that this Perrin is our Unnamed God?'

'There is strong evidence to support it, sir. Three weeks ago, our operatives attempted to make contact with Mr Perrin at his home in the West Country but his wife informed them that he is currently working in Bahrain until the middle of next month. However, further investigation has revealed that, rather than being in Arabia, Mr Perrin was at the time resident in Surrey, a few miles south of Guildford, where he has, for the last several years, been pursuing an alternative romantic liaison and living under an assumed name: Jonah Royston.'

'What a dastardly scoundrel, Jones! And have your men spoken to this *other* woman… one presumes it's a woman?'

'Indeed. We have learned from this mistress, a Ms Sophie Denham, that Mr Perrin is currently in Intensive Care in the Neurological Unit at Southampton General Hospital, having suffered a skull fracture and brain damage.'

'Good Lord. How unfortunate.'

'Indeed, sir. But I'm afraid there is an additional complication which might explain his recent and very inconvenient reluctance to continue supplying his services. It would seem that Robert Perrin, aka Jonah Royston, is now the subject of an investigation by the Serious Fraud Office and also, I believe, the NCA. Apparently, he is implicated in the misappropriation of considerable amounts of cash into off-shore accounts, it seems via a few of his self-generated false identities. Although much of this cash would seem to have been derived from sources other than the Organisation, Mr Perrin might be in possession of data that could compromise our network.'

'Quite. So, our bad man has been spreading his interests has he?' Again, Sir Hugh checked his pocket watch. 'Well, we'd better get the operatives to pursue this matter further. A thorough search of the home and business premises for anything incriminating, and perhaps a delayed recovery until we can fully assess the situation. Perhaps you could arrange that?'

'It has already been arranged, Sir Hugh.'

'Good, good. And, tell me, Jones, is there anything from the Source regarding the police investigation of the dead girl?'

'As yet, there has been no identification, although I gather that the NCA have approached Europol to assist in the investigation.

They are unlikely to be successful, given the length of time since acquisition.'

'And the infants?'

'Successfully placed and awaiting their certification and journey home to Arizona with the proud sponsors.'

'Excellent. Now, is that everything, Jones? I have a meeting with the Home Secretary in forty minutes.'

'There is just one thing, Sir Hugh. Regarding the Masked Ball, I have managed to secure the desired venue for the first half of November. If you would instruct me regarding guests and their special preferences, I will start to make arrangements...'

'Ever discreetly, Jones. And perhaps you can let me have additional images of our two most recent assets.'

'Of course, Sir Hugh.'

20

Laura woke at six twenty, bright and needy. Sophie left her with Sam and staggered around in the kitchen preparing her milk. When she returned, she found Laura lying enthralled, listening to Sam's impression of Richard Burton reading *The Rime of the Ancient Mariner*:

> *And I had done a hellish thing,*
> *And it would work 'em woe:*
> *For all averred, I had killed the bird*
> *That made the breeze to blow.*

Later, over toast, Sam explained, 'It's the enrapturing effect of Coleridge's meter and the Welsh sibilance. It always worked with Jake and Benz.'

—

Sam left straight after breakfast and Sophie took the opportunity to practise reading Coleridge's poem in a Welsh accent. Laura responded by emptying her toys out of the playpen. Mid-morning, Rosemary Perrin phoned. She was going to visit Robert tomorrow morning. Could she drive up and have a chat? Had Sophie managed to contact Heidi?

Sophie gave Rosemary instructions regarding car parks, lied that she hadn't yet managed to contact Jonah's other woman, then rang off and sat watching Laura crushing pink unicorn's head for a full five minutes until her mobile shattered her stupor. Lately, Sophie had been experiencing a burst of reflux every time her phone sounded, and this second tidal wave of acid in less than ten minutes was now eroding its way towards her throat. She was half-relieved to hear Katie's voice.

'Sophie?'

'Hi, what's up? Are you phoning from the office?'

'No, I'm driving. I'm co-ordinating a seminar this afternoon. In Guildford. More people talking crap about crap. Soph, you've got to tell me what to do about Jesse.'

'What about Jesse?'

'We got talking last night, you know, in the street. And the car park. And he's asked me to dinner with you and Sam. On Friday.'

'Well, what's wrong with that?'

'Everything! I've already acted like a complete bitch in front of him and you know I can't help myself. Look what happened with Paul. I'll argue with him. And I don't want to argue with him.'

'Well, don't. Are you using hands-free?'

'Yes.'

'Right, well, go and run your seminar. And phone me this evening.'

'OK. Any news from the hospital?'

'Yes, Jonah's regained consciousness and his wife's driving up to see him tomorrow.'

'Well, if you see her, don't forget to tell her he's not your problem.'

'Katie, do not start that again. We'll speak later, OK?'

–

Sophie put her phone on silent, set it down on the hall table and forbade it to ring again. After a moment or two of letting her stomach reclaim its contents, she hoisted Laura from her playpen to take her upstairs for her nap time which, hopefully, once she'd sorted through her bank statements, she would be able to share. But as she was passing the hall table her phone started to vibrate its way towards the edge. OK, that was the lining of her oesophagus written off for the rest of the day. She grabbed the phone as it was about to plummet to the floor and answered the call. It was Inspector Blake asking if he might call round to clear up a few unanswered questions. Sophie said early afternoon would be best. Then she carried Laura upstairs, determined to locate her paperwork, assess her state of destitution and then just sleep.

Now, anybody who has ever lain awake until the dawn will know that there is a strange three-way conflict that exists between sleep, tiredness and the human mind. You might expect that the more tired you are, the more likely you are to sleep but, sadly, that is not always the case, because the mind can flood that simple equation with worries that make sleep impossible. On the other hand, occasionally, when you have important things to do, like sit your finals or write a report by the following morning, tiredness can utterly override the mind's imperatives and send you into the deepest dreamless sleep you've had for as long as you can remember. Sophie was simultaneously experiencing both those predicaments: her brain knew she had to review her financial crisis but tiredness was making her senseless, demanding that she sleep. However, her brain was also reminding her repeatedly that Inspector Blake wanted to clear up some questions. The upshot was that Sophie found herself unable to keep her eyes focussed on the bank statements in front of her, but, falling back onto her welcoming pillow, she was then unable to sleep until just before Laura woke up demanding lunch. Sam returned at around twelve thirty, strode into the kitchen and came to a halt. 'Soph, you're spooning that into Laura's ear.'

'What? Oh God, I'm so tired.'

'Me too, although I did manage to doze off for twenty minutes in the car. When Jesse was ordering tiles. Let me feed her. Go and lie down. And by the way, Katie's joining us for dinner on Friday.'

'I know. I'm trying not to think about it.'

Sophie woke to the sound of voices downstairs. She checked the clock: 2:49, pulled herself up, grabbed her hairbrush, tried to organise the mess then hurried downstairs. The lounge door was closed. It was never closed. Sam and Inspector Blake both got to their feet as she walked in.

'Sophie, I was about to wake you. Inspector Blake has a few questions for you. About Jonah's contacts.'

'We would appreciate Mr Perrin's two mobile phones, if you would like to hand those over voluntarily. Without the need for legal seizure.'

'Seizure won't be necessary, Inspector,' said Sophie. 'Sam, they're still in the tea towel drawer.' Sam hurried away. Sophie sat down close to the playpen and attempted to organise her thoughts. 'Did you find something when you searched Jonah's office?'

Inspector Blake sat down. 'There was a lot of hardware. We're currently attempting to gain access to two desktop computers, but, apparently, he has them both encrypted and a wrong step might erase everything. Would you happen to know where he would keep a list of passwords and the like? Perhaps a notebook?'

'I'm sorry, I've never involved myself with Jonah's affairs. He always carried a laptop with him so perhaps his passwords are on that.'

'No laptop has been recovered during the searches.'

'Well, it isn't here,' said Sam, stepping back in and handing the phones to Inspector Blake. 'And I searched his car when I moved it.'

'Maybe he'd already taken it to his new girlfriend's place,' said Sophie. 'That's where he was going when the accident happened.'

Inspector Blake asked Sophie if she had contact details for this girlfriend. Sophie paused, uncomfortable about dragging Suzie into this, especially in her current state. But she had no choice. She fetched Suzie's business card and handed it over. Inspector Blake slipped the card into his notepad. 'We're currently sifting through Mr Perrin's paperwork, hoping to identify any significant contacts. One document has a list of names, two of whom Mr Barnes has confirmed are college employees.'

'Soph, you remember I attended a faculty meeting last week? Because a couple of staff member's bank accounts had been tampered with. They might have been used to bounce cash overseas. It's undoubtedly easier to access existing accounts and use them as temporary conduits rather than go to the bother of creating new ones. Jonah must have been getting lazy. Anyway, those two people were on his list.'

Officer Blake cleared his throat. 'We have a unit investigating cybercrime networks. It would seem that Mr Perrin may be peripherally involved, to the extent of misappropriating personal data. He may also have been creating false identities, possibly for use other than by himself. Making them available to third parties. Presumably at a price, which would be a possible source of the money he appears to have been transferring overseas. We were wondering whether you had any information regarding his business contacts.'

'No, I'm sorry. Jonah always dealt with clients at his office.'

'So, you are saying that, in all the time you were together, you did not meet any of Mr Perrin's business acquaintances? Did you not think that was strange?'

'Not really. Jonah kept his business and home lives separate.'

'Perhaps he introduced these people as friends?'

'Jonah didn't have friends. He worked alone so I suppose he didn't get much opportunity to meet people. Perhaps he knew people in Exeter. Did you ask his wife these questions when you searched his Exeter house?'

'The Devon Police found nothing related to Mr Perrin's company or finances in his marital home. It was the opinion of the investigating officers that he was very structured in his domestic affairs and that his business affairs were conducted elsewhere.'

Sophie shrugged. 'I'm sorry I can't be more helpful.'

Inspector Blake got to his feet. 'Ms Denham, there is one more thing I have to ask: when we were investigating Mr Perrin's business premises, it was clear that someone had been searching ahead of us. It's possible that, if this person or persons failed to find what they were looking for, they will continue their search. Have you had any strange calls, suspicious people coming to the house? Observing the house from outside?'

Sophie's stomach churned. She looked at Sam. 'There *were* those two men. The ones that Rosemary thought were Special Branch. Do you think it was them searching Jonah's office?'

'Special Branch?' said Inspector Blake, casting a questioning glance towards Sam.

Sam shook his head. 'Sophie, do *not* start worrying about that. Just be grateful that Jonah kept his private and business lives separate.'

'But *they* don't know that, do they? Inspector, the money we gave you, it might have been theirs. What if—'

'I'm sure you have nothing to worry about,' interrupted Inspector Blake. Again, he glanced at Sam. 'But, if Mr Barnes would bring you to the station, you might like to look at some photos. In the meantime, if you see anything suspicious, please inform us immediately.'

Sam saw Inspector Blake out, chatted to him on the doorstep, then returned to calm Sophie, who was now approaching a whole new level of hysteria.

'Sam, what if somebody breaks in when we're asleep?'

'Soph, if there's the slightest possibility of a threat, we'll pack up your stuff and go to my place. Jesse's got more security than Fort Knox.'

Sophie pulled her unsuspecting daughter out of her playpen and hugged her. 'Rosemary phoned. She's driving up tomorrow to visit Jonah and find out what's in store. I ought to go over and speak to someone before she does.'

'OK. If we go now, we can be back by Laura's bedtime.'

21

From outside the glass, Jonah didn't look any different to the last time Sophie had seen him. His bandages were, perhaps, not so huge but he still looked unconscious. Suddenly a nurse was standing alongside her, asking if she would like to go in and speak to him. Actually, Sophie didn't want to speak to Jonah ever again, but if she refused it would look terrible; callous. So, she said, 'Just for a few minutes. How is he?'

'He's doing very well,' said the nurse. 'His friend came to see him this morning but we had to advise him that only family members were allowed to visit at the moment.'

Sophie stared at her. 'His friend?'

'Yes. A huge bald chap with a beard.'

Sophie tried not to overreact, tried to communicate vague recognition and allowed the nurse to escort her to Jonah's bedside. In anticipation of visitors, the room was now graced with an uncomfortable-looking chair. The nurse pulled it close to Jonah's bed, warned Sophie not to expect too much, then left. Sophie considered running straight back down to Sam and telling him about Jonah's visitor but, instead, she sat down and watched the ventilator, the waves and spikes monitoring Jonah's life. She glanced around to make sure there was nobody watching then stood up and leaned close to inspect the swathe of bandages. The slit over Jonah's mouth still provided entry for the fat plastic tubing, but there was now another slit over his eyes. He really did look like that early Hollywood version of the Invisible Man. Apart from the fact that his closed eyes were visible through the slit.

She thought about saying something but her mind was devoid of inspiration. Perhaps she should ask him whether he had any feelings for his daughter who was now downstairs being cared for by another man. She jumped back as the monitor emitted a short beep, waited to see if anyone was going to rush in then leaned forward when they didn't. She would say Laura's name. That's the least she could do. But she was on the same side as his reattached ear, so she leaned across to address the other side of his head. 'Your daughter Laura's downstairs.' But, as she said it, she realised the inherent confusion in that statement and corrected herself. 'Your youngest daughter, Laura Royston...' She noticed the spikes on the monitor alter, maybe in response to what she had just said. She leaned even closer, her chin almost touching the bandages. 'Jonah? Robert?' she whispered. But, as she did so, the eyes in the slit flashed open. Wide, bloodshot, filled with panic. Just inches away from her own.

Sophie leapt backwards, backed away towards the door, opened it and backed out into the corridor, all the while checking that Jonah wasn't rising up and staggering towards her, arms outstretched, trailing bandages. She closed the door, caught the attention of the same nurse, who was standing at some distance, next to a water dispenser. 'His eyes opened!' she shouted.

The nurse hurried over. 'I should have warned you about that. It's just a reflex reaction. It's not likely that he's actually registering any images just yet.'

–

Sam looked up as Sophie approached. 'Hi. I managed to speak to Mrs B before she left. Apparently, Jonah's making good progress. But it'll be some time before he gets out of here. She suggested you call her tomorrow. Sometime after nine.' He paused. 'How did it go?'

'He opened his eyes. But the nurse said it was just a reflex. Can we go home?'

'Yes, of course.' He started to collect Laura's things together. 'You OK, Soph?'

Sophie said yes, she was OK. But, really, she wasn't.

–

On the way home Sophie watched the road ahead and tried to force from her mind the memory of Jonah's eyes staring out through the slit in their white bandage pall, unaware that his corrupt world was being deconstructed as he lay there. Impotent. Exposed. She felt Sam touch her arm.

'Soph, what's wrong?'

She turned to look at him. 'Five whole years and I never doubted him. It's why he was with me such a long time. All his other women guessed what he was up to but I just carried on believing his lies, oblivious to the fact that he was getting himself involved in…' She paused. 'Sam! A bald man with a beard tried to visit Jonah. Earlier today. He said he was Jonah's friend. But Jonah doesn't have friends. I think it was one of those guys that came to the house. Although, this time he was on his own.'

'The ginger guy was probably scared some dermatologist might spot his pulsating mole and not let him leave. We'll tell the cops next time they call round. Stop worrying about it.'

Moments passed. 'Sam, I'm sorry you're having to witness all this fallout from Jonah's lies. Gangsters breaking in and murdering us while we sleep.'

'I really don't think it will come to that, Soph. And I'm a bit pissed off that Blake raised the subject of suspicious characters coming to the house. I asked him, before you came down, to consider what a toll this was already taking on you.'

'How long was he there before I came down?'

'Not long. Maybe twenty minutes.'

'But it was long enough for him to show you that list.'

'What's that supposed to mean?'

'I just think it's strange how willing he is to allow you to speak for me. I didn't think the police did that. What else did you talk about?'

'We talked about football. Sophie, he knew I worked at the college. That list included college email addresses. Are you angry with me for involving myself in your affairs? I was only trying to help.'

'I know. I'm sorry. This whole mess is making me crazy.'

–

Sophie woke several times that night, each time expecting to see some mole-faced killer looming over her, and each time waking Sam from his own restless dreams. At ten past three she collected Laura, without waking her, and put her in bed between them so they could all get some decent sleep. At three thirty Sam got up and dragged the chest of drawers across the bedroom door. Just before seven, Sophie jumped awake, sat up and addressed the room. 'He said tell Robert that Joe and Col asked after him. The gangsters are called Joe and Col.'

–

Straight after breakfast Sam phoned a security company about fitting an intruder alarm then nipped into town to purchase some iron bolts. Sophie immediately phoned May Barnet and discovered that Jonah was responding to being spoken to. Sophie mentioned Rosemary Perrin's imminent visit and stressed the practical difficulties that might arise with Robert's accommodation, following his discharge from the rehabilitation unit. Mrs Barnet had made the quite reasonable suggestion that these problems should best be addressed when Mr Perrin's post-recovery status had been assessed. Sam left for a meeting late morning and Rosemary arrived in a harassed state an hour or so later.

'I wasn't really prepared for that, Sophie,' she said.

'You mean the ventilator?'

'It wasn't so much that, it was his eyes looking out through those slits in the bandages.'

Sophie indicated the lounge. 'Have you had lunch?'

'No, I'm not hungry. Not after that.'

'OK, what about a drink? Tea? Coffee? Prosecco? Did they tell you anything?'

'They said he was improving quicker than expected. His eyes move towards noises. That's freakin' scary. And one of his hands moves. They said he's in a *minimally conscious state*, which is due to the sedation. They can start to reduce that when they remove the ventilator. Then they'll be able to assess the damage. They said his reflexes are all good. I asked them how long he'd be in the ICU and they gave me one of those "it depends" answers. I spoke to that weird woman, May Barnet, with that fixed look on her face. Like the Virgin Mary smiling down on the wicked. She said she'd keep me informed. I told her I was driving over to see you and I thought she was going to pee herself. Sophie, I'd kill for a prosecco.'

—

When Sam arrived home, Sophie was showing Rosemary photos of her five years with Jonah. He walked over to take a look. 'You'd never know, would you? Such a consummate liar. I think they should all be burnt because Jonah Royston doesn't exist.'

'Unfortunately, Robert Perrin does,' said Rosemary. She got to her feet. 'Nothing personal, Sam, but I'd better be getting back. Or I'll have another glass of prosecco and then you'll never get rid of me. And by the way, loving the new haircut, Sam. Classy.'

Sam watched her pulling her things together. 'I presume Sophie mentioned that the police have found evidence of Jonah's involvement in various kinds of computer crime. Including the manipulation of false identities. I gather they searched your home?'

'Yes. But I don't think they found anything. I've always imagined that the only false identities Robert was concerned with were his own.'

Sam glanced at Sophie. 'It's just that we're quite concerned about the kind of people he might have been involved with. Did Robert ever have any suspicious-looking characters come to the house? You mentioned those two detectives that called. You thought they might have been Special Branch. Have they reappeared? And you said people often pull into your drive to ask directions. Has that happened lately?'

'Not since you visited. Why? Should I start to worry? We've got loads of alarms.'

'No, don't worry. Just call the police if you see anything suspicious.'

'OK, Sam, thanks for scaring the life out of me.' She gave him a quick peck on the cheek. 'Sophie, stay in touch. Phone as soon as you hear anything and I'll do the same.' She waved at Laura. 'Bye sweetheart. Happy birthday for tomorrow.'

Sophie saw Rosemary to the door. When she walked back into the lounge, Sam was collecting up photos. 'That is one strange alliance,' he said. 'Perrin's wife and mistress conspiring together. It reeks of the aristocracy of seventeenth-century France. Infidelity in the court of Louis Quatorze. The writing of Molière and Racine.'

'Sam, I have no idea what you're talking about.'

He handed her the photos. 'Did you tell her about Suzie?'

'I said that, so far, we hadn't managed to contact Heidi. I never mentioned Suzie.'

'Right. Is there any prosecco, or did you two drain the bottle?'

–

Sophie glanced up from scraping the last of the peanut butter out of the jar and noticed Sam slumped onto the kitchen table, frowning at her. 'Are you cross about something?'

'What? No! No, I'm not cross.'

She put the jar in the sink, carried the loaded spoon over and stood next to him. 'I'm sorry if this whole Jonah thing is getting you down. It must be…'

'Sophie, don't be silly. It's just that…' He exhaled frustration. 'I love you.'

'Oh! Are you cross about *that*?' She curled her tongue around the edge of the spoon.

'No. I just… Sophie, we need to talk…'

She put her finger across his lips. 'You need to know that I'm not just suffering from rebound syndrome, right? Well I'm not. I love you desperately. And if you make me hot chocolate, I promise I'll love you for ever.' She held the spoon towards him. 'Do you want some? We've already shared germs.'

He laughed and prodded her hand away. 'No! And it's twenty past ten. You'll get indigestion.'

'I never get indigestion.'

The Gift of Life

'And this video demonstration, you feel, will replace the need for you to explain in person?'

'Yes, Thaddeus.'

'And will it be available in other languages?'

'No more than I have been available in other languages.'

'And any likely questions that might arise?'

'Are unlikely to require my input, and in all cases can be answered by other team members. Will you allow me to show you the presentation before you offer any further critique?'

'Indeed, Dr Matthews. I...'

The wide screen filled with a young infant lying in a cot, watching a mobile above its head, occasionally lifting a small, chubby arm in an attempt to touch one of the ducks orbiting to a version of Brahms' lullaby pranged out by the combs of a musical box. The image faded to be replaced by the words:

PROGENTA
THE GIFT OF LIFE

which in turn faded to a group of people discussing something around a conference table and then to a laboratory where a white-coated man was inviting a grey-suited woman to observe something down the eyepiece of a microscope. Throughout this sequence a voiceover explained that the London-based Human Fertilisation and Embryology Authority regulates assisted reproduction research and practice in the UK, and is responsible for granting licences for these activities. The commentary continued as the screen filled with footage of *in vitro* fertilisation and chromosome duplication in a dividing cell. It described the removal of embryo cells for the purposes of pre-implantation diagnosis and embryo selection. An animation of embryo development was then accompanied by a woman's voice explaining that, whilst permitting embryo selection to prevent the implantation of abnormal embryos, the Embryo Authority does not licence the selection of embryos to satisfy social preferences. Prospective parents wishing to choose the gender of their child are denied this choice. The footage became that of a grateful couple with three sons holding a pink-wrapped newborn. This choice, the voice explained, is given to couples in some other countries, notably the United States, where parents may seek gender selection for no reason other than what is referred to as 'family balancing'.

The screen filled with laboratory workers observing DNA printouts, the voiceover explaining that in the PROGENTA laboratories they use a range of techniques to eliminate abnormal embryos, but also in association with their laboratories in the Middle East, to guarantee required gender and to offer an advanced degree of gene editing. The woman went on to explain that the Authority also prohibits embryo splitting for the purposes of multiple implantation since this is regarded as human cloning. An animation demonstrated a single embryo giving rise to several pregnancies. The woman's voice mellowed to explain that this prohibition was unfortunate, since early embryos can be safely divided to provide couples that have been able to produce only one viable embryo with more than one opportunity for pregnancy. This is indeed cloning, but cloning in much the same way as occurs in monozygotic twin births. Moreover, this prohibited cloning is associated with less risk since, with multiple implantations, each of the foetuses invariably has an individual placenta, thus eliminating any risk of compromised placental sharing.

The footage became that of egg harvesting, more fertilisation, and the plunging of embryos into a fuming canister for cryopreservation, explaining that, at PROGENTA, embryos are routinely selected, cloned, implanted or frozen for future implantation into the biological mother. When necessary, PROGENTA can provide gametes and healthy embryos donated by third and fourth parties. However – once again the voice mellowed – PROGENTA offers an additional service: the gestation of embryos by a carefully selected third party referred to as a surrogate. An animation presented a pregnant surrogate standing between sponsoring parents, and then the newly not-pregnant surrogate standing amongst her own three children, waving goodbye to the sponsoring parents and their newborn.

The surrogates, the voice explained, are provided with comprehensive antenatal care and are not usually recruited to provide surrogacy on more than one occasion. In most circumstances, to protect all parties, PROGENTA advises that the surrogate remains anonymous, although the parents are kept informed throughout the pregnancy. The surrogacies are managed according to legally valid contracts and appropriate certification is undertaken by PROGENTA, who will also arrange accommodation for couples wishing to take up residency in the UK for some or all of the gestational period. The screen filled with an image of a Georgian building in expansive grounds. The final footage showed nursing staff handing twin babies to a commissioning couple.

Thaddeus Jones allowed the promotion to come to an end then touched his fingers together.

'Dr Matthews, there seems to be no mention of same-sex parenting by client couples, contracts for which contribute significantly to our commissioning base.'

'There is an alternative presentation with same-sex parenting included. The sequence was omitted from the standard presentation since some clients, whilst happy to go against God's plan with regard to conception, are antagonistic towards homosexuality, bisexuality and probably cross-dressing.'

'Quite. Well, this has been most excellent, Dr Matthews. So very clearly explained.' Thaddeus Jones pressed his fingertips hard against one another. 'My only other critique might be that there is a tad too much technical jargon, which might be a problem for our non–English-speaking clients.'

'My dear Mr Jones, my use of jargon will succeed in crushing any attempts by *all* our clients to comprehend the extent of our malpractice. Our non–English-speaking clients will have very little idea about any of the footage. But if you are dissatisfied with this effort on my part, I suggest you get my successor to provide an alternative.'

Thaddeus Jones's fingers jolted between one another. 'Your successor?'

'Yes, Thaddeus, I have decided to choose this moment to retire from practice. I have two, possibly three, recommendations for team leader, which you might pursue. Which I suggest you do without further delay. I will see the current confinements through to their conclusion, but I will cease to initiate any further pregnancies.'

'Last month's fatality was unfortunate. I am assured it will not happen again. I…'

'That may well be the case, but I have made my decision based on reasons other than that poor young woman's fate. I will not be dissuaded.'

22

Thursday morning, Jesse dispatched one of his carpenters to fit Sophie's bolts, and a representative from the security company called round to quote for an intruder alarm and security cameras to be fitted as an emergency: possibly tomorrow week. From lunchtime, Sophie felt no safer. To lift her from her incipient despondency, Sam insisted that she and Laura came to visit his piles of bricks, shuttering and cement mixers.

Sam's site was bordered on three sides by woodland, with the emergent foundations being located a good distance from the road. Sophie was staggered at the size of the plot. She checked the pushchair wasn't about to roll away and tip Laura into a hole. 'Which way's north?' she asked. Sam pointed. She did a slow spin. 'So, everything is south-facing. That's perfect. You could plant your apple trees towards the back, over there, and a couple of plums and pears. You don't want a monospecific orchard. That's just asking for trouble. And a greenhouse there, with the big vegetables in front, leading up to a kitchen parterre garden. Herbs and salads. I think you should have a rose walk this side of the orchard. And you'll need a cage for the soft fruits. And… why are you laughing?'

'I'm just delighted we've got all that sorted out. Although I'm going to insist upon dandelions. And baking potatoes. They're big vegetables, aren't they?'

She frowned. 'Who owns the adjacent land?'

'Jesse's purchased the eastern plot. He says he might build a multi-storey car park on it and would I mind. And the woodland to the west and the rear belong to Stroud's Farm. If I win the lottery, I'll put a bid in for the land at the back.'

'You're joking about the car park, right?'

'Right.'

'Sometimes I'm not sure. So, how long is it all going to take?'

'The Project Manager estimates three months for the outside shell and services and the same amount again for most of the internal work. Probably another month to finish and get off site. Can you wait seven months?'

'Can *I* wait seven months?'

'Well, you don't expect me to move into our house on my own, do you?'

Sophie released the brake and manoeuvred the pushchair round on the uneven ground. 'Will we still be together in seven months?'

'I'll do whatever it takes to make sure we are.' Sophie went to push Laura forward but Sam caught her arm. 'Soph, I mean that. Tell me you'll come and live with me and we can plant our garden together.'

She didn't answer. But she did smile and say. 'I like dandelions.'

'Is that a yes?'

'It's an extremely possible. Come on, it's birthday tea time.'

–

The following afternoon Sophie learned that, although still only intermittently conscious, Jonah had proved himself able to respire without the help of a ventilator. Of course, Sophie's far greater concern was the evening about to happen, when she and Sam would have to witness another round of Katie's over-supper conversation. Sam had insisted they should stay over in his attic afterwards, an insistence about which Sophie was silently ecstatic. And, to save any major haulage of baby equipment, Jesse had moved a playpen and cot to the top floor. As they drove over late-afternoon, Sophie fought to disguise her breathless anticipation. Her efforts collapsed when Greenfield's tall iron gates registered their arrival and began to open, permitting their access into a long, rising, gravel drive, bordered on either side by tall rhodo-dendrons, laurels, euonymus and limes. As they approached the house, its splendid façade could be seen rising out of the greenery.

'The house was constructed in the nineteen thirties,' explained Sam, 'but Jesse's rebuilt it from the inside out, so it's really the shell of a pre-war house with an eco-living space on the inside. You'll like it.'

Sophie chewed her lip in awe. 'I already like it.'

They pulled up outside the main door where Jesse was waiting to greet them, the gates having informed him of their arrival. He hurried forward to hug Sophie, relieved her of the bags and escorted her into his reception hall. She looked around in amazement. 'Jesse, this is wonderful! I can't believe Sam has chosen to come and stay in my tiny three-up-two-down box instead of here.' She cast her eyes right, through a wide archway into the vast open-plan living area. 'You must need a staff of thousands to help you.'

'Just a couple of cleaners and an occasional handyman. It's large open spaces that are the answer: no walls to stand unnecessary pieces of furniture against. So, no unnecessary things can stand on the unnecessary furniture, collecting spiders and dust.'

'But what about your books and papers? And DVDs and CDs?'

Jesse pointed to a door on the left. 'The library-cum-office is through there. So, the books are in there, although Sam prefers to keep his on his floor. And the music and films are all comput-erised. Centrally organised. Your ex-partner would be impressed. There's a gym through there as well. And a panic room.'

'All guests are expected to do twenty minutes on the treadmill before breakfast,' said Sam. 'Jesse diverts the energy to heating the water.'

Sophie was suddenly apprehensive. 'Sam's joking, right?'

'Not completely,' said Jesse. 'But there are several back-up systems, so the treadmill isn't compulsory. Do you want to take Laura straight up? Or have you got time for a drink?'

'We'll take her up,' said Sam. 'But why don't you come up and have a drink with us? Where are the boys?'

'They're with Barbara for the night.'

'And when's Katie expected?' Sophie asked.

Jesse ran his fingers through his hair. 'Seven thirty for eight.'

–

An acceptably wide staircase led up to the top floor, which was a relief since all the attics Sophie had ever frequented were reached via some kind of ladder. 'Is all this stuff Jesse's?' she said, surveying Sam's single large living space: the leather sofas, steel lamps, the rugs, the occasional oriental item, the dining area, the kitchen crammed with appliances that would make Jamie Oliver green with envy. The giant TV.

'What you mean all this unnecessary furniture? No, it's mine. The master bedroom's through there and Laura's room, otherwise known as the study, is beyond that.' He put Laura down on the rug and after a moment's apprehension she crawled over to the long coffee table to tear the magazines.

'English lecturer salary must be better than I thought, Mr Barnes.'

–

Katie arrived just as Jesse was transferring a large poached salmon to its platter of cucumber and samphire, so Sam and Sophie hurried through to welcome her. They exchanged kisses and Sam accepted the bottle of Bollinger she was offering. 'You look nice,' he said. 'And surprisingly sophisticated. Jesse likes white. He's just putting the finishing touches to his culinary masterpiece.'

Katie looked horrified. 'Oh no, am I early?'

'No,' said Sophie. 'We've all been desperate for you to arrive. You look really lovely.'

Katie grabbed on to Sophie's arm, leaned close and whispered, 'Is this all Jesse's?'

'Yes,' she whispered back. 'Amazing, isn't it?'

Jesse looked up as they approached, strode round and kissed Katie's cheek, a bristlier kiss than the one she had just received from his brother. 'Would you like a champagne cocktail?' he said. 'I'm afraid Sam and his woman have been drinking ever since they arrived but I'm completely sober and in charge of kitchen equipment.'

'That sounds great... the cocktail, I mean. Although the kitchen equipment also looks great. But I have to go slow because I'm driving.'

'Oh, I wouldn't worry about that,' said Sam. 'We can dump you in one of Jesse's spare rooms. Have you brought your toothbrush with you?'

'Please excuse my brother,' said Jesse. 'He has no idea how to behave. Although there are several guest rooms if you'd like to stay over. I should have mentioned that before.'

Katie said nothing. In fact, Katie continued to say virtually nothing through the canapés and cocktails, speaking only to reply to direct questions. Eventually Sophie had to ask, 'Katie, why aren't you insulting people? You've hardly said anything.'

'I've decided that the best way of *not* insulting people is to say nothing.'

Jesse laughed. 'But the only reason I asked you to supper is because I crave your tactless observations. Surely you're not going to leave your Übermenschlich host disappointed.'

Katie looked at him and folded her arms. 'OK, I like your house. It's very big.'

Jesse raised an eyebrow. 'And?'

'I'd prefer an extra wall or two. And you must get lonely here, just you and the boys.' She grinned. 'Do you need an au pair? I can make toast.'

–

For the next three hours, Katie's critiques fell within the bounds of the almost acceptable, and after thanking Jesse for their marvellous supper, Sophie and Sam made a discreet retreat up to the attic, leaving Katie and Jesse to discuss sleeping arrangements.

Sometime later, Sam located *The Complete Poems* of John Keats and read to Sophie as she drifted into sleep:

And can I ever bid these joys farewell?
Yes, I must pass them for a nobler life,
Where I may find the agonies, the strife
Of human hearts…

The following morning, Sam was investigating the use-by date on a box of eggs, when his phone rang. It was Jesse inviting them all to breakfast. Sam said they'd love to join them then hurried through to help with Laura.

'Brace yourself, Soph, we're breakfasting with the golden couple.'

'Do you think they, you know, spent the night together?'

Sam shrugged. 'Don't know. Jesse's never been averse to casual sex, in fact, after Sandi, it's the only kind of sex he's interested in. And I can't see your best friend turning down the opportunity. So, probably yes. Let's go see.'

Downstairs, a highchair had been made ready and, wearing an apron over a lush white bathrobe, Katie was helping set out breakfast on the big marble eat station. Jesse glanced up. 'I've made salmon kedgeree with last night's leftovers but there's standard English, whatever you prefer. I'd tuck in as fast as you can because the kids will be back any minute.'

'There's yoghurt and strawberries for Laura,' said Katie, pulling out the stool next to Sophie, 'and watermelon.'

'Fantastic,' said Sophie, trying to discern, from outward appearances, whether Katie and Jesse had spent the whole night engaged in rampant sex.

They ate and chatted and indulged Laura until the front door burst open and Grandma Buckley ushered her grandsons inside. Jesse jumped up to introduce his mother-in-law. There followed two pecks on the grandmotherly cheek from Jesse and Sam and some earnest handshaking. Benz and Jake dragged and forced stools between Sophie and Katie. Jesse snapped at them not to be impolite, but Grandma Buckley tapped his arm. 'Jesse, your sons crave the attention of younger women, who might have the slightest idea about Lego *Star Wars* and *Scooby-Doo*.' She frowned at her grandsons leaning across the table top helping themselves to plates and food. 'As you can see, Jesse, I have starved them.'

'Barbara,' said Sam, 'will you join us?'

'No, no, dear. I have an old lady to visit.' She glanced over at Katie and smiled. 'Let you all get yourselves sorted out. I'll see myself out. Bye, boys, and behave yourselves.'

Benz yelled goodbye then turned to Katie and said, 'Are you Dad's girlfriend now?'

'Benz!' said Jesse, 'don't be so rude!'

'Actually, Sophie and I have been wondering the same thing,' said Sam.

'For your information, *Sam*, I haven't yet discussed any such arrangements with my supper guest. I was hoping to test the water a little before presuming to seek a commitment.'

Katie took a bite of croissant and spoke with her cheek full. 'After my night with the Übermensch, I'm hardly likely to refuse.'

–

Despite the luxuries of penthouse living, Sam and Sophie elected to return to Sophie's three-up-two-down that afternoon, essentially because they thought it best to let Jesse and Katie negotiate their relationship without the distractions that two other adults might offer.

–

The following Wednesday morning, DI Blake phoned to tell Sophie that the investigation into Jonah's business activities was continuing and they needed to keep his phones for the time being. Had she thought of anything that might help their enquiries? She said sorry, no. The phone rang again. It was the hospital informing her that, though sedated, Jonah was now fully conscious for extended periods and that he would be transferred to a normal ward, probably after the weekend. His progress was good, although he was experiencing some confusion, and he seemed also to be suffering severe retrograde memory loss. His psychotherapist wondered if Sophie was contemplating a visit in the near future since a familiar voice might succeed in evoking reactions that would help assess the temporary or permanent nature of this memory aberration. Mrs Perrin was unable to make the journey from Devon any time soon. Sophie ended the call, then sat and stared at the surface of the table. The front door opened and closed and Sam strode into the kitchen, carrying groceries. 'I've got duck eggs and... what's up?'

'Jonah's psychotherapist wants me to go in and speak to him. To help him remember.'

'What? Tell them you won't do it. What about Rosemary? Tell them to ask her.'

'They already have. And she said she's not available.'

'Well, neither are you. I'm not letting you do it, Soph. I want that bastard out of our lives.'

'So do I. But, Sam, I really have to do this. Just to get closure.'

Sam became silent. He just put away the shopping then picked Laura out of her highchair. 'I'll take her into the garden and let her smell the lavender. It's supposed to be good for the nerves. And if you insist upon involving yourself with Robert Perrin, then I'll drive you over tomorrow afternoon, after I've been to the site. I need to check they're building the walls straight. And remembering to leave holes for the windows.'

Watkins

The door eased open. 'Hello, Mr Watkins, you may remember me, DI Barnes, National Crime Agency.' The door opened a little wider. Leonard Watkins remained silent. 'I wonder if I might ask you a few questions regarding your discovery of the young woman's body… four weeks ago. If I might come inside? This won't take too much of your time. We just need to get a few things cleared up.' The door opened wide. Sam stepped inside and was instantly struck by the stench, a cocktail of wet bark, public urinals and pet food. He had never before suffered breathing difficulties but felt if he were ever to experience them it would be during the next few minutes. He followed Watkins into a damp and dingy lean-to kitchen populated by more cats than he cared to count. 'Mr Watkins,' he began, 'at the crime scene, I was given to believe that you had been made aware of the critical nature of the investigation relating to your discovery and of the need to prevent any details making their way into the press. I gathered that you had agreed not to contact the media. However, I am now informed, by my superior officer, that details of the poor woman's fate are about to appear in the local newspaper. Do you…'

'I was within my rights,' whinged Watkins.

'Sorry?'

'I never signed anything… official secrets or whatnot. What-ever you people use to keep things from the public. It was merely a spoken request. A gentlemen's agreement.'

Gentlemen? 'So, you admit that it was you that informed the local newspaper?'

Watkins picked up a large cat that was sniffing around a heap of wet, brown toadstools lying next to the sink. He stroked its neck and, in the shaft of sunlight penetrating through the moss-covered glass, Sam could see long grey hairs floating free with every swipe of Watkins' hand. He went to take a deep breath then decided against it. 'Our concern is obviously the panic that such news might cause, not only locally but further afield. I need to ask you exactly how and what you told them. Did you make an anonymous phone call?'

Watkins gave a half-sneer. 'They can trace phone calls. And emails.'

'Quite.'

'Actually, I wrote a note to the editor, cut out of bits of newspaper. Whilst wearing disposable gloves.'

Prat. 'I see. And do you have a copy of this note?'

'I went to the library and photocopied it.'

'So, you have a copy? Might I see? It would be in everyone's interest if we knew what the papers are likely to print.'

Watkins set the cat down on the table amidst a flurry of hair, retrieved a folded sheet from a pile of papers and handed it to Sam. Sam observed the note. It was reminiscent of something you would expect to see in a very bad TV crime series from the 1960s: words and letters cut out and pasted onto a sheet of paper. He had to admit he quite liked it. It read:

> WOMAN'S NAKED BODY DISCOVERED IN LOCAL WOODS. POLICE HAVE CORDONED OFF THE AREA FOR THE LAST 4 WEEKS. WHAT ARE THEY HIDING?

Sam could feel his throat prickling with hair. He took out his phone, checked for Watkins' approval, and photographed the sheet of paper. He glanced up. Watkins was watching him, an air of belligerence about him. 'This must have taken you some time, Mr Watkins. Tell me, if, despite your precautions, you are traced by reporters or the like, do you intend to offer additional information? Perhaps regarding how the unfortunate woman died? Was she strangled? Perhaps a gun crime?'

'I don't know how she died. And I don't want to know. I kept my distance. She was probably raped.'

Sam nodded.

'Or erotic asphyxiation. That's more common than you think.'

Tosser. 'Yes. The police are still investigating possible cause of death. Mr Watkins, can I ask why, after four weeks, you have now decided to contact the press?'

'Because the authorities have no right to prevent access to such a large area. I have tried to collect twice in the last week and have been forced to enter a cordoned-off area where I found fresh young cep, *Boletus edulis*, trampled into the ground and unlikely to recover this season. This whole overreaction has caused me significant financial loss. Indeed, I would have been morally justified in selling my experiences to the newspaper to compensate, rather than merely informing them.'

'And may I ask why you did not *sell* your experiences?'

'I disapprove of cheque-book journalism,' he said with a full sneer.

Sam studied Watkins for a moment. 'Well, I can only apologise about the inconvenience your discovery has caused you and I assure you that our investigation of the areas adjacent to the crime scene is reaching its conclusion. In the meantime, I should caution you not to cross police barriers.'

Sam left Watkins to his cats and hurried back to his car where he phoned Director Short and assured him that, as far as he could gather, the press had been given very little information, but probably enough to cause the perpetrators to speculate and quite possibly take some precautionary action or other.

23

Once again, Sophie left Sam and Laura in Costa while she visited Intensive Care where a tall, white-coated woman introduced herself as Dr Thea Graves, the resident psychotherapist. She explained that scans had confirmed that Mr Perrin's injuries were restricted to the superficial brain tissue, with circulation within the brain returning to normal as the swelling and inflammation decreased. She further explained that the area of brain affected would not necessarily be associated with memory defects. Memory and other aspects of higher neurological function were deep-seated within the brain, although it was possible that additional trauma might have resulted from sudden impact as with some closed head injuries, and this might explain the memory loss. She was hoping to observe his responses upon encountering someone with whom he was previously familiar, and cautioned that, although he *was* able to respond to requests, he was not yet able to offer complete sentences. They were also experiencing a slight dilemma related to his aversion to the smell of disinfectant and was this an existing problem?

'Jonah… I'm sorry, Robert, has always been hypersensitive to strong smells. They give him really bad migraines. I did wonder whether it would be a problem when he regained consciousness. The disinfectant, that is.'

'Well, there's not much we can do about the smell of disinfectant in a hospital, is there? Anyway, I'd like to thank you for coming in like this. It must be very difficult for you.'

Sophie forced a smile then followed Dr Graves to the side room, wondering if everyone in the entire hospital knew that she had been living with an adulterer for the last five years and was now pathetic enough to still agree to aiding his recovery. She was surprised to find Jonah raised up on pillows, his bandages reduced mostly to one side of his head, his face almost fully uncovered apart from a thin strip across his forehead. His eyes watched her as she stepped into the room. Dr Graves indicated the chair for Sophie to sit down. 'Hello, Robert,' she said. 'I've brought someone to see you.'

Sophie cringed at the patronising tone, clearly reserved not only for the very young, the very old and the very pregnant, but also for the recently brain-damaged. Jonah continued to watch for a few moments then closed his eyes. 'Stinks,' he said. 'Stinks!'

Dr Graves gave a half-smile, half-grimace. 'Robert, do you know who this is? It's your friend, Sophie. Would you like Sophie to speak to you?'

Jonah opened his eyes but said nothing. Sophie experienced a wave of uncertainty. She had lived with this man, had his child, and yet right then and there she couldn't think of a single thing to say to him. She wasn't even sure what to call him. So, she fell back upon the obvious. 'The doctors say you're making excellent progress. And we're all hoping you'll get well very soon.' Five years and nothing but platitudes. 'Do you remember me? We've known each other for a long time. Do you remember Laura?'

'Issy and Laura,' he mumbled.

Sophie looked at Dr Graves. 'They're his...'

'Yes, I'm aware of that.' She leaned towards him. 'Do you know why you're here, Robert?' There was no response. 'Do you remember what happened to you? Would you like Sophie to say what happened to you? To help you remember? Sophie, would you like to remind us what happened that day?'

Sophie took a deep breath. What could she say? How about: *Completely out of the blue after living with me for five years you drove to our house with your new girlfriend in the car and told me you were leaving me and your daughter, you bastard?* No, that wouldn't do. 'We used to live together. And I used to call you Jonah. And one day three weeks ago, you were putting things into your car and you fell and hurt your head. Do you remember that, Jonah?'

'Where's Rosie?' he said.

Another deep breath. 'She's at home at the moment. She came to see you when you were not properly awake. But she sends her love.' *Like hell she does.* 'She'll come and see you again soon.' *Actually, I'm the only fool who's willing to waste my time coming here and you don't even recognise me.*

Jonah stared at her. A fixed stare with no expression attached. Then, all at once, the traces on the monitor were becoming erratic. He leaned forward, dragged taut the tube that was feeding into the crook of his arm and tried to touch Sophie's hand. 'Stinks!'

Sophie recoiled from the threat of contact. Dr Graves leaned forward to pat his arm. 'It's OK, Robert, we're trying to do something about the smell. It will be better once you're up on the wards. I'll leave you and Sophie to have a chat.' She got to her feet. 'I'll wait for you outside, Sophie. Take your time.'

Thea Graves left. Sophie wanted to leave too, but, curious to understand the plight of this man she had lived with for so long, she lingered. She lied that everything was fine, that all his things were safely packed away. Jonah watched her speaking then, without warning, threw himself upright and towards her, again dragging the line but this time managing to close his fingers around her wrist. Sophie gasped as his skin touched hers. It felt laminated, too smooth to be alive, just like that day, stroking her mother's cold, lifeless cheek as she lay in the funeral parlour. She managed to pull free then backed away towards the door, watched his outstretched hand begging her return. Then, clear as anything, she heard him say, 'Don't give it to them, Sophie.'

–

For the first half of the journey home, Sophie refused to talk about her time with Jonah but eventually, when she was convinced that her thoughts were going to burst straight out of her head if she didn't release them, she said, 'He asked about Rosemary. And Issy and Laura.' She twiddled with the strap of her bag. 'He's freaking out about the disinfectant. It's a shame he didn't lose his sense of smell instead of his memory. He's a bit paralysed down one side, but they think it's only temporary.'

'Do they think his memory loss is temporary?'

'I think so. He seemed to be recovering bits and pieces while I was there. At first, he didn't know who I was but then, just as I was leaving, he said, "Don't give it to them, Sophie".'

'Don't give them what?'

'Perhaps he meant his laptop.'

'You didn't ask him what he meant?'

'No. I don't care what he meant.'

'Sophie, if he *has* secreted something, the laptop or whatever, somewhere in your house, and there are people looking for it, then we need to find it first, so we can give it to the police.' He blew out a lungful of air. 'I want you and Laura to move to my place. ASAP.'

'But they're fitting the alarm tomorrow.'

'I don't care. I want you out of your house until we're sure what Jonah was referring to. I need to know you're both safe. I mean it, Soph.'

'But what about Jesse?'

'I've already spoken to him about it.'

She sighed. 'So, how did it go today?'

Sam glanced at her. 'Sorry?'

'At the site. You wanted to make sure they were leaving holes for the windows.'

'Oh yes. Loads of windows. Doors too.'

Sophie lifted a crinkly grey hair from Sam's sleeve. 'Are you having an affair with a curly pensioner?'

—

Fitting the intruder alarm took most of the next morning. Sam stayed home to make sure that none of the security engineers were gangsters in disguise and Sophie continued with the packing she had started the previous evening: just the things she and Laura might need for a warm, late August that sooner or later just had to turn to rain. As she folded her clothes into her mother's old suitcase, she couldn't help remembering Jonah's similar undertaking those three fateful weeks ago, remembered his library book, last seen lying in the road, never to be returned, the fine mounting up indefinitely. She thought about the missing laptop. She ought to ask Suzie about it but, in truth, she'd avoided contacting her ever since she'd shopped her to the police. She heard Sam thanking the security team and closing the door behind them, quietly so as not to wake Laura. Moments later the doorbell rang. Laura stirred but didn't wake. Sam could be heard directing someone along the hallway. Voices behind a closed door. Sophie hurried downstairs and discovered Inspector Blake and two other officers in the kitchen. Sam instantly reassured her that there was nothing to worry about, which is what people usually say when there *is* something to worry about.

'Inspector Blake has a warrant to search the house. It means that if they find anything, it will be permissible evidence. Allowed in court.'

'But why do they need a warrant? I never said they couldn't search?'

'It's really just a formality,' said Inspector Blake. 'You have been very helpful at every point in our investigation. But, given the latest circumstances, we now have to do things by the book. Constables Barry Lane and Susan Rice will assist me in the search.'

'What latest circumstances?'

'Last Saturday, Jonah's car was stolen from the Business Park,' said Sam. 'It was found dismantled and burnt out on a disused refuse site. There's also been a break-in at Jonah's Exeter house. Yesterday morning. They were all out at the time, apart from the dog, which seems to have slept through it. Apparently, nothing was taken but the place was turned over.'

'But what about the alarms? Rosemary's house was covered in alarms.'

'All alarms can be defeated by someone,' said Inspector Blake. 'It was a professional job undertaken by individuals who were experienced at thievery. The Devon police concluded that several perpetrators were involved. And the fact that they have broken into Mr Perrin's home, would suggest they failed to find what they were after when they searched his business premises.' He glanced at Sam. 'And we must presume that, if their search of the Perrin residence was also unsuccessful, they'll continue to search elsewhere. If there is anything incriminating hidden in your home, we need to be the first to find it.'

Sophie immediately felt threatened. 'Inspector, when I visited Jonah yesterday he was very confused, but as I was leaving he said "Don't give it to them". Do you think he was referring to his laptop? And that's what they're looking for?'

'That's possible.'

Sophie frowned. 'Have you asked Suzie Kay about it?'

'When questioned, she had no knowledge of a laptop. We have also acquired a warrant to search Miss Kay's home.' Again, he glanced at Sam. 'Mr Barnes has informed me that you will be moving over to his premises for the time being. I believe that might be a wise move. At least until we know what we're dealing with here.'

—

Sam accompanied the officers from room to room. They started by excavating the contents of the cupboard under the stairs. Sophie cringed at the piles of junk being pulled out into the hallway. They found nothing, so Sam escorted Officers Blake and Lane into the lounge whilst Sophie helped Constable Rice load everything back under the stairs. A shrill scream interrupted their awkward conversation. 'It's my daughter's lunchtime,' explained Sophie. She hurried upstairs to collect Laura, uncertain what kind of psychological damage she might suffer watching strangers pulling her house apart. Half an hour later, having phoned Rosemary to offer condolences about the break-in,

Sophie carried Laura into the lounge and discovered her sofa on its side. Constable Lane was investigating its innards by poking a camera through a hole in the fabric across its base. 'How would Jonah have put anything in there without me knowing?' asked Sophie.

Officer Lane stepped over and handed Sophie a gold locket and chain. 'So far this and some loose change is all we've found. Down the back of the armchair.'

Sophie rubbed the dusty locket between her fingers. 'It was my mother's. I thought my sister had all her jewellery in Ireland.' She eased her fingernail into the small indentation in the side and it flipped open to reveal two tiny, faded photos: two little girls, perhaps five and six. She tried to remember her mother wearing it but Laura started to wriggle so she left them to their searching, hurried upstairs, shut herself and Laura in the main bedroom and resumed packing. But after a few hectic minutes of Laura pulling things down on top of herself, Sophie lifted her into her travel cot with her caterpillar book and sat down on the bed to take another look at her mother's locket. She looked up as Sam stepped into the room.

'Are you all right?'

'Not really. It makes me sad to imagine what my mother would have thought about her house being pulled apart like this. And it scares me how you can't know what fate has in store for you.' She handed him the locket. 'That's me and Josie, when we were little, with our whole lives ahead of us. We had so many plans. About all the things we were going to do together. And now Josie's in Ireland married to a farmer and I'm an abandoned single mother with the police rummaging through my possessions.'

'Sophie, these little girls and their plans belong to the past.'

'But the past is all you can be sure of. Although, I suppose I can't even be sure of that.'

Sam closed the locket and handed it back. 'The greater part of your life is still ahead of you. And it's going to be the best part because it will have me in it. And however disastrous the last few years might seem right now, you have Laura to compensate.' He smiled. 'Although we need to teach her to read her books rather than eat them.'

-

The search of Sophie's house continued for several hours, with little success until they came, at last, to the spare room. They removed a number of things into evidence bags and then prepared to leave, but Sophie was reluctant to let Inspector Blake escape without some further explanation. 'Inspector, what do you think could possibly warrant this degree of searching? What on earth do you think Jonah was involved in?'

Inspector Blake chose his words carefully. 'Over the last few days, we have retrieved data from Mr Perrin's computers and phones that confirm his involvement with individuals Serious Crime have been trying to link to certain criminal activities. In addition, we now suspect not only that he was involved in wrongful access to both private and business bank accounts, in order to move funds into as yet untraceable accounts abroad, but also that he has been trading in false identities for use in criminal practices. The break-ins might be related to individuals attempting to claim services they have already paid for. But an additional concern, indeed DCI Gardener's main concern, for yourself and others, is that Mr Perrin might have secured his own safety by holding incriminating information on the individuals he was dealing with. And they would be keen that such information did not find its way into police hands. Considering Mr Perrin's passion for conundrums, it is likely that the data is held in more than one location.'

'Have you checked his puzzle books?'

'Yes, and I have to say, the man has an astounding appetite for such things. We've already had someone working on those retrieved from the Topsham Road property but there appears to be nothing significant in any of them. Just a few red herrings.'

Sophie sighed. 'What kind of criminal practices, Inspector?'

'I'm afraid I'm not at liberty to share that information at the present time. Suffice it to say that your ex-partner might well be implicated in what is an ongoing criminal investigation by the National Crime Agency. There is every possibility that he was not fully aware of what he was involved in.'

Sam saw the officers to the door. When he walked back into the lounge he spoke with a sense of urgency. 'Sophie, we're out of here *now*. Just get whatever things you need for the next few days and don't forget it's Bank Holiday weekend. We'll come back for some more stuff when you need it.' Sophie didn't argue. She just concentrated on packing whilst Sam watched Laura and the pavement outside.

24

Sophie glanced up from checking the fridge just as Sam was carrying the last of the bags downstairs. 'Can we collect some more of Laura's toys tomorrow, before she starts to miss them? And I've also got to sort out my things for going back to work. I haven't even thought about it with all this going on. There's only two weeks before I've got to turn up looking professional. And I don't think any of my pre-pregnancy clothes will fit.'

Sam dropped the bags and walked through to put his arms around her. 'Why, have you grown taller?'

'No, just a little wider around the waist. And possibly the boobs. Although that will probably change when I stop feeding. In fact, I'll probably do that before I go back.'

'That's a shame,' said Sam. 'I've quite enjoyed it.'

Sophie poked his shoulder. Then she frowned. 'Sam, what's the National Crime Agency? Is it like Special Branch?'

Sam stepped back and furrowed his brow. 'I think they deal with things like computer crime and drug trafficking. Child prostitution. Things like that.'

'And they think Jonah was…?'

'Like Blake said, he might not have realised what he was getting himself into. He might not even have been involved anyway. Come on, let's go.'

–

When they arrived at Greenfields, Sophie went straight to Jesse to provide a crisis update. He listened without interrupting. Eventually, she paused for him to respond.

'Sophie, you'll be safe here. Please stay for as long as you can bear to live with my brother's chaos. And there's a lot of storage space above the middle garage if you need it.'

'Jesse, that's very kind of you.'

'My pleasure. And, to be honest, I have a vested interest. I'll be able to call you down if Katie starts to frighten me. She's coming over to stay for the weekend.'

—

By the following morning, Katie had managed not to reduce anyone to rage. Indeed, over breakfast, Sophie was intrigued to witness her trying her hardest to avoid provocation. But at the back of Sophie's mind there was a constant, low-level dread about how Jonah's clandestine affairs seemed to be unravelling her previously uncomplicated life and how they might adversely affect the people she was currently breakfasting with. Sam interrupted her thoughts.

'Sophie, shall we nip back and collect your things? Then we'll be free to enjoy the rest of the weekend. Jess, would you and Katie mind Laura?'

—

Sophie's new security system registered no intrusions. In fact, everything looked the same as it had when they'd left those few hours ago and, as Sophie watered her plants, she began to feel that Sam might have overreacted about the threat to her safety. Back inside, she selected various uninspiring office outfits and a few extras for Laura. But, as she was forcing yet another stuffed toy into an IKEA bag, she remembered Jesse's offer of space above his garage and thought of her mother's jugs and teapots and vases. She didn't think it likely that gangsters would be interested in such a collection but she felt uncomfortable leaving them there, abandoned in their spidery larder. She hurried downstairs to find Sam watching the local news on mute. She asked him if he thought Jesse would mind her mother's collection of china being stored above his garage.

Sam gave a cautious smile. 'Is it a big collection?'

'It's five boxes in the back of the larder. Some of the vases are vintage Moorcroft.'

'Wasn't that Sherlock Holmes's brother? Oh no, that was Mycroft.'

Sam excavated the boxes, carried them one at a time to the back road, tessellated them into the Range Rover, then came back for the IKEA bags, by which time Sophie had decided that she would also like to store her mother's Victorian vanity unit.

'You mean the one that's screwed onto the bedroom wall?'

'Yes.'

'Did Jonah have a toolkit? Apart from the one that took his ear off.'

'I don't think so. There's a mini set of screwdrivers that came out of a Christmas cracker. In the pot on the mantelpiece.'

Sam rolled his eyes. 'I've got one in the car. I'll take these round and fetch it. I'll have to unload everything. Do not open the door to anyone, under any circumstances. Right?'

'Right.' She watched him leave then returned to the larder to check for overlooked teapots. The doorbell rang. Sam must have forgotten his keys. She hurried through and opened the door. 'Oh! Hello, Mrs Davies.'

'Hello, Sophie. I saw you were here and I thought I'd drop round with this dear little dolly for Laura.' She handed Sophie a small gift bag. 'Handmade by the natives in Sardinia.' Sophie invited Mrs Davies inside, asked if she would like a cup of tea. Mrs Davies said that would be lovely then walked ahead of Sophie into the kitchen, bustled herself into a chair and made ready. 'Well now, how are things with you, dear? Mrs Bartram, number 58, said Mr Royston had a bit of an accident. Right outside his door. Such a dangerous road. You keep your eye on little Laura when she starts her walking. Don't want her running around in the traffic, do you? And Mrs Bartram said you've had trouble with the police coming. More than once, she said. I hope it's nothing serious?'

Mrs Davies' partiality for gossip was legendary and Sophie was aware that this gift-bearing visit was in part a contrivance to glean transferrable information. She also realised that it was within her power to decide exactly what Mrs Davies would have on offer in the days that followed. She decided to opt for the entire package. 'It was terrible, Mrs Davies. Jonah was just packing his case into his car and he fell onto his toolbox and fractured his skull. He's been in Southampton General ever since. He was in a controlled coma for a couple of weeks. But he's slowly improving. I'll just make the tea.'

Sophie filled the kettle. Decided to let her neighbour fester a little. Eventually the wait became insufferable. Mrs Davies leaned forward, her eyes bright with enquiry. 'I told Mrs Bartram, the police were probably here because they needed to sort out all those little bumps and scrapes with people's cars. And, my goodness, she said there was a huge lorry right across the road.'

'Yes, there was. But, mostly, the police have been coming here about Jonah.' Mrs Davies moved even further forward, like a vacuum cleaner eager for dirt. And Sophie felt that all the dirt should be about Jonah. 'I've discovered that Jonah is not who I believed him to be. His real name is Robert Perrin. And he has a wife and two daughters. Living in Exeter.'

Mrs Davies' eyes widened at the prospect of scandal beyond expectation. 'Good Lord. How terrible for you, Sophie, dear. And with nobody for you to turn to, what with your poor mother being gone.'

Sophie continued to make the tea. She could feel Mrs Davies watching her, waiting for the next nugget of gossip. Finally, she handed her a mug and sat down opposite. 'I must admit I did feel a bit shell-shocked for the first few days.'

'Dear, dear. Mrs Bartram said she would have popped in, but Mr Bartram has been in bed with the doctor, and she was worried you might think she was interfering.' She took a sip of tea. 'And where is dear little Laura? Is she having her nap?'

'Er, she's not here at the moment. We've been staying with a friend.'

'With that nice young girl that helped me with my letter to the gas board?'

'Katie? No, not Katie. We've...'

Just then the front door opened and Sam strode in carrying a toolbox. 'Sophie, the car's full. There's just room for you and me, the vanity unit and possibly a book of postage stamps... Oh, hello!'

Sophie jumped up. 'Sam, this is Mrs Davies from next door.'

Sam offered his hand and Mrs Davies accepted it, with all the delight of a woman full to the brim with enough information to establish her primacy for the next month. And Sam performed perfectly: he poured himself tea, offered Mrs Davies an in-date packet of chocolate digestives and agreed with her about the escalating price of food. And to top it all, as he saw her to the door, he asked her to keep an eye on Sophie's house whilst she was away. When he stepped back into the kitchen, Sophie was still seated and waiting.

'Sam Barnes, you are an elderly-lady tart.'

He folded his arms. 'And you are totally hopeless. I asked you not to open the door to anyone. What if she'd been one of Jonah's partners in crime?'

'Well, she wasn't, was she? And you're still a tart.'

He bent over and kissed her cheek. 'Be that as it may, I must now prove my handyman skills by removing your mother's shelves, without demolishing the wall.'

Warning

'The message was received and decoded this morning, Sir Hugh. It states quite clearly that it has been automatically generated as a result of Robert Perrin failing to prevent its dispatch: that obviously being due to his present unfortunate circumstances. It also suggests that, if he should further be unable to prevent it, a detailed log of incriminating data will automatically be dispatched to the National Crime Agency.'

'Yes, yes, Jones, I can see all that here.' Sir Hugh scanned the printout. 'But is this it? Does this disgusting rodent make no suggestion of a timescale?'

'No, sir. This message may have been set up recently, at the same time as the announcement of his intention to cease all dealings with the Organisation. And we should consider the possibility that the suggested dispatch of incriminating data might be an empty threat. Indeed, this warning may be the full extent of our problem.'

Sir Hugh re-read the printout. 'Have you been able to determine its source?'

'The message seems to have been bounced around various IP addresses.'

'An *earthly* location, Jones?'

'Sir Hugh, Mr Perrin has, in the past, proved himself to be supremely capable of defeating the most advanced IP locating software. Our preliminary search of the Royston Computer Solutions offices and last week's extensive search of Perrin's Exeter property have both provided nothing. The Source informs us that the police have confiscated the remaining hardware from Perrin's business premises, although so far, as our operatives concluded, they have not managed to access anything that needs concern us directly. A further attempt will be made to question Mr Perrin as soon as he is moved from the Intensive Care Unit. And I have arranged for a team of operatives to undertake an immediate search of the Denham property.'

'Yes, yes. But, let us be clear, Jones. There are to be no more bodies.'

'Obviously, Sir Hugh. My operatives will be very discreet.'

25

The long weekend passed undramatically, as did most of the following week, until a Thursday early-evening trip back to water Sophie's abandoned plants and gather up her crop of tomatoes. At first glance, it seemed that nothing had changed. The security system continued to declare no intruders and Sophie began to seriously regret wasting her limited resources on a system that was now obliged to record nothing. It was not until she stepped into her yard that her swallowing reflex informed her that something was wrong. It was too green. Her tomato plants were missing their tomatoes, not just the ripe red ones but all of them, even the tiny pale green ones. The trusses were bare to their very tips. She knelt down to check around the pots: perhaps some strange affliction had caused her plants to shed their fruit. She knew that was a daft idea but she checked anyway. She glanced up as Sam appeared in the doorway. Framed alongside an unfamiliar smiley face roughly chalked beside the kitchen window.

'Soph, we must have left the landing light on last time we were here… What's up?'

'Someone's stolen my tomatoes.'

'What?'

She pointed at the wall. Sam stepped outside to take a look, grabbed Sophie's arm and pulled her back into the kitchen, closed the back door and locked it, pulled her along to open the front door and told her to wait on the step whilst he checked the house. Sophie watched him look in the lounge. She stepped inside and tugged at his arm as he went to climb the stairs. 'Do you think somebody's been inside the house?'

'Yes.'

'But the security camera hasn't recorded anything.'

'Like Blake said, no security system defeats everyone.' He inclined his head towards the lounge. 'Things have been moved.'

'What things?' She edged towards the lounge door and peered inside. It took her a moment to realise what was different. Laura's playpen had been turned upside down.

Sam pulled her arm. 'Go back outside. I'll check the bedrooms.'

'But what if someone's up there? In a wardrobe or...'

'Sophie, that's not likely. Just wait outside.'

Sophie stood on the bottom step and tried to hear above the sound of traffic. Five minutes passed. Then ten. She was about to yell through the front door when Sam appeared and beckoned for her to come back inside.

'I think there's been a pretty thorough search. But whoever's been here, they're good. No evidence apart from things they wanted you to see. Your tomatoes are in the toilet. And there's a message on the bathroom mirror.'

'What message?'

'Another smiley face. I phoned Blake. He's meeting me here later. I'll take you back to Greenfields first.'

'Are you sure there's no one up there?'

'Yes. Get your things.'

'I ought to water my tomatoes.'

'They're in the toilet.'

'There are tomato flowers.'

'Right. Hurry up.'

–

On the drive back, Sophie WhatsApped Jesse to check on Laura and discovered a message from Suzie sent two days earlier: *Sorry about lack of communication. At my mother's til end next week. Nauseous. Hope all well. Suzie x*

Sophie texted back: *Just rest. Call me when you're back.*

'Who are you texting?' said Sam.

'Suzie. She's at her mum's feeling sick.'

He said nothing so Sophie resumed checking her messages. But something started to niggle at her. She stared through the windscreen and tried to work out what it was. It had to be something to do with Suzie because that's when the niggle had started. About her staying with her mother? Being pregnant? Then she frowned. 'Sam, I've been thinking about Suzie telling the police she had no knowledge of Jonah's laptop. But he'd been seeing her for three months. Staying over with her when he was supposedly away on business. So, she must have seen it because he always had it with him. He used to play Solitaire on it if he couldn't sleep.'

'They didn't find it when they searched her flat.'

Sophie watched him for a moment. 'How do *you* know?'

'Because Blake phoned me back. When you were watering your plants. To let me know the crime scene investigators would be accompanying him. I asked him about the laptop.'

'And he told you?'

'Yes. And he said it was advisable for us to stay with Jesse until it's located.'

Sophie folded her arms, which tended to help her thought processes. 'But if he thinks there might be people looking for it, I ought to warn Suzie, in case they know about her. I'll wait and phone her next week, so I don't spoil her holiday.' Sam drove on and Sophie continued to mull things over. 'It must have been terrible for her that day, seeing Jonah carried away in an ambulance then discovering he'd been lying to her.' She glanced at Sam but he seemed preoccupied. 'I feel really sorry for her.' She frowned. 'Sam, are you listening to me? I said I feel sorry for Suzie.'

'Me too.'

–

When they arrived back at Greenfields, Katie's car was there. 'Sam, do you think Katie and Jesse will move in together?'

'Do you mean, will Katie come and live here in Jesse's Kingdom?'

'Yes, I suppose that's what I mean.'

'Don't ask me. I'm as much an observer as you are.'

'Hasn't he said anything?'

'Only that he was relieved that immediately after the sex act she didn't stab him and consume his remains.'

–

The following day, Inspector Blake phoned Sophie to say that forensics had failed to find any additional evidence of the intrusion into Sophie's property. They were clearly dealing with experienced lawbreakers with a macabre sense of humour. The security system had been compromised and was essentially useless against the intention of such adept criminals. As, indeed, were most security systems. Sophie hurried through, primarily to tell Sam but also to find out whether, this time, the inspector had actually opted to communicate with her first. She found him watching the local news. The screen showed an image of a crumpled car...

> ...*Hampshire police are investigating a fatal accident, which occurred in the early hours of this morning along the A354 south of Salisbury. No other vehicles were involved and it is believed that the driver, who has been identified as a Mr Leonard Watkins of Farnham, might have fallen asleep at the wheel. Apparently, Mr Watkins' car left the carriageway and collided with a tree. Police are advising motorists that if they feel tiredness coming on to pull over immediately and take a sleep before continuing their journey... And here is Carl Dawson with the weather...*

'Sam, did Inspector Blake phone you to say forensics found nothing of any use?'

Sam switched off the TV. 'Yeh. I told him to phone you directly.'

Europol

'Officer Barnes, perhaps you would like to talk me through these latest developments?'

'Yes, sir. Essentially, we believe we have identified the Downs body. Following confirmation from forensics regarding the likely age and origins of the victim's tattoo, we've been coordinating with Europol. More particularly with the Czech police. We requested that an investigation be carried out on their missing-persons records, particularly those concerning minors that disappeared during the last seven years. We presumed that this would more than cover the likely period of incarceration suggested by the three successive pregnancies. Available DNAs were compared with those of the victim, but nothing was discovered. However, the Czech police elected to investigate earlier cases and came up with a partial match with a sibling of Galina Novák, abducted at the age of seven and recorded as having a small heart-shaped tattoo on her left shoulder.'

Director Short shook his head. 'Seven years old? But this means that the child would have been confined for, what, ten years or more?'

'Just over eleven years from time of abduction to her death. Apparently, the family have never stopped trying to trace her. Although both parents are now deceased, the search has been taken up by three older siblings. Arrangements are being made for two of the sisters to see the body. This might well be closure for them, although not the kind of closure they'll be happy with. It's worth mentioning that the successful match has led to further joint investigations of instances of the abduction of young girls over the last *twenty* years. And there seems to be another possible: early indications that a young woman washed up in Plymouth last year is a match with a nine-year-old child that went missing in Romania thirteen years ago.'

'*Thirteen years?* Barnes, this seems to be an extraordinarily long period of time for these practices to have stayed beneath our radar.'

'Indeed, sir, and that would, in turn, suggest a very sophisticated level of organisation. And, from what we can gather, a significant amount of *professional* assistance.'

'Are you saying you suspect…'

'Sir, the investigation is ongoing.'

26

Living together in their three-roomed penthouse continued well into a second week, without a single harsh word, despite Sam's inconvenience at having to pack most of his books into cardboard boxes. Sophie stood, arms folded, watching him to guarantee that he didn't crawl into a corner and start reading. Laura also encouraged the packing process by sitting on his 1945 first edition of *Sparkling Cyanide*. Sophie quickly imprisoned her in her playpen. Her mobile rang. Sam picked it up.

'It's Rosemary.'

Sophie hurried over and grabbed her phone, asked if everything was OK. Yes, Rosemary said, everything was almost OK, although the hospital had been in contact about future plans for Robert. He was improving remarkably for someone who had suffered a skull fracture just five weeks earlier and had been moved to a general ward. Apparently, he was now quite lucid and had regained full use of his leg and fingers. However, his memory was still not right. Although he was able to remember his Exeter life, he was still very vague about the previous five years and had no recollection of the time immediately prior to the accident.

Sophie's stomach churned as the subject of her last week or so of denial was jettisoned back into her life. She mentioned the break-in at her house and her move to Sam's attic. Rosemary made supportive comments. Then came her bombshell: since she had no intention of having Robert back living with her, she had consulted a lawyer about the likelihood of her being able to keep her house and had been advised that, since the property was jointly owned, the courts would probably decide in her daughters' favour. Sophie asked if she had detailed Robert's injuries. Rosemary said she'd mentioned them. Sophie asked where Robert was expected to go upon leaving the rehabilitation unit and Rosemary said in no uncertain terms that she didn't care where he went as long as it wasn't anywhere near her. He'd need care and she had no intention of providing it. And, by the way, had she managed to contact Heidi? Sophie said yes, but she was actually called Suzie and was not really in the picture, thanked Rosemary for the update and ended the call.

Sam looked at her over his non-glasses. 'What was all that about?' Sophie summarised. Sam listened stony-faced. 'Right, well, this is nothing to do with you now.' He watched her say nothing. 'Sophie, love, tell me you are not going to involve yourself further in this disgusting man's life.' Still she said nothing. Sam looked irritated. 'OK, tell me what crazy ideas are currently going through your head.'

'He'll have to have carers to start with.'

'Not you, Sophie. No way!'

'I know. Social Services will have to arrange it.'

'And?'

'Well, he'll have to be living somewhere Social Services can attend him.'

Sam walked over and leant against his desk. 'Please tell me you're not thinking of letting him move back into your house.'

'It's empty. And his things are there.'

'Not all of them. Most of them are in Exeter.'

'Sam, I really have to do this.'

'No, you don't!'

'I do. Sam, how could I ever tell Laura that I let her injured father be homeless? I know he was abandoning us. But I'm here with you now. So, I won't even have to see him.'

'And who do you think will be cooking his meals and doing his washing and listening to the lying bastard moan about smells?'

'Social Services will sort it out.'

'They won't. Not long-term. Once he's deemed able to fend for himself, any extras will have to be paid for. Who's going to do that? I would imagine all his accounts are frozen pending criminal investigation. And if they can prove he's been wrongfully acquiring money, then his assets will be sequestered until judgement. Sophie, it would be craziness to involve yourself in his dealings. And what about Josie? The house is half hers. She won't want to be charitable towards him. Even if *you* don't want anything, Josie would expect him to pay rent.'

'How do you know what Josie would expect?'

'I phoned her.'

'What? When did you phone her?'

'Yesterday. I got her number off your phone. You really ought to put a password on it.'

'Why didn't you tell me you'd spoken to her?'

'Because I phoned to introduce myself, and to reassure her that you were safe with me. And I discovered that she'd never heard of me. So, I've been nervous to mention it.'

'Did you tell her about Jonah being Robert Perrin and about Rosemary and the police?'

'No. I just said we were friends and you were staying with me because you were not happy living in the house where it all happened. Sophie, she still thinks you're with Jonah.'

Sophie turned away and caught sight of Laura accusing her through the bars of her playpen and, suddenly desperate for air and solitude, she fled out onto the landing. Sam called after her but she was already running down the stairs, out the front door, round past the rose beds and through the gate into the water gardens. She found a seat, threw herself down and at last embraced the tears she had been denying herself since, well, since the last time she'd cried. Time passed. But not very much time. And suddenly someone was sitting beside her.

'What's up?' said Jesse.

Clearly, there was no way that Sophie could summon language whilst sobbing into her hands. She felt Jesse's arm around her and feared she might asphyxiate.

'Hey, come on, Soph, you'll be sick if you carry on like this. Tell me what's happened. Is Laura OK? You haven't accidentally broken my brother, have you?'

She turned her head into his chest and smelled that same reassuring perfume that was Sam's. He let her cry uninterrupted until…

'Jess, would you take Laura for a minute?'

Sophie looked up to see Sam standing beside his brother, Laura wriggling in his arms. She pulled herself upright, spluttered an apology and tried unsuccessfully to wipe the tear splodges away from Jesse's shirt. He stood up, took charge of Laura and carried her away to feed the fish. Sam took his place, his hands in his lap. 'I'm sorry, Soph. I shouldn't have phoned Josie without telling you. And I should have realised how hurt you must still be. I just haven't wanted to believe you still have feelings for Jonah. But…'

'No!' Sophie wiped her face. 'I don't have feelings for him. That man in hospital is a man I never knew. A poisonous man, who used all his considerable intelligence to cheat people. I'm embarrassed I believed his lies, and I didn't want my little sister to know how foolish I've been. When my dad left and my mum fell apart, Josie needed me to make sense of it all. I didn't want her to think that history was repeating itself.' She paused to breathe. 'I'll phone her this evening and tell her everything. And, Sam, Jonah can't hurt me as long as I have you. But I know it wouldn't be right to let him be homeless while the house he's lived in is standing empty. Please don't hate me for it, because if I lost you…'

Sam touched his finger against her lips. 'I understand. I'm not happy about it, but I understand, OK? And, sweetheart, I could never hate you. Whatever happens. We'll sort this out between us. Get some advice about limited tenancies. And we can speak to Josie about rent.' He sighed. 'And, this Saturday, we'll ask Jess and Katie to sit Laura while we go and visit Jonah and his alter ego. See for ourselves what he can and can't remember. You can introduce me as the new man in your life and see how the bastard handles it.'

Early evening, Sophie phoned her sister to tell her what she had already guessed about Sam. What Josie had not guessed was that Sophie had been co-habiting with a criminal fornicator for the last five years. She listened without interrupting then responded by inviting Sophie and Sam to come and watch the cows as soon as possible. Sophie said that they would love to do that, rang off and spent the next ten minutes rehearsing her call to Suzie, fearful that she might inadvertently blurt out some random declaration about gangsters. Eventually, with Sam beside her, she put the phone on speaker and dialled. It was Suzie's mother who answered so there was an unanticipated wait whilst she fetched her daughter, during which time Sophie's resolve disintegrated.

'Hello, Sophie, has something happened?'

'No, I just thought I'd update you on Jonah. He's apparently much improved. And I need to warn you that…'

'Have you been to see him?'

'Not recently. We're driving down this Saturday. Suzie, the police…'

'Do you know if he remembers me?'

'I think he has some memory problems. But, Suzie, I need to…'

'So, he probably doesn't remember me.'

Sophie looked at Sam and raised her eyebrows. She took a deep breath and changed tack. 'Anyway, Suzie, how are you? Is the nausea still bad?'

'It's not too awful if I eat something every twenty minutes.'

'Yes, I remember that. Suzie, the police are trying to find Jonah's laptop and Inspector Blake, the detective in charge, says you had no idea where it is. It seems to have gone missing and there's a lot of really important…'

'I hid it in my car.'

Sam got to his feet and mimed something Sophie didn't understand.

'Suzie, I think you should give it to the police. I mean, if you like, Sam and I can drive over and collect it and take it to the police for you.' She noticed Sam nodding. 'When are you going to be home?'

'I'll be back around Sunday lunchtime.'

Sam signalled to say he was going to check Laura and left Sophie and Suzie chatting. When, eventually, he stepped back into the room, Sophie was staring at her silent phone. 'Sam, even if we collect the laptop and take it to the police, the gangsters won't know Suzie doesn't have it. So, she might still be in danger.'

'But you didn't say that to her?'

'No. What shall we do?'

He shook his head. 'I suppose we'd better warn her.'

–

Saturday arrived too soon. Sophie was frantically unrelaxed about seeing Jonah in his newly sentient state and all attempts by Sam to calm her were met with stony silence, so he resigned himself to watching her fret over a Costa coffee. However, realising that the caffeine was making things worse, he pushed their mugs together and got to his feet. 'Come on, there's no putting this off. We could call into the shop and buy him some grapes.'

'He doesn't like grapes.'

'OK, maybe some peppermint creams for the man in our life.'

'Sam, please stop pissing me off!'

'Right! You coming?'

She sagged forward. 'I'm sorry. I really don't want to do this.'

–

Since being moved to the general ward, the sister explained, Jonah had been unpleasant to anybody that had been placed in an adjacent bed, so that morning he had been transferred to a side room normally reserved for private patients. Sophie apologised on his behalf, but that seemed to come nowhere near to compensating for the inconvenience. The sister offered a few details about the rehabilitation programme then directed Sophie and Sam to a side room, where Jonah lay in obnoxious isolation, apparently asleep, a single monitor recording his status. His bandages had been removed to reveal his ear, back where it ought to be, although at first glance – actually at all further glances – Sophie thought that they might have reattached it slightly askew.

'Do you think we should wake him?' she whispered.

Jonah opened his eyes and looked at her. 'Who are you?' he snapped.

Sophie felt Sam's hand on her arm. 'I'm Sophie. And this is my partner, Sam.'

Jonah's mouth twitched into a momentary sneer. 'What do you want?'

She fought to maintain enthusiasm. 'We've come to see how you are. Sister says you're recovering at record speed. And we're all trying to work out what's best for—'

'Where's Rosie?' he interrupted.

'Rosemary's fine. And Issy and Laura. They're at home. But—'

'Where's my car?'

Sam broke his silence. 'Unfortunately, it was stolen, so you'll need to make a claim when you get out of here.' He fetched the chair for Sophie then wandered over to look out of the window whilst she struggled on with the conversation.

'We've put all your things in the spare room,' she said. Actually, most of his things went to the tip and his phones and the bag of money were with the police, but Sophie saw no point in complicating things with the truth. After all, Jonah never did. 'Sister said you'll need a few weeks' rehabilitation. And then you'll just visit as an outpatient. You'll probably need some help at first. I think Social Services…'

'When's Rosie driving over?'

Sam turned to speak. 'We get the impression she has no immediate plans to do so. Issy and Laura are back at school so she doesn't have a lot of spare time.' Jonah glared at him and said nothing, although the monitor beside him displayed a few peaks of concern. Sam approached the bed. 'Summer's over, Jonah. You've missed all the good weather in here. And young Suzie's had to cancel your holiday plans. Edinburgh, wasn't it?' Sophie touched Sam's arm for him to stop, so he returned to the window and resumed his observation of the concrete outside.

She staggered on. 'Suzie has been asking after you…'

'I don't know who she is.'

Sam was unable to remain silent. 'It would really upset Suzie to hear that, Jonah. She's pregnant, you know. We're calling in to see her tomorrow to pick up your laptop and take it to the police. To help them with their enquiries.' He watched Jonah's eyes go wide. 'And it's a pity you can't remember Sophie, because she's your best bet for having somewhere to go when you leave this place. And by the way, we've given your bag of money to the police.'

Sophie gasped. Jonah closed his eyes. The traces on the monitor became very busy, so busy that an alarm must have sounded somewhere because a nurse came hurrying into the room to assess the situation. She looked at Sophie. 'Mr Perrin seems to be distressed. Perhaps it would be better if you stepped outside for the moment. The doctors think it's best to avoid any upsets for the time being. You can wait in…'

'No, that's OK,' said Sam, walking towards the door. 'We have to be getting back to relieve the babysitter.'

Sophie wished Jonah goodbye then hurried after Sam. As soon as they were clear of the ward, she pulled at his arm. 'Why on earth did you goad him like that?'

'I wanted to see exactly what would upset the bastard.'

'What?'

'He's lying, Soph. That guy's bloody unbelievable. Despite all the trauma, and the brain damage, he's still *compos mentis* enough to be able to spin his lies. Pretending that he doesn't know who Suzie is, doesn't remember you, although he remembers his car. Remembers that Rosemary has to *drive over* to get here. And he's clearly concerned about that laptop. Don't worry, we can phone later to see if I've actually managed to kill the creep.'

–

The following afternoon, Sam and Sophie drove over to collect Jonah's laptop and Sophie discovered that Suzie was renting a small, one-bedroomed flat in a gated development awash with security cameras. She experienced a slight additional insult that Jonah had been leaving her comparatively desirable house to move into such a minute rented property, but then, there really was no understanding his priorities. Although, how he thought he was ever going to fit the TV, the Bose and the new freezer into that tiny place was unimaginable.

They stayed with Suzie for a while to tell her about the police investigation and the various break-ins, tried to warn her to lock her doors and keep a look out for any suspicious people loitering around, but she didn't seem to be unduly interested. In fact, despite her previous declarations, all she appeared to be interested in was hearing more news about Jonah. Sophie wondered whether she saw herself having any further involvement with him when she ought to be distancing herself as far away from him as possible. Although, she recalled, pregnancy did change the way you thought about things.

In the Air

'Ah, Mr Mann, Mr Sokolov, how did the errand proceed today?'

'Very well, Mr Jones. I 'ad a nice talk with Mr Perrin and I managed to persuade 'im to tell me all about that automatic messaging system of 'is. And we are now able to reassure you that the warning which was received is all there is to worry about for the moment.'

'Are you telling me that *no* incriminating data will automatically be dispatched to the National Crime Agency?'

'Yes, Mr Jones. 'owever, I did gather that to guarantee 'is own safety, Mr Perrin 'as indeed accumulated a great deal of information concerning various bodies, including the Organisation, which is 'id away where no one will find it. And, if we leave 'im alone then no one will ever see it.'

Thaddeus Jones clasped his hands together. 'Was there any indication as to what form this data takes? I presume it would be held on some kind of digital storage device. A hard drive? A USB flash? Something of the kind?'

'Well, sir, Mr Sokolov believes it might be in the air, on account of us 'aving thoroughly searched all Mr Perrin's properties and found nothing.'

'You mean in the cloud?'

'Yes, sir.'

'What else did Perrin tell you?'

'Not very much, sir. On account of 'is being taken poorly during my visit.'

Thaddeus Jones wandered over to his window to observe the Westminster skyline. 'Mr Mann, whatever assurances Mr Perrin offers, we cannot allow this data's continued existence. It needs to be acquired and destroyed. Do whatever it takes.'

27

After the initial enthusiastic greetings, as Sophie reclaimed her place in the office hierarchy, things slowly took a turn for the worse. Unlike Sophie, office politics had not enjoyed a year's worth of maternity leave. A few people she almost remembered had disappeared without trace and a couple of vibrant young things, both women, had taken their place and seemed to be attracting more attention than Sophie thought appropriate. One of them, Viola, had been given a desk in Sophie's old office on the second floor. In fact, she had been given Sophie's desk in Sophie's old office on the second floor and a different, slightly more dilapidated desk had been moved in alongside it for Sophie's return. Viola immediately saw Sophie's presence as a kind of demotion. That, in itself, would not have bothered Sophie, but what did bother her was Viola's incessant habit of whispering to herself as she prodded her keyboard. By mid-morning on that first day back, Sophie was already toying with the idea of handing in her notice, but she wasn't sure whether she would have to pay all her Statutory Maternity Pay back if she did so, because if that were the case she would be in financial ruin.

Just after noon, Viola's co-golden girl, Bella, dropped by to collect Viola for lunch, gave Sophie a condescending smile and then bustled Viola out of the door with some giggle-worthy anecdote about a pilot she had met at the weekend. Sophie's desire to condemn young women's brainlessness was tempered by the realisation that she was merely watching a rerun of herself, maybe six or seven years ago. In the days before her stable, long-term relationship with Jonah the unstable. She waited until the giggling had faded into the distance then phoned Sam to check that Laura was OK. Sam said he was teaching her to play the guitar. Slightly relieved, Sophie headed down to the coffee machine on the ground floor, where she ran into her one-time speed-dating buddy, Joanna.

'Sophie, why didn't you tell me you were back.' Joanna hurried over and they traded hugs. 'God, it hasn't been a whole year, has it? How's the baby… Laura? How's Jonah?'

Sophie took a step back and smiled. 'He's Robert.' The explanation, punctuated by gasps from Joanna, took the entire cup of coffee. And some.

Inevitably, Joanna asked, 'What are you going to do about it?'

Sophie spent another few minutes telling her about Sam. Joanna listened intently, determined not to allow a single detail to pass unrecorded, until her Supervisor popped his head through the door to tell her there was a call for her in the office. She re-hugged Sophie and hurried away. Sophie watched the door swing closed behind her, knowing with certainty that, by the end of the day, everybody in the entire organisation would be fully informed of her current status. On the positive side, it meant she wouldn't have to keep repeating herself.

The afternoon was quieter. Viola's need to whisper was clearly dulled by alcohol. Sophie threw herself into unravelling the explanation behind a missing consignment of Biohazard suits, edited an internal document regarding access to clinical trial data and by the end of the day was convinced that to continue working there was a crime against her own humanity.

–

Sophie trudged through Tuesday, spent Wednesday fretting about Thursday and Thursday rewriting her Section Manager's article in *Biowise*, the company magazine, whilst listening to Viola summarise her catalogue of previous boyfriends. The only thing driving her on was the promise of the next three days at home with Sam and Laura. That evening, with Laura asleep, she awarded herself a pre-supper bath, deep and redolent with the scent of wild rose and jasmine. And gradually, as she watched the candlelight flickering in the bubbles around her, her mind freed itself from the horror of her first week back at work. Sam brought her a glass of something sparkling. 'It might interest you to know that I'm considering a very large, circular bathtub for our new house. Jesse's having a breakdown about it since it offends his commitment to straight lines. It's for you to decide. Pie's ready in thirty minutes.'

Twenty minutes later, Sophie pulled on her bathrobe, hurried into the bedroom and came to a halt. She could hear music coming from the lounge, wandered through and found Sam sitting on the coffee table, playing his guitar. She sat down beside him and listened to him accompany himself to a perfect performance of *Make You Feel My Love*. He stopped playing and waited for Sophie's reaction. She ran her fingers along his sleeve.

'I didn't know you could play the guitar like that.'

'Ah, Sophie, my love, there are many things you don't know about me.'

–

Time passed. Inspector Blake made a brief weekend appearance at Greenfields to explain that a great deal of supplementary information had been recovered from Jonah's laptop, but would remain inconclusive without some additional key data needed to link names and trace the beneficiaries of Jonah's catalogue of false identities. With the guile of a committed puzzler, he had clearly stored these elsewhere. What they had so far was, at best, circumstantial. Essentially, they were still not able to nail him for anything other than tax fraud and money laundering. Remote site activity was being investigated but, so far, with zero success. Sophie explained that Jonah would never store data remotely on the understanding that cloud sites were the most efficient way of making your data available to the entire world. She asked Inspector Blake to keep her informed then left Sam to show him out whilst she returned to the summerhouse where Benz's party was still underway. After half an hour, she began to wonder why Sam hadn't appeared so she went to investigate and found him sitting at their dining table studying his computer screen.

'I was wondering where you were.'

Sam looked up unsmiling. 'You'd better see this. It's a piece of video footage that was on Jonah's laptop. Blake went against procedure and removed it on your behalf.' He pulled a chair next to him and waited as Sophie sat down. Then he started the sequence. It was a good half a minute before Sophie realised that she was watching herself, naked, her right side towards the camera, her hair swaying rhythmically across her face. The man she was astride was not easily identified since his head was not in the field of view but, since Jonah was the only person she had ever had sex with whilst being pregnant, very heavily pregnant, she had to presume it was him. She watched in disbelief. Sam interrupted her mounting hysteria.

'There's audio if you'd like to hear yourself. The best bit's coming up.'

'Sam, how the hell…!'

'Did you know about this?'

'Of course I didn't!'

'What a sick bastard. You look as if you're about to give birth.'

'I was. I was overdue. We'd not had sex for weeks. And, if you have sex, the prostaglandins in the semen can help induce labour. And if you have an orgasm…'

'That's about another three minutes away.'

'…It encourages the uterus to contract. Jonah was up for it. But I didn't know he was filming it. I would never have agreed to that. I don't remember seeing a camera.'

'It would have probably been concealed. Did it induce labour?'

'Yes. Laura was born the following afternoon. Oh my God, I'm about to…' She threw her hands over her eyes. 'Sam, turn it off!' Sam turned it off and sat back in his chair. Sophie looked at him. 'Please do not start with the wisecracks. I'm sorry you had to watch that. I'd hate to see you… Oh, God, who else has seen it? Did Inspector Blake watch it?'

'He didn't go into detail. Soph, I've given him my keys so he can check whether that camera's still there. Check out whether it's still filming and uploading to some remote site. It could be motion sensitive. Not likely, but it's a possibility.'

'What? You think it's been recording me since then?'

'And your latest partner.' He started to laugh. 'Sexy Sam the porno star.'

'Sam, you can't think this is funny.'

He became serious. 'Of course I don't. I'm hoping Jonah just made the video for his own entertainment, which, without your consent, is an infringement of your rights.'

Sophie got up and wandered over to collapse into the sofa. 'This is awful.'

'Actually, I thought it was hot. Can we have an early night?'

-

More time passed: Inspector Blake informed Sam that a small disconnected camera had been found inside the double socket above Sophie's dressing table; Sam resumed his teaching load at the college; the students moved back in next door to Sophie's empty house; Laura settled into her three days a week at the nursery; and Sophie became desensitised to Viola's morning whisperings and managed to complete her fourth week of churning out official documents without losing her mind.

Then on a Friday afternoon in early October, Sophie was at home waiting for Sam to get back after his morning lectures, when her mobile rang. It was May Barnet. After four weeks of conscientiously not thinking about him, Jonah was back in Sophie's life. Apparently, after a minor setback, which may have been stress-induced, he had rallied, although he was still suffering episodes of confusion. Functional MRI scans had been inconclusive regarding his memory loss, although, now that the tissue swelling was reduced, CT scans had indicated a much earlier skull fracture.

Sophie suffered an avalanche of guilt as she recalled Jonah's distress over Sam's deliberate provocation. She asked when the setback had occurred and was relieved when Mrs Barnet said that it had been just over three weeks ago, but different fears were awakened when she added that Mr Perrin's episode had occurred during a friend's visit. A rather rough-looking man who had not reappeared since. This may have been a coincidence, although the nursing staff had been instructed to report further visits from this same individual. Following two full weeks of rehabilitation, the doctors had decided it was almost time to consider accompanied trips to a permanent address. Perhaps towards the end of the month. Mrs Barnet's voice began to wobble slightly as she informed Sophie that Mrs Perrin had stated categorically that she would not accommodate her husband and was filing for divorce on the grounds of adultery and criminal behaviour. She had suggested that her husband might more appropriately return to his previous address in Surrey now that it was unoccupied.

Sophie felt her lips go numb. Rosemary had stitched her up. She needed to present her case before things got out of hand. 'Mrs Barnet, as Mrs Perrin mentioned, I no longer live in the house I shared with Mr Perrin, although I still part-own the house with my sister. My sister and I will allow Mr Perrin to occupy our property, for a limited period until it's sold.' She hadn't actually spoken to Josie about accommodating Jonah and was still sending her rent from her paltry wages. 'And I ought to point out that, since I have returned to work, I will not be available during Mr Perrin's visits to the house or to assist in any subsequent periods when he might be living there whilst seeking more permanent accommodation. I will try to arrange a trip over to discuss details, perhaps this coming Wednesday, when I will be happy to dispense keys into Social Services' safe-keeping.' Thank goodness for the last four weeks of garbage-speak.

Mrs Barnet paused before saying that would all be most kind, and the conversation was terminated. Sophie collapsed into the sofa and recalled her last discussion with Sam regarding Jonah's future accommodation. So, she did what anyone would do in the circumstances: she imprisoned Laura in her playpen then sat and stared mindlessly into the distance. Eventually, when she heard Sam's car pulling up outside, she quickly tidied around, switched on the coffee machine and selected the Prokofiev violin concerto she knew was his favourite. Moments later, Sam strode in, threw his satchel down and came to a halt.

'What's wrong, Soph?'

'What makes you ask that?'

'I'm used to coming home to baby squalor and nineties pop music. What's happened?'

Sophie sank back into the sofa. 'I've just had a call from May Barnet.'

'And?'

'About Jonah's living accommodation.'

He folded his arms. '*And?*'

'There's no need to be aggressive.'

'Sophie, I don't want you having anything to do with him.'

'I don't want to have anything to do with him either. I've told May Barnet he can be taken to my mother's house for the time being but that I won't be involved in the visits or when he's staying there. She said he still can't remember his recent past, which presumably means me and Laura. So, we're not really involved anyway.'

Sam pushed both his hands through his hair. 'Sophie, he's lying. I know he had a brain injury but it wasn't invasive enough for him to have retrograde amnesia.'

'So, suddenly you're an expert on the central nervous system, are you?'

'Now *you're* being aggressive. Sophie, this guy will ruin our lives if you let him.'

'I won't let him. I'm going over to see May Barnet next Wednesday. To give her my spare keys. I'll catch a train. So, you won't have to know anything about it.'

Sam exhaled frustration. 'My lectures are cancelled next Wednesday. There's a theatre trip: *Macbeth*. I already know the ending. I'll get someone to go instead of me so I can drive you there.' He stepped over and lifted her chin. 'Let's not argue about him.' He kissed her forehead. 'Now, shall we have some of your music?' He picked up the remote. 'What about *Bitter Sweet Symphony*? That seems appropriate.'

'I'd rather have nothing. There's enough noise in my head already. Sam, I think that bald gangster paid Jonah another visit. And, from what May Barnet said, it seems that whatever went on between them caused Jonah to take a turn for the worse.'

'Sounds like my kind of gangster. Did she say when it happened? Perhaps he's been captured on a security video. It'll give Inspector Blake something else to watch.'

–

That evening they drank a lot of prosecco and avoided the subject of Jonah. By nine thirty, Sophie was finding it difficult to keep her eyes open.

'I'm boring you already and we've only been together two months.'

'I'm just tired. We have to leave so much earlier to get Laura settled ever since that little boy, Hadrian, snatched Clown-face away from her.'

'I think that counts as foreplay in the under-twos.'

'And I can't be late into work. They're probably looking for an excuse to replace me with another young flunky who earns less.'

'You ought to tell them to stuff their job. I can support us both.'

'On part-time lecturer's pay? I already don't understand how you can afford your new house. With all those expensive tiles.'

'I told you, I get mate's rates. And, besides, my mother left me and Jesse a fair bit, so if you play your cards right…'

28

The meeting with May Barnet went well enough. Having reduced the waving at Laura to a minimum, she thanked Sophie for her Christian act of allowing Mr Perrin to occupy her house after he had treated her in such a disreputable manner, although Sophie got the distinct impression that Mrs Barnet disapproved of her speedily-found recovery with Sam. Or perhaps she disapproved of Sam; there was definitely an air of brusqueness in her voice whenever she spoke to him. But, quite honestly, Sophie didn't care. She handed over the keys and promised to check the house and remove all her personal effects, took Laura from Sam's arms and was about to go when May Barnet interrupted her leaving.

'Ms Denham, Social Services have contacted me regarding Mr Perrin's long-term care. His accounts appear to have been frozen, so that his financial contribution to his care package will not be available without lengthy application. Would you...'

Sam intervened. 'Mrs Barnet, Sophie is already paying her sister rent on Mr Perrin's behalf, for a house which could otherwise provide her with income. She has no shared finances with Mr Perrin and no further obligation, financial or otherwise, to his care. His wife, however, who I gather is attempting to take full possession of his Exeter property, would undoubtedly have joint assets. Have Social Services communicated with her?'

'Not with any success, Mr Barnes. Although, obviously, that route of support will continue to be investigated.' She clasped her hands together and Sophie wondered whether she was about to offer a prayer. But she didn't. Instead, she said, 'Mr Perrin's current *girlfriend* mentioned a large amount of jointly-owned cash that was in Mr Perrin's car at the time of his accident.' Her cheeks flushed with disapproval. 'Several thousands of pounds, I believe.'

Sophie stared at her. 'Suzie? You've spoken to Suzie Kay?'

Mrs Barnet looked apprehensive. 'She was here yesterday. Also, I believe, twice last week. I—'

Again, Sam interrupted. 'The money was handed over to the police. They regarded almost thirty-seven thousand pounds in the boot of a car as suspicious. If Miss Kay believes she has claim to some of it she will need to take that up with them.'

May Barnet offered an insincere smile. She turned to Sophie, who frowned back at her.

'Has Miss Kay often visited Mr Perrin?'

'Only the three times, as far as I'm aware.'

'Did he remember who she was?'

'I'm sorry, I don't know. It seems his ability to recall varies from day to day.'

Sophie felt Sam touch her arm.

'Soph, I'm sure Mrs Barnet will contact you if she needs to.'

Sophie paused then held out her hand. 'May, thank you for all your help.'

May Barnet seemed relieved that the meeting had come to an end. She stood to shake Sophie's hand then followed her to the door, waited whilst she secured Laura into her pushchair then waved. 'God bless, Laura. You be a good girl and help mummy.' She turned her diminishing smile towards Sam and watched as they walked away.

As Sam pushed Laura towards the main exit, Sophie leaned close and whispered, 'She really doesn't like you, does she?'

'I'm utterly heartbroken.'

–

Sam paid the parking machine then wheeled out into the fresh autumn air. Sophie watched him negotiate the pushchair between the rows of parked cars and wondered why May Barnet could possibly not like him. Perhaps it was because he had been so ready to step into Jonah's vacated shoes. Or perhaps she was contemptuous of the whole adultery–infidelity–unmarried-sex situation and she needed someone upon whom she could focus her disgust. Perhaps. As they were pulling away, she considered May Barnet's recent revelation.

'Sam, what do you think about Suzie visiting Jonah?'

'Maybe she was checking out her cash.'

'Do you think some of it really was hers?'

'God knows.' He slotted the exit card into the barrier, waited for the bar to rise and drove out towards the road. 'Let's eat, I'm starving.'

Sophie's brow furrowed. 'But why would they need all that cash?'

'I dread to think. Perhaps they were planning to go somewhere or do something and Jonah didn't want to leave a card trail. Perhaps he didn't want to risk Suzie discovering his name on his credit cards. Whatever the reason, if it involved Jonah, it involved deceit.'

Sophie sighed. 'Do you think Jonah will be safe at the house? What if those people try to get that missing data from him?'

'I couldn't fucking care less, Soph. I just hope that, if they decide to kill him, they don't damage your house in the process.'

–

Sophie festered for the rest of the week and the weekend, desperate to know how much Suzie had contributed to Jonah's blue-bag hoard of cash. So, on Monday, she waited for Viola to leave and rang Suzie, inviting her to meet for a quick lunch, perhaps on Thursday, that is if she could take a longer lunch break. After a brief and pregnant silence, Suzie said she'd love to.

–

They were both well into their pizzas when Sophie broached the subject of Suzie's visits to Jonah's bedside.

'May Barnet mentioned you'd been to see Jonah a couple of times.' Suzie failed to respond. 'I was wondering how he is.' Suzie remained silent. 'I haven't seen him since last month and they've stopped giving me updates. And I'm not sure whether it's appropriate for me to call.'

'He's much better. They're taking him to your house for assessment. It was kind of you to let him go back there.'

Sophie smiled and changed the subject, mentioned her return to office drudgery, Laura's crèche and eventually homed in on her underlying purpose. 'Suzie, why did you give Jonah all that money? We found it in his car and gave it to the police. We had no way of knowing some of it was yours. You never mentioned it to me.'

'I didn't know whether you'd found it. And I was embarrassed to mention it.'

'But why did you and Jonah need all that cash? How much of it was yours?'

'Ten thousand. It was towards our deposit on a house. The person who was selling it said they'd reduce the price if we paid in cash.' She rummaged in her bag and pulled out some folded sheets, opened them out and showed Sophie an estate agent's details. At least it looked like an estate agent's details. But what she actually showed Sophie was two sheets detailing the Perrins' Topsham Road house located at an address in Bournemouth. The photo of the lounge included a small, sleeping dog. 'It's probably sold by now,' said Suzie. Sophie handed back the sheets and said she was sure Suzie would eventually get her money back.

That evening Sophie told Sam about her conversation with Suzie. He was irritated that she'd failed to mentioned her lunch date before it happened. She brushed his irritation aside. 'Given the fact that Jonah was not hoping to purchase the house that he already owned, what do you think he needed thirty-seven thousand pounds for?'

'I don't know, Soph. Time will tell.'

–

The weeks passed. Sophie and Sam continued to observe the tumultuous relationship that was building between Sam's brother and Sophie's best friend and, whenever possible, they visited Sam's site and watched Jesse's architectural vision emerge from the chaos of bricks and cement. College reading week began and Sam was at home and able to take care of Laura and save her from the evil advances of Hadrian the bully. Then, the following mid-week, Sophie received a call informing her that, the coming Monday, Jonah was to be accompanied on his first visit to her house. Sam responded to the news by purchasing Sophie a new mobile with a new number, arranging a new email address and setting up replacement bank, Ebay and Amazon accounts. Sophie hoped this might be an overreaction.

'Do you really think all this is necessary?'

'I'm not risking Jonah knowing where you are. You're still officially at the same address.'

'But why do I have to have a new mobile number? I've had that same one for years.'

'Because as soon as he gets his hands on any computer equipment, he'll be able to trace the location of your phone, and if he doesn't know the number it will slow him down. He'll undoubtedly be able to work it out by checking the call histories of people you contact. People like Suzie and Rosemary. So, make as many calls as you can from the office. And delete all texts and logged calls immediately. And don't download emails.' He handed her a slim silver case. 'And keep your phone in here when you're not using it.'

'What this?'

'It's an expensive and very stylish radiodense mobile case. I've cancelled geolocation on your new phone, but this will block any attempts at tracking. And it'll prevent the screen from cracking next time you drop it on the floor.'

'Why do you know all this stuff?'

'Because I'm an aspiring criminal.'

Social Services emailed Sophie regarding Jonah's progress and by the end of the second week of visits, they reported that he was deemed capable of moving into the house, with daily supervision to confirm that he was coping. Sophie forced all this from her mind and spent her days at home working on a duplicate site map, marking out Sam's new gardens. Jesse nipped up to take a look at her work and was impressed.

'Have you had much experience with garden design?'

'I did some courses a few years back. And I used to volunteer at Mately Gardens. There was an old gardener there, who used to say "it's all very well you young people drawing your plans on pieces of paper, but what you really have to do to be a Capability Brown or a Gertrude Jekyll is be able to imagine the finished garden inside your mind. You have to be able to smell the herbs in the herb garden and the scent of the honeysuckle and stock in the early evening. And you have to be able to see the irises reflected in the water and feel the wind blowing through the trees long after you've become dust."'

'And can you do that?'

'Yes, I think so.'

He put his head to one side and looked at her. Then he resumed reading her notes. After a while, he sat back and folded his arms. 'So, why are you working in a crappy office writing short-term corporate garbage when you could be creating beautiful gardens for the future?'

'My mother wasn't sure gardening was an appropriate job for a *gal*.'

'I see.' He laughed. 'When I told my mother I wanted to be an architect she said, "*They're just glorified builders, dear.*" But I was able to change her mind by building this. Sandi and I brought her here to see the finished thing a couple of months before she died.' He paused. 'Benz was just over a year old. She never saw Jake but she knew Sandi was pregnant again. She knew Jake was on his way.'

Sophie had never heard Jesse say his wife's name before. She didn't know how to respond but she knew that silence would be worse. 'Was Sam in Hong Kong when your mother died?'

'He got home in time to see her. He came home for good to help with the boys when I lost Sandi.'

'Sam told me. It must have been terrible for you. With two little boys. But they are the most marvellous kids I've ever met. You and Sam have done a great job.'

Jesse smiled. 'It's amazing what you can achieve by showering children with gifts and letting them do whatever they please.'

'Don't talk rot. They're perfectly behaved tiny gentleman.'

'I'm probably not going to tell them that. It might go to their heads.'

Other Women

'I would like to assure you, Mr and Mrs Carrington, that we manage every aspect of our sponsorships with the utmost discretion. I gather that you would prefer anonymity during your stay in the United Kingdom and I am pleased to be able to offer luxury accommodation, support and, should the need arise, temporary identities for you both.'

'In order for the validity of my wife's pregnancy not to be challenged within our community, Mr Jones, we would need to be resident in the UK for an extended period, preferably a ten-month period.'

'Quite so. This is, indeed, a highly recommended option but obviously not always possible for sponsoring parents due to the obvious cost of such a long sojourn.'

'Cost is not a consideration.'

'Quite. I...'

'And my wife has expressed concerns regarding the status of the surrogate mother.'

'Our host mothers are chosen with the utmost care. All details of their medical history are thoroughly checked. These women that have chosen to offer their services are all happily married with children of their own. Many of them profess to enjoying the pregnant state but in addition they are pleased to be able to offer to other couples the happiness that children can bestow upon a family. I notice that you have opted for a multiple.'

'Yes, identical twin boys. How are you able to guarantee this?'

'The techniques which we have pioneered here, and in our additional laboratories in Dubai, boast a very high degree of certainty of outcome, as our explanatory documentary will demonstrate. So, now, if you have no further questions, I will ask Nurse Megan to escort you to our small media lounge where all will be explained. Light refreshments will, of course, be available. If, following this demonstration, you have any further questions, I will be only too pleased to assist.'

29

Sophie preferred not to think about Jonah living in her house and, instead, concentrated on the things at hand: the inanity of her job; Laura's displeasure at having to share a crèche with an infant sociopath; the slowly evolving house that she was to share with Sam; and the proximity of Christmas. It was approaching Tuesday lunch hour, towards the end of November when it occurred to her that her Christmas tree decorations were in the loft at her mother's house. She hadn't thought of them all those weeks ago, when she'd been squashing things into Jesse's van. She didn't want them to be there, imprisoned in a house occupied by Jonah, denied a Christmas tree for the first time since she was a child, so she waited for Viola to leave then phoned Sam. She was about to ring off when he answered.

'Soph. Anything wrong?'

'No.' She could hear raucous laughter in the background, laughter too deep and vulgar to belong to students. 'Are you in a pub?'

'Blimey, I knew you'd been tracking me. I'm at a spur-of-the-moment faculty meeting. But I'm only drinking shandy. Are you OK?'

Sophie rolled her eyes at her keyboard. 'Yes, but I've just realised that all my Christmas decorations are in the loft at my mother's place.'

'They're probably OK. I can't see Jonah going up to have a poke about. There's no light up there. The cops had to use torches when they were checking it out.' He paused. 'Are you about to tell me you want me to go over and ask Jonah if I can look in his loft? Can't we buy new decorations?'

'They're the same ones I've had since I was little.'

'Right. I'll drive over later.'

'Sam, I can hardly hear you.'

'I said, I'll drive over later.'

She paused. 'I'd better come too… I mean… you'll never find them.'

'Ah, Sophie! OK, why don't you text Jesse and ask if he'll sit Laura. And phone Social Services and explain that we'll be visiting Jonah around seven.'

–

They parked in the back road and walked round to the front door, but just as they drew even with Mrs Davies' closed curtains, Sophie tugged at Sam's sleeve. 'What if he overreacts?'

'Social Services told him to expect us, didn't they?'

'I assumed they would, but they didn't actually say they were going to. And I don't think there'd be anyone there with him. I think they just visit during the daytime.'

'Well, we've come this far. Come on, it's your house. And besides, I get the impression you're more than a little curious. A little interested to see how he's managing without you.'

'I'm not!'

'Right. Well, I am.' He pulled her towards the door, climbed the steps, rang the doorbell then stepped down beside her.

At first there was no answer, but at last footsteps could be heard approaching. The door opened and Sophie took a step back in surprise. 'Suzie!'

Suzie returned the surprise. 'Sophie!'

'Didn't anyone mention we were calling round?' said Sam.

Suzie looked nonplussed. 'I don't think so. Would you like to come in? I'm making supper.'

Sophie was caught between a polite response, whereby she ought to offer to come back later, and downright outrage at being asked whether she wanted to go into her own house, which was currently accommodating, rent-free, her cheating ex-partner and quite possibly his treat-me-like-a-doormat pregnant other woman. 'Are you living here, Suzie?'

Suzie seemed oblivious to the unreasonableness of the situation. 'I come over most evenings to make supper. After the carer leaves. We watch a bit of TV and I make sure he gets to bed OK.' She moved aside to invite them in. 'I'd better check the casserole.' She hurried away to the kitchen. *Doormat*.

As Sophie stepped into her hallway, she caught sight of Jonah, sitting in her lounge, on her sofa that had been violated in a search for evidence of his villainy. Damn it, she was not going to allow the absurdity of the situation get the better of her. She strode straight in to confront him and, with confident familiarity, said, 'Hello, Jonah, do you remember me now?'

Jonah glanced up from his crossword book. 'Sophie, isn't it?'

Sam was right behind her. 'You know damn well it is. We've come over to collect some things from the loft.' He squeezed Sophie's arm. 'I presume the ladder is still in the back porch. Are you OK here?'

'Yes.' She touched his hand. 'There are three boxes with "Xmas" written on them.' She watched him leave. Then, without taking her eyes off Jonah, she put her bag down on the coffee table, removed her coat and sat down in the armchair. 'How are you, Jonah? Or, should I say, Robert?'

'I'm improving every day, they say.'

'Didn't they tell you I was coming over?' She noticed Jonah's copy of *Lord of the Rings* back on the side table. His pewter tankard beside it.

'I'm not sure. I forget things,' he said. The corner of his mouth twitched upward. 'They tell me this is your house. And that I used to live here. It's very kind of you to let me stay while Suzie helps me sort out my affairs.'

Sophie could feel her blood turning to bile. 'Why don't you cut the crap, Jonah? We both know this is all a performance and poor Suzie's your latest victim.'

'She tells me I'm the father of her child.'

Sophie stared in disbelief, but their exchange was interrupted by the sound of an approaching ladder. Sam stopped to check Sophie was OK then carried on up the stairs.

'Be careful,' called Jonah. He smirked at Sophie. 'He seems like a nice guy.'

In that instant, Sophie truly hated him. 'Josie wants us to sell this place as soon as possible. I presume that if the police don't clap you in irons, you'll try and set up home with Suzie, although God knows how you think you'll manage with Suzie pregnant and no money coming in. I take it you know Rosemary's planning to have your Exeter house.'

Jonah glanced towards the empty hall. 'She'll be lucky. The ungrateful cow! If she thinks she's going to stay there with her dumb-blond lover boy, she's mistaken.'

Sophie was appalled. She felt the need to defend Rosemary but, just at that moment, Suzie stepped into the room, carrying a tray with Jonah's obligatory pre-supper glass of milk and digestive biscuit. As she bent over to balance the tray on his lap, Jonah caught Sophie's eye and gave an unpleasant smile. 'Thank you, Suzie darling,' he said.

Suzie beamed at him, asked Sophie if she would like some tea. Sophie said thank you but no, she wanted to get back. And she ought to check Sam was OK. She stepped into the hallway and called. Sam's complaints echoed down from the loft: the spiders were bigger than the ones in the larder. She yelled for him to take care then went to the kitchen to wait for Suzie. She needed to say something to her even though it would most certainly be ignored. Eventually Suzie walked back in.

'Suzie, are you sure you know what you're doing?'

Suzie's cheeks flushed. 'I'm just doing what you did.'

'Yes, but I did it in ignorance. You *know* he's a bastard.' Suzie checked the casserole, and said nothing. Sophie realised it was hopeless. 'How are you? What are you, twenty weeks?'

'Twenty-two. It's a boy.'

'Fantastic! So, more than halfway, then. The middle trimester's much easier. I remember feeling really gorgeous.'

Suzie's cheeks were now crimson. 'Yes, I… Sophie, I know you think I'm crazy but I didn't want to be on my own. I know his memory's not as bad as he says it is, but while the police think he's not fit to be charged then things can stay as they are. And day to day, when I'm here with him, I pretend everything's going to be OK.'

Sophie sighed. Pretending everything's going to be OK. That's what most people do. But eventually it's not OK. Eventually, there's always a bitter end. That's man's fate. But, in the meantime, nobody lets inevitable fate interfere with the delusion that it's all going to be OK. So, if Suzie wanted to delude herself, who was she to prevent her from doing so? 'Suzie, you need to take care of yourself. Are you driving backwards and forwards each day?'

'I come straight after work.'

'Why don't you stay over?'

Suzie's cheeks became so red Sophie thought she might explode. 'Jonah thinks it's best if he's on his own. You know what he can be like in the middle of the night. And the doctors say that he mustn't get stressed or excited. So, sex is out of the question.'

Now it was Sophie's turn to blush. Yes, she did remember what Jonah had been like in the middle of the night, and the memory made her want to run away and hide. Or, maybe, vomit. She heard Sam calling from the top of the stairs.

'I'll throw the first box down. Are you ready to catch?'

She ran into the hall. 'Sam, they're made of gla—'

He was just reaching the bottom stair. 'Joking! I'll take this round and come back for more. Let me in.'

Sophie returned to the conversation in the kitchen. 'He was joking.'

'He does that a lot, doesn't he?'

Sophie smiled. *Better than downright lying*. She watched Suzie fussing over cutlery, folding napkins. Young and stupid and pregnant. And treading a very dangerous path. 'Suzie, if you need to speak to someone, you know you can call me any time, right?' The doorbell rang. Sophie hurried to open it but Jonah was already there, his tray under his arm, an empty glass in his hand. He said nothing, just opened the door then brushed past her into the kitchen.

'He's all charm, isn't he?' Sam whispered. 'I'll fetch the others then we're out of here.'

'I'll get my things.' Sophie wandered into the lounge and pulled on her coat but, as she lifted her bag from the coffee table, she noticed Jonah's crossword book open beneath it. She picked it up and frowned, flicked through a few of the pages and her blood ran cold. The puzzle grids were mostly blank. But quite clear, running down or across on each of the grids was a string of letters: DON'T LET THEM HAVE IT. She threw down the book. Had Jonah gone completely mad? Was Suzie safe? She hurried back into the kitchen where Jonah was seated in his usual place at the head of the table, rubbing Suzie's pregnant waist as she loaded casserole onto his plate. Sophie needed to get out of there straight away. Fortunately, at that very moment, Sam carried the ladder through the kitchen and said everything was ready to go. Suzie saw them out. Jonah barely acknowledged their leaving.

As he stepped down onto the pavement, Sam paused. 'Suzie, you haven't had any weird people calling, have you? Apart from us, that is?'

'No, nobody. Not even the neighbours to ask how he is.'

–

As soon as Sam pulled away, Sophie told him about the puzzle book. He frowned. '*Don't let them have it?* On all the pages? The guy needs to be sectioned.'

'Do you think he's gone mad?'

'When was he ever not?'

30

November did not end well. Sophie was disturbed from her Wednesday lie-in by raised voices. Indistinguishable words. Anger. She felt for her phone: 8:15. Laura was grumbling next door; there were more indistinguishable words. Sophie slipped out of bed and hurried through to her daughter, who was trying to reach through the cot bars to retrieve her bottle of milk which she'd lobbed out onto the floor, probably in response to the shouting. Babies have a heightened ability to detect anger. Sophie picked up the milk and returned it just as the front door slammed so loudly that the house shook. She briefly wondered whether Jesse's wall-less planning could withstand such a tremor. But the upstairs didn't seem to be collapsing into the downstairs, so she hurried over to the window just in time to see the Z4 disappearing down the drive, leaving a spray of fine shingle in its wake. She ought to investigate. She carried Laura downstairs and found Sam sitting in the kitchen, glaring at a half-eaten boiled egg. 'The trouble with no doors,' she said, 'is that you can't shout at each other without waking the people on the top floor. Have you and Jesse had a row?'

Sam looked up from the egg. 'No. Yes.'

'What about?'

'Nothing.'

'It didn't sound like nothing. Did the boys get off to school OK?'

'Barbara collected them. Do you want tea?'

'Yes please. Why were you and Jesse shouting at each other?'

'It's nothing. Just a trivial brotherly disagreement.'

Sophie inserted Laura into her chair and sat down beside her. Watched Sam making tea, recycling the remains of his breakfast into the organic waste. 'Was it about me and Laura staying here? Co-habiting always causes tension.'

He spun round. 'Don't be ridiculous! Jesse loves having you here.'

'Me and my criminal intrigue? A cheated woman and her illegitimate daughter pushing his hospitality beyond reasonable limits when he's trying to court probably the most difficult woman he's ever met?'

Sam returned to the tea-making. 'That's mostly what's wrong. Jesse and Katie have had a lovers' spat and he's taking it out on everyone else.'

'What did they fight about?'

'Nothing.'

'Everything's about nothing, is it?' She watched him avoiding eye contact. 'I'll find out if you're lying, Sam.'

He sighed with exasperation. 'I'm not lying. Katie's not coming over this weekend. She said she needs her own space.' He handed her a mug. 'I'd better get going. I've got a class at eleven.' He stooped to kiss her cheek. 'Hamlet for the disinterested.' Then he was hurrying away, up the stairs.

Laura mumbled something. Probably an infant declaration that her mother's consort had, in the last fifteen minutes, failed to engage with her. Sophie handed her a stray slice of toast and recognised the stirrings of panic rising within her. Sam was lying to her, she was sure of that. And there was no way she would accept another round of being lied to. She'd leave rather than let that happen. She watched Laura dismantling the toast and, for the first time, acknowledged the truth of her situation. Her mother's house was currently occupied by a criminal madman. She had nowhere to go. She heard Sam hurrying back downstairs, watched him hurry over to kiss Laura.

'Soph, I'll be back about four. Leave all this. The cleaners will be here any minute. I'll pick up something special for supper.

Love you. And I'd never lie to you, OK?' A quick peck on the cheek and then he was gone.

And, as usual, Sophie believed him.

–

That evening Jesse was with a client so Sophie fed all three children and packed them off to their beds, leaving Sam free to mark a pile of mostly unexceptional essays on the influence the Decadent Movement had had upon British literature of the late nineteenth century. She discovered him, papers spread across the dining table, pen poised in one hand, raking his hair with the other. He glanced up. 'This kid has written the most fantastic essay about homoeroticism in *The Picture of Dorian Grey*.'

'Isn't that where the main character has a portrait in his attic that does all the ageing while he stays young and handsome?'

'Yes, but it's also about aestheticism and moral perversion. A falling away of values. Art for Art's sake.'

Sophie sat down at a safe distance from his essay classification system. 'Jesse's viburnums are full of flower. And the *Ilex* berries will be fantastic by Christmas.'

Sam sat back and frowned. 'Are you suggesting we have nothing in common, Ms Denham?'

'Possibly, Mr Barnes.' She glanced dismissively at the piles of paper. 'Have you spoken to Jesse since this morning?'

'No.'

'Well, I've tried contacting Katie all day but she's been incommunicado. I've just got a text from her to say she's thinking her way through a situation. What did they quarrel about?'

'Soph, let it rest! I'll catch up with him later. Try and talk him through it. Do you need me to clear all this away or can we eat in front of the TV?'

'Have you got time to eat?'

'Not really.'

'OK. I'll eat in front of the TV. You eat on top of that lot. Get it finished so you'll have enough time to *catch up* with your brother.'

Things at Greenfields remained tense and unexplained for the next two days but, fortunately, by Friday evening Katie had obviously succeeded in thinking her way through her situation and was back in residence and resigned to merely bickering with Jesse about which ski resort to visit for the boys' next half-term.

December began uneventfully. Sophie tested Sam's shopping tolerance to the point of crabbiness, assuaged only by her promise that, if he behaved himself, Santa would bring him the definitive DVD collection of Basil Rathbone's *Sherlock Holmes*. She decorated their modest penthouse tree as soon as she could get Sam to collect it from the garden centre and Jesse erected a giant Nordmann fir in the main living area. Sophie had to admit that the absence of walls really did enhance its splendour. Then, on the second Thursday of the month, Sophie was in her office, eating her lunch and avoiding the season to be merry when her phone vibrated beneath the proofs of the Special Christmas Edition of *Biowise*. It was Suzie. She was sobbing so much that Sophie could barely make out what she was saying. She was phoning from the emergency department of the Royal Surrey Hospital. Sophie immediately feared for the baby. She was, what, twenty-three, twenty-four weeks? Too early. Lots of babies survive as early as that but lots of them don't. And the ones that do are tiny, at–risk little things, with fragile lungs not ready to cope with air.

'Suzie, try and stay calm. Tell me what's happened.'

'Jonah pushed me.' More sobbing.

'What? Is the baby all right?'

'I think so. They're monitoring him and he seems to be OK. I was only unconscious for a few minutes and the doctors said that wouldn't affect him.'

'Jonah knocked you out? Why? What happened?'

'I stayed over. And this morning, over breakfast, I asked him about my money and he went crazy and yelled at me because I gave the police his laptop. And then he pushed me and I fell against the sink. I went next door and Mrs Davies called an ambulance. I told her I fell over. Sophie, I'm scared to go back there.'

'Well don't go back there!'

'But my car's parked on the back road.'

'I'll get Sam to collect it. Where's Jonah now?'

'I don't know. He wasn't there when I came round. Sophie, I've been so stupid. I didn't know who else to call.'

Sophie took a moment to consider that last statement. Sophie Denham, the woman stupid people call when they find themselves in crisis. 'Suzie, listen, just try not to worry. I'll get Sam to drive me over after work. And phone your mum and ask her to come and look after you. Mums do that. And, for now, just lie there listening to the monitor because that's your baby telling you he can't wait to meet you.'

'Thanks, Sophie. Sophie, my car keys are beside the toaster.'

–

Sophie texted Sam that there was a crisis involving Suzie. He phoned back straight away and she gave a summary of the situation. He said he'd pick Laura up early and ask Jesse to watch her while they were away. 'So, where is the bastard right now?'

'She doesn't know.'

–

Sophie spent the afternoon trying to write enthusiasm into the biographies of the year's finalists for the employer of the year award. Three men and two women from various departments whose day-to-day commitment had caused them to shine above all others. On the other hand, Sophie's day-to-day commitment was currently plummeting well below zero. Her daughter was being terrorised in an expensive nursery; her friend, albeit a friend who was her ex-lover's other woman, was *in extremis*; and Christmas was coming and she had some impossibly important gift ideas to conjure up out of nowhere. Yet she was sitting in a claustrophobic office, three days a week, churning out garbage. She glanced over at Viola, who was engrossed in her latest copy of *Marie Claire*. She should have been working on the Section Manager's Christmas message. Heaven forbid, if she didn't get that finished in time. What were they both doing with their lives? Answer: wasting them.

-

Suzie had been moved to a ward and was still attached to a monitor when Sophie and Sam walked into the small side room. She seemed to be asleep so they waited in silence but after a few moments she turned her head towards them and opened her eyes. Sophie gasped at the bruising down the side of her face.

'Suzie, did Jonah do that to you?' said Sam.

Suzie's eyes filled with tears. Sophie hurried to her side. 'Are they keeping you in?'

'I don't know. The nurse says my blood pressure is high. I'm waiting for the doctor to tell me whether I have to stay in overnight. I'm sorry if you've come here for nothing.'

'Suzie, we've come to see you. Have you contacted your mother?'

'No, I don't want to worry her.'

'That's ridiculous. She'd be angry if she knew you were like this and not telling her.'

'I don't think he meant to hurt me, Soph.' She glanced over at the door. 'I think that's the doctor.' She grabbed Sophie's arm. 'They'll make you leave.'

'No, they won't.'

The door opened and the ward sister stepped into the room ahead of a young doctor. 'Can we ask you both to step outside whilst the doctor sees to Miss Kay?' she said.

'I'm her birth partner,' said Sophie, in a moment of inspiration.

The sister acknowledged Sophie's newly-conceived status then escorted Sam outside. The doctor shook Sophie's hand and introduced himself as Simon Grant. He checked the monitor then examined the side of Suzie's face. 'Suzie has taken a bad fall. The damage is superficial, but her blood pressure is quite high at the moment, quite possibly unrelated to the fall. It was slightly raised at the last antenatal visit.'

'She's been trying to do too much,' said Sophie.

'That's not unusual. So much to prepare. Sister will contact you if it becomes necessary.' Sophie's stomach churned: did he think she might go into labour? He continued. 'Although there's no sign that anything drastic is going to happen. Baby seems quite happy where he is.' He smiled at Suzie. 'We'll keep you in for a couple of days. Make sure you don't take any more tumbles.'

Sophie had no intention of letting that lie continue. 'Dr Grant, Suzie was pushed over. By the baby's father.'

Simon Grant's brow furrowed. 'Is that the case, Suzie?' Suzie started to cry. He turned back to Sophie. 'Does she have somewhere else to go?'

'Yes, she has her own place.' She patted Suzie's hand. 'Suzie, we'll sort this out. Just think of the baby and let everything else just happen around you.'

'Good advice,' said Dr Grant. 'Suzie, we'll get you fed and watered and give you something to help you sleep, OK?' He took another look at the monitor then left.

A few moments later Sister returned to take Sophie's details. So, for the moment, Sophie was the official birth partner for her ex-lover's latest mistress. On the way home, Sam said that he had spoken to the doctor, who said that the cause of Suzie's injuries was now on record and that they were obliged to inform the police.

'Let's hope this will finally sever the hold he has on her,' said Sophie.

'Yeh. Unfortunately, domestic violence rarely ends as easily as that.'

—

Back in the attic, Sophie hurried through to check Laura whilst Sam cleared sufficient space on the dining table to accommodate two plates. She returned to find him apron-clad and reading the proofs of the Christmas edition of *Biowise*. He glanced up. 'Did you write this?'

'Most of it. It's one of the brain-numbing things my contract requires of me. Please do not offer a critical analysis.'

'It's extremely well-written crap.'

'Thanks.'

'So, remind me what your company actually *does*.'

'It produces biopharmaceuticals. Testing kits, immunological agents, things like that.'

'And Jonah set up their computer system?'

'Yes, I told you. It's when we met. He maintained it for a couple of years.'

'But not more recently than that.'

'I don't think so.'

31

That Saturday, Sophie received an early morning call from Mrs Davies. Mr Perrin had lit a bonfire next door. Yesterday evening. There had been a lot of smoke. She'd been worried it was getting out of control. She'd thought of calling the fire brigade but then it stopped suddenly. She had nipped round to ring the bell. The lights were on but there was no answer. She hadn't seen Mr Perrin since having to call the ambulance for his young lady on Thursday, although he'd had two visitors yesterday morning. Two men she hadn't seen before. One of them was bald and very unshaven and the other one had a mole on his cheek. She always noticed things like that. She was wondering if Mr Perrin's young lady was all right, being pregnant and taking a tumble like that. Sophie assured her that Suzie was fine, thanked her for calling then flopped back onto her pillow.

Sam sat up and rubbed his eyes. 'What now?'

'Mrs Davies said there was a fire next door.'

'With a bit of luck, Jonah suffered spontaneous combustion.'

'It was a bonfire, in the back garden. She said there was a lot of smoke.'

'So, how come she knows your new number?'

'I might have phoned her about the house.'

'I'll get dressed.'

'No, I'll go over and check everything's OK. I want to know what he was burning and I can't expect you to keep attending my disasters. You look after Laura. I'll get the train.'

'You expect me to sit here playing with Laura while you go and confront that mistress-basher? Text Katie and warn her she's looking after her favourite baby.'

Sophie sighed. 'I think Jonah might have had a visit from Joe and Col.'

Mrs Davies was waiting by her curtains as Sam and Sophie strode past at nine thirty. She hurried out, eager to join them and, in truth, Sophie was glad of her presence. Sam rang Sophie's doorbell and, when there was no response, opened the front door with his key. He called but there was no reply, so they stepped inside. All the lights were on and there was, indeed, a strong smell of burning. Cautiously, they wandered through to the kitchen. Mrs Davies gasped at the shambles. Everything had been emptied out of the larder onto the floor. Packets of rice, sugar, flour had spilled their contents. There were pieces of broken glass and a smashed Portmeirion teapot that Sophie must have overlooked. She was thankful she'd moved the rest of her mother's china to the safety of Jesse's garage. The back door was slightly ajar, which explained the arctic conditions inside the house. She stepped over to close it and froze. Sam hurried to see what had caused her reaction and they stood, all three of them, staring at a scene of desolation. The charred remains of Laura's cot, complete with mattress, were in the middle of the yard atop a wet heap of what was left of Sophie's plants, which had been emptied out and burnt, their pots smashed against the garage wall. Pieces of mattress foam were blowing around the yard.

'Who could have done this?' said Sophie, stepping outside. She prodded one of the cot bars and it snapped at her touch. 'Perhaps it was Mole-face and Bald Man.'

'But his visitors were only here for an hour, no more,' said Mrs Davies clutching her hands together. 'And the smoke was in the evening.'

Sam pulled Sophie back inside and asked Mrs Davies if she'd go next door and make some tea while he phoned the police. He told Sophie to go with her but she refused.

'Sam, we need to check upstairs. But, Mrs Davies, I'd be really grateful for that tea.'

They watched her leave then checked the lounge: more destruction. Sam went upstairs to investigate and called down to say that Jonah's bed didn't look slept in. Sophie hurried up to the landing, watched Sam check the spare room. He shook his head. 'Where the hell is he? We'd better check Laura's room. Why on earth did he do that to her cot?'

Sophie pushed open the door to her daughter's little room and fell back against Sam. The room was wrecked, Laura's things smashed and torn apart and thrown on the floor. And Jonah was lying face down in the middle of them. His hair and hands and clothes were covered in soil. Sam hurried over and felt his neck. 'He's alive. He doesn't look injured. But it's difficult to tell underneath all the filth.' He pulled out his phone and called an ambulance, gave details, all the while watching Sophie slumped against the doorframe, wringing her hands and growing paler by the minute. 'Soph, go next door. I'll phone Blake.'

'Should we move him into recovery position?'

'There's nothing to be gained by moving him before the ambulance gets here. *Sophie, go next door!*' But as he issued his instruction, Jonah emitted a long, low groan. Sophie uttered a squeak of horror. Sam stepped over and took her by the arm and led her towards the stairs. 'Sophie, go next door. I'll wait with him. I'll phone if the police need to talk to you.'

–

Sophie watched Elvira Davies keeping vigil by her window, waiting for the ambulance to draw up outside and cause mayhem. This was clearly the vantage point from which she monitored the local comings and goings. Much to Mrs Davies' consternation, the police car arrived first and Sophie joined her to observe Inspector Blake step out and instruct the patrol officer to park on the back road. She saw the Inspector greet someone as he climbed the steps so Sam must have been waiting for him. She was distressed at how much her involvement with Jonah was polluting his life. There would have to be a breaking point sooner or later. She found herself wishing Jonah would just go ahead and die, then hated herself for thinking that about Laura's father. Moments later, a siren announced the arrival of the ambulance, which pulled up half on the pavement, its lights flashing. An ambulance crew ran into the house and, almost immediately, one of the paramedics came back outside to collect a stretcher. The patrol officer hurried past their window and began directing traffic. After another short while, Jonah was stretchered out. Mrs Davies threw her hand across her mouth. 'Good God, Sophie, he's covered in dirt!'

Within minutes Jonah was sealed inside the ambulance and the patrol officer was holding up the traffic to allow it to pull away. Mrs Davies was now free to pour the tea. Sophie waited, the fragrance of cheaply-scented candles encouraging her anxieties. She accepted the mug Mrs Davies was offering her. For once her neighbour seemed uncertain about the virtue of further interrogation, so Sophie saved her the bother. 'Jonah's girlfriend, who fell over – Suzie – Jonah pushed her.'

'Oh, dear. Such a pretty little thing too.'

'Jonah was leaving me to move in with her. I didn't suspect anything.'

'There's terrible.'

Yes, it was terrible. Sophie's phone rang. It was Sam. Inspector Blake was still looking around. Perhaps another ten minutes, which Sophie took to mean stay away for another ten minutes. When she eventually let herself back into her house, the inspector was about to leave. 'Miss Denham,' he said, 'this is definitely one to test the imagination.'

'Do you think Jonah did all this?'

'It does look that way. The security cameras show no indication of anyone visiting the house yesterday other than the two gentlemen callers your neighbour saw. They stayed for less than an hour. And there is very clear footage of Mr Perrin searching for something after they left, and of his lighting the bonfire several hours later.'

Sophie looked at Sam. 'But Laura's cot! All her things pulled apart.'

He shrugged. 'It must have been something he remembered hiding in Laura's room. It's the sort of creepy thing he might have done.'

'But, Sam, what about all the stuff pulled out of the larder?'

'Perhaps he thought it had been found and re-hidden. Most likely by you.'

'Miss Denham,' said Inspector Blake, 'it's seems that the two men that visited yesterday were the same two that called here in August, one of whom you believe visited Mr Perrin in hospital, although unfortunately he was not captured on the security cameras. We'll run a face recognition check on today's footage. If these individuals are, indeed, involved in criminal activities, it's likely they're working for someone else, who chooses not to dirty their fingers with the likes of Mr Perrin.'

Sophie frowned at the mess. Then something occurred to her. 'What if whoever is behind this believes that I *have* found what they're after? And they come looking for it?'

'Ms Denham,' said Inspector Blake, 'I think you'll be safe with Mr Barnes.'

–

Inspector Blake left and Sam and Sophie cleared much of the wreckage into refuse bags. Sophie found Suzie's car keys in the rubble on the kitchen floor. She gave them to Sam and pulled him to leave. The rest of the desolation could wait. On the journey back, Sam phoned Jesse to check on Laura and to summarise the latest instalment in the tale of 'Jonah the Psycho'. Sophie added detail, about the cot and her burned pansies and lavenders, because it meant that, whilst she was talking about the morning's experience, she wasn't actually thinking about it. And she really didn't want to be thinking about it. Back at Greenfields, she hurried straight through to reclaim Laura, who was sitting contentedly in a hastily-constructed cardboard grotto that the boys had manufactured from the packaging around Jesse's new-for-Christmas TV. Katie looked up from her magazine.

'It's a laugh a minute with you and Jonah, isn't it?'

'And yet another sensitive remark from Mrs Hurst,' observed Jesse.

Katie hurried over to give Sophie a hug. 'Sophie knows I'm always in her corner, whatever happens.' She stepped back and held Sophie's arms. 'The boys have baked some gingerbread men to cheer you up.'

'Laura helped,' said Benz.

'We have since redecorated,' said Jesse. 'Do you know what state he's in, Sam?'

'I'm about to phone. They were taking him to the Royal Surrey.'

'Is Suzie still there?' said Katie.

Sophie checked the time. 'Her mum was picking her up this morning. Her car's still parked on the back road. I'd rather they didn't go there in case they run into him.'

'Do you think Jonah will be back there any time soon?' asked Jesse.

Sam pulled out his phone. 'He was coming round as they were carrying him out. And I don't suppose the hospital will want to hang on to him.'

'Surely they wouldn't discharge him back to living on his own,' said Katie. 'If you ask me, he ought to be certified insane.'

Sam scrolled through his contacts. 'The loony bins won't be looking for any new inmates this side of Christmas.'

Sophie followed him into the hall, listened to him breaking through the security barricades to speak to Accident and Emergency. Eventually he handed her the phone since they would only speak to Jonah's partner. Sophie gathered that he had experienced a stress-induced episode, which although it may have caused a period of semi-consciousness, had not been life-threatening. In fact, he might have merely been phasing in and out of sleep for much of the time, particularly if he had taken his usual evening sedatives. He was being transferred to a ward for observation. The doctor added that, in the light of this latest incident, it would be wise for Mr Perrin to avoid further stressful situations that might exacerbate a more serious attack. And was she intending to accompany him when he was discharged? Sophie said that Mr Perrin was now in the hands of Social Services.

–

The following day Sam and Jesse took one of the vans over to Sophie's house and spent the morning clearing the wreckage. Sam drove Suzie's car over to Guildford and chatted to her and her mother while he waited for Jesse to pick him up. He asked Suzie why she'd hidden Jonah's laptop and she confessed that she'd been hoping to use it as leverage to get her money back.

On Monday morning, Social Services phoned Sophie to tell her that Mr Perrin was being discharged that afternoon and would continue to be visited once daily by the Care Team. Again, Sophie experienced a deep desire for Jonah's life to end. She called Suzie and was relieved at how much happier she seemed. Her blood pressure was fine and she now realised how misguided she'd been to re-establish her relationship with Jonah.

Immediately the call ended Sophie's mobile rang. It was Rosemary. That morning she'd received a letter from Social Services, informing her that they had obtained details of joint accounts Jonah held with her, and that she would be expected to arrange payment for additional expenses incurred in his ongoing care package. She had checked her accounts and discovered that money had been transferred from her personal account to the joint account, apparently by herself. She had contacted her solicitor to continue the conversation regarding her rights to the house and had learned that a letter was in the post to inform her that, after checking with Land Registry, it was now clear that Mr

Perrin was the sole owner of the property and that any charges against Mr Perrin's estate might require that the house be sold. She was therefore faced with destitution if Social Services or any of Robert's creditors were to successfully file claims against him. Sophie wasn't sure how to respond to all this. She told Rosemary about Jonah's bonfire episode and him rekindling his relationship with Suzie, about Suzie being pregnant and about Jonah attacking her. Rosemary fell silent.

'Rosemary, are you still there?' She was. 'I thought we'd been cut off. Rosemary, there's nothing I can do to help. I'm already paying my sister rent so he can live in my house, which he's slowly destroying.'

'He's ruining our lives, Sophie. We'll never be free while he's alive.'

–

Early evening, Sophie took a call from Suzie's mother, Ella Roberts. She was in Sainsbury's and Suzie was unaware that she was calling. Apparently, Jonah had been trying to contact Suzie: six missed calls and a text message, apologising about losing his temper last week and asking if they could meet. Suzie was determined not to reply but this harassment, if it continued, would be sure to take its toll. Sophie said she was glad Suzie wasn't on her own at the moment. Loneliness makes people do stupid things. She promised to phone Suzie but not mention the Sainsbury's call. Mrs Roberts thanked her and added, by way of a farewell, that she wished Jonah were dead.

Sam handed Sophie a glass of merlot. 'He's trying to contact her, is he? The bastard's living in your house and he's trying to get Suzie back in there to skivvy for him? That guy really needs to fall off a cliff.'

Sophie agreed then phoned Suzie, who told her about Jonah's calls and text. She insisted she had no intention of responding to any attempts by Jonah to make contact and that sometimes she thought it would have been better for everyone if he had died last summer when he fell against his toolbox and broke his brain.

So, thought Sophie, pretty much unanimous as far as Jonah-cum-Robert's continued existence was concerned.

Lost

'What do you mean, he's lost it?'

Thaddeus Jones chose his words advisedly. 'Our operatives approached Mr Perrin to discuss surrendering the data in exchange for assistance in relocation and he seemed willing to accept the offer...'

'Is the man a fool?'

'...but when the operatives returned to *collect*, he informed them that, following their visit, he had attempted to retrieve the relevant data device and found that it was no longer where he had concealed it. At this point, Mr Perrin undertook a thorough search of the property and was able to find no trace. He has since repeated his assurances that without the key data, all other data would remain useless. He suggested that there was a slight possibility that his ex-mistress, Ms Sophie Denham, who, in fact, owns the property, had discovered the data device and had re-hidden it or taken it with her, quite possibly unaware of its significance.'

'And do we know this Ms Denham's whereabouts?'

'Mr Perrin is attempting to determine her new address, Sir Hugh. He does, however, know which nursery her daughter is attending.'

'Well, arrange something, Jones.'

'Yes, sir.'

'And, Jones, in the meantime, I gather that the sponsors of the most advanced double surrogacy have taken up residence in the Belgrave apartment. I do not want any complications. Have all parties been informed? Are the emergency protocols in place?'

'Yes sir, the infants will be delivered on Christmas Day as requested. The Winchester team are on standby.'

'Excellent. I'll inform the Organisation.'

32

By the Tuesday of the last working week before Christmas, Portway Biotech was awash with tinsel – the corridors, the offices and even the ladies' washroom. And Clive Mason from the post room had started early on his mistletoe tour of the female staff. In response, Sophie and Viola had stuck a notice on the door:

MISTLETOE NOT ALLOWED.

GO AWAY CLIVE.

Sophie's Special Christmas Edition of *Biowise* had been very well received and, as she flicked through the pages of inane anecdotes about the previous year, she cringed at the thought of all those people reading her words and at the waste of her time that those words represented. Viola suggested she come to lunch, just this once, and for once she did. But as soon as Sophie stepped into the crush in the Slug and Lettuce, she wished she hadn't. She felt too old and troubled to be standing amongst all these not-necessarily-younger, apparently carefree people. She'd forgotten how to do all this.

Bella fought her way through to the bar for a bottle of Shiraz and Viola looked around for somewhere to sit. There was little hope of success but suddenly Sophie caught sight of Joanna, waving at her above the crowd. She was pointing at the people next to her, who were vacating their seats. Sophie forced her way through the crush – at least she hadn't forgotten how to do that – and she and Viola waited for the people to leave then claimed their seats. Bella joined them with a bottle and three glasses and squashed in next to Viola. Suddenly Clive's flaccid body was looming beside Sophie.

'Fuck off, Clive,' said Bella.

'Oh, excuse me for living,' said Clive, undeterred. 'I've just come over to see Sophie. I've got something for her.'

Oh Christ, thought Sophie, not the mistletoe. But, instead of mistletoe, Clive handed her a white envelope. 'What's this?' she said.

'Christmas card I presume. This guy said he wanted you to have it straight away, so when I saw you heading this way, I grabbed it and brought it with me.'

'What guy?' said Sophie, pulling out a sparkly card.

'Never seen him before. But, if you ask me, him and his mate looked like ruffians.'

Sophie opened the card: a single word, *Rosemead*, was written in an untidy hand, an all too familiar smiley face beside it. She frowned up at Clive. 'There were two of them?'

'Yeh, one of them was bald with a beard, really ugly. And the other one, he was also ugly, with, like, ginger hair.'

Sophie threw her hand against her chest.

'What's up, Soph?' said Viola.

'I've got to phone Sam!' She pushed past Clive and forced her way to the street, pulled out her phone and dropped her bag on the ground. People stopped to stare at her. Joanna and Clive hurried out to join her, picked up her things and watched her prodding her phone, pressing the wrong number. Trying again. Sam picked up straight away. 'Sam, those two thugs came to the office. I'm scared they're going to take Laura.'

'*What?*'

Joanna touched her arm but Sophie shook her away and tried to speak calmly. 'The two gangsters. They delivered a card to the office. To me. It just had *Rosemead* written inside. And a smiley face. Sam, I think they're going to go to the nursery. Maybe they're there already. How can I get there before them?'

'I'll drive you there,' interrupted Clive. 'I'll fetch the car. It's just down the road.'

'Who was that?'

'Clive.'

'Look, Sophie, try not to panic. I'll phone the police. They'll probably get there before me. Phone the nursery and warn them about the two men, right? I'll ring off now, OK?'

She watched the call end. Joanna put her arm around her. Viola and Bella joined them on the pavement. Bella was still clutching the bottle of Shiraz. She told the gathering crowd to piss off and mind their own business; some guy called her a slag. Clive pulled up alongside them and Sophie hurried into the car. She looked at Clive, hoped he wasn't in on the whole thing, with Bald Man and Mole Man, like he would have been if this was one of Sam's detective novels. But he wasn't in with them. He was just Clive.

Sophie gave directions, phoned and tried to control the tremor in her voice as she spoke to Mrs Bain, the Rosemead Manager, who understood her concern but assured her that the two men she described had not put in an appearance and that Rosemead's security system would defy all attempts at entry other than with a battering ram. She would look out for the police and check their credentials before allowing them onto the premises. Sophie thanked her, rang off and looked at Clive. 'She says she hasn't seen anyone suspicious.'

'Is it to do with your ex?'

'Yes. He's muddled up in something I never knew about. It's the next on the left.'

–

By the time Clive pulled up in front of the nursery, a police car was already parked outside and a police officer was standing at the main entrance, talking to Mrs Bain. Sophie picked up her bag. 'Thanks so much, Clive. Sam will be here soon. So, there's no need to stay. I'm so grateful.'

'Glad I could help. But I'd better hang around. Just in case they need me to make a statement about those two villains. And it's a good excuse not to go back to the office. I'm sick of all those lovelorn women breaking into the post room to snog me.'

Sophie left Clive moving his car and hurried towards the nursery entrance.

'This is Laura's mother, Constable Banks,' explained Mrs Bain.

The policeman turned. 'Ms Denham? We've been informed that this is a situation that ought to be followed up with caution. Part of an existing investigation.' Sophie noticed Mrs Bain's look of disapproval. Perhaps she should have mentioned on Laura's application that her father was a criminal sociopath. The officer continued. 'I gather that two men delivered a note to your place of work this morning? And that it contained a reference to this nursery.'

'Yes.' Sophie handed over the card. 'When the post guy described them to me, I recognised them as two men that had been threatening Laura's father.' Another look of disapproval from Mrs Bain. 'Is Laura safe, Mrs Bain?'

'Yes, of course, Miss Denham. The little ones are having their afternoon rest at the moment.' She looked up as Clive approached. 'And this is?'

'This is my colleague, Clive Mason. He was kind enough to drive me here. It was Clive who alerted me to the two men. They gave him the card and asked him to give it to me.'

Mrs Bain acknowledged Clive with a brief nod of her head. 'Perhaps we should continue this inside,' she said.

'I ought to wait outside until my partner gets here,' said Sophie.

'Isn't that Sam now?' said Clive. 'In the Range Rover.'

They watched Sam pull in behind the patrol car, jump out and hurry towards them. 'What's the situation, Officer?' he said, taking Sophie's hand.

'All seems to be well at the moment, sir,' said Constable Banks. 'No sign of the men in question. It was Mr Mason here who they approached.'

Yet another car pulled up. Sophie watched DI Blake and Officer Lane stepping out but, just as they did so, there was a screech of tyres and a car sped past on the opposite side of the road. 'That's them!' shouted Clive.

Sam and Clive ran towards the road. Sam pulled a pen out of his pocket and wrote on his palm as he and Clive watched the low black saloon disappear. Sophie hurried over to join them.

'Was that the two men?' asked the inspector.

'Yes,' said Clive. 'And that was a 2015 Ford Mustang 2.3 Fastback V8 with replacement alloys. Obviously, I'm in the wrong job.'

Sam held up his palm. 'This is the licence.'

'I'll get that checked out,' said Inspector Blake. He looked at Sophie. 'We clearly arrived just in time, although it's possible that this was just an attempt to frighten you.'

'Well, they certainly achieved that,' said Sophie.

'It was most likely a nicked car.'

'Quite so, Mr Barnes,' said Inspector Blake. 'But, for now, we'd better go and explain ourselves to that severe-looking lady standing in the entrance. If I were you, I'd take Ms Denham and her daughter home straight away and, perhaps, make alternative arrangements for her day care. No point in taking chances.'

–

They left Clive giving details to Officer Lane. Inspector Blake accompanied Sophie and Sam to Mrs Bain's office where the atmosphere was decidedly unrelaxed. Essentially, Mrs Bain felt that the other parents would be most concerned when they learned about today's crisis. And, not to put too fine a point on it, she thought that, for the time being, it might be safer for all concerned at the nursery if Laura ceased to attend. Sophie both understood Mrs Bain's fears and loathed her for expressing them in such a way that suggested Laura was somehow to blame. 'I wouldn't feel safe sending her here after today, Mrs Bain.'

Mrs Bain bristled. 'Our security system is top-drawer!'

'As long as it's never tested,' said Sophie. 'If I may collect my daughter, you will see no more of us. So, please, reassure the other parents accordingly. And please keep any overpayment as a contribution to the paddling pool fund.'

'Miss Denham, we usually expect two months' notice, so this amount will remain outstanding.'

'Then sue me,' said Sophie. 'Sam, would you help me collect Laura's things? Inspector Blake, if you need to speak to me further, please wait for me outside.'

Sam and Officer Blake clearly realised it would be wise to say nothing. Sophie followed Mrs Bain out of the room. Sam hurried along behind them and in no time at all, Laura was secured in her car seat and Sophie was in the passenger seat fuming. Sam got in beside her and Inspector Blake leaned low to speak to them. 'Officer Lane has confirmed that the car the men were driving was stolen yesterday from a spa centre just outside Oxford. The two assailants, who we have previously identified from your security footage, are the recently unbearded Joseph Mann. And the redhead is a Russian called Kolya Sokolov, who seems to have developed a large melanoma since his last mugshot. I'm sure this episode was an attempt to scare you, Ms Denham.'

'But, Inspector, why?'

'Perhaps they believe that you know the whereabouts of – or, indeed, are in possession of – whatever it was that Mr Perrin was searching for last week, and that the kind of intimidation we have just witnessed will cause you to surrender it.' He paused. 'When questioned, following his discharge from the Royal Surrey Hospital, Mr Perrin was unable to explain last Friday's damage to your property. I believe Social Services are arranging repairs.'

–

It was dark by the time they arrived home. Sam went through to update Jesse and Sophie carried Laura up to their rooms and fussed around getting her tea and trying to supress a burgeoning sense of dread. By the time Sam joined her, she was in tears, the kind of tears that spill out because your head's so full of anxieties that it has to start bailing out. He tried to get her to talk about it but she couldn't. The anxieties were too primal: pre-linguistic. She felt like a distressed ape in the days before language was invented. So, Sam just helped put Laura to bed and then they sat in silence. Eventually, Jesse and the boys joined them for supper, which meant Jesse carried a large venison casserole up two flights of stairs and placed it on Sam's hob to reheat it, which was just as well since neither Sophie or Sam were inclined to open the fridge door to find food. The boys hurried over to sit beside Sophie.

'Dad said we could stay up late and be with you,' said Benz, 'because our vile behaviour will take your mind off the shit storm.'

Jesse stopped what he was doing. 'Benz, that's disgusting language!'

'You said it.'

'That's got nothing to do with it. If I hear you say that again, I'll phone Father Christmas and tell him to take your parcels to some more deserving children.'

'But, Dad, not my iPad,' said Jake.

'He doesn't mean it,' whispered Benz. He turned to Sophie. 'He just doesn't like us swearing. In case we do it in front of the teachers.' He rolled his eyes. 'But Jake and I are not stupid, are we, Jake?'

'No way,' said Jake.

—

Sleep did not come easy so, as the house settled, Sam reached for Coleridge.Sophie listened, but after only a few verses Sam placed the book back on his bedside table. 'Soph, I don't want you going back into work this side of New Year. I'll phone and say you're suffering from stress. It means we're both free for the duration.'

'OK. Sam, do you think Jonah's in danger?'

'I sincerely hope so.'

33

Sam phoned the Portway personnel department to say that Sophie was suffering severe stress following yesterday's incident and would not be in until after New Year, which, given her total lack of severe stress, made her feel a little like she was playing truant. It felt good. So, free for the build-up to Christmas, the penthouse contingent joined Jesse and the boys for breakfast. Sophie made scrambled eggs, aware that her acceptability as a family member might depend upon not sticking it to the bottom of the pan. She ladled it onto the plates and waited as the various brothers sampled it.

'Almost perfect,' said Sam.

'Almost?'

'Yes. You've given Jesse more than me.'

'They were my eggs,' said Jesse.

Sophie frowned and moved a small dollop from her plate to Sam's.

'I was only joking,' he said.

'One joke too many, Mr Barnes.'

'Well said,' exclaimed Jesse, helping himself to smoked salmon. 'Soph?'

Sophie looked up, fully expecting some culinary criticism. 'Yeh?'

'Why don't you quit your job and come and work for me?'

'She's not that good a bricklayer,' said Sam.

'You've never seen me lay bricks.'

Jesse persisted. 'I could do with a garden designer. I usually bring one in from outside.'

'But, Jesse, I've never done anything properly professional.'

'Don't worry, Soph, he's not thinking of paying you.'

'Sam, will you shut up for once!' Jesse rolled his eyes. 'We could give you a try with Sam's place. Then, if everything dies, we'll pretend we never had this conversation, OK?' He glanced at his brother. 'If you interrupt, I'll kill you.' Sam smirked and said nothing.

'But I don't drive,' said Sophie. 'I'd need to be able to do that, wouldn't I?'

Sam held up his hand. 'I've picked up an application for a provisional licence.'

'What? For me?'

'Well, I already have a licence, Soph. And Laura's far too young. And…'

'Shut up, Sam!' said Jesse. He smiled at Sophie. 'So, done deal?'

–

For several weeks now, Sam's study had been established as Laura's room. His books and papers were in boxes on the landing, and the floor, once his open-plan library, was now covered in Laura's toys. Sophie wandered through into the lounge. 'Sam, I can't find Blue Bear.'

Sam looked up from his book. 'Did she take it in the car this morning?'

'I don't think so. I usually make sure it stays home in case it's lost and she never sleeps again.'

'Have you looked down the back of the cot? She's always stuffing things down there.' He started to search under cushions. 'I'll go ask Jesse if he's seen it.'

Sophie listened to him hurrying downstairs, tried to remember whether Blue Bear had accompanied Laura into bed with them that morning. She decided to recheck their bedroom. Laura tumbled in after her. Sophie pulled back the duvet, checked under the pillows then climbed up onto the bed to look down behind the carved wooden headboard. And there it was: way down and to one side. She tried to reach down but her arm wasn't long enough. Indeed, it would have been a very strange human whose arm had been long enough. She stood a better chance of reaching it from Sam's side of the bed, so she climbed down, removed the lamp and books from Sam's bedside cabinet and started to ease it away. It was heavy, full of more books no doubt, but at last it started to slide, providing her with enough space to squeeze in beside the bed and reach Blue Bear. Easier said than done. She sat down and edged herself in until her back was against the wall. Laura was looking at her in disbelief. Blue Bear was tantalisingly close. She needed to move the cabinet further away so she pushed as hard as she was able in her sitting position, levered herself against the cabinet and reached behind the bed, caught hold of a blue ear and yanked the wretched creature to freedom, tossed it at Laura and collapsed back against the wall exhausted.

She was just about to edge herself back out, when she caught sight of something taped to the back of the cabinet. She twisted herself round to take a look. It was a package of some kind, wrapped in plastic and duct-taped to the cabinet's recessed back panel. With renewed effort, she reached round and eased it away then managed to successfully escape from the furniture. She sat on the bed and turned the package over in her hands. It was quite heavy, wrapped in layers of thick grey plastic. Was it something Sam had hidden there and forgotten about? She listened but she couldn't hear him coming back so she decided to take a peek, started to unwrap the layers, but as they unfurled she became prematurely aware of what she was holding. She threw it down onto the bed and as it landed the final folds fell away to reveal what she had already guessed was inside: a very convincing matt-black gun.

Sophie understood very little about guns, just enough to know that they were dangerous, illegal and they killed people. She hurried over to pick up Laura and carried her a safe distance, right away from the direction towards which the gun seemed to be pointing. After a few moments of watching it to confirm that it wasn't going to spontaneously leap into action, she carried

Laura and Blue Bear over to the little sofa, sat down and waited. Eventually she heard Sam clumping back up the stairs. He called from the main room then stepped into the bedroom. 'Jesse's not seen it but he said would we nip down and try his mince pies... Oh, you found bashed-up bear. What's up?'

Sophie inclined her head towards the bed. He followed her eyes and froze as he caught sight of what was lying in the mass of grey plastic. He went to speak. But she pre-empted him. 'It was taped behind your bedside cabinet. If I'm not very much mistaken, it's a gun.'

Sam ran his hands through his hair. 'Yes... it's a handgun. I forgot it was there.'

'You forgot it was there? You *forgot* that a gun was taped to the back of your bedside cabinet, right next to where we sleep?'

Sam grappled for an explanation. 'It's something I brought back from Hong Kong. A kind of souvenir.'

'Oh, I see, a souvenir. Like some people bring cardboard lanterns and plastic shit... and you bring a gun? Why was it taped to the back of a piece of furniture?'

'It's illegal to own it in the UK.'

'Sam, Laura could have found it and shot herself.'

'It's not loaded, Soph.'

'Oh, well, that's all right then.'

Sam picked up the offending weapon and flicked it open. 'See, there's no ammo inside. It's just a lump of metal. But it's still illegal, even when it's not loaded.'

'Why did you have a gun in Hong Kong?'

'Because... loads of people have guns in Hong Kong. I mean, you have to have licences, but I used to belong to a Shooting Club. It's a Glock 19 semi-automatic. Essential hardware for the modern-day cattle rustler.' He sighed. 'Soph, I'm sorry. I really did forget it was there. I'll put it somewhere else. I'll get rid of it if you want. Chuck it down a well, lob it into the Thames, like in the movies. The bed of the Thames must be covered in weaponry. Really, Soph, it could never have hurt Laura. Let's go and have a mince pie.'

'Are you lying to me?'

'Of course not. I'll get Jesse to lock it in his gun cupboard.'

'What gun cupboard?'

'He keeps the shotguns in a metal cupboard bolted to the wall… well, you're obliged by law to do that.'

'Jesse has shotguns?'

'Yes, several. And a couple of air rifles.'

'Does he shoot things?'

'Only clays. We both do. Jesse's won prizes.' He wrapped the gun back in its plastic and carried it into the kitchen. 'I'll put it in the top cupboard for now, I don't think Jesse knows I've got it up here. He'll probably go mad when he finds out.'

Sophie sighed and believed him. Who wouldn't?

–

As Christmas approached, Sophie began to experience unreasonable waves of regret. She waited for what she considered an appropriate moment to express her concerns. 'Sam, I don't like to think of anyone being on their own at Christmas. I know Jonah's vile but…'

'Would you like me to go and spend the day with him?'

'No! But I could send him a hamper. Anonymously. Just for old times' sake.'

'Sophie, that's absolute insanity! There's no old times' sake with Jonah. And it's Christmas Eve tomorrow. How exactly are you thinking of sending this hamper? Shall we drive over and leave it on the step with a message from Father Christmas?'

'I could ask Mrs Davies to give it to him. She could say it was delivered to the wrong address.'

Sam tugged at his hair. 'Sophie, the poor old girl is terrified of him!'

'You're angry.'

'Yes, I'm bloody furious! I don't want to hear any more about Jonah, right! I'm going down to watch the boys. Jesse's having lunch with a client.' He picked up his book and left.

Sophie sagged into a chair, wishing she could erase that whole conversation. It was so short-sighted of her not to realise that, despite Sam's long tolerance of the worries Jonah had imposed upon his life, and his indulgence of her occasional crazy ideas, there had to come a breaking point. And he had just reached it – two days before Christmas. She sat berating herself for a full five minutes before going to remove Laura from her playpen. Laura screamed her disapproval but, eventually, stopped thrashing around sufficiently for Sophie to be able to carry her downstairs, where she found Sam and Jesse huddled over an opened package. She put Laura on the floor with the boys. 'I thought you were going to lunch, Jesse,' she said.

'I'm leaving in ten minutes to pick up Katie. I'm about to risk introducing her to a client.' He smiled but his expression was one of concern.

Sophie looked at Sam. His brow was furrowed with anger. 'Is something wrong, Sam?' she asked.

'Yes. This just arrived. Special delivery. It's addressed to Laura.'

'And you've opened it?'

'The sender is J.C. Royston. We opened it in case it contained something unpleasant. It's a jigsaw puzzle.' He handed it to her along with a card, already opened.

Sophie looked at the puzzle. 'It says 3+. So, he nearly got it right.' She read out the card: '"To Laura, Merry Christmas from Daddy xxx." That's nice,' she said.

'He's toying with you,' said Sam.

'Perhaps he's just sending his daughter a Christmas present.'

'After having not had the slightest interest in her since the day he walked out on you both? Anyway, that's not the worst of it.'

Sophie could feel the stirrings of anger. 'Well, Sam, what *is* the *worst of it*?'

It was Jesse who answered. 'Sophie, the fact that it was delivered to Laura here indicates that Jonah, and quite possibly the people he's dealing with, know exactly where you're living. It's likely that the sole reason this has been sent is to make it perfectly clear that he knows where you are.'

Jesse left, Sophie made lunch and Sam's mood slowly mellowed. He herded the boys to their places, strapped Laura in her chair then helped Sophie with the pizza. 'I'm sorry I lost my rag. We can phone and get something sent to him if that's what you want.' He turned his attention to the battle that was brewing over the grated mozzarella.

Sophie touched his arm. 'Jesse's security system is good, isn't it?'

34

Christmas Eve morning, Sophie woke to discover a text from Jonah thanking her for the anonymous hamper. She wouldn't reply. Wouldn't even think about replying. And there was no way she was going to tell Sam about it. Enough was enough and Christmas Eve was a day not to be marred by anxieties. It didn't occur to her to wonder how Jonah had acquired her new mobile number. She glanced at the alarm and was horrified that it was after nine, but just as she was about to panic that she might be alone in the house, Sam nudged open the bedroom door to bring her Laura and a mug of tea. He manoeuvred himself and Laura into bed beside her. 'So, what are we doing today? Not shopping, I beg you.'

'It's all done. I just want to be here.'

'In bed?'

She peered at him over the top of her mug. 'Some of the time.'

–

Katie was now in residence until the New Year. Sophie decamped downstairs to help her wrap, which she enjoyed, her only concern being that it was quite clear Katie had spent more money on Jesse than she'd spent on Sam. Later, with Christmas Eve lunch enjoyed, Sophie dragged Sam upstairs and persuaded Laura to take her afternoon nap:

>...*I love thee with the breath,*
>*Smiles, tears, of all my life; and, if God choose,*
>*I shall but love thee better after death.*

Sam flicked pages. Sophie interrupted his search. 'What's a panic room, exactly?'

He turned to face her. 'Amazing!'

'What?'

'Your non-sequiturs. I make passionate love to you, I read you the outpourings of adoration of Mrs Barrett Browning and the only response I get is for you to ask me "*what's a panic room?*". Well, for your information, it's a reinforced room with no outside walls, which you lock from the inside. And it has everything you need to survive an attack by a marauding tribe of madwomen. Jesse built his early on in the days when he and Sandi used to smoke a lot of weed. He uses it to store Christmas decorations when it's not Christmas.'

'Is it like a nuclear bunker?'

'Hardly. It vents out to the roof, so any passing megacuries would have no problem working their way down there. Why do you ask? Are you planning something?'

'I just remembered Jesse mentioning it.'

'I'll get him to show you it.' He glanced at his watch. 'We'd better get organised. Barbara's due to arrive and Katie needs support.'

'Why?'

'Jesse says she's scared Barbara will think she's trying to step into Sandi's shoes.'

'Is it likely Barbara will think that?'

'Not in the least.'

–

Christmas Eve supper was cleared away, Laura was put into her snowman sleepsuit and everyone gathered around the fire to hear Sam read *The Night Before Christmas* followed by the boys singing their school Nativity songs. Sophie watched the sparkle in Barbara's eyes as she listened to her grandsons sing. She wished her mother could have known grandchildren but Josie and Francis had decided to have cows instead of children and her mother had died before Laura was born. Sam interrupted her thoughts. 'Shall I take her up?'

Sophie said no, she'd do it. In truth, she wanted to be on her own for a while to feel sad about her mother and she didn't want the misery to spill out and spoil the evening. So, she carried Laura up to her room, set the baby monitor then took a moment to just clear her head. She wandered into their lounge and over to the huge panoramic window that looked out over the gardens around Jesse's beautiful house. From where she was standing she could see above the trees towards the front entrance, see the lights of the cars passing by on the road, their passengers on their way towards their own versions of Christmas Eve.

'We were wondering where you'd got to.' Sam was standing behind her.

She turned to smile. 'I was just thinking how different my life is this Christmas.'

'Different in a good way?'

She put her arms around him. Kissed his chin. 'In a *very* good way.' She went to step away but he held on to her, pushed her hair behind her shoulder, kissed her neck… then he let her go. 'We'd better leave this for later. Or people will start to talk.' He took her hand. 'Come on, Jesse wants to make an announcement.'

'About what?'

'God knows. He's probably given the turkey to the poor.'

–

A jug of vodka snowball was waiting as Sam and Sophie stepped into the room. Sam pulled Sophie over to a sofa. 'What have we missed?'

Katie filled Sophie's glass. 'It seems that Jesse is about to move in mysterious ways. Would you boys like some more chocolate milk?'

'I want a snowball,' said Benz.

'That is never going to happen. And you two are twenty minutes to bedtime, that is, if you want the weird bearded man to creep into your room and leave presents.'

Jesse looked at Barbara and rolled his eyes. 'Katie, sit down for a minute. I've been building up to this all day.' He pulled a small, silver wrapped, ribbon-splattered cube from his pocket and held it towards her. She put down the jug and accepted it.

'What's this? It's not Christmas until tomorrow.'

'This is not about Christmas,' he said. 'It's about you and me. And the boys.'

Sophie felt Sam take her hand and, together, they watched Katie tug at the silver wrap to release a small white leather box containing a significant diamond solitaire. Time seemed to take a pause. Jesse interrupted the silence. 'I think it's the right size.' Katie stared at him. Everything became awkward. Again, Jesse broke the silence. 'Well?'

'It's a ring.'

'Yes. An engagement ring.'

'Jesse, I don't know what to say.'

'Well, saying yes would save a whole lot of embarrassment.'

Katie flashed Sophie a grimace of desperation, looked at the ring, turned it in the lights of the Christmas tree. 'God, I can't stand that I'm going to say this in front of everybody but, Jesse, you know I love you to pieces. And I love Jake and Benz.' Her voice started to break. 'And I could never ever be happier than I've been here with the three of you. But...' She touched her throat with her free hand. 'But, Jesse, if you're not happy for things to stay the way they are, then I ought to go now, before things get any more complex.'

Sophie's desire to interfere was almost suffocating but she managed to stay silent.

Jesse spoke through the anxiety. 'Why on earth would you say that?'

Katie glanced at the two boys sitting beside one another, staring back at her. 'Because I can't risk the same thing... Jesse, if something happens to me, you and the boys will finish up with nothing but heartache all over again.' She closed the little box and placed it on the coffee table. 'I can't let that happen to you.'

The room fell silent. And then, just when life, time and Christmas seemed to have reached an impasse, Benz calmly sliced through the atmosphere, walked over to pick up the box and held it towards Katie. 'At least this time Jake and I will remember.'

His brother hurried to his side. 'Katie, please marry Dad. Because we really love you.'

Sophie felt her throat constrict, which was just as well because at least that meant she was unable to speak. There was a lengthy pause and, all credit to Katie, she was the first to recover the power of speech. She wiped her eyes on her sleeve and took the ring. 'If I marry your dad, will you promise to teach me to play Angry Birds?' She hugged them, looked at Jesse over their heads and mouthed. 'Are you sure?'

Jesse strode over. 'Make way, lads. Let's put it on her finger before she changes her mind.'

—

Benz and Jake were finally persuaded to their beds with a cocktail of threats and promises, and then the large-scale fetching and stacking of presents began. Sophie collapsed back into her chair and wondered at the vast display of privilege and generosity piled around the tree and, once again, felt her throat closing over. Sam sat down beside her. 'Jesse never warned me about the proposal. But just in case you suspect that my commitment to you is any less than my brother's is to Katie, I'd like you to have this.' He lifted her hand, turned it over and placed his chain and St Christopher into her palm.

'It's your good luck.'

'No, Sophie, you're my good luck.' But their romantic exchange was interrupted by Jesse demanding Sam help fill the log basket. So, he kissed Sophie and followed his brother outside. Sophie fastened the chain around her neck and wandered over to join Barbara's firelight appreciation of Katie's ring. It must have cost a fortune, but more than that, Jesse must have thought deeply about giving it. And he must have spoken to his boys and Barbara about it because they all seemed to know what was at stake. They all turned as Sam and Jesse came clumping into the room either side of a huge basket of logs. Everyone stepped back to allow them through and, as they staggered past, Sophie could feel the cold radiating off them. 'It must be freezing out there,' she said. 'You're like ice men.'

'There's a really thick frost,' said Sam. 'I hope Santa's got his anti-slip boots on. We don't want him sliding off the roof and landing in the drive.'

'It was getting that way this afternoon,' said Barbara. 'Those poor men working on your gate must have been perished. I don't know how you managed to get them to come out on Christmas Eve.'

Jesse stepped away from the log basket. 'What men working on the gate?'

'There were three of them. I had to toot them out of the way. They said they were servicing your gates, because they'd registered a malfunction. They must have fixed them though, because they opened perfectly.'

Jesse went over and pulled open a tall, flat panel just inside the archway to reveal a concealed system of lights, a wide monitor and a keypad. He typed in a series of numbers and spent a few moments staring at the screen. Sam walked over to join him. 'Is there anything to suggest a malfunction?'

'There's a gap in the video footage for the main entrance. It hasn't caught Barbara arriving. See there...' He pointed to the screen. 'There's a jump forward in time and it suddenly gets dark.' Jesse shook his head. 'I'd better phone.'

'You'll be lucky on Christmas Eve,' said Katie.

Jesse made the call. Somebody answered straight away and from Jesse's half of the conversation it was clear that no engineers had been dispatched to check the security system and as far as central monitoring was concerned, there had been no interruption of signal that day, although footage was not currently retrievable. When Jesse put down the phone his expression was serious. 'Nothing. From their end, the system doesn't appear to have been compromised. No record of on-site maintenance. I'm going to change the codes. They'll text a confirmation.' Everyone stood silent as Jesse poked around on the control panel then waited for an incoming text. It arrived.

'Barbara, can you describe those three guys?' said Sam.

'Well, it was getting dark but they were wearing those bright yellow coats. Two of them were big and well-built and the third one was shorter.'

'What colour hair did they have,' he asked.

'I don't know. They were all wearing Father Christmas hats. I remember that one of the big ones had a beard and the shortest one had really thick black eyebrows. He was the one that was doing all the work. The other two were just watching.'

'Sam, it's Jonah!' All eyes turned towards Sophie.

'What would Jonah be doing, fiddling around with Jesse's gate?' said Katie.

Sam raked his hair. 'Collecting data to give those two thugs access.'

'But, Sam,' said Katie, '…how?'

'I don't know but…'

'If there was a way, I'm sure Jonah would find it,' said Sophie. 'He once told me that, if he wanted to, he'd be able to penetrate Pentagon security and find the missile codes and start World War III.'

'But he didn't, did he?' said Sam. 'That's a load of crap. Nobody can do that. Not even Jonah. And it probably wasn't Jonah anyway. Loads of people… God, are we safe, Jesse?'

'I think so.' He glanced at Sam. 'You should call… the police.'

'Yeh. I'm sure there's a whole battalion of cops just waiting to sort this one out on Christmas Eve.' He looked at Sophie. 'I'll go up and check Laura at the same time.'

'Shall I come too?'

'No, stay here. I probably won't get through to anyone. It's after ten.'

After more than twenty minutes, Sam stepped back into the room and reported that DI Blake, clearly with no good reason to go home, had listened to his concerns and had assured him that a patrol car would check Greenfields at intervals over the Christmas period. He did not envisage any invasion by gangsters and suggested that Jonah just might not be involved, that the three men might well have been casing the house and that the break in the video footage was probably a glitch in the system. There were sighs of relief, indicating the enormous faith that innocent people place in those who are committed to upholding the law.

Jesse returned to the control panel and set the video footage to stream through the large TV beyond the dining suite, and his guests were slightly reassured by the split-screen images of six uneventful views of the outside of the house. Besides, as Barbara pointed out, it was far too cold for anybody to be up to anything that involved going outside. Katie added that even criminals would be reluctant to work over Christmas.

35

By midnight things were calm, as they were throughout Christmas morning, apart of course, from the hysteria that accompanied unwrapping parcels. Christmas lunch was a triumph, after which Jesse suggested a post-prandial walk in the gardens. Katie said that she'd rather die and on this one occasion, and no other, she would prefer to clear away. Sophie suggested that the menfolk should take this opportunity to bond with each other and, besides, if she tried to walk after eating that much turkey she would also die. Benz and Jake refused to look up from their iPads and Barbara retired to a sofa to doze and wait for the Queen's speech. So, after pulling on numerous scarves and sweaters, Sam and Jesse strode out onto the back patio looking like the waxed-jacket brigade. Katie eased off her ring and placed it on the side. 'I don't want that falling into the dishwasher.' She sighed at the pile of greasy plates. 'Soph, I'll do this. Why don't you make some more coffee? They'll need something to thaw them out when they come back in.'

'OK. I'd better take the princess up for her nap first. She put the kettle on then scooped Laura up from the mountain of used wrapping paper that she was shredding and carried her upstairs. She was asleep almost as soon as her head touched down. Sophie checked the monitor then wandered through into her bedroom and over to the window that overlooked the water gardens. It was a stunning scene, snowier than snow, framed by the ice that was clinging to the outside of the window. The ground, the trees and shrubs were covered in a thick white layer of frost. She could make out two tall figures standing over by the frozen pond. It was impossible to tell them apart at that distance. They were both staring down into the frost-covered ice. It was all so white and still, no movement of the trees, not a bird in the cloudless sky. A moment outside of time. Spectacular.

Then something caught her eye, something moving slowly above the tree tops. The size of a large bird. She thought of the albatross in Coleridge's poem. But it wasn't an albatross. Then she noticed Sam or Jesse, she couldn't tell which, pointing up at it, and then the pair of them running towards the house. What on earth was wrong? Her mobile rang in her pocket. It was Sam.

'Sophie, where are you? Is Laura with you?'

'I'm in the bedroom. Laura's in her cot. What's that flying thing?'

'A drone. Sophie, listen, lock yourself in the bedroom, right now. And pull the sofa against the door.'

'What's happening?'

'Just do as I say. Keep your phone on. Are you locking yourself in?'

'Yes.' She hurried over to lock the door into the lounge. She could hear Jesse issuing frantic instructions to Katie to take everyone into the panic room and stay there until he told them to come out, a confusion of questions and fear coming from Katie: 'What's happening? Jesse, the TV by the dining table's gone crazy. Sophie and Laura are upstairs. There's a flying thing outside the window…'

'Katie, just get Barbara and the boys into the panic room.'

Then Sam: 'Sophie, are you locked in? We're at the house.'

'Yes. What's happening? The sofa weighs a ton. But I've done it.'

Jesse: 'Get the shotguns. Cupboard's unlocked. Where's your gun?'

'Upstairs. Loaded it last night. Jesus, Jesse, the front door's open!'

'Katie, are you and the boys in the panic room?'

'Yes, and Barbara. There's hardly any signal in here. What's happening?'

Jesse or Sam: 'There's someone inside.'

Sophie felt terror. She ran over to the door to Laura's room, pulled the key from the inside, locked it from the outside and threw the key behind the bed, ran back and pulled the big dragon chest over towards the lounge door. But as she was pushing it up against the sofa, there was a loud crack and the sofa jolted towards her. She could see the upright of the doorframe splitting along its length and then, just like in the worst horror movie ever, a gun in a gloved hand started to work its way through the crack. Sophie looked around in desperation. She could hear rough voices in the next room, Sam's voice still coming out of her phone. Breaking up. Then the screen went black. She heard a sharp explosion, a gunshot, so loud it made the glass in the windows rattle. She backed away towards the bathroom. Another gunshot. Closer. And then with some massive force the sofa moved fast away from the door and two huge men were striding in past it, wielding guns and heading straight for her. She cringed against the bathroom door, fumbled to grab hold of the handle but one of the men had her arm and was pulling her towards the bed.

Sophie's mind was a chaos of fears. About Laura asleep in her cot, about Sam, about whom the guns had been pointing at when they were fired, about the sweat-smelling man who was gripping her arm. About the other man who was pointing a gun at her. They were barking instructions at each other. She wanted Laura to be safe. She wanted Sam not to be hurt. Jesse not to be hurt. Another man was coming through the door: this man she recognised. It was the bald man with the beard. But now his beard was dripping blood, which was issuing from his ear.

'Fuck, Joe, you been hit?'

'Bastard winged me. Col's fucked. Don't know 'ow bad.' He grabbed Sam's white pullover from the sofa and held it against his ear. 'Keep 'old of the bitch.' He started to push the sofa back against the door. 'Give us an 'and, Bill. Keep the two fairies out of the way. Fairies with fucking shotguns. For killing ickle wabbits.'

'They shoot clays!' Sophie couldn't believe she had just shouted that, but whatever her brain thought she might achieve by doing so, what it actually achieved was a slap across the side of her face which was so hard that it made her teeth ache. She fell backwards onto the bed, watched the two men pushing the sofa but it began to move back towards them. She remembered how strong Sam was. She hoped it was Sam. Then Bald Man turned his gun towards the door and fired and now Sophie hoped it wasn't Sam pushing the sofa. The bullet took a large chunk out of the thick wood. It might have gone through. Sophie didn't understand about bullets. She heard Jesse's voice.

'The police are on their way. Sophie, are you there?'

'Yes. Where's Sam?'

'He's coming.'

The man holding her was about to hit her again, but Bald Man shouted that he didn't want her unconscious. They needed the kid. 'It's not downstairs.' He walked over and grabbed Sophie's hair. 'Where's the baby?'

'She's downstairs in her playpen.'

He shot at the wall behind her. 'Don't lie to me. Where is she?' But he needed to ask no more because a scream rang out in the next room. He let go of Sophie's hair, hurried to push his weight back against the sofa and instructed Bill to knock Laura's door down.

'No!' Sophie screamed. 'Leave her alone!' But at that very moment, as the big man's shoulder impacted with the door and loosened it from its hinges, a deafening explosion caused the huge window to shatter into tiny, sparkling fragments. Like frozen snow. And suddenly Sam was leaping through the empty frame, a shotgun in one hand and a familiar handgun in the other. He spun round and fired the Glock towards Laura's room. Bill's large body fell to the floor, unmoving. The man holding Sophie turned his gun towards Sam. Sophie tried to push his hand sideways. But his arm seemed to be made of iron. A dull shot sounded and in that moment Sophie's mind emptied of everything other than an image of Sam's lucky St Christopher, which was around her neck instead of his. Sam's shotgun fell to the floor. He staggered.

She could see blood splattered across his arm and chest as he recovered his balance, leapt towards the man who was holding her and brought the Glock down on the side of his thick neck so hard that he fell to the floor like a lump of cement.

Sam turned to confront Bald Man but he had moved fast to grab Sophie and now had an arm around her neck and his gun pressed against her temple. She could feel the hard steel cold against her skin. Sam dropped his gun and held up his palms in surrender. 'Don't hurt her.' Blood was dripping off his wrist. 'What can you possibly gain by hurting her.'

Bald Man gripped her tighter and laughed. 'Satisfaction.'

She heard the gun click then a loud explosion and saw Sam's face drenched in blood and something else that looked like pink and red blancmange. She wondered if she was dead but the fact that she was wondering suggested she wasn't. She felt Bald Man's arm slide away from her neck. She was falling, being pulled down by him. She saw Sam's hands move to catch her. Felt his one arm fail him, his other levering her to the bed. 'Don't look down,' he said. But, of course, she did. Bald Man was slumped against the bed. The top of his head was missing and what was left of it looked like a bowl full of blood clots. One of his hands was twitching the way her decapitated frog had twitched in A Level biology class.

'That was a fucking difficult angle!' Jesse was standing in front of the sofa, shotgun in hand. 'Are you OK, Sophie?' He picked up Sam's ruined sweater and threw it over Bald Man's half-head. 'Sam, let me have a look at your arm. And we'd better get all that shit cleaned off your face.'

'Check the others first. Sophie, are you hurt? Just lie still.'

Sophie could feel her heart thumping in her ears. 'Laura,' she managed to say. Then everything ceased.

First there was silence. And within this silence, language evolved to communicate truth. The deliberate misrepresentation of truth came later when dishonesty took on evolutionary significance and deception offered a survival advantage: an advantage that relied absolutely upon the assumption of truth. But lies have proliferated. And there is now every fear that, if this proliferation continues, the assumption of truth will cease to be valid and language itself will no longer be trusted. Communication will become meaningless and mankind will be returned to silence.

From *A Natural History of Lies* by J. Clarke

36

Sophie was sporadically aware of her pillow, soft against her aching jaw, voices phasing in and out, the sound of heavy feet coming and going. She opened her eyes. Katie was sitting on the bed beside her. A man was pressing her wrist, fingers against her pulse. Sam was in a chair pulled close, his hair matted with dried blood, his bare chest smeared burgundy and brown. Another man was applying a dressing to the top of his arm. There were bloodied wipes over his lap. She could feel her chest heaving. 'Where's Laura?'

Sam leaned slightly towards her. 'Downstairs. With Barbara. She's fine.'

Sophie tried to push herself up, but she was trembling so badly that her arms wouldn't support her. Her head felt as if someone was hitting it with a mallet. 'He shot you.'

'I'm OK.' Sam winced as the paramedic wound a tight bandage over the dressing.

'Luckily the bullet went straight through. Didn't hit anything important. Might have nicked the bone.' It was Jesse's voice. 'They'll have to take him in and patch him up.'

Sophie tried to turn her head but the pain in her neck made that impossible. 'Are you sure Laura's all right?'

Now Jesse was beside Katie. 'Perfect. But we had to remove the door to get to her.'

Sophie tried to think but her mind was full of the memory of a bloody half-head. Cold steel pressed against her temple. That hard, polished piece of metal just moments away from penetrating her skull. Beyond Sam she could see the door lying inside Laura's room, its hinges still attached to the frame. She looked down at the crumpled sheet of plastic on the floor and realised what it was. 'Is he dead?'

'Yes,' said Katie. 'Two dead, two unconscious. Good riddance to the lot of them.'

Suddenly, three men in black protective gear were stomping past the foot of the bed, heading for the corpse, throwing down a stretcher. As one of them turned away from her, Sophie could see the letters NCA in white across his back. 'Just this one to go, boys,' he said.

Sam pulled away from the paramedic and barked instructions. 'Officers, stand down! I don't want her seeing any more of this.'

'Yes, sir,' said one of the men. He turned to the others. 'Leave this until Officer Barnes's girlfriend is out of here.' He turned back to Sam. 'Would you like one of the men to carry her downstairs, sir?'

'I'll take her,' said Jesse.

Sophie looked at the man, at Jesse. At Sam. She caught her breath as realisation gouged its way through her aching head. 'You've lied to me.'

Sam began to sag forward. 'Sophie, I'll explain. I didn't... I merrrr...' The paramedic caught him before he fell forward onto the floor.

Jesse hurried to help, held his brother's head down over his lap. 'Just take it easy, Sam.' The three NCA officers stood observing the scene.

'Is he OK?' said Katie.

'It's probably shock,' said one of the officers.

'That never happens on the TV.'

Jesse looked at her. 'Katie, love, the people that write that stuff have probably never been shot and most of them wouldn't have actually killed anybody.'

Sophie tried to sit up. 'What if there was poison on the bullet?'

Jesse helped Sam pull himself upright. 'Sam, you've got to stop Sophie reading that crappy crime fiction of yours. You OK? Any poison careering through your veins?'

'I'm good. Sophie, let Jesse take you downstairs. I'll follow you down.'

Jesse carried Sophie down to one of the guest suites on the first floor and laid her on the bed. Katie followed them in with a glass of water and some codeine, waited as Sophie gulped them down then left to check that Barbara was managing with the children. A stampede of heavy boots went thundering past the door. Sophie tried not to think about what was being carried downstairs. 'Are we safe, Jesse?'

'Yes. The house is awash with Christmas policemen.'

'Is Sam OK?'

'I think so. Just lie still and let the painkillers work. I'll stay with you.'

Suddenly, Sam was standing in the doorway, a shiny blanket around his shoulders, two paramedics supporting him. He pulled himself away, walked over and sat on the bed, close enough to take Sophie's hand but not taking her hand, his face deathly pale, pieces of his blond hair adhering to the dried blood on his forehead. She could hear his breathing, each inhalation laboured, each exhalation erratic.

'Sophie, I need to explain.'

'You've been lying to me the whole time.'

'Yes, but I… I was…'

Jesse touched his shoulder. 'Sam, you're not up to this.'

'Jess, I need to say this.'

He tried to touch Sophie's hand but she pulled it away. 'What are you, Sam?'

He took a deep breath. 'I was seconded from the home police force to work undercover as an SI, a senior investigating officer, with the NCA, investigating organised crime. Just after I came back to the UK.'

Sophie felt sick with disbelief, her mind a chaos of all the time she had known him, right back to that first moment she caught sight of him, a bent bicycle wheel in his hand. 'So, you weren't just cycling past that day?'

'That day I really was going to my mother's grave. But I'd been watching your house for a couple of weeks. Sophie, the NCA have been investigating a cybercrime network: identity theft. But worse than that, there were links to prostitution… child trafficking and exploitation. That's what I was working on in the Far East. With the Hong Kong and Thai Police. But I needed to quit my posting and come home for Jesse.' He caught the blanket as it was about to slide off his shoulder and winced with pain. 'Then, last July, the Agency received intelligence that Robert Perrin might be peripherally involved. Brokering identities. We discovered he'd been manipulating a chain of compromised accounts to facilitate the movement of money overseas. We traced him to his Exeter address but Rosemary insisted he was in Bahrain…'

'You knew he was married to Rosemary? When we first met?'

'I couldn't tell you. We accessed his accounts. Investigated his employees. You were the only one that checked out. We traced his car and discovered he was living with you. Leading his dual life between Exeter and…'

'You knew about the pretend employees before Inspector Blake told me about them?'

'That's when I told Blake who I was. I told him we'd been monitoring the people visiting the house.'

'Like Mrs Davies? And Katie?'

'No. People that might have been doing business with Jonah. Sophie, that first day, I knew straight away that you had no idea what was going on.'

'But you still carried on lying to me.'

'I had no choice; I was undercover. Telling you the truth would have compromised the investigation and put you in danger. So, I stayed close. And fell in love with you. Sophie, whatever these people are trying to find, it's clear it will spill the beans on something very nasty, involving people that don't grubby themselves with the kind of carnage we've just witnessed. Those were four paid thugs.' He began to sag forward. Jesse stepped closer but he raised his hand in reassurance, causing the blanket to fall away from his shoulders and reveal his chest, still smeared with his own and Bald Man's blood. Jesse pulled it back over him.

'Sam, you need to go to hospital.'

'I need to say this now, Jess.' He took a moment to breathe. 'Sophie, keeping you and Laura safe is all I've cared about. I didn't want to carry on deceiving you. I'm so sorry.'

With difficulty, Sophie pushed herself upright. Now that the headache was slowly decreasing, she was aware that all her teeth felt too close together. She recalled that smack on her jaw and tried to remember whether or not the man that had done it was one of the dead ones. But it had all happened so fast. She looked at Sam. His pallor was worsening. He stretched to touch her arm and started to slide forward. Jesse moved to catch him. 'Come on, mate. There's an ambulance waiting.'

The paramedics hurried over to help but Sam shook himself back. 'Sorry. I'm being a complete wimp. Sophie, when I get back, I'll explain everything.'

Sophie leaned close to hold his cold hand. 'Just go and get mended, OK?'

–

Sophie listened as Sam was escorted downstairs and away into the frozen darkness. She remembered some random TV episode where a person had been shot and the bullet had hit a bone and caused it to leak something or other and the person had died of a pulmonary embolism. 'Will he be all right, Jesse?'

'He should be.' His face was lined with worry.

'Are *you* OK?'

'Almost. But blowing someone's brains out is never easy. I prefer clays.'

'Jesse, did you know about Sam being a… whatever?'

'Yes.'

'And when you came to my house that first time, were you helping him check me out?'

'No. I told you at the time. Sam had come home that previous night desperately upset. So, I came to speak to you. To try and tell you about him without actually telling you *everything* about him. I was just trying to prevent my brother collapsing into another mental wipeout.' He sat down on the bed. He looked exhausted. 'And if you're at all interested, I'd like you to know that, after meeting you that first time, I told Sam that he should hurry and get this case out of the way and concentrate on sorting his life out. With you and Laura.'

Sophie tried to smile. 'So, I suppose this means you've been lying to Katie.'

He exhaled audibly. 'No. Against Sam's insistence, I told her about Sam's undercover work. At the university…'

'So, he does actually teach English then?'

'Yes, he does. Anyway, Katie went crazy. She wanted to tell you. We had a huge bust up about it. But after a couple of days of not speaking to me she agreed it was best if you didn't know the truth.'

'That was when you and Sam were yelling at each other, right? So, everyone's been lying to me. Even Katie.'

'She hated keeping secrets from you.'

'Secrets? They were not just secrets, Jesse. They were lies.'

37

By early evening, a clean-up team had sealed the penthouse window and removed the blood-soaked carpet, and the two broken doors and their frames. And Laura's cot had been carried down to the guest suite. Sam phoned to let Jesse know that Officers Blake and Rice would be giving him a lift home from the hospital with a view to immediate debriefing before the evening's alcohol erased all memories of the day's events. Sophie said nothing. She just sat watching the fire, clutching Laura and waiting for the time when she could next take some painkillers.

Katie sat down beside her. 'Would you like me to take her up. She's fast asleep.'

'No, I'll do it, but I could do with a hand. Every time I lean forward, my teeth hurt.'

On the way up the first flight of stairs, it was difficult not to notice the wide, dark stain in the otherwise beautiful white oak. 'Jesse thinks he can bleach it,' said Katie. 'It was the ginger guy. He's not dead, but if you ask me that mole might kill him anyway.'

'Did you see him.'

'Only with a hole in him. I'll need therapy about that.'

'Do you know who shot him?'

'It was Jesse.'

'He seems quite unfazed by it all. Anybody would think he was used to killing people.'

'He used to be in the army. That's what they do, isn't it? And he'd never let Benz and Jake see him fall apart. He'll probably do that later when we're alone.'

'Sam never mentioned Jesse had been in the army.'

'Yeh. Jesse in the army and Sam a policeman. Who would have guessed?'

'Well, I didn't.'

—

Katie helped persuade Laura into her sleeping bag then she and Sophie made their way downstairs for the debrief. They discovered Inspector Blake waiting in the hall. He informed them that Sam had gone up to his apartment to clean up. Jesse was with him. The inspector escorted them into the main room where Jake and Benz were giving Officer Rice their version of events, which was essentially Dad phoning up in a state and everyone locking themselves in the panic room. They'd taken their iPads in with them so it wasn't too bad. Barbara and Katie were able to offer little more, other than Katie recalling the security monitor going haywire and Barbara remembering that, just as they were ushering the boys along, she heard the front door bang open. Of course, Jesse, Sam and Sophie's recollections were what were required so, amid protests, Katie and Barbara escorted the boys to their room whilst the officers waited for Sam to appear.

Inspector Blake turned a cautious smile towards Sophie. 'Officer Barnes has insisted, at every juncture, that you are not placed in danger but, sad to say, the situation today was beyond anyone's control.'

'Inspector Blake, in my experience, most *situations* are beyond anyone's control. In this case, despite Jesse's comprehensive security system, these people were able to break in and threaten us all. It could have ended very badly. Well, I suppose for the, what do you call them, for the assailants, it did end very badly.'

Inspector Blake gave a grim nod. 'We will maintain an armed police presence in and around the grounds for the next forty-eight hours, until Mr Barnes's security system is up and running. So, do try not to worry. But, Ms Denham, I have to ask, do you think your ex-partner was involved in this incursion? The use of high-tech equipment, the compromise of a highly-sophisticated security system…'

'Ron, I said I didn't want Sophie questioned until I was with her! We'll follow correct procedures, if you don't mind.' Sam was striding through the archway, wearing a clean shirt and the jeans Sophie had given him that morning, his arm in a sling.

Inspector Blake got to his feet. 'Sorry, Sam, I…'

Sam waved his hand to dismiss any formalities. 'Officers, let's get this over with.'

—

The three versions of the afternoon were recalled and taped. Sam and then Jesse accompanied the two officers to the library, where their individual recollections would be free of any external influences. However, Sophie was allowed to give her account beside the fire with Sam at her side and everyone listening. She found it very difficult to relive those moments, almost more difficult than originally living them, because reliving them involved more thinking about detail, more analysis. But, despite her dull headache, she managed to stay focussed. When she arrived at the moment when Bald Man was demanding to know where Laura was, Sam interrupted. 'Did he actually say her name, Soph?'

'I don't think so. He just said "Where's the baby?". Why were they looking for her?'

'I don't know. Jonah clearly has at least some involvement in all this. And it can't be a coincidence that Laura's room at your mother's house was completely wrecked and her cot and mattress were torn apart and burned. He must have hidden something in her room. Perhaps they think you still have it.'

'But, Sam, everything we brought here has been used.'

'It's probably something small like a notebook, a hard drive, perhaps a memory stick with account details and passwords. Links to people who wouldn't want the data to fall into police hands.'

'We could go and tell Jonah that we haven't got whatever it is they want.'

'No bloody way, Sophie! Don't even suggest it. He gave those murdering thugs access to this house.'

'You can't be certain it was him.'

'Maybe not. But only a person with his expertise would have been able to break through Jesse's security. Use that drone to jam the phones and cameras. We have to assume that someone is putting pressure on him.'

Sophie sighed. 'Sam, I need to stop talking about this or I'll go mad.'

'Just tell us the last bit. As much as you can remember. Then we can both collapse.'

'What, you mean the bit where you jumped through the window like Superman. With a rifle in one hand and your Hong Kong shooting club gun in the other?'

'Yeh, that bit.'

–

Inspector Blake and Constable Rice finally left and the room fell silent save for the sound of fresh logs hissing and spitting in the heat of the fire. Sophie suppressed a yawn which hurt her jaw. She noticed Sam watching her. 'Is that the first time you've been shot?'

'Strangely, yes. And I can't say I recommend it.'

'Did they give you a tetanus jab?' asked Jesse.

'Yeh. And some anticoagulants and a dose of horse-strength antibiotics. I've got a bagful of the stuff to last into the New Year. And a bottle of diazepam in case I get anxious.' He tapped Sophie's thigh. 'We can share it. Come on, I need sleep.'

Sophie dragged herself up but before she let Sam pull her up the stairs, she went over and gave Jesse a hug. 'Jesse. I'm sorry I've brought all this trouble to your family.'

'It's not your fault, Soph. And, on the bright side, it's encouraged me to upgrade the security system. I've always been worried about that external access. They said it was impenetrable but they obviously failed to take account of the likes of your ex.'

'Well, thank you for saving my life today. I owe you.'

'Don't worry, I'll think of a way you can repay me.'

—

Sophie eased Sam's pyjama sleeve past the thick layer of bandage just to the left of his heart. Another two inches and she would have lost him. What if she'd pushed that thug's arm the wrong way? It didn't bear thinking about, although it was the one thing that Sophie couldn't stop thinking about. She helped with his other sleeve, fastened buttons then climbed over to her side of the bed. 'Does it hurt really badly?'

'Only when I move, and breathe. And think about it.'

She watched him swallow down a small blue tablet. 'So, all this time I've been sleeping with an undercover cop and I didn't know it. But I suppose that's better than sleeping with an evil psychopath and not knowing it.'

'Do you want a Valium?'

'No. In case Laura wakes up and I don't hear her.'

'Well, if you can't sleep, take one, right?' He climbed in beside her and tried unsuccessfully to find a position that didn't involve agony. Eventually, he resorted to lying on his back, perfectly still, his breathing ragged, not so much with the pain but with a guilt that required exorcism. He sighed. 'Sophie, I'm so sorry. I almost broke protocol and told you the truth so many times. And then the longer I didn't tell you the more impossible it became.'

'That's what happens with lies.'

'I was terrified that knowing the truth would put you in danger and, more selfishly, I was scared you'd throw me out.'

'I probably would have done. But then I was living here, so I couldn't have thrown you out. But you still didn't tell me the truth. It's what you and Jesse were shouting about. He told me.' She edged closer. 'But I don't want to talk about it. Those lies can rot away in the past. Sam, we could have died today.'

'But none of us did.' He felt for her hand. 'So, let's be grateful.'

'I am grateful. But I can't stop thinking about those disgusting people, looking for Laura. What if they thought she'd swallowed the thing they wanted and…' She pulled her hand away to cover her eyes, '…and they were going to cut her open and look for it?'

Sam moved to comfort her and winced with pain. 'Soph, you have to stop thinking things like that. And Laura can't even swallow chocolate buttons without retching. She'd hardly be able to swallow a flash drive. Or a notebook. Why don't you take a Valium? It will make thoughts like that go away.'

'But not for good. And when the Valium wears off, the thoughts will still be there, demanding more Valium. I need to deal with this myself.' She exhaled a lungful of anxiety. 'You were very brave today.'

'Does that surprise you?'

'Not really. What was that thing you did to that man's neck?'

'It was… it was a Glock-assisted karate chop. If you do it right you can hit the vagus nerve and the carotid artery and make a person unconscious.'

'Do you know karate?'

'I was working with the Hong Kong Police for six years. It would be odd if I didn't. Although I was a member of a Shotokan dojo, which is Japanese and not that popular in…'

'Could it have killed him?'

'If I'd wanted to kill him I would have hit his throat and collapsed his windpipe. I prefer to take prisoners alive, but it's not always possible. Sophie, please take a Valium. The monitor's right next to your ear. You'll be bound to wake up. I don't want you lying here all night thinking about people being killed.'

'Have you ever killed anyone before?'

'Not to my knowledge.'

'It must be awful shooting someone for the first time.'

'I didn't say I hadn't shot anyone before. It's just, the people I've shot haven't previously finished up dead.'

'People?'

'Yes. Sweetheart, go to sleep.' Silence descended, but not for long. 'Soph?'

'Mm?'

'You don't think any less of me, do you? Because of what I do?'

'No, it's just…'

'Just what… Bloody hell I feel like I'm being anaesthetised. It's just what?'

'It's just that I don't like you having such a dangerous job.'

'Sophie, we'll talk about it tomorrow. I think I'm unconscious.'

'I don't want you getting hurt again.'

'Mmm.'

She felt his body sinking towards sleep, saw the lines of tension disappearing from his face. Saw a different person beside her that night and realised that she had to come to terms with the fact that the sonnet-quoting, gentle man she had known for the last five months had a different, darker side. One that involved violence and damaged lives. 'Sam?'

'Mmmm.'

'I think I'm pregnant.'

38

Sophie lay awake for some time, staring up at the ceiling, a screen for the memories of that afternoon, particularly the clear image she had of Bald Man's half-head filled with mulched brain. And the more she tried to sleep, the more vivid the memories became, each one accompanied by a burst of fear and panic that took her breath away. When the palpitations became unmanageable, she got up and walked round to help herself to a Valium, thought of the new baby and staggered back to her side of the bed, unmedicated and resigned to watching the ceiling until daybreak. But she must have fallen asleep because suddenly the sun was forcing her awake. Sam was sitting on the edge of the bed, offering her a mug of tea. She sat up and took a moment to remember.

'Where's Laura?'

'With Katie. How's your head?'

'It feels like I've had amateur dental work.' She took the mug. 'How's your arm?'

'It didn't fall off in the night. So, it'll probably be OK.'

'What time is it?'

'Just after ten. We thought we'd let you have a lie-in.' He touched her leg through the duvet. 'Soph, did you tell me something? As I was falling asleep? Or did I dream it?'

'Dream what?'

'I was just passing out and I...'

'I told you that I think I'm pregnant.'

Sam stared at her. 'What does the *think* bit of that mean?'

'It means I'm pregnant. I wasn't sure but yesterday before lunch I did the test and then I was. Then everything happened and there wasn't any chance to tell you. Sometimes the pill doesn't work. That's what happened last time. Are you cross?'

'Cross? No, of course I'm not cross. I… look, Soph, I'll leave my job, my NCA job. And the police. I'll just be an English teacher. I'd prefer that anyway, trying to force people to care about books. We won't have enough money to go on holiday ever but… Sophie, I'll never lie to you again. I am the father, right? I mean, Jonah's been out of the picture for months and…'

'And unless I'm an armadillo or a fruit bat or, if I remember correctly, a kangaroo, and I'm able to pause implantation, then yes, you are the father.' She touched his arm. 'Sam, it's your baby, OK?'

'OK. When do we tell people?'

'When we're sure.'

'I thought you were sure.'

'I am.'

'Right. Sophie logic. Katie said do you want her to bring you some breakfast?'

'No, but I'd like someone to bring me Laura so I can know she's OK.'

–

Over a ham and cold turkey lunch, everybody avoided mentioning the horrors of the previous day, which unfortunately failed to prevent Sophie from constantly mulling them over in her mind. So, as soon as lunch had been cleared away, she excused herself and took Laura up for her afternoon nap and the promise of solitude. Sam knew better than to let her be alone.

'Is she asleep?'

Sophie turned from observing the driveway. 'She's playing with Clown-face.'

'Are you feeling all right?'

'I'm fine. Every five minutes or so my stomach churns in my throat but I'm getting used to it. I think I might stay up here for a while. Give them some time to themselves.'

'And where do I fit into that plan?' Sophie tried to answer but her throat was aching too much to allow further conversation. Sam put his good arm around her. 'Soph, we're all OK.'

'But…' She grappled the words into sentences. 'Whatever Jesse says, this has all been my fault. I put all their lives in danger. Their lives are probably still in danger.'

'Nobody blames you for yesterday. Come downstairs. Everyone's worried about you.'

There was a gentle tap-tap. 'It's me,' said Katie. 'Is it safe to come in?'

Sam walked over and opened the door. 'Safe as houses.'

'Very funny. Soph, the boys want you to watch *Home Alone* with them. Because it's about baddies breaking into a house and getting bashed up. Barbara's making popcorn. Just in case anyone has a small empty space in their spare stomach.' She frowned. 'Are you OK?'

Sophie wiped her face on her sleeve. 'Yeh. Could you ask them to give me twenty minutes? I ought to cover up the blotches on my face.'

'I'll tell them they have to wait until you're unblotched. Do you fancy a coffee?'

'No thanks.'

Katie folded her arms. 'No coffee? And you had hardly any of Jesse's finest Burgundy at lunch. Are you demented or pregnant?'

'Witch,' whispered Sam.

She gaped at him. 'Good God, Sophie, are you pregnant?'

Sophie considered her reply. 'Probably.'

'Great! Hurry up and sort your face out. I'm going down to break the news.'

–

Sam waited and, after not much time at all, Sophie emerged from the bathroom looking and feeling a lot better. But there were things she needed to get straight. 'Sam, you said you only realised you'd already met Jonah when you saw that picture of him at Katie's wedding and you recognised him from when he was working at the college. But, if you'd been watching my house you must have seen him loads of times, coming and going.'

Sam gave a tired sigh. 'It was July. August. Whenever I saw him he was wearing sunglasses. And at that point we didn't have a decent photo of him. I just didn't recognise him. Sophie, I am NOT lying to you any more. You have to stop doubting me.'

'Yes. Because that would be unreasonable, wouldn't it? Tell me what you've been doing at the uni for the last couple of years, pretending to be an English lecturer. Were you checking out your cybercrime and just waiting for Jonah to blunder into view? And how come you know all that literature stuff? Did they hammer it all into you at Undercover Academy.'

'Actually, Ms Denham, I have a Masters in English Liter-ature. I had been studying for my doctorate but, just before he died, my father... who was a senior army officer, expressed his and my mother's deep regrets that, unlike my brother, I had chosen a namby-pamby career. So, ever willing to please, I abandoned academia and became a cop. OK?' Sam pushed his wrong hand through his hair. 'And as far as my part-time teaching post is concerned, to begin with I was checking out foreign students. And some of the staff. Institutes of higher education have traditionally been regarded as hotbeds of sedition. These days, those worries extend to terrorism. We'd had a heads up about possible links with Syria. The introduction into the UK of foreign nationals posing as student family members. It's not usual for an officer as senior as myself, a detective inspector, to be assigned to undercover work but there was not a big choice of lower-ranking personnel able to take on an academic post. Then I got pulled back into organised crime, human trafficking. And became a senior investigator with the National Crime Agency. And last year Robert Perrin really *did* land on my patch.' He sighed. 'Is there anything else bothering you?'

'Yes. Why did you let me imagine Jonah's wife was called Heidi when you already knew she was called Rosemary?'

'Because I couldn't be sure that wasn't what he called her. It didn't seem likely that there was a third woman in the equation. Then I discovered that mobile number was registered to someone living in Bridport. Ella Roberts. Turned out to be Suzie's mother. Is there anything else?'

'Yes, there is… When we first made love, were you still checking me out?'

'No, of course not. I… I was hopelessly attracted to you.'

'So, tell me, Officer DI-SI Sam, how can I ever really believe that?'

'I can't answer that, Soph. All I can do is promise you it's true.'

'That's the problem, isn't it? How can anybody believe anything they're told? You checked Jonah's phones behind my back, didn't you? It's why you stayed with me? So you could find out more about Jonah.'

Sam just shook his head. 'That might have been true to start off with but, as soon as I got to know you, everything changed. Sophie, there are no more secrets.'

'You can't write all this off as secrets, Sam. Secrets are things you keep to yourself. Lies are what you tell. But I'm as much to blame as anyone. Because I was stupid enough to believe you.' She watched him sit down on the bed as if that last statement had drained the energy he needed to stand. She didn't want that to be happening. 'But, like I said, we need to leave those lies in the past.'

'OK. But, Soph, I've got to ask you not to mention my work with the NCA, or what happened yesterday, to anyone outside of this house. Can you promise me that?'

'You want me to promise not to tell the truth?'

'I just want you to promise to be economical with it.'

'Right. Economical. Shall we go and watch Kevin beat up the baddies?'

39

Jesse was taking no chances. The day after Boxing Day, the house was full of engineers replacing the security system. Jesse and Sam spent a lot of time following them around asking questions. By the afternoon, the constant testing and retesting of alarms was beginning to drive Sophie crazy, so she went up to the top floor to pack some more things to transfer downstairs. She was just forcing toys into an IKEA bag when her phone rang. It was Mrs Davies. She thanked Sophie for the Christmas hamper and then, by way of conversation, mentioned that there had been a lot of banging next door for the last few days. She added that the same two men as before had visited Jonah just before Christmas, although they hadn't been there since. No, and they won't be, thought Sophie. She told Mrs Davies not to worry then wandered through to her bed, now resting on bare, blood-stained floorboards, sat down and worried. After a while, her phone rang again. It was Suzie.

Suzie wasn't sure what to do. Some of her things were still at the house with Jonah and she was frightened to go there to collect them. Sophie gripped the phone nearer her ear. 'No, Suzie, don't go there. I'll ask Sam to collect them for you. How much is there?' Suzie said just her new boots and her pyjamas. And her antenatal record pack and she needed that for her appointment the day after tomorrow. Sophie thought it was quite likely that Jonah would have put it all in the bin, or perhaps tossed it onto his ceremonial bonfire in the back yard. She told Suzie she'd ring her back, wandered over to the window seat and resumed worrying.

It was as she was staring aimlessly through the window at the sunlit grass, wondering at the speed with which things change, that she came to a decision. She needed to know what Jonah was up to, banging around in her mother's house. And she knew how important it was for Suzie to have her baby logbook. And, to be honest, Sam would go crazy if she asked him to visit Jonah. She rang Suzie back. 'Hi, it's Sophie, are you still all right to drive?' Of course she was. 'Well, why don't you drive over to Jesse's place and pick me up? I'll text instructions. We can go take a look at the sales, and if we're feeling courageous, we can go on over and collect your things. And I can check my house is all right.' After a brief pause, it was agreed that Suzie would pick Sophie up the following day, around noon. She'd tell her mother they were checking out prams. Her mother would be relieved because she hated shopping. Sophie said that sounded like a plan, rang off and went downstairs to tell Sam that Suzie had phoned to ask her to go pram shopping. He offered to come with them although he'd rather die and Sophie said such things were best done in the absence of a suicidal man. Then she sat, riddled with guilt, and watched Laura forcing Clown-face into a cardboard box.

–

Suzie picked Sophie up as arranged, and having negotiated her exit through Jesse's new check-in, check-out licence-recognition procedure, she took the road to the after-Christmas sales.

'Sophie, that's a very thorough security system Jesse has. It will be a miracle if anybody ever visits him.'

'We had a bit of trouble with the old system over Christmas, so he's upgraded.'

'Anything serious?'

'Not really.' Sophie didn't think there was anything to be gained in worrying Suzie with details, especially when she was driving with twenty-six weeks of pregnancy between herself and the steering wheel. Besides, Sam had asked her to tell no one.

They parked in the multi-storey and after a cursory glance at prams, a quick hot chocolate, and dismissing all good sense, they made their way towards Sophie's house. Sophie climbed her steps and rang the doorbell, waited, peeked through the letterbox. 'I don't think he's there. Shall I use my key?'

'We'll just pick up my things and go.'

'OK.' Sophie opened the door and stepped into the freezing hallway, called Jonah's name, prayed that he wasn't lying on the floor upstairs, walked ahead of Suzie to the kitchen and was appalled at the squalor: food trodden into the floor, dirty dishes. She looked though the back window at the few remaining pieces of debris from before, then, together, they checked the lounge. It was messy with computer components, wires and metal boxes.

'It's colder in here than it is outside,' said Sophie. 'Were your things upstairs?'

'Yes. In Jonah's bedroom. What if he's up there?'

'We'll say we're checking that he's been managing all right over Christmas.'

Cautiously Sophie climbed the stairs. As she reached the landing, she was able to see through into Jonah's bedroom. The bed was unmade, clothes all over the floor. She peered in through the doorway, reluctant to go inside. 'He's living like a pig. I thought Social Services were visiting him every day.'

'Maybe he's frightened them away,' said Suzie, finding the courage to go inside and investigate the wardrobe. 'I can't see my things anywhere.' She stepped back onto the landing and wandered off to the spare room.

With trepidation, Sophie walked along and prodded the door to Laura's room, which, as it eased open, revealed everything she had feared but really hadn't expected. It was as if a pack of rabid dogs had been cut loose inside. Things that had survived the previous onslaught had been torn to pieces, the wardrobe had been emptied, tiny coat hangers snapped, clothes thrown onto the wooden floorboards, some of which had been levered up and not replaced. That would probably explain the banging Mrs Davies had heard. Sophie felt the need to run home and tell Sam that Jonah had obliterated Laura's little pink bedroom, but she realised that her deceit made that impossible. She pulled the door closed, took a moment to gather herself then hurried to the spare room to tell Suzie they should leave straight away. She found her standing beside the bed, shaking her head in frustration.

'There's nothing in here, Soph. Apart from his stupid model aeroplanes.'

Sophie walked over to investigate. The bed, once covered in Jonah's stacked possessions, was now covered in the hardware of his latest project. She pulled out her phone and took a few hurried photos. 'They're not model aeroplanes, Suzie. They're drones.'

'What?' But as Sophie went to explain, she heard the front door open and close, felt Suzie grip her arm.

'Sophie, what shall we do?'

'Just stay calm.' She pulled Suzie out onto the landing and yelled downstairs. 'Is that you, Jonah? It's Sophie. And Suzie's with me. We dropped by to collect Suzie's things.'

Jonah was standing at the bottom of the stairs. Scowling up at her. She took a deep breath and started down towards him. 'We rang the bell but we realised you were out. We were just looking for Suzie's antenatal papers.' Jonah said nothing. He just watched her drawing closer. She stopped three steps from the bottom. She felt vulnerable, terrified of this man she had lived with all that time. She managed a little laugh, steadied her voice. 'You guessed it was me that sent the hamper.'

He continued to stare at her. Then suddenly his mouth twitched and, to Sophie's great relief, he turned away and headed for the kitchen. She heard the squeaky stair and was aware that Suzie was standing right behind her. She knew they ought to leave right then and there but, despite Suzie tugging at her arm to do so, some inconvenient curiosity forced her to do otherwise. She left Suzie pulling at the front door and followed Jonah into the kitchen. He pulled out a chair and sat down. Glanced past her. 'What's wrong with *her*?'

'Her mother's expecting her home five minutes ago.'

Again, his mouth twitched. 'And she's Suzie, is she? I think I remember her coming here before. Did you have a good Christmas?'

Sophie was overcome with a deep desire to denounce him as a lying cheat but, instead, she countered his lies with lies of her own: 'Yes. Although, there was a bit of a break-in at my boyfriend's house, but nothing was taken. Anyway, we'd better be going. Suzie's a bit nervous driving in the dark.' She turned to leave. Heard Jonah's chair move. Turned back hoping her face was not displaying the terror she felt. He was standing, shaking his head.

'They won't stop until they have it, Soph,' he said. 'There's too much at stake.'

For a brief moment, Sophie caught a hint of the man she had once lived with and believed. But then it was gone and he was the crook who had visited horror upon the people she cared about, had enabled those murderers to gain access to Laura. He took a couple of steps towards her. She fought not to run to the front door and away. 'Jonah, I truly don't know what you think I have.'

'Please yourself. But, be assured, those morons were not the only thugs they have at their disposal.' He turned his back on her and walked away to the sink.

Sophie watched him for a moment. He was more or less admitting that he was involved in the break-in. She needed to interrogate him, ask him to explain, but she could hear Suzie calling her. She glanced along the hallway. Suzie was now standing on the top step, holding the front door open and flapping her hand in desperation. Sophie took a last look at Jonah's back then hurried to join her but, as she stepped out into the cold late-afternoon drizzle and pulled the door closed, she heard Jonah's final words, clear and unmistakable.

'It was under her mattress.'

—

Back at Greenfields, Sophie stepped out of the car and watched Suzie drive away, stood for a moment, staring down at the wet gravel, convincing herself that she'd done nothing wrong, then hurried inside out of the rain. She discovered Katie and Barbara watching *Dr Zhivago*. Apparently, Sam had taken Laura up for her nap over two hours ago and hadn't reappeared. Sophie frowned. 'I hope he's not let her sleep all that time. She'll never go down this evening if he has.' She hurried up to the big guest room and found Sam sitting on the profusely-cushioned daybed, his hands on his knees, the sling on the seat beside him, his face serious. Laura was amusing herself in the playpen.

'How was your shopping trip?'

'Good.' She could see he was angry. She pulled off her coat and threw it on the bed.

'See anything interesting?'

'Not really.' Something was wrong.

Sam got to his feet. 'Would you like to tell me where you've been?'

'I'm sorry we're a bit late. Town was full and...'

'Sophie!'

Good God, he knew. 'We went to... how did you find out?'

'You mean, how did I find out that you've been to see Jonah?' She chewed her lip. 'Yes.'

He threw back his head in frustration. 'Sophie, did it not occur to you that Jonah is still under surveillance? Blake phoned me to ask why I'd risked you going there with just a girlfriend with you. Have you any idea how stupid it was to do that? The guy's unstable. He's mixed up in God knows what. I've been worried sick. Why didn't you answer your phone?'

'Oh! I think it's on silent. But I'm OK.'

He walked over and held her arm. 'Sophie, it's not just about you now, is it? Please tell me what possessed you to risk confronting him like that.'

She mumbled into his chest. 'Suzie left some of her things there and she was scared to go there on her own. And Mrs Davies phoned to say Jonah had been banging around next door and I didn't want to worry you with it. He's pulled up the floorboards in Laura's room.'

Sam pulled her over to sit down. 'Tell me exactly what happened.' It was Sophie's second debrief in three days. Sam listened without interrupting until her narrative reached Laura's room. 'My God, Sophie, you should have left right then and there.'

'I went to tell Suzie we should do just that. She was in the spare room. Jonah's things are all back around the house. But the bed was covered in… I'll show you.' She fetched her phone, opened Photos and handed it over.

Sam flicked through the images. 'This was in the spare room?'

'Yes. They're drones, aren't they? That proves he was involved, doesn't it?'

'Yes, it does, but circumstantial evidence like this might not be admissible in court. I'll have to check. Jonah could argue that you photographed his possessions without informing him that you were going to go into the house in his absence and undertake a search.'

She sat down beside him. 'But it's half my house.'

'I know.' His tone mellowed. 'But, it does do away with any doubts we might have had about Jonah's involvement in our Christmas Day massacre. Tell me what happened next.' So, Sophie told him about Jonah coming home, the lies, his warning and his final statement.

'He actually said it was under her mattress?'

'Yes.'

'What a sick bastard! Did he say what it was?'

'No. And he probably still thinks I have it, despite the fact that I told him I didn't know what he was talking about. And… I was scared to ask. I wish he was dead.'

Sam rubbed his hand down his face. 'You're going to have to repeat all this to Inspector Blake. Although I'd advise you not to include the bit about wishing he was dead.'

'OK. Are you still mad at me?'

'Yes! Absolutely. After all your protests about my deceiving you, you deliberately lied to me. Promise you'll never do anything as crazy as that again.'

'I promise. I… Are the police parked somewhere, watching my mum's house?'

'Not exactly. There *have* been periods of intermittent surveillance by officers, including myself, but over the last six months that's placed too much strain on resources.' He almost smiled. 'However... *The Regulation ofInvestigatory Powers Act* allows for the surveillance of individuals...' He mimed air quotes. '...*for the purposes of preventing or detecting crimeviathe use of covert human intelligence sources*.'

'What does that mean?'

'Informers.'

'What informers?'

'Mrs Davies next door and her friend down the road.' He actually smiled. 'Mrs D. saw you walking past her window and phoned Inspector Blake.' He laughed. 'Sophie, love, you'd make a really lousy criminal.'

Sophie sighed. 'What will Josie say when she discovers what he's done to the house?'

'We'll fix it. But, first, we need to get him out of there. Prison would be the best option. If only we could nail the bastard. Cybercrime think they've located a likely darknet portal: *Deus Innominatus*. If they're correct, well, you've spent five years living with a man who has no qualms about who and what he deals with. The Agency are now looking into his possible involvement in the falsification of drug trials. Providing bogus clinical subjects to speed up the acquisition of marketing authorisation licences for drugs that run into problems during their clinical trials. The Bundespolizei and the Swiss Federal Police are aiding the investigation.'

'But adverse drug reactions can be lethal.'

Sam shrugged 'I think Jonah's moral compass is a little defective.'

Sophie glanced over at the playpen where Laura was attempting to pull the head off a talking tortoise that Jake had given to her on long loan. 'I hope moral compasses are not dominantly inherited.' She slumped into the cushions. 'Sam, what did you mean when you said Jonah might have been involved with exploitation of children?'

'It's best you don't know.'

'You don't get to say that any more. Tell me!'

He sighed. 'You might be aware that it's not uncommon for young girls to be smuggled into the UK, many of them from Eastern Europe, to be used for prostitution and – in the network we've been investigating – for the gestation of babies that can be sold for adoption or, we think, as part of some kind of surrogacy enterprise. Also, during their repeated pregnancies, these young girls fetch a higher rental price since some individuals have a predilection for pregnant women. Obviously, the girls' families attempt to find them, so they need to be provided with new identities. It's also likely that the sale of farmed babies requires falsification of birth certificates. Something about which Jonah has personal experience.'

Sophie shook her head in disbelief. 'I can't believe Jonah would get himself involved in such things. Money laundering maybe, but not using young girls to farm babies. For God's sake, he has three daughters of his own.'

'As Blake said, he might not have been aware of what he was involved in.'

Disaster Management

Sir Hugh Grenville swallowed a large dose of scotch. 'Jones, this has been an unmitigated disaster! Have you managed to contact the Source?'

'Yes, sir.'

'And?'

'As you are aware, the Royston child was not taken. But from what has been gathered during the aftermath of the failed incursion, it seems that this would have been a pointless intimidation strategy, since, according to Perrin, it is now clear that the data is not in the possession of his ex-partner, the child's mother. More significant, however, is the revelation that the mother's new partner of several months is, in fact, a police detective working undercover as a senior investigating officer with the National Crime Agency.'

'Good God! What? Can this wretched situation get any worse?'

'Sir Hugh, I assure you that the situation is not as bad as one might imagine. Given the involvement of this NCA officer, Samuel Barnes, we can rest assured that if any incriminating information had come into the hands of the Agency, action would already have been taken. As it stands, none of our facilities have reported any problems. I think we can safely assume that, as Mr Perrin has suggested, the data is lost. Which means that the only threat would be from details known only to Robert Perrin himself.'

'And what of Perrin?'

'Given his knowledge of our enterprises and his involvement in the Xmas incursion it would probably be advisable if our unnamed god met with another unfortunate turn of fate.'

'We cannot risk any further compromise, Jones.'

'No, Sir Hugh. Absolutely.'

40

'Soph, can I come in? I'm desperate.'

Sophie looked up from sorting socks. 'What's up?'

'We're going for drinks with that new client and I can't find my concealer. Can I borrow one? I'll bring it back as soon as I get home.'

'In my bag.' Sophie pointed. 'Front pocket. Take your pick.' She resumed comparing shades of black. 'I don't know whether the washing machine is eating socks or generating them. Jonah always bought the same socks so it was never a problem.' She watched Katie rummaging in her bag. 'Have you found one?'

'Yeh, I think the dark one's the closest. Can I...?'

'Can you what?'

Katie held up three slim boxes. 'When did you change to Rigevidon? Is it as good? Or do you think that's why you're pregnant?'

Sophie walked over and took the pills. 'Nothing works a hundred percent of the time.'

'Certainly not in your case, Soph. That's quite a collection and none of them opened.' She folded her arms. 'When did you stop taking them?'

'What do you mean, I...? Three months ago. Don't tell Sam!'

'I wouldn't dream of it. But, if I were you, I'd flush them down the toilet, just in case he decides to investigate your bag.'

–

The old year stumbled to an end and became the new year without further trauma. Barbara Buckley went home to prepare for her long trip to see her daughter in Australia. And Sophie paid a quick visit to her GP who confirmed her pregnancy and reassured her that being beaten and frightened into unconsciousness was unlikely to have affected her baby, because if that were not the case there would not be so many healthy yet doomed babies born in war zones. In response to this confirmation, Jesse hassled his workforce and managed to get the penthouse repairs completed by the end of the first week of January so that Sam and Sophie were able to move back prior to their return to work and Laura's initiation into a new crèche, which at least promised no further emotional abuse from the vile infant Hadrian.

Unsurprisingly, Katie put her apartment on the market and began the stressful task of moving her possessions into Greenfields. She received an offer of purchase within two hours, which relapsed her into a heightened state of unreasonableness. Jesse handled her mood swings with saint-like tolerance and on the Sunday evening that marked the end of their long and eventful Christmas break, he prepared a last supper of comforting fish pie and apple crumble. Over coffees and hot chocolate for one he revisited his suggestion that Sophie give up her office grind and come to work with him, planting gardens that would survive long after all those office papers had been shredded into oblivion.

'Jesse, I'm going to be a complete physical liability in the next year.'

'Why do you say that, Soph?'

'Because I'm pregnant?'

'Well, that shouldn't stop you hurling instructions at your workforce. And when you get too large to sit behind the steering wheel of your car, we'll arrange a driver.' He took a mouthful of coffee. 'Will you consider it? Instead of your four-day week in the waste paper factory?'

Sophie was confused. 'What car?'

'Your company car,' said Sam, pushing a pink plastic card towards her. 'As you can see, I've been opening your mail. I've booked lessons for you, which you'll need to confirm.'

Sophie frowned at the Provisional Driving Licence in front of her. 'Where did you get that photo. It's nothing like me!'

Sam looked at his brother and shook his head. 'It's the one from your passport.'

Sophie continued to frown at the card. 'Is that my signature?'

'Yes, I forged it. I'm a policeman, I'm allowed to.'

'But Sam, I can't learn to drive and be pregnant at the same time!'

'It never said anything about that on the application form.'

Closure

On Monday morning, Sam helped escort Laura to her new crèche, dropped Sophie off at the office, cancelled his morning tutorial then drove up to the Forensic Pathology Unit.

'Hi, James. Happy New Year. Am I interrupting anything important?'

James Moran looked up from the mass of blasted brain tissue. 'Sam! Happy New Year! I gather you had an eventful Christmas. How's the arm?'

'Still hanging there. Is that who I think it is?'

'Yes. Allow me to introduce the late Joseph Mann. Your brother made a real mess of his haircut.'

'Jesse's better with clays. I thought I'd nip up and take a look. Get closure.'

'Sure. I've already done yours. William Bartholomew Langley-Jones. Quite an upmarket name for a murdering thug.'

'His parents probably didn't realise he was going to be a gang-ster.'

'Probably not. He's back on ice.' He pulled off his gloves and indicated the stacked refrigeration system to one side, escorted Sam over and pulled open one of the steel units. A covered cadaver emerged feet first. 'Hello, Billy Boy. And how are you today?'

Sam watched him pull back the smooth white sheet to reveal a person whose face Sam failed to recognise. He looked at the yellow-grey body, at the hole where the bullet had entered and the Y-shaped repair that rose up alongside it. 'He was breaking into the baby's room. I fired the Glock straight at him. No time to aim.'

'Well, it was a nice shot. Straight through the dorsal aorta. Out like a light. Unfortunately, he knew nothing about it. Is the missus OK?'

'Yeh. We're all pretending it didn't happen. That one of us didn't almost finish up lying here on one of your slabs.'

'From where I'm standing, it looks like you came pretty close, my friend.' James Moran took a step back. 'You've been in the game a long time. Was he your first fatality?'

'First in the UK. I don't count the ones in the Orient.'

'You know there's counselling if you…'

'I'm OK. And I've seen enough. Put him away.' Sam watched the unit slide back. 'This whole incident's made me realise how what I do threatens the people around me. It's never felt like a problem before. I'm thinking of asking for a desk job. Maybe early retirement.'

'Is that an option?'

'I'll let you know. I'm speaking to a Careers Advisor next week. In the meantime, James, we will be pursuing our inquiries regarding half-headed Joe's possible contacts.'

'An unenviable task, Sam.'

'Yeh.'

41

That same Monday morning, Sophie popped in to tell her Section Manager that she was pregnant again and that she thought it was only fair to hand in her notice sometime in the next few months so that the company was not forced to pay her another year's worth of maternity leave. Mandy Drew, the misandrist who headed up PR, contacted her within twenty minutes to assure her that she would be within her rights to have as many babies as she liked one after the other and her contract would be protected. Sophie said that, although she valued her current employ, she could not bear to envision a future when her efficiency and contribution to the company would be compromised by difficulties with child care; she would prefer to go out in a blaze of colour. She did not mention that the future which she now envisioned included a company car, her own workforce and a free hand to buy as many and whatever plants she chose, aromatic or otherwise, in order to build a brighter, greener world.

Her friend, Joanna, called in to see her just before lunch to ask whether she would like her to organise a farewell party. Clearly, everyone knew that Sophie was moving on.

That afternoon, Sophie took a call from a distressed Rosemary, who had, immediately after Christmas, received a letter from Robert's solicitor, informing her that Mr Perrin was now forced either to sell his Exeter property to raise funds for his care, or to charge her an appropriate rent if she wished to continue to live in his house. Therefore, would she make arrangements to vacate the property or contact them immediately to discuss a rental agreement. She was driving up tomorrow. Robert had granted her audience on Wednesday morning. She was going to appeal to him: Zane needed time to raise money.

Sophie said she thought it would be dangerous visiting Jonah-cum-Robert because he was unstable, but Rosemary said that her life was on the verge of ruin and she had to do something about it, however dangerous he might be. She was staying over in the Premier Inn. Perhaps they could meet for supper. Perhaps Suzie would like to come along too. She'd love to meet her.

After Rosemary rang off, Sophie went down to the coffee machine, bought a latte and sat on her own thinking about her five years with Jonah. She progressed to fantasising about the various directions her life might have taken if she had never become involved with him, but all of them included no Laura and no Sam. So, she just had to accept that she *was* involved. As was poor Suzie. She decided to give her a call and wish her Happy New Year. Suzie returned the good wishes but said that, so far, her new year had not been happy. She'd had three texts from Jonah in as many days begging her forgiveness. When he'd seen her that day, just after Christmas, he had realised how much he missed her. He'd do anything to make amends because he didn't want his son to grow up not knowing his father.

Sophie resisted her need to curse. 'Suzie, please tell me you're not going to let him lie his way back into your life. Quite apart from the fact that he's hoping to use you as some kind of chambermaid, he's also muddled up with some really violent people.'

'No, Sophie, I'm not as stupid as that. I just wish he'd leave me alone. What if he tries to demand visiting rights to see his son?'

'They'd never grant him visiting rights.' Actually, Sophie had no idea whether that was true. But Sam had never seen his son and she was sure he would have done if it was possible. She listened to the silence at the other end of the phone. 'Look, Suzie, Rosemary's driving up tomorrow and staying over. She's meeting Jonah Wednesday morning to try and negotiate a way of staying in her house. I'm having supper with her. She suggested you come along too.'

That evening Sophie told Sam about her dinner date with Jonah's wife and mistress. 'I think they're keen to meet each other. Maybe find out whether they have anything in common… other than Jonah.'

'Just supper, right?'

Sophie frowned. 'Yes.'

'And, presumably, you'll go straight from the office?'

'Yes, straight to Pizza Express.'

'Right. I'll pick Laura up as usual. I should be back in time.'

'Back from where?'

'I'm checking out one of half-headed Joe's contacts. He had a burner on him at the time of his comeuppance.'

'What's a *burner*?'

'It's a disposable phone. Untraceable. Popular with criminals. And adulterers. It's a wonder Jonah didn't have a drawerful of them.'

'Will it be dangerous?'

'I shouldn't think so. It's a rental company: Arcadia Jay Retreats.'

'Well, be careful anyway.'

'I always am. I'll drive back over and pick you up.'

'I'll catch the train. I—'

'I'll pick you up.'

Thaddeus Jones

Thaddeus Jones glanced across at the security monitor. He frowned. Allowed his phone to ring a few times. 'Miss Holmes? I insisted no interruptions.'

'Mr Jones, there's a Detective Inspector Barnes to see you. He says it's urgent.'

Thaddeus Jones took a moment to calm himself. 'Well, tell him I'll see him in five minutes… no, ten. I'm in the middle of a phone call, which is also urgent. Offer him coffee.' He cancelled the call and sat for a moment watching the monitor, watched the tall Inspector Barnes fold his arms then turn to stare straight at the camera. Thaddeus Jones flinched, turned away and started to collect up the files he'd been annotating and the photo identities of a couple of prospective clients, chose a few documents that it was safe to leave on display. He glanced several times at the monitor. Barnes was still standing, arms still folded, glancing every now and then at the camera. Thaddeus Jones felt observed. He reached for the remote and switched off the security monitor, pressed the intercom and asked for DI Barnes to be shown in.

Sam stepped into the palatial office, made immediate eye contact with the expensively suited, finely coiffured man sitting at the desk and watched Thaddeus Jones get to his feet and indicate the seat opposite.

'To what do I owe this pleasure, Inspector Barnes? Hopefully nothing too serious. I do believe my TV licence is up-to-date.'

Sam sat. Initial value judgement: slimebag. 'Mr Jones, this inquiry is in response to a violent and fatal altercation, which occurred over the Christmas period.'

Thaddeus Jones sat back down and placed his palm against his chest. 'My Good Lord! And you imagine that I might be of assistance in such a… Where did this dreadful incident take place?'

'That is of no consequence, Mr Jones. Our only interest in your good self rests upon the fact that one of the fatalities, a Mr Joseph Mann, was in possession of a prepaid mobile phone and of only six calls made, two of them were to you. So, clearly, we are interested in any dealings you might have had with this man.'

Thaddeus Jones shook his head. 'Can you tell me when these calls were made, Inspector?'

'They were made on the 23rd and the 24thof December.'

'To this office number?'

'Yes.'

'Obviously, I receive many calls. Particularly throughout the holiday season. But I'm afraid I don't recognise the name. *Mann*, did you say?'

Sam felt in his breast pocket and pulled out a photo. 'This is the individual in question. It's not a particularly recent photo. The beard has been added to assist identification.' He paused. 'In our more recent image of Mr Mann, he is missing the top half of his head.'

For a brief moment Thaddeus Jones seemed to lose his cool. Then he rallied. He took the photo. Looked confused. 'Actually, I do recognise this character, but he was not using the name you mentioned. He had a foreign name, Polish or the like.'

Sam frowned. 'Sokolov?'

'Yes, that's it! He came here on a single occasion, looking for a short-term retreat. It must have been early December. Quite clearly, he had the funds… from what I gathered… but he was not the kind of person we do business with. So, I sent him on his way with a promise to get back to him if anything should become available.'

Sam nodded. 'And what kind of people do you do business with, Mr Jones?'

'The kind of people that would not usually find themselves losing the tops of their heads, Inspector Barnes. Mr… Mann or whatever, phoned me after, perhaps two weeks, to enquire as to whether anything had become available. And, not satisfied, he tried calling again. That must explain the two phone calls. On the second occasion, he was most abusive. I can't say that I regret the fact that our paths will not cross again. A most uncouth gentleman.'

Sam took the opportunity to look around the room: at the framed photos of town houses, aerial shots of country estates. He indicated the blank monitor. 'The surveillance footage piped in from your reception area, do you retain the data?'

'We are very particular about the people we deal with, Inspector Barnes. Most of our clients come recommended but occasionally undesirables do slip through the net, in which case it is appropriate that we have a record. However, all footage is deleted after two weeks. Our clients expect a high degree of confidentiality.'

'I'm sure they do.' Again, Sam looked at the properties on display. 'Do you let properties throughout the entire UK?'

Thaddeus Jones bristled. 'We arrange luxury retreats for a discerning clientele. Our fine residences are distributed widely throughout the United Kingdom, however we have found that most clients prefer to sojourn in the southern counties.'

Sam watched him reach for a file.

'I regret that I cannot offer more assistance in your inquiries, Inspector, but if there is nothing else I can help you with, I am expecting an important telephone call in just under fifteen minutes.'

Sam got to his feet. 'Well, thank you for your time, Mr Jones. I'll see myself out. Although there is just one last thing: has Miss Holmes been with you long?'

'New this week. Agency staff. No point in letting them get their feet under the desk.'

Sam left Thaddeus Jones reading his notes. Overall impression: definite slimebag. And, undoubtedly, a well-practised liar. There was no way that half-headed Joe had been contemplating a luxury sojourn. So, what business had he been pursuing with Mr Jones?

42

Sophie met Suzie in the car park and they walked the short distance to Pizza Express, where Rosemary was already into her second glass of chardonnay. After hugs and introductions, they gave their orders and the conversation turned to the issue at hand. Apparently, Rosemary's solicitor had advised her that, if things continued as they were, she stood little chance of any claim on Robert's house since, despite her daughters, her desire to live in his property with her new partner should not be allowed to compromise the funding of his ongoing care. Alternatively, if he were to be found guilty of financial fraud, embezzlement or the like, his property would become forfeit and she would continue to have no claim on any proceeds. On the other hand, if Robert were to die before charges could be brought against him, she would stand a chance of securing at least some of his estate owing to her and her dependants' lack of complicity in Mr Perrin's perfidious behaviour.

'So, ladies, I'm hoping for his sudden death. I did think of going there tomorrow and offering him one last vigorous shag in an attempt to kill him. I tried suggesting it as a bargaining chip but apparently he has to avoid "arousal".'

'Good Lord,' said Sophie. 'Can he still not have sex?'

Suzie leaned closer. 'In his last email, asking me to move back in, he said he knew that I'd understand his forced celibacy. He said that even when he tried to pleasure himself, his headache became unbearable.'

Sophie gaped at her. 'He put that in an email?'

'Actually, he said *wank*.'

'That's real irony for you,' said Sophie. 'To think that after his previous priapic commitment he's now an obligate celibate.'

They shared a discrete snigger.

Their drinks arrived, another chardonnay and two mint teas. Rosemary reached over to pat Suzie's hand. 'So, sweetie, how's the bump? Robert always wanted a son.'

'We're both fine,' said Suzie.

'And Sophie's pregnant too. I hope it's not contagious!'

'Suzie's worried that Robert will try and get visiting rights.'

'Is that possible, Sophie?'

Suzie sighed. 'With Jonah, anything's possible. I just wish they'd put him in prison.'

A waitress brought their starters. Sophie waited for her to leave. 'Prison doesn't last as long as dead does. He's wrecking my house and Sam's solicitor said getting him out before he causes any more damage would be difficult given his medical circumstances. I was stupid to let him move back in there. He's even pulled the floorboards up looking for… They think it's a notebook or a hard drive or a memory stick. Something holding information that certain people want to get their hands on.'

'And you've absolutely no idea where this thing could be?' said Rosemary.

Sophie looked at Rosemary, who was currently comparing the size of her tiger prawns with Suzie's, and dismissed her momentary suspicions. 'It seems he hid it under Laura's mattress but we never took the cot with us. And I've searched through everything. I think it must have been thrown away when I was sorting through things to take to Sam's. Jonah thinks I found it and re-hid it, which is why he's wrecked my house and why a load of thugs turned up at Jesse's house over Christmas.'

'What thugs?' said Suzie.

Sophie paused. She might already have said too much. 'I didn't tell you. It was to do with the people Jonah's got himself involved with. We informed the police. They said not to worry. But I'm scared that, whatever happens to Jonah, none of us will be safe until those people realise that what they're looking for doesn't exist any more.'

Rosemary put down her fork. 'And you're sure about that are you, Sophie? That this, whatever it is, doesn't exist any more?'

Sophie watched her reach for her glass. 'Rosemary, it's *lost*.'

Rosemary sipped her wine. 'Well, lost or not, our lives would be a whole lot easier if Jonah was out of the equation.'

'But he isn't out of the equation, is he? And all this rubbish about amnesia and confusion... he's obviously decided it's the way he can stay in my house, and get Suzie to skivvy for him, and take your house away from you.'

'He's been lying to us all,' mumbled Suzie.

'Well then, why don't we make him realise he's not going to get away with it.' Rosemary emptied her glass. 'Like, if we convince him that there's no way he can set us against each other, that Sophie will evict him if he tries to take my house. And that neither of us will let him threaten you and your son, Suzie. Put an end to his lies once and for all.'

43

Sam drove Laura to the crèche before dropping Sophie outside her office block. She pecked his cheek then hurried through the rain into the building and, as she often did, she watched his car drive away. But, as she never did, she called a cab and waited in the lobby for it to arrive… As arranged, Suzie and Rosemary were waiting for her in the Premier Inn car park and, with Rosemary at the wheel, and the windscreen wipers distracting their thoughts, they drove together to the town centre, parked, grabbed umbrellas and made their way towards Sophie's house.

'Sophie, are you sure Mrs Davies visits her daughter *every* Wednesday?' said Suzie.

'Yes, without fail.' She hoped without fail. But she was reassured by the *Sorry We Missed You* note slotted through Mrs Davies' brass door knocker, and with this reassurance she climbed the two steps to her mother's house, inserted her key in the lock and knocked hard as she was opening the front door. 'Are you there, Jonah? It's Sophie. I've come along with Rosemary to give her moral support. I don't think the doorbell's working.'

Jonah emerged from the kitchen and came to an abrupt halt when he caught sight of his wife and two mistresses. His surprise was palpable. 'All three of you? I presume introductions aren't necessary.'

'No, we're all acquainted,' said Rosemary.

'You were supposed to get here at eleven. It's twenty past nine.'

'We couldn't wait to see you,' said Sophie.

Jonah watched as they propped their umbrellas against the wall. Then he retreated into the kitchen, strode over and opened the door into the yard wide.

'God, Jonah, it's already freezing in here,' complained Rose-mary, stepping into the kitchen. 'Is my perfume bothering you?'

He remained by the open door. 'Yes, as I'm sure you realised it would. And it's *Jonah* now is it?'

'Well, as far as the three of us are concerned, Jonah seems the most popular choice.'

He sneered. 'Look, shall we get this over with, Rosie. There's nothing to discuss. The house is mine and it needs to be sold in order to pay for my care. Either that, or you pay me to let you stay there. I really don't know what you think your new friends can do about it.'

Sophie fought to stay silent. This was not a man who was suffering any kind of mental fragility. All pretence of confusion was abandoned. Unexpectedly, Suzie broke the silence. 'But, Jonah, if I go back to helping you, then it won't cost anything, will it?' Jonah was visibly taken aback.

'And, I'd step in as needs be,' said Rosemary, 'so I could stay in the house with the girls. We can discuss how much rent you'd need to charge me with Suzie helping out.'

As he turned his attention towards her, Sophie detected a clear chink in his armour. 'I'd be happy for you to stay here until you can find somewhere better. Obviously, Josie…'

But suddenly his expression changed. He placed his hand over his reattached ear. 'Is this some kind of laugh you're having at my expense?'

'No, of course not,' said Rosemary. 'We've all discussed it and we've concluded that it would be in all our best interests if Suzie went back to helping you. She was your most recent choice, after all.'

Jonah stepped away from the door, caught hold of a chair and lowered himself into it.

'Are you all right?' said Suzie.

He eyed Sophie taking the chair opposite him, his face now twisted with discomfort, his hand firmly against his ear, as if he was trying to prevent it breaking away.

'Oh dear, Jonah,' said Rosemary. 'Is it one of your migraines? Perhaps you should have a lie down. We can have our little talk later.'

'There's nothing to talk about! I want you all to leave!'

'We can't leave you like this,' said Rosemary. 'You've gone terribly pale.'

Sophie watched Jonah sag forward onto his arms and began to seriously doubt whether their charade should continue. All they were supposed to be doing was warning him off. Not stressing him to death. She moved her hand to touch him but thought better of it, asked if he was still taking the same migraine medication. He raised his head briefly and pointed to a white tub beside the microwave. Suzie hurried to fetch it but, as she reached out to pick it up, Rosemary caught her wrist, told her to fetch him some water, then grabbed the tub, tipped its contents into her palm, walked over to the open door and cast Jonah's medication wide into the rain outside.

Sophie leapt up. 'What are you doing, Rosemary?' She hurried round to Jonah and touched his shoulder. Spoke to his downturned head, worried about what might be going on inside it. 'Jonah, can you make it through to the lounge so you can lie down? Suzie come and help. I'll take his weight.'

Suzie banged the glass of water down on the work surface and helped Sophie manage Jonah up out of the chair and along the hallway. She looked frightened. 'Sophie, do you think we should phone for a doctor?' she whispered.

'No!' snapped Rosemary. She was right behind them, the glass of water in her hand.

They reached the lounge door. Sophie grabbed the frame to steady herself. This wasn't supposed to be happening. 'Suzie, just help get him to the sofa. He just needs to sleep when he's like this.'

With no contribution from Rosemary, Sophie swiped plugs and wires aside and they managed to manoeuvre Jonah along the length of the sofa. He lay there, eyes closed, his breathing irregular. Sophie felt in her coat pocket and pulled out her phone. But before she was able to make a call, Rosemary nudged her aside, perched herself beside Jonah's tense body and spoke quietly into his good ear. 'Try and take some sips of this. It will make you feel better.' She lifted his head slightly and held the glass to his lips, waited as he drank, his eyes still closed, then placed the half-empty glass on the coffee table. Began to stroke her hand along his thigh.

Suzie ran out of the room but Sophie remained, horrified. 'Rosemary, what on earth are you doing?'

What on earth was she doing? Jonah groaned, turned his head towards them. His eyes open, bloodshot, dashing from side to side, displaying the same desperation Sophie had witnessed through that slit in the bandages. He threw his hands up to his temples as if he was trying to hold his head together and cried out in anguish. Sophie didn't know what to do so she just stood, incapable, listening to his cries becoming quieter, then quieter still, then slurred. His right leg gave a single jerk. And then, in no time at all, he was quiet, his breathing slow but regular. Sophie felt sick, faint; she stepped over to the coffee table, picked up the glass and lifted it to her lips. Rosemary jumped up and snatched it from her.

'Don't… I'll get you some fresh.'

Sophie looked at the glass. She was scared. Scared for Jonah. Scared that Sam might ever find out that she had been there. Rosemary was reassuring her: it would all be OK, but they should leave right away. Sophie was speechless. She remembered Suzie, found her in the kitchen clutching the back of a chair. 'What was happening to him, Sophie?' she said.

'It's just a really bad migraine.' She walked over and closed the back door.

Rosemary stepped into the kitchen, hurried over to the sink, rinsed out the glass, let the warm water wash everything away. Then she rinsed it again, dried it and put it back in the cupboard. 'Nobody needs to know you were here,' she said. 'I'll phone Social

Services as soon as I'm back at the hotel, and tell them that Jonah felt unwell during our meeting and I was concerned about him.'

'Were you planning this all along, Rosemary?'

'Planning what?' said Suzie.

'I just came to ask him not to drive his daughters out of their home.'

'What did you put in that glass?'

'Nothing! I… I just didn't think you ought to be drinking out of the same glass as him in your condition. God knows who he mixes with these days.'

Suzie looked at the cupboard. 'What did you do, Rosemary. Is he going to die?'

'No, of course not,' said Sophie. 'But, Rosemary, we ought to phone now.'

'I really will do it as soon as we're back at the hotel.'

–

They drove back to the Premier Inn and parted company with Rosemary's assurance that she would alert Social Services straight away. Suzie drove Sophie back to work. They barely spoke. When she asked what had happened after she'd left the room, Sophie said that Jonah had just started to quieten down and fall asleep. That always happened with his migraines. She had almost convinced herself that was the explanation. She promised to phone, stepped out of the car and hurried up to her office.

Viola glanced up from filing her nails. 'Hi, how did it go?'

'The baby's due August 23rd.'

'Do you know what sex it's going to be?'

'No, you can't know that until about eighteen weeks.'

'Oh. Do you fancy lunch? With me and Bella?'

'Thanks, but I'm feeling a bit woozy and I've got some catching up to do.'

–

Sam had already collected Laura by the time he drew up outside the office. Sophie climbed into the Range Rover, leant over and kissed him and felt horribly guilty, a feeling which she thought might be with her for ever. Sam asked her a couple of times on the way home if she was feeling all right and she said it was just those first weeks of being pregnant when your whole physiology is reorganising itself.

Just before supper, Sam took a call from Ron Blake informing him that Robert Perrin had been discovered unconscious by Social Services late that afternoon and he was now back in Intensive Care at Southampton General. His condition was critical. Sophie instantly felt sick, announced that she wasn't able to eat anything and hurried upstairs to the bathroom, where she locked herself in and texted Suzie. Then she deleted the line of texts, flushed the toilet and ran the taps. Sam's voice came from outside the bathroom door. She stepped out to reassure him. 'I wasn't sick. I just thought I might be.'

'Sophie, don't upset yourself about him.'

'I'm not. I ought to phone Rosemary. Make sure she knows.'

'I'll call her, if you want.'

'No, I'll do it. I'll come down in a minute. Tell Jesse it wasn't the promise of his pizza that made me feel sick.' She waited for Sam to leave then called Rosemary to relay the news, particularly the part about Social Services not discovering Jonah until late afternoon. Rosemary said that the hospital had already called her and that she couldn't explain the delay because she had phoned straight away. Sophie didn't believe her but saw no point in telling her so. She ended the call then wandered through to where Laura lay sleeping, unaware of the part her mother had played in her father's latest crisis.

—

Downstairs, Sam had just taken another call from Inspector Blake. He stepped over to take Sophie's hand. 'I have to go over to the house. Officially, we're just confirming there are no suspicious circumstances but Blake also wants me to check out those drones and anything else that might link Jonah to what happened Christmas Day.'

Sophie's stomach took a dive. 'Suspicious circumstances?'

'Whether someone's still sending thugs to harass him. See if there are any signs of an intrusion. Blake's over there at the moment. I presume Rosemary told you, it seems Jonah had a migraine attack during her visit. She phoned Social Services to get them to check he was OK and they found him unconscious.'

Sam left. Sophie made her apologies and sought the silence of her room, where she sat, trying to recapture details which her mind was refusing to remember. Evidence that she might have been there. Had she taken anything out of her bag? She wasn't sure. She had her phone and she'd used her umbrella on the way back to the car… and her scarf was lying on the daybed. She recalled her psychology notes: serious stress inhibits memory processing. And she *was* seriously stressed. But she was sure of one thing: that Rosemary had gone to her meeting with Jonah with an altogether different intention to the one they had previously discussed. And she had drawn her and Suzie into her plans with lies and deceit.

Hours passed. Katie brought tea, hot chocolate. The house fell silent. Then at last Sophie heard Sam's car pull up outside. She listened to his feet coming up the stairs. She'd be able to tell from his face if he'd found anything wrong, anything suspicious.

He stepped into the room. 'How are you feeling?' he said. 'You shouldn't have waited up like this.'

'I'm fine. I was worried that you were taking so long.' She hoped fear wasn't obvious in her voice. 'Did you find anything?'

He sat down beside her. 'We checked out the house then I drove down to Southampton. Jonah's back in his old room. They're reasonably certain he suffered a spontaneous episode. There were no outward signs. They're recording it as a major bleed. Something that was just waiting to happen, quite possibly unrelated to the accident last August. Apparently, scans carried out last October revealed a previous skull fracture, although there was nothing recorded in his medical notes.' He took her hand in his. 'He's not expected to recover. Which doesn't help our investigation but it will certainly relieve any emotional burdens upon the people whose lives he's been destroying.' Sophie could feel her hand shaking in his. He squeezed it steady. 'Soph, there's nothing to worry about. You're in the clear.'

She sat back and looked at him. 'What?'

'Sophie, you need to tell me what happened. Shall we start from the beginning? From when I dropped you at work and you waved at me through those big glass windows?'

Sophie put her head in her hands. After too long a silence, she took a deep breath. 'It really started yesterday evening. Over supper…'

Sam listened to Sophie's account without once interrupting. She insisted that she and Suzie had gone along just to show Jonah that he was no longer dealing with individual victims but with three women who would support each other against his machinations. As far as they were concerned it was to be a demonstration of solidarity but Rosemary must have had some ulterior motive, she must have been hoping that seeing the three of them together would upset him. She told Sam about Rosemary throwing Jonah's migraine pills into the rain, but failed to mention her snatching the glass away; it frightened her to even consider why she had done that. And she insisted that Rosemary had promised to phone straight away and she clearly hadn't because straight away would have been earlier than late afternoon. She stopped talking and waited for Sam to comment but he didn't, which is the best way of guaranteeing that the guilty will say too much. But Sophie just said, 'Mrs Davies usually goes to her daughter on Wednesdays…'

'It wasn't Mrs Davies who revealed you were there,' said Sam.

She frowned. 'So, who told Inspector Blake we were there?'

'Nobody told Inspector Blake. We checked out the drones then I decided to take another look around and I found this

357

amongst some wires, down beside the sofa. You were wearing it in the shower this morning.'

Sophie watched him put his hand in his jacket pocket and pull out a small St Christopher hanging on a silver chain. Pointlessly, her fingers went to her neck. She felt his arm close around her.

'Don't worry, Sophie. You're free of him now.'

Lost in the System

'James, any luck with that blood?'

James Moran looked up from his sandwich, reached across his desk and uncovered a slim folder. He started to read: 'A lot of what you'd expect: beta blocker, anti-psychotic, traces of sodium valproate... probably anti-migraine...' He got to his feet. 'But then, just when you'd least expect it, a whole heap of ephedrine hydrochloride.'

'What?'

'Ephedrine. Strange given that Mr Perrin was not listed as an asthma sufferer, was probably not dieting in preparation for his new summer wardrobe, and was actually taking drugs to reduce his blood pressure not increase it. There was enough there to blow anyone's brains out. Way beyond recreational use.'

'Jesus!'

'Yeh.' He handed Sam the folder. 'Your call. Analyses officially logged in as pertaining to a Mr John Doe. Who, incidentally, had a serious cholesterol problem.'

'James, could we possibly file this for the time being?'

'Sam, my friend, that is the only printed copy.' He returned to his sandwich. 'The digital version is about to become lost somewhere in the system.'

44

Sophie phoned each day to ask after Jonah, requesting each time that she be contacted if there was any improvement. But improvement there was not. And improvement there was never likely to be. She was plagued constantly by memories of his last sentient moments, those last slurred cries for the pain to stop. And Sam's reassurances helped not a jot.

'It's been over two weeks and he's not got any worse. And last time he recovered.'

'Soph, it's not the same as before. You have to stop blaming yourself.'

She chewed her lip. 'I spoke to Rosemary earlier. She doesn't seem to be suffering any kind of remorse at all. She said she's thinking of nipping over to tell his mother that her son is being punished for his sins and is on his way to Hell.'

Sam furrowed his brow. 'Jonah's mother's still alive?'

'Yes, well... she was last summer. She's in a home. I think she has dementia. Jonah used to go sit with her every Sunday when he was in Exeter.'

'You never mentioned that before.'

'Rosemary told me. When we visited her that time.'

'And he visited her every Sunday?'

'Yes. Why?'

'Well, perhaps he stashed something with his mother. I wouldn't put it past him. I'll find out where she is. Don't tell Rosemary, but I think it's time Jonah's mother was introduced to her youngest granddaughter.'

The trip to Devon was less arduous on a drizzly January Sunday than it had been in the glaring sunshine last August. They took the time to have lunch at their favourite Topsham Hotel and then, mid-afternoon, drove to Snowberry Residential Care Home, where they were escorted past vases of petrol-station chrysanthemums to Laura Perrin's room. Her priest was just folding his stole and crucifix into his case, as the care assistant knocked and stepped inside, so it was a very righteous and forgiven elderly woman that scowled up at them as they were introduced: Sophie as the mother of Robert's youngest daughter and Sam as her partner. Father Leary left without much attempt at communication. Clearly the two tainted heathens that carried poor Mrs Perrin's illegitimate grandchild into the room were not worthy of conversation. Laura Perrin senior fixed her eyes on her granddaughter and crossed herself. Undeterred, Sophie attempted to apologise about not having visited before, and communicated Rosemary's best wishes.

'Whore!' exclaimed Mrs Perrin.

Uncertain as to which whore she was referring, Sophie continued with her attempts at conversation, whilst Laura wriggled in her pushchair and Sam scanned the spartan decor: no books, a plain wooden box on top of a chest of drawers, a large family bible on the bedside cabinet, a demanding wooden cross on the wall above the bed, a faded print of Holman Hunt's *Light of the World* hanging next to the window and a single coat hanging on the back of the door. Then, all at once, as if she was alone in the room, Mrs Perrin got up from her chair and shuffled away into her bathroom.

'You can see where Jonah learned his pleasantries,' said Sam, quickly checking the drawer of the bedside cabinet and the cupboard beneath. He opened the bible, checked its binding then hurried over to investigate the wooden box. It opened easily to reveal no contents whatsoever. He turned his attention to the two large drawers, rooted around in the top drawer, lifted a few things, closed it, opened the bottom drawer and felt around beneath the clothing.

'Sam, hurry up! What if she comes back?'

He looked behind the chest of drawers, under the bed, lifted the curtains, checked in the coat pockets. 'Nothing! I'll ask the matron if she's got anything stored elsewhere. For insurance purposes. I'll show her a cop card if necessary.' The toilet flushed.

'Sam, she's coming back!'

Sam hurried to stand next to the pushchair just as Jonah's mother stepped back into the room. She looked at them in surprise.

'Hello, are you visiting me? What day is it?'

Sophie glanced at Sam. 'It's Sunday. We've brought Laura to see you. She's your granddaughter. Robert's daughter.'

'Robert's daughter? I had a boy called Robert. But he died when he was little.'

'Oh dear. That's sad.' Sophie glanced around for inspiration. 'Do you have any photos of him? Photos of Robert? When he was little?'

Mrs Perrin stared at her blankly then shuffled over to her chair, sat down, reached under her pillow and pulled out a rusted biscuit tin with *Royal Wedding Shortbread* and a decades-old image of Charles and Diana on its lid. She lifted the tin onto her lap and, with her shaky yellow fingers, prised it open to reveal a few curled photos. But it was not the photos that caught Sam's eye. It was the passport that was amongst them. Sophie noticed it too. She picked out a photo of two boys: dark eyebrows, dark hair, one of them obviously Jonah, although she wasn't sure which. She held it towards the window and asked Jonah's mother which of the boys was Robert. Mrs Perrin pushed the tin onto the bed and leaned over to take a closer look, providing Sam with the opportunity to nip behind her chair, lift the passport and slip it into his jacket pocket.

Mrs Perrin pointed over to the bathroom. 'They were bad boys. The Lord had to punish them for their sins. He sent them into the cupboard and they never came out. I couldn't find them anywhere.'

Sam caught Sophie's attention and indicated the door. So, Sophie handed Mrs Perrin her photo, wished her goodbye and told Laura to wave. They left her waving back.

As they were signing out, the Matron-Manager stepped over to speak to them. 'Going so soon? I hope she wasn't rude to you. She has her good days and her bad days.'

'This was one of her good days,' said Sam. 'We were wondering if you could help. The family have been searching for an old endowment policy but Mrs Perrin doesn't seem to have any papers with her.'

'As far as I know, her son keeps all her documentation. I gather that he's been quite unwell lately.'

–

Sam waited until they were a safe distance from the Care Home before pulling into a layby to investigate the passport. He opened the data page, took a moment then handed it to Sophie. It was a more recent photo than the one on Robert Perrin's driving licence, and this time the name alongside it was Brady and beneath that Anthony Patrick. Sophie handed it back and, as she did so, a small folded piece of paper fell out. Sam opened it. An alphanumeric reference was written across the fold, and beneath it, two long strings of numbers.

'That can't be what they're looking for, can it?' said Sophie.

'I don't think so. I think the top one's a flight reference. The other two might be bank codes and account numbers. I'll get them checked out.' He sighed. 'It's not what I was hoping for but it's something.' He placed the passport back in his pocket and pulled away.

–

By the time he picked Sophie up the following day, Sam was able to reveal the next instalment in Jonah's abortive plans. The booking reference was for a flight from Heathrow to Istanbul which had left on 11th August last year. The booking had been made some weeks before Jonah's collision with his toolbox, for one person only and that person, a Mr Anthony Brady, had failed to make the flight.

'There's a possibility that Jonah rumbled the fact that he'd been found out and he was planning to make a dash for it. The passport's issue date was early July. He must have paid his mother a quick visit and stashed it there where no one was likely to find it. The two other numbers are for a Spanish account with 1.2 million Euros and a Cayman Island account with just over two million dollars. Both accounts, held by Anthony Brady, have been active during the last two months. Seems he was still hoping to get away.'

'So, back last summer, Jonah was leaving me, Rosemary and Suzie.'

'Looks like it.'

'And my TV and freezer were going to be Suzie's consolation prize?'

'Perhaps Suzie's place was somewhere to lay low until Robert Perrin became Anthony Brady.'

Sophie shook her head. 'Sam, don't tell Suzie he was planning to leave without her.'

'OK. Anyway, how did your antenatal go this morning?'

'Fine.'

'I'll come with you next time. If you want… I mean, if that's appropriate.'

'OK.' She tapped her lips slowly as she watched him drive.

He glanced round. 'What?'

'You must have thought I was a complete dope believing all those lies.'

Sam sighed. 'Is this going to be a lengthy conversation?'

'Not really.' She opened her bag. 'You carried on checking my house after we moved out, didn't you? Going there and telling me you were going into uni.'

Another sigh. 'Yes, particularly when it became obvious that Jonah had hidden something there.' He pulled into the crèche car park and cut the engine. 'I was just trying to protect you both.'

'That was very considerate of you, Officer Barnes.' She pulled out a small black and white photo and handed it to him.

Sam frowned. 'What's this?'

'They scanned me today. They think I'm more pregnant than I calculated.'

Sam's frown deepened. 'I don't know what I'm looking at.' He pointed to a curved bit. 'Is that a head?'

Sophie also pointed. 'Yes, and that's another one.'

—

Over the next three weeks Jonah's condition at first failed to improve and then started to decline. Then a very ordinary noso-comial infection rapidly became a ventilator-associated pneu-monia which exacerbated further strokes. Rosemary phoned Sophie on the Thursday of the third week to say that the hospital had contacted her for a decision about the continuation of life support and resuscitation if it became necessary. She was driving up the following day and would appreciate Sophie being with her when she visited Jonah for what was to be the last time. She had also asked Suzie to be there. So, that Friday, Sam accom-panied Sophie to the Neurological Unit. Suzie and her mother were already there, waiting beside Zane. Rosemary had gone ahead into Jonah's room to spend a few moments alone with her husband. Sophie could see her through the glass partition, looking down on her handiwork.

Dr Donovan arrived and escorted Sophie and Suzie in to join Rosemary at Jonah's bedside. He made a much-practised state-ment about the absolute unlikelihood of recovery from what was essentially brain stem death and explained that, when the venti-lator was turned off, Jonah would be unable to breath, oxygen would fail to reach his brain and heart and life would end. Suzie started to cry. Sophie put her arm around her. Rosemary turned to do the same and Sophie could see that she was also crying. She feared that she might be the only heartless one there. And then she felt tears running down her own cheeks and was grateful that if this had to be happening, she was sharing this dreadful situation with these two other women that Jonah had forced into her life.

As Jonah's next of kin, it fell to Rosemary to hand the signed forms to Dr Donovan and ask him to proceed. It was a simple process: turning somebody's life off like that. It took no effort at all. Dr Donovan told them to take all the time they needed and then left. The room became deathly quiet. The machinery that had been maintaining Jonah's life was now silent. The monitor was still registering something, but the peaks were getting lower and further apart. Sophie waited for that long whine that always signified people flatlining in the movies but it didn't happen. The monitor just slowly stopped recording anything.

Sophie looked at Jonah lying there, coming to an end, and felt an irrational desire to hear his voice one last time. But his voice was gone to Hell with the rest of him. They stood in silence for a while, the three of them just watching what remained of the man who had fathered their four children. Then, slowly, Rosemary stepped forward to stroke his hand. 'So sorry, my love,' she whispered, 'but you gave me no choice.' With that, she turned to leave. 'Ladies,' she said. 'It's time to move on.'

-

Robert Perrin's cremation was a brief affair attended by just six adults, who, once the fine oak casket had been dispatched towards the incinerator, and instructions had been given for Jonah's ashes to be strewn in the Memorial Garden, stepped out into the late-February sunshine and repaired to Carluccio's for lunch and reminiscences. Late afternoon, with promises to stay in touch, they went their separate ways and Sophie was now free to tell Sam about the snatched-away glass, but she found it much easier to pretend that those few moments had never happened. And so, as summer drew near and life became gloriously routine, the guilt that Sophie feared might follow her to her grave slowly withered away.

Resignation

'Ah, Officer Barnes, do take a seat. I've been reading your interim report. It seems that the search for the Perrin data has reached a terminal impasse.'

'I'm afraid so, sir. I believe we have to resign ourselves to the fact that the data is lost.'

'And do you think that those whose practices and reputations are threatened by it will also regard it as lost?'

'In time, with the lack of arrests, I think it will become obvious. In the meantime, I'm continuing to follow up on a couple of leads and my colleagues are pursuing parallel enquiries regarding the Downs and Plymouth bodies and any possible links to surrogacy practices. The only positive thing we can draw from Robert Perrin's death is that organised crime has lost a significant resource.'

Director Short grunted his dissatisfaction. He indicated two handwritten sheets on his desk. 'I have also been reading your request for a cessation of field duties. I gather that you wish to pursue a more didactic career within the police force and you are asking me to recommend you for this post at the Academy? A post which would not seem to require a knowledge of Coleridge and Shakespeare, Detective Barnes.'

'I realise that, Commander Short, however, personal circumstances make it impossible for me to continue my undercover work as efficiently as before. And I feel that my knowledge and experience would be better diverted towards…'

'Barnes, you have been a valued officer in the NCA. Your field skills are not easily replaced. And I was under the impression that you were very happy teaching reluctant students at that university of yours.'

Sam held his voice steady. 'Sir, if I am successful in this application, I intend to resign from my existing teaching post… other than, perhaps, as a visiting lecturer in eighteenth and nineteenth century literature…' He noticed Director Short roll his eyes. 'Recently, as you may be aware, my circumstances have changed. And are continuing to change…'

'And how is your partner?'

'Very well, sir. We are both looking forward to a hectic autumn. Indeed, sir, this is not the least of the reasons that I feel I am no longer able to offer the Agency the absolute priority that is required for the safety of myself and my men.'

Director Short sighed with resignation and reached for a wide envelope. 'Officer Barnes… Sam, this is my recommendation for your appointment at the Academy. I will provide it on one condition.'

'Sir?'

'I will provide it on condition that you remain a Special Officer in the NCA, advising, but also involving yourself in field operations whenever unusual circumstances require it.'

'Which *unusual* circumstances… sir?'

'All those circumstances that would appear to be *not usual*, Officer Barnes.'

Some lies are more costly than others.

From *A Natural History of Lies* by J. Clarke

Loose Ends

...Dr Phillip Matthews, obstetrician and an early pioneer of embryo diagnosis was found hanged in his home in the remote Scottish Highlands earlier this week. Foul play is not suspected. Dr Matthews was recently in the news...

...And now the Shipping Forecast issued by the Met. Office on behalf of the Maritime and Coastguard Agency at 00.15 on Friday 4th May... Thames, Dover, Wight, Portland, Plymouth south-westerly 4 or 5 becoming 6. Occasional rain. Good becoming moderate...

-

At the break of a sunny May morning, slightly more than two months after Robert Perrin... aka Jonah Royston... had finally been put to rest, the two plus two crew of the magnificent fifty-eight-foot *Sweet Dreams II* prepared to leave port.

'Rosie, darling, what's wrong? Are you having second thoughts?'

'About the crossing? No, not at all. I was just remembering that day. You have to allow me a small regret. He was their father. And this feels like we're finally leaving him behind.'

'Sweetheart, he left you no choice. You had to do it. Robert was a threat to us all. To Sophie and poor Suzie. And he was going to take our girls' home away from them. And he was a threat to the Organisation and the desperate people it tries to help. And Mr Jones has rewarded us well. More than we expected.'

'Yes, a lot more than we expected. It makes you wonder what else Robert was muddled up in.'

'Mr Jones said he was involved with child abduction. And prostitution. That's terrible stuff. We have two girls to protect. People like Robert have to be stopped.'

'I know. I just can't believe he knew what he'd got himself into. Zane, do you think we know too much?'

'Too much what?'

'Too much for them to let us just sail away into the sunset?'

'Crumbs, Rosie. We should be in Roscoff before sunset. There's a strong breeze mid-channel and it's in our favour.'

Rosemary shook her head and sighed, sat back and allowed the engine to gain confidence, watched the ordered exodus leaving the harbour and tried to imagine those carefree, sunny days working their way down the French coast.

Zane leapt onto the pontoon, untied the rope and threw it onto the deck, then jumped aboard. 'Get ready to fend off, Laura. Izzy, you're too near the edge.' He walked over and took the wheel. 'Here we go, ladies, we should be there in time for tea.'

Rosie laughed. 'In time for Vin du Pays, sweetie. Nothing in front of us but a blue sky and the open sea.'

–

And on that same sunny May morning, Sir Hugh Grenville regarded the thick folder with irritation. 'Exactly how much of this do I need to read, Jones?'

'Perhaps the contents page would suffice, Sir Hugh. The rest includes the personal details of the current sponsors, twenty-three sponsorships in all, the financial and security checks, disclaimers, medical data… information regarding surrogates, genetic markers, requested birth dates. Also, two requests to sponsor which are being investigated. The printed copies do seem more daunting than the digital files, but you insisted that we revert to such… due to the lack of ease by which they might be duplicated.'

'Yes, yes. Quite! And tell me, Jones, the gestations are proceeding according to plan?'

'Yes, Sir Hugh. All contracts are in order. And the new obstetric team are a vast improvement. If you remember, the most advanced cohort of seven multiple sponsorships are all currently resident in the UK awaiting completion.'

'Excellent!' He flipped open the folder. 'And the Perrin data?'

'The Source has confirmed the final investigation report, which concludes that the data, if it did indeed exist, is lost.'

'And there is no possibility of linking the wretched man's activities to this office?'

'None whatsoever.'

Sir Hugh Grenville cast the folder aside. 'And the Perrin wife's involvement?'

'Officially, she remains beyond suspicion.'

'However, people share confidences, become overwhelmed by the need to confess. As ever, Jones, we do not want any more... loose ends.'

'Quite so. But I do assure you that the wheels are already in motion. Or should I say that the gentle sea breezes are already in motion. An unfortunate nautical incident, Sir Hugh... and the very last of our *loose ends* dealt with absolutely.'

45

Elsewhere, Sam Barnes was sitting at the kitchen table in his new eco-home, reading his laptop, when Sophie carried through an armful of washing.

'Suzie phoned. She's bringing the baby over later this morning. Are you working?'

He glanced up. 'I'm just reading Blake's report about our failure to find Jonah's data. It's pretty hopeless. We know some of those people Jonah had dealings with were involved in serious crime, and moving large amounts of cash abroad, but we can't match the actions to the individuals. And we can't source the money. And there are some really notable contacts on Jonah's lists.'

'So, what has to happen?'

'We wait for some other lead. Jonah was our big hope. But there'll be others.' He sat back and folded his arms. 'Anyway, I've informed my Commanding Officer that I'm not willing to be reassigned in the field. So, you see before you an occasional English teacher, who has just received confirmation of his appointment to a full-time post, training cops to use their truncheons properly. It pays quite well. We'll be able to buy Mr and Mrs Bump that ridiculously expensive pram you have your eye on.'

'Is that true?'

'Yes, on all counts. I'll stay on the books as an NCA Special. You never know when my knowledge of literature might come in handy.' He pointed to the top of Sophie's pile. 'Are you going to put one-eyed bear in the machine? Won't he drown?'

'He's supposed to be washable. And he's covered in macaroni cheese.'

'What if you ruin him? Laura will never sleep again.'

'I'm watching one on Ebay just in case. Anyway, she likes him ruined. I can't count the number of times I've had to mend his ears and sow his sides back up. She's always making holes in him and poking her finger inside.'

'I hope she hasn't inherited that tendency for abuse from her father.' He watched Sophie carry everything through to the laundry room, load the washing machine, throw in a capsule and turn the dial. Then, just as the rush of water announced the beginning of the wash cycle, he yelled, 'Stop!' He hurried through and switched the machine off at the wall. 'Can we open it?'

'You have to wait until it clicks.' She rubbed her back. 'What's wrong?'

'Blue Bear!'

'What?'

'We need to get him out!'

'Why? I think he'll be OK.'

The machine clicked, Sam pulled open the door and hauled out the washing, extricated the bedraggled bear, carried him back to the kitchen table and began to dry off the superficial water. Then he started to press his chest.

Sophie moved to his side. 'Are you trying to resuscitate him?'

'No, I… God, Sophie, there's something there. Where did we put the scissors?'

Sophie fetched her bag, rummaged around and handed him her nail scissors. He started to undo some of Sophie's past stitching. She watched him snip open Blue Bear's side, feel around in the thick stuffing and pull out a thin silver object less than an inch long. He held it in his palm. 'It's a mini flash. She must have found it and managed to stuff it through a hole and has spent the best part of a year trying to retrieve it. And every time she nearly did you sowed him back up.'

'My God, is that what everyone's been searching for?'

'I think it might be. And Blue Bear's had it all along.' He hurried over to pull a small contraption out of his brief case and plugged it into his laptop.

'What's that?' said Sophie, retrieving Blue Bear's violated remains.

'Virus-blocker. Just in case Blue Bear's flash is booby-trapped.' He inserted the tiny memory stick and studied his computer screen. Sophie watched as he scrolled down menus, opened spreadsheets that revealed a whole complex of data, arranged into categories, magnificently tagged and indexed for ease of cross-referencing to names, contact details, strings of numbers, dates. He clicked on a folder that opened to display clear images: birth certificates, visas.

'I've never seen anything like this, Soph. Jesus, all these names!' He paused. 'And look who we have here. My goodness, Mr Jones, what have you been up to?' He started to transfer the data onto his laptop. 'I'll get all this copied and send it to HQ. There are going to be some interesting resignations in the next few days.' He glanced up. 'This is an absolute Godsend. Soph, we've got the bastards at last!'

Sophie slowly shook her head. '*We've* got the bastards, Inspector Barnes?'

'Well, Soph, I'll obviously have to…'